PENGUIN BOOKS
SELECTED STORIES

SAADAT HASAN MANTO, the most widely read and the most controversial short-story writer in Urdu, was born on 11 May 1912 at Samrala in Punjab's Ludhiana district. In a literary, journalistic, radio scripting and film-writing career spread over more than two decades, he produced twenty-two collections of short stories, one novel, five collections of radio plays, three collections of essays, two collections of personal sketches and many scripts for films. He was tried for obscenity half a dozen times, thrice before and thrice after independence. Some of Manto's greatest work was produced in the last seven years of his life, a time of great financial and emotional hardship for him. He died several months short of his forty-third birthday, in January 1955, in Lahore.

KHALID HASAN, journalist, writer and translator, was born in Srinagar, Kashmir. He has translated most of Saadat Hasan Manto's work. He has also translated the stories of Ghulam Abbas and the poetry of Faiz Ahmed Faiz. Khalid Hasan's own publications include *Scorecard*, *Give Us Back Our Onions*, *The Umpire Strikes Back*, *Private View* and *Rearview Mirror*.

He lives in Washington and is US correspondent of *Daily Times* and the *Friday Times*, Lahore.

_Kolkata,_
_India_
_2018_

# Selected Stories

SAADAT HASAN MANTO

_Translated from the Urdu with an introduction by_
KHALID HASAN

PENGUIN BOOKS

PENGUIN BOOKS

USA | Canada | UK | Ireland | Australia
New Zealand | India | South Africa | China

Penguin Books is part of the Penguin Random House group of companies
whose addresses can be found at global.penguinrandomhouse.com

Published by Penguin Random House India Pvt. Ltd
7th Floor, Infinity Tower C, DLF Cyber City,
Gurgaon 122 002, Haryana, India

| Penguin
Random House
India

First published by Penguin Books India 2007

Translation and Introduction copyright © Khalid Hasan 2007

All rights reserved

18  17  16  15  14  13

ISBN 9780143102182

Typeset in Perpetua by R. Ajith Kumar, New Delhi
Printed at Repro Knowledgecast Limited, India

www.penguin.co.in

*This book is dedicated to the memory of Saadat Hasan Manto and his wife, Safia, who stayed by his side through good times and bad. And to his favourite nephew and literary executor, the late Hamid Jalal, and his wife, Zakia Jalal. But, above all, this book is for Manto's three daughters, Nighat, Nuzhat and Nusrat.*

# CONTENTS

# INTRODUCTION

SAADAT HASAN MANTO WROTE HIS OWN EPITAPH SIX MONTHS BEFORE HE died, though it does not appear on his grave in Lahore. This is what it said: 'Here lies Saadat Hasan Manto and with him lie buried all the secrets and mysteries of the art of short-story writing. Under tons of earth he lies, still wondering who among the two is the greater short-story writer: God or he. Saadat Hasan Manto, 18 August 1954'

Born into a middle-class Kashmiri family of Amritsar, Manto showed little enthusiasm for formal education. Close to his mother and always in awe of his stern father, who scoffed at his first attempt at writing, Manto was instinctively a rebel, questioning what others took for granted. Manto considered himself a reject of the family because he was always being told to be like his older step-brothers, who were lawyers. He was fortunate in finding a mentor in the historian and journalist Bari Alig, who encouraged him to write and to translate a number of literary works, including Victor Hugo's *The Last Days of a Condemned Man* and Oscar Wilde's play *Vera*. About Alig, Manto wrote, 'He it was who encouraged me to take to writing. Had I not run into him in Amritsar, I would either have died as an unknown man and been forgotten or I would have been serving a long sentence in jail for armed robbery.'

Manto failed his school-leaving examination twice in a row; ironically, one of the subjects he was unable to pass was Urdu, in which he was to produce such a powerful and original body of work in the years to come, blooming into one of the language's great stylists. Manto entered college in Amritsar in 1931, failed his first-year examination twice, and dropped out. He was also at Aligarh for a short while but ill health forced him to abandon his studies. He neither completed his education nor was he interested in doing so, but under Bari's influence and his own inquiring and sceptical mind, he read a great deal. It is poetic justice that the very institutions where he could not complete his education now have his work placed in the textbooks they teach.

Those were heady times. Manto was a boy of seven in 1919 when the horrific Jallianwala Bagh massacre took place in Amritsar, an event that left a deep and bloody imprint on the Raj, one from which it never recovered. Not surprisingly, Manto was greatly inspired by revolutionary ideas. As he later wrote, he and his friends, walking the streets of Amritsar, would pretend that they were in Moscow launching a revolution. He was also much taken with the firebrand Punjabi revolutionary and Indian nationalist Bhagat Singh, who was hanged in Lahore for the murder of a British police officer. There was a smell of revolt in the air and, for the first time, it appeared possible to force the British out of India.

Manto's first job took him to Lahore where he worked for a magazine, but he kept returning to Amritsar, only a couple of hours away by train. Soon after, he went to Bombay where he worked briefly for a film journal. But he fell out with the owner-editor and left for Delhi where he found work at the All India Radio, already home to many writers and poets, including Krishen Chander, Upindar Nath Ashok, Meeraji and Noor Meem

Raashed. Manto produced a large number of radio plays for AIR and scripted very many other presentations. Only some of his radio plays survive and these have been published in one volume.

Eventually, it was Bombay where his heart was set and where he settled down. His love affair with Bombay was to last throughout his life, though he left the city twice, once only briefly in 1941 but for good the second time, after Partition in 1947. In his powerful memoir about his friend the actor Shyam, he summed up his feelings about Bombay and the trauma of Partition and his departure for Pakistan. 'I found it impossible to decide which of the two countries was now my homeland—India or Pakistan?' Manto would have felt sad, were he alive today, that Bombay has been renamed Mumbai by an intolerant, revivalist party of religious zealots, the kind of people he hated passionately all his life.

Why did he leave Bombay? Manto himself has not written about it but his wife, Safia, wrote to one of Manto's Indian biographers, Brij Premi, on 6 April 1968: 'He was always treated unjustly by everyone. The truth is that he had no intention of leaving India, but a few months before Partition, Filmistan handed him a notice of termination and that, believe me, broke his heart. For a long time, he kept it hidden from me because he was proud of his friendship with Mr Mukerjee and Ashok Kumar. So how could he tell me that he had been served with a notice? That was when he started drinking heavily which in the end claimed his life. I had come over earlier; he came in January 1948. While he was alone in Bombay, his drinking got completely out of hand. Here his life was full of worries. You can yourself imagine the state he was in and if it was conducive in any sense. His health had also become poor. But one thing he did. He wrote prodigiously, almost a story a day, until the day he died. That is all I know.' Whether Manto was sacked or whether he left on his own, one day in January 1948, he packed his bags and boarded a ship for Karachi, the first capital of the new Muslim homeland of Pakistan.

Manto wrote with amazing speed and never revised what he had once written. Writing a hand that was neat and calligraphic, he would sometimes complete a very long story in one sitting with the final page as neat and legible as the first. Manto was the first to write about what had until then been forbidden territory in Urdu literature: sex and the sexual urge. Some of his most celebrated stories revolve around this theme. He wrote about the onset of puberty in a young boy, about a torrid encounter on a wet afternoon between a young man and an earthy woman, the powerful memory of which makes his bridal night by comparison a lacklustre, unexciting experience. When accused of pornographic writing, he asked how he could possibly disrobe a society that was already naked. He did not beautify what was ugly nor hide what he felt should be exposed. He did not moralize. Manto had great empathy with those on the outer fringes of society. He had a natural feeling of oneness with the poor and the despised. He could identify with the alienated because he had felt that alienation in his own life from his own family. He also had contempt for the hypocrisy and double standards of so-called 'respectable' society.

However it is Manto's Partition stories that are most read and anthologized. No one has written about the holocaust of Partition with greater power than Manto. What distinguishes his writing from that of others are his deep humanism and his refusal to treat people as Hindu or Muslim or Sikh. To him, they are all human beings. What he finds incomprehensible is why they turned on each other with such savagery at a time which should have been their greatest moment of joy: independence from alien rule. The greatest of Manto's Partition stories is 'Toba Tek Singh', which recalls the madness that had gripped the subcontinent at the time of independence, permeating even lunatic asylums, inducing decision makers in the two countries to exchange their inmates on the basis of religion. Others included in this collection are 'The Return', 'Colder Than Ice' and 'The Assignment' all of which chillingly illustrate the savage irony of those times. 'The Last Salute', set in the war in Kashmir in the wake of independence, underscores the dilemma of yesterday's comrades having become today's enemies because of a line drawn across the map.

Manto's classic 'The New Constitution', written several years before independence, is the story of a tonga driver who hates the British passionately and beats up a Tommy who abuses him on the day the 1935 India Act is promulgated because he mistakenly believes that 'we are now free'. His rude awakening comes when he is told at the police station that the same old law is still in force and nothing has changed. 'Khushia' is about a procurer whose manhood is challenged by the girl he provides to his customers when she tells him to walk into her place although she is stark naked. He returns to her later, but in a different capacity: as a customer. Manto could also write a pure love story, such as the moving and lyrical 'On the Balcony', which is included in this collection. His light and satirical stories are a special pleasure to read. 'Upstairs Downstairs' is a rib-tickling account of an old couple that plans to 'risk' having sex but is not sure if that is what the doctor would recommend or approve. As a counterpoint, Manto moves us to the quarters of the domestic help, where we find the young couple fit and ready to get into what their masters are scared to death of attempting.

No other Urdu writer's work has been as extensively translated in English as that of Manto, though the quality of the translations has tended to remain indifferent. Manto has also been translated in very many languages spoken in the subcontinent. A collection of his stories has been published in Japanese translation; and here and there in English-language anthologies, the odd Manto story continues to appear.

In translating Manto, I have tried to retain the bite and sharpness, no less than the infrequent but moving lyricism of his style, to capture the essence of his style—or perhaps I should call it the sound of his voice. However, like all translators, I am painfully aware that all translations are approximations of the original, at best. My only aim, if not my ambition, was and has been to bring the work of one of the greatest writers of Urdu prose to the attention of as large an audience beyond the subcontinent as possible.

Khalid Hasan

# A Wet Afternoon

ON HIS WAY TO SCHOOL, MASOOD WALKED PAST A BUTCHER CARRYING A huge basket on his head that contained two recently slaughtered sheep. Their skins had been removed and from the bare flesh rose a misty vapour. The carcasses were so fresh that they were still throbbing. He saw it and his body trembled, bringing a glow to his cold cheeks and reminding him of the way one of his eyelids sometimes throbbed.

It was a quarter past nine but, because of a dull, low cloud, it felt like the early hours of the morning. There was no bite in the cold but he could see the breath coming out of people's mouths as they went their way. It was like puffs of steam pouring forth from the nozzle of a samovar. There was a heaviness in the air as if it was weighted down by the overhanging clouds. This weather gave him the same feeling that walking in rubber shoes did. And while there were many people up and about in the bazaar, and the shops were beginning to show signs of life, the level of noise was low, like a whispered conversation. People were moving slowly as if they were afraid of having their footsteps heard.

Masood moved lazily; his satchel was under his arm. When he had seen the vapour rising from the freshly slaughtered sheep, he had experienced a strange pleasure, experienced a certain warmth rise in his body. It felt good and he wished he could experience the same comforting sensation when, on cold days, he was caned on his outstretched hands by the teacher.

The light of the day was not clear but diffuse. Everything

seemed to be coated with a thin layer of mist making the atmosphere heavy, but it did not strain the eyes because the contours of everything were indistinct.

When Masood arrived at the school, his classmates told him there would be no classes because of the death of the school secretary. They looked happy; in fact, they had already begun to play in the school yard, having flung their satchels to the ground. Some had gone home, while others were gathered at the school noticeboard, reading the school closure announcement over and over again.

The news brought Masood no joy. He felt no emotion at all. He was not the least bit sorry that the school secretary had died. He thought of the time the year before when his grandfather had died and there had been much difficulty with the burial because of rain. He had accompanied the body to the graveyard and almost slipped into the open pit because the ground was so muddy. He remembered it distinctly. It was very cold and there were red blotches of mud all over his white clothes. His hands were blue with cold and, when he pressed them for warmth, whitish spots appeared under the skin. His nose felt like an icicle. He remembered coming home, washing his hands and changing into fresh clothes. The school secretary's death had brought all that back. He was sure when they carried him for burial, it would begin to rain and the graveyard would get muddy. Many people would slip and suffer painful injury.

He made straight for the classroom, unlocked his desk, took out the books he was going to bring in the next day and left them in. Then he picked up his satchel and began to walk home.

On the way, he again came upon those two freshly slaughtered sheep. One of them was now hanging by a hook in the butcher's shop and the other was lying across a large cutting board. Masood had an urge to touch the flesh from which he had seen vapour rising. He stopped and touched the still throbbing part with his cold finger. It felt good. The butcher was busy sharpening his knives, which encouraged him to touch the flesh again before walking off.

When he told his mother about the school secretary's death, she said that his father had gone for the funeral. That left only two people in the house, his mother, who was cooking in the kitchen, and his sister Kalsoom who, her hands placed for warmth over a small fire, was trying to memorize the musical scale of the raag Darbari.

Since his friends from the neighbourhood all went to Government School, the death of the secretary of Islamia School had earned them no holiday. That meant there was no one to play with, nor any homework to do. In any case, whatever there was to be learnt in the sixth form, his father had already taught him at home. He had no particular game to play with either, except a dirty pack of cards lying in the alcove. Masood was not interested. The board games that his sister played with her friends were beyond his comprehension. Since he was simply not interested in them, he had never even tried to learn the rules.

He placed his satchel in its customary niche, took off his jacket and went to the kitchen to sit next to his mother. He could hear his sister intoning the scale of the raag with its repetition of *sa*, *ga* and *ma*. His mother was chopping spinach which she now threw into a saucepan and, as the heat reached the wet and finely cut green leaves, a whitish vapour began to rise from them. This reminded Masood of the two slaughtered sheep.

'Ammi jan,' he said, 'I saw two sheep at the butcher's shop

today. They had been skinned and the flesh was sending up a misty vapour just like my breath on cold mornings.'

'Oh yes!' his mother said absent-mindedly, as she tried to stroke the fire.

'And I touched the flesh with my finger. It was warm.'

'Oh yes!' she said, moving the saucepan in which she had washed the spinach, before leaving the kitchen.

'And this flesh throbbed at so many spots.'

'Oh yes!' This was Masood's sister who, forgetting her exercise, was suddenly attentive. 'How did it throb?'

'Like this . . . like this,' Masood said, snapping his fingers.

'What happened then?'

Masood thought for a moment. 'What then? Nothing, I just told you what I saw at the butcher's shop. I even touched it. It was warm.'

'It was warm . . . now come here and do something for me.'

'What?'

'Come with me first.'

'No, first tell me what.'

'Come with me first.'

'No, first tell me.'

'All right, my back is hurting badly . . . I will lie on the bed and you press the sore areas with your feet . . . Aren't you my darling brother! I swear it really hurts.' Then she began to pound her back with clenched fists.

'What is wrong with your back? It is always hurting. And I am the one you always pick on to press it. Why don't you ask your friends to do that? They are always hanging around here.'

He stood up. 'All right, I will do it but no more than ten minutes.'

'Good boy, good boy!' she said, and put away the exercise book from which she was trying to memorize her musical scales and went into the room where both of them slept.

To get to the room, they had to walk across a small open courtyard. Kalsoom paused there for a moment, stretched herself, looked up at the sky which was overcast and said, 'Masood, it will definitely rain today.' But Masood was already in the room, sprawled on his bed.

Kalsoom came in and threw herself on her bed, face down. Masood stood up and looked at the clock which said ten minutes to eleven. 'At exactly eleven, I will stop,' he announced.

'All right, but get on with it. And do it well; otherwise I will pull your ears.' Resting his hands against the wall along which the bed lay, Masood climbed on Kalsoom's back and began to work her waist rhythmically with his feet, pressing the flesh in, then relieving the pressure, like construction workers mixing clay with their feet. Kalsoom began to moan softly.

Whenever Masood's feet happened to fall on Kalsoom's buttocks, he felt as if he was gently pounding the butchered sheep's flesh that he had touched that morning. He felt somewhat confused, not quite sure what was passing through his mind.

Once or twice, it seemed to him that Kalsoom's flesh was throbbing under his feet, just like the sheep's that morning at the butcher's shop. Having started half-heartedly, he now was beginning to enjoy what he had earlier seen as a chore. Under his weight, Kalsoom was moaning softly, her oos and ahs keeping time with the movement of his feet and making him feel good.

The clock said it was past eleven but Masood kept on. After some time, she turned around and lying flat on her back said, 'Now Masood, nice brother, do the same up front.'

Balancing himself against the wall, he placed his feet on her thighs but, every time he did that, he slipped. She began to giggle, almost making him lose his balance. Resting his hands against the wall once again, he placed his feet on her thighs firmly and began to work his feet under which he could feel her flesh throbbing. 'Why do you keep giggling? Lie still,' he said.

Kalsoom straightened herself and said, 'I feel funny. You kick in like a savage.'

'I promise, I will not put my full weight on you this time . . . I will be careful so that you don't feel any discomfort,' he said.

Once again, balancing himself against the wall with his hands, he placed his feet carefully on Kalsoom's thighs so that she should only feel half his body weight. He began to press her thighs dexterously as the flesh under his feet rippled from side to side. Masood thought of the tightrope walker who had once come to perform at his school. He felt like one himself.

It was not the first time he had pressed Kalsoom's legs but never before had he felt this way. His mind kept going back to the butcher's shop with that misty vapour rising from the slaughtered sheep's bare flesh. What if Kalsoom was slaughtered and skinned? Would the same kind of vapour rise from her flesh, he wondered. But he immediately wiped off this thought from his mind just as he wiped off the writing on his slate with a sponge.

'That's enough, that's enough,' Kalsoom said, sounding exhausted.

Masood thought of teasing her a little and, as he stepped down from the bed, he began to tickle her in her armpits, sending her into convulsions. She was so weak with laughter that she did not have the strength to push him away. She tried to kick him once but he was quicker and jumped off. Then he picked up his slippers and ran out of the room.

When he walked into the courtyard, a gentle rain had begun to fall, the raindrops disappearing in the brick floor as soon as they touched it. The clouds had come even lower. Masood's body felt warm and the wind felt good on his cheeks. The raindrops sent a shudder through his body. On the roof of the house across the street, a pair of pigeons sat, their feathers fluffed up. He was sure they were warm like a clay pot that has been on a low fire all night. The chrysanthemums in the courtyard looked clean and washed. A strange drowsiness hung in the air, wrapping him up like a warm woollen shawl.

Masood felt overwrought but he could not understand his thoughts. Whatever it was, it felt nice.

He stood in the rain till his hands went cold. When he pressed them, he saw whitish spots that disappeared just as quickly. He clenched his fists and began to blow on them. He felt warmer though wet. Then he walked into the kitchen. The food was ready and he began to eat. His father returned from the burial. They did not talk. Masood's mother rose and went into her room, followed by her husband. He heard the two of them talking in low voices.

After he had eaten, Masood went to the living room, opened the window and lay down on the carpeted floor. Because of the rain, it had become colder. A wind had also risen. But Masood did not find it unpleasant, though his muscles hurt slightly. Once or twice, he stretched himself and it felt good. It seemed to him that there was some strange presence in his body, but where exactly it was, he couldn't tell. A feeling of restlessness washed over him. His body seemed to be getting longer.

After tossing and turning on the floor for some time, he stood up, went to the kitchen and from there walked into the courtyard. Nobody was around. The rain had stopped. Masood pulled out his hockey stick and ball from where he always kept them and began to play. Once when the ball hit a door with a loud bang, his father screamed, 'Who is that?'

'It is I, Masood.'

'What are you doing?' his father asked.

'Playing.'

'All right, play,' then after some time, 'your mother is pressing my head so don't make noise.'

Masood let the ball rest where it was and, hockey stick in hand, walked towards the bedroom. One door was shut while the other was half open. On tiptoe, Masood moved forward and threw the doors ajar. Kalsoom and her friend Bimla screamed, then covered themselves with a quilt. But he had seen what they were doing.

Bimla's blouse was unbuttoned and Kalsoom was staring at her breasts.

Masood could not quite understand. His brain felt foggy. He returned to the living room and sat down. A surge of power rose in his body, paralysing his ability to think.

He picked up the hockey stick, placed it across his thighs and wondered if it would snap if he were to push it down at both ends with all his strength. He began to do that but could only manage to bend it slightly. He wrestled with it for some time and, finally, in frustration, he chucked it away.

# Toba Tek Singh

A COUPLE OF YEARS AFTER THE PARTITION OF THE COUNTRY, IT OCCURRED to the respective governments of India and Pakistan that inmates of lunatic asylums, like prisoners, should also be exchanged. Muslim lunatics in India should be transferred to Pakistan and Hindu and Sikh lunatics in Pakistani asylums should be sent to India.

Whether this was a reasonable or an unreasonable idea is difficult to say. One thing, however, is clear. It took many conferences of important officials from the two sides to come to the decision. Final details, like the date of actual exchange, were carefully worked out. Muslim lunatics whose families were still residing in India were to be left undisturbed, the rest moved to the border for the exchange. The situation in Pakistan was slightly different, since almost the entire population of Hindus and Sikhs had already migrated to India. The question of keeping non-Muslim lunatics in Pakistan did not, therefore, arise.

While it is not known what the reaction in India was, when the news reached the Lahore lunatic asylum, it immediately became the subject of heated discussion. One Muslim lunatic, a regular reader of the fire-eating daily newspaper *Zamindar*, when asked what Pakistan was, replied after deep reflection, 'The name of a place in India where cut-throat razors are manufactured.'

This profound observation was received with visible satisfaction.

A Sikh lunatic asked another Sikh, 'Sardarji, why are we being sent to India? We don't even know the language they speak in that country.'

The man smiled. 'I know the language of the Hindostoras. These devils always strut about as if they were the lords of the earth.'

One day a Muslim lunatic, while taking his bath, raised the slogan 'Pakistan Zindabad' with such enthusiasm that he lost his balance and was later found lying on the floor unconscious.

Not all inmates were mad. Some were perfectly normal, except that they were murderers. To spare them the hangman's noose, their families had managed to get them committed after bribing officials down the line. They probably had a vague idea why India was being divided and what Pakistan was, but, as for the present situation, they were equally clueless.

Newspapers were no help either, and the asylum guards were ignorant, if not illiterate. Nor was there anything to be learnt by eavesdropping on their conversations. Some said there was this man by the name Muhammad Ali Jinnah, or the Quaid-e-Azam, who had set up a separate country for Muslims, called Pakistan.

As to where Pakistan was located, the inmates knew nothing. That was why both the mad and the partially mad were unable to decide whether they were now in India or in Pakistan. If they were in India, where on earth was Pakistan? And if they were in Pakistan, then how come that until only the other day it was India?

One inmate had got so badly caught up in this India–Pakistan–Pakistan–India rigmarole that one day, while sweeping the floor, he dropped everything, climbed the nearest tree and installed himself on a branch, from which vantage point he spoke for two hours on the delicate problem of India and Pakistan. The guards asked him to get down; instead he went a branch higher, and when threatened with punishment, declared, 'I wish to live neither in India nor in Pakistan. I wish to live in this tree.'

When he was finally persuaded to come down, he began embracing his Sikh and Hindu friends, tears running down his cheeks, fully convinced that they were about to leave him and go to India.

A Muslim radio engineer, who had an MSc degree, and never mixed with anyone, given as he was to taking long walks by himself all day, was so affected by the current debate that one day he took off all his clothes, gave the bundle to one of the attendants and ran into the garden stark naked.

A Muslim lunatic from Chaniot, who used to be one of the most devoted workers of the All India Muslim League, and obsessed with bathing himself fifteen or sixteen times a day, had suddenly stopped doing that and announced his name was Muhammad Ali—that he was Quaid-e-Azam Muhammad Ali Jinnah. This had led a Sikh inmate to declare himself Master Tara Singh, the leader of the Sikhs. Apprehending serious communal trouble, the authorities declared them dangerous, and shut them up in separate cells.

There was a young Hindu lawyer from Lahore who had gone off his head after an unhappy love affair. When told that Amritsar was to become a part of India, he went into a depression because his beloved lived in Amritsar, something he had not forgotten even in his madness. That day he abused every major and minor Hindu and Muslim leader who had cut India into two, turning his beloved into an Indian and him into a Pakistani.

When news of the exchange reached the asylum, his friends offered him congratulations, because he was now to be sent to

India, the country of his beloved. However, he declared that he had no intention of leaving Lahore, because his practice would not flourish in Amritsar.

There were two Anglo-Indian lunatics in the European ward. When told that the British had decided to go home after granting independence to India, they went into a state of deep shock and were seen conferring with each other in whispers the entire afternoon. They were worried about their changed status after independence. Would there be a European ward or would it be abolished? Would breakfast continue to be served or would they have to subsist on bloody Indian chapatti?

There was another inmate, a Sikh, who had been confined for the last fifteen years. Whenever he spoke, it was the same mysterious gibberish: *'Uper the gur gur the annexe the bay dhayana the mung the dal of the laltain.'* Guards said he had not slept a wink in fifteen years. Occasionally, he could be observed leaning against a wall, but the rest of the time, he was always to be found standing. Because of this, his legs were permanently swollen, something that did not appear to bother him. Recently, he had started to listen carefully to discussions about the forthcoming exchange of Indian and Pakistani lunatics. When asked his opinion, he observed solemnly, *'Uper the gur gur the annexe the bay dhayana the mung the dal of the Government of Pakistan.'*

Of late, however, the Government of Pakistan had been replaced by the government of Toba Tek Singh, a small town in the Punjab which was his home. He had also begun inquiring where Toba Tek Singh was to go. However, nobody was quite sure whether it was in India or Pakistan.

Those who had tried to solve this mystery had become utterly confused when told that Sialkot, which used to be in India, was now in Pakistan. It was anybody's guess what was going to happen to Lahore, which was currently in Pakistan, but could slide into India any moment. It was also possible that the entire subcontinent of India might become Pakistan. And who could say if both India and Pakistan might not entirely vanish from the map of the world one day?

The old man's hair was almost gone and what little was left had become a part of the beard, giving him a strange, even frightening, appearance. However, he was a harmless fellow and had never been known to get into fights. Older attendants at the asylum said that he was a fairly prosperous landlord from Toba Tek Singh, who had quite suddenly gone mad. His family had brought him in, bound and fettered. That was fifteen years ago.

Once a month, he used to have visitors but, since the start of communal troubles in the Punjab, they had stopped coming. His real name was Bishen Singh, but everybody called him Toba Tek Singh. He lived in a kind of limbo, having no idea what day of the week it was, or month, or how many years had passed since his confinement. However, he had developed a sixth sense about the day of the visit, when he used to bathe himself, soap his body, oil and comb his hair and put on clean clothes. He never said a word during these meetings, except occasional outbursts of, *'Uper the gur gur the annexe the bay dhayana the mung the dal of the laltain.'*

When he was first confined, he had left an infant daughter behind, now a pretty, young girl of fifteen. She would come occasionally, and sit in front of him with tears rolling down her cheeks. In the strange world that he inhabited, hers was just another face.

Since the start of this India—Pakistan caboodle, he had got into the habit of asking fellow inmates where exactly Toba Tek Singh was, without receiving a satisfactory answer, because nobody knew. The visits had also suddenly stopped. He was increasingly restless, but, more than that, curious. The sixth sense, which used to alert him to the day of the visit, had also atrophied.

He missed his family, the gifts they used to bring and the concern with which they used to speak to him. He was sure they would have told him whether Toba Tek Singh was in India or Pakistan. He also had a feeling that they came from Toba Tek Singh, where he used to have his home.

One of the inmates had declared himself God. Bishen Singh asked him one day if Toba Tek Singh was in India or Pakistan. The man chuckled. 'Neither in India nor in Pakistan, because, so far, we have issued no orders in this respect.'

Bishen Singh begged 'God' to issue the necessary orders so that his problem could be solved, but he was disappointed, as 'God' appeared to be preoccupied with more pressing matters. Finally, he told him angrily, *'Uper the gur gur the annexe the mung the dal of Guruji da Khalsa and Guruji ki fateh . . . jo boley so nihal sat sri akal.'*

What he wanted to say was, 'You don't answer my prayers because you are a Muslim god. Had you been a Sikh god, you would have been more of a sport.'

A few days before the exchange was to take place, one of Bishen Singh's Muslim friends from Toba Tek Singh came to see him—the first time in fifteen years. Bishen Singh looked at him once and turned away, until a guard said to him, 'This is your old friend Fazal Din. He has come all the way to meet you.'

Bishen Singh looked at Fazal Din and began to mumble

something. Fazal Din placed his hand on his friend's shoulder and said, 'I have been meaning to come for some time to bring you news. All your family is well and has gone to India safely. I did what I could to help. Your daughter Roop Kaur . . .'—he hesitated—'She is safe too . . . in India.'

Bishen Singh kept quiet; Fazal Din continued, 'Your family wanted me to make sure you were well. Soon you will be moving to India. What can I say, except that you should remember me to bhai Balbir Singh, bhai Vadhawa Singh and bahain Amrit Kaur. Tell bhai Balbir Singh that Fazal Din is well by the grace of God. The two brown buffaloes he left behind are well too. Both of them gave birth to calves, but, unfortunately, one of them died after six days. Say I think of them often and to write to me if there is anything I can do.'

Then he added, 'Here, I brought you a nice treat from home.'

Bishen Singh took the gift and handed it to one of the guards. 'Where is Toba Tek Singh?' he asked.

'Where? Why, it is where it has always been.'

'In India or in Pakistan?'

'In India . . . no, in Pakistan.'

Without saying another word, Bishen Singh walked away, murmuring, *'Uper the gur gur the annexe the bay dhayana the mung the dal of the Pakistan and Hindustan dur fittay moun.'*

Meanwhile, the exchange arrangements were rapidly being finalized. Lists of lunatics from the two sides had been exchanged between the governments, and the date of transfer fixed.

On a cold winter evening, buses full of Hindu and Sikh lunatics, accompanied by armed police and officials, began moving out of the Lahore asylum towards Wagha, the dividing line between India and Pakistan. Senior officials from the two sides in charge of exchange arrangements met, signed documents and the transfer got under way.

It was quite a job getting the men out of the buses and handing them over to officials. Some just refused to leave. Those who were persuaded to do so began to run pell-mell in every direction. Some were stark naked. All efforts to get them to cover themselves had failed because they couldn't be kept from tearing off their garments. Some were shouting abuse or singing. Others were weeping bitterly. Many fights broke out.

In short, complete confusion prevailed. Female lunatics were also being exchanged and they were even nosier. It was bitterly cold.

Most of the inmates appeared to be dead set against the entire operation. They simply could not understand why they were being forcibly removed, thrown into buses and driven to this strange place. There were slogans of 'Pakistan Zindabad' and 'Pakistan Murdabad', followed by fights.

When Bishen Singh was brought out and asked to give his name so that it could be recorded in a register, he asked the official behind the desk, 'Where is Toba Tek Singh? In India or Pakistan?'

'Pakistan,' he answered with a vulgar laugh.

Bishen Singh tried to run, but was overpowered by the Pakistani guards who tried to push him across the dividing line towards India. However, he wouldn't move. 'This is Toba Tek Singh,' he announced. *'Uper the gur gur the annexe the bay dhayana mung the dal of Toba Tek Singh and Pakistan.'*

Many efforts were made to explain to him that Toba Tek Singh had already been moved to India, or would be moved immediately, but it had no effect on Bishen Singh. The guards even tried force, but soon gave up.

There he stood in no-man's-land on his swollen legs like a colossus.

Since he was a harmless old man, no further attempt was made to push him into India. He was allowed to stand where he wanted, while the exchange continued. The night wore on.

Just before sunrise, Bishen Singh, the man who had stood on his legs for fifteen years, screamed and as officials from the two sides rushed towards him, he collapsed to the ground.

There, behind barbed wire, on one side, lay India and behind more barbed wire, on the other side, lay Pakistan. In between, on a bit of earth, which had no name, lay Toba Tek Singh.

# Colder Than Ice

AS ISHWAR SINGH ENTERED THE ROOM, KALWANT KAUR ROSE FROM THE bed and locked the door from the inside. It was past midnight. A strange and ominous silence seemed to have descended on the city.

Kalwant Kaur returned to the bed, crossed her legs and sat down in the middle. Ishwar Singh stood quietly in a corner, holding his kirpan absent-mindedly. Anxiety and confusion were writ large on his handsome face.

Kalwant Kaur, apparently dissatisfied with her defiant posture, moved to the edge and sat down, swinging her legs suggestively. Ishwar Singh still had not spoken.

Kalwant Kaur was a big woman with generous hips, fleshy thighs and unusually high breasts. Her eyes were sharp and bright and over her upper lip there was faint bluish down. Her chin suggested great strength and resolution.

Ishwar Singh had not moved from his corner. His turban, which he always kept smartly in place, was loose and his hands trembled from time to time. However, from his strapping, manly figure, it was apparent that he had just what it took to be Kalwant Kaur's lover.

More time passed. Kalwant Kaur was getting restive. 'Ishr Sian,' she said in a sharp voice.

Ishwar Singh raised his head, then turned it away, unable to deal with Kalwant Kaur's fiery gaze.

This time she screamed, 'Ishr Sian.' Then she lowered her

voice and added, 'Where have you been all this time?'

Ishwar Singh moistened his parched lips and said, 'I don't know.'

Kalwant Kaur lost her temper. 'What sort of a motherfucking answer is that!'

Ishwar Singh threw his kirpan aside and slumped on the bed. He looked unwell. She stared at him and her anger seemed to have left her. Putting her hand on his forehead, she asked gently, 'Jani, what's wrong?'

'Kalwant.' He turned his gaze from the ceiling and looked at her. There was pain in his voice and it melted all of Kalwant Kaur. She bit her lower lip. 'Yes jani.'

Ishwar Singh took off his turban. He slapped her thigh and said, more to himself than to her, 'I feel strange.'

His long hair came undone and Kalwant Kaur began to run her fingers through it playfully. 'Ishr Sian, where have you been all this time?'

'In the bed of my enemy's mother,' he said jocularly. Then he pulled Kalwant Kaur towards him and began to knead her breasts with both hands. 'I swear by the Guru, there's no other woman like you.'

Flirtatiously, she pushed him aside. 'Swear over my head. Did you go to the city?'

He gathered his hair in a bun and replied, 'No.'

Kalwant Kaur was irritated. 'Yes, you did go to the city and you looted a lot more money and you don't want to tell me about it.'

'May I not be my father's son if I lie to you,' he said.

She was silent for a while, then she exploded, 'Tell me what happened to you the last night you were here. You were lying next to me and you had made me wear all those gold ornaments you had looted from the houses of the Muslims in the city and you were kissing me all over and then, suddenly, God only knows what came over you, you put on your clothes and walked out.'

Ishwar Singh went pale. 'See how your face has fallen,' Kalwant Kaur snapped. 'Ishr Sian,' she said, emphasizing every word, 'you're not the man you were eight days ago. Something has happened.'

Ishwar Singh did not answer, but he was stung. He suddenly took Kalwant Kaur in his arms and began to hug and kiss her ferociously. 'Jani, I'm what I always was. Squeeze me tighter so that the heat in your bones cools off.'

Kalwant Kaur did not resist him, but she kept asking, 'What went wrong that night?'

'Nothing.'

'Why don't you tell me?'

'There's nothing to tell.'

'Ishr Sian, may you cremate my body with your own hands if you lie to me!'

Ishwar Singh did not reply. He dug his lips into hers. His moustache tickled her nostrils and she sneezed. They burst out laughing.

Ishwar Singh began to take off his clothes, ogling Kalwant Kaur lasciviously. 'It's time for a game of cards.'

Beads of perspiration appeared over her upper lip. She rolled her eyes coquettishly and said, 'Get lost.'

Ishwar Singh pinched her lip and she leapt aside. 'Ishr Sian, don't do that. It hurts.'

Ishwar Singh began to suck her lower lip and Kalwant Kaur

melted. He took off the rest of his clothes. 'Time for a round of trumps,' he said.

Kalwant Kaur's upper lip began to quiver. He peeled her shirt off, as if he was skinning a banana. He fondled her naked body and pinched her arm. 'Kalwant, I swear by the Guru, you're not a woman, you're a delicacy,' he said between kisses.

Kalwant Kaur examined the skin he had pinched. It was red. 'Ishr Sian, you're a brute.'

Ishwar Singh smiled through his thick moustache. 'Then let there be a lot of brutality tonight.' And he began to prove what he had said.

He bit her lower lip, nibbled at her earlobes, kneaded her breasts, slapped her glowing hip resoundingly and planted big, wet kisses on her cheeks.

Kalwant Kaur began to boil with passion like a kettle on high fire.

But there was something wrong.

Ishwar Singh, despite his vigorous efforts at foreplay, could not feel the fire which leads to the final and inevitable act of love. Like a wrestler who is being had the better of, he employed every trick he knew to ignite the fire in his loins, but it eluded him. He felt cold.

Kalwant Kaur was now like an overtuned instrument. 'Ishr Sian,' she whispered languidly, 'you have shuffled me enough, it is time to produce your trump.'

Ishwar Singh felt as if the entire deck of cards had slipped from his hands on to the floor.

He laid himself against her, breathing irregularly. Drops of cold perspiration appeared on his brow. Kalwant Kaur made frantic efforts to arouse him, but in the end she gave up.

In a fury, she sprang out of bed and covered herself with a sheet. 'Ishr Sian, tell me the name of the bitch you have been with who has squeezed you dry.'

Ishwar Singh just lay there panting.

'Who was that bitch?' she screamed.

'No one, Kalwant, no one,' he replied in a barely audible voice.

Kalwant Kaur placed her hands on her hips. 'Ishr Sian, I'm going to get to the bottom of this. Swear to me on the Guru's sacred name, is there a woman?'

She did not let him speak. 'Before you swear by the Guru, don't forget who I am. I am Sardar Nihal Singh's daughter. I will cut you to pieces. Is there a woman in this?'

He nodded his head in assent, his pain obvious from his face.

Like a wild and demented creature, Kalwant Kaur picked up Ishwar Singh's kirpan, unsheathed it and plunged it in his neck. Blood spluttered out of the deep gash like water out of a fountain. Then she began to pull at his hair and scratch his face, cursing her unknown rival as she continued tearing at him.

'Let go, Kalwant, let go now,' Ishwar Singh begged.

She paused. His beard and chest were drenched in blood. 'You acted impetuously,' he said, 'but what you did I deserved.'

'Tell me the name of that woman of yours,' she screamed.

A thin line of blood ran into his mouth. He shivered as he felt its taste.

'Kalwant, with this kirpan I have killed six men . . . with this kirpan with which you . . .'

'Who was the bitch, I ask you?' she repeated.

Ishwar Singh's dimming eyes sparked into momentary life. 'Don't call her a bitch,' he implored.

'Who was she?' she screamed.

Ishwar Singh's voice was failing. 'I'll tell you.' He ran his hand over his throat, then looked at it, smiling wanly. 'What a motherfucking creature man is!'

'Ishr Sian, answer my question,' Kalwant Kaur said.

He began to speak, very slowly, his face coated with cold sweat.

'Kalwant, jani, you can have no idea what happened to me. When they began to loot Muslim shops and houses in the city, I joined one of the gangs. All the cash and ornaments that fell to my share, I brought back to you. There was only one thing I hid from you.'

He began to groan. His pain was becoming unbearable, but she was unconcerned. 'Go on,' she said in a merciless voice.

'There was this house I broke into . . . there were seven people in there, six of them men whom I killed with my kirpan one by one . . . and there was one girl . . . she was so beautiful . . . I didn't kill her . . . I took her away.'

She sat on the edge of the bed, listening to him.

'Kalwant jani, I can't even begin to describe to you how beautiful she was . . . I could have slashed her throat but I didn't . . . I said to myself . . . Ishr Sian, you gorge yourself on Kalwant Kaur every day . . . how about a mouthful of this luscious fruit!

'I thought she had gone into a faint, so I carried her over my shoulder all the way to the canal which runs outside the city . . . then I laid her down on the grass, behind some bushes and . . . first I thought I would shuffle her a bit . . . but then I decided to trump her right away . . .'

'What happened?' she asked.

'I threw the trump . . . but, but . . .'

His voice sank.

Kalwant Kaur shook him violently. 'What happened?'

Ishwar Singh opened his eyes. 'She was dead . . . I had carried a dead body . . . a heap of cold flesh . . . jani, give me your hand.'

Kalwant Kaur placed her hand on his. It was colder than ice.

# The Assignment

BEGINNING WITH ISOLATED INCIDENTS OF STABBING, IT HAD NOW developed into full-scale communal violence, with no holds barred. Even home-made bombs were being used.

The general view in Amritsar was that the riots could not last long. They were seen as no more than a manifestation of temporarily inflamed political passions which were bound to cool down before long. After all, these were not the first communal riots the city had known. There had been so many of them in the past. They never lasted long. The pattern was familiar. Two weeks or so of unrest and then business as usual. On the basis of experience, therefore, the people were quite justified in believing that the current troubles would also run their course in a few days. But this did not happen. They not only continued, but grew in intensity.

Muslims living in Hindu localities began to leave for safer places, and Hindus in Muslim majority areas followed suit. However, everyone saw these adjustments as strictly temporary. The atmosphere would soon be clear of this communal madness, they told themselves.

Retired judge Mian Abdul Hai was absolutely confident that things would return to normal soon, which was why he wasn't worried. He had two children, a boy of eleven and a girl of seventeen. In addition, there was an old servant who was now pushing seventy. It was a small family. When the troubles started, Mian sahib, being an extra cautious man, had stocked up on food . . . just in case. So on one count, at least, there were no worries.

His daughter, Sughra, was less sure of things. They lived in a three-storey house with a view of almost the entire city. Sughra could not help noticing that, whenever she went on the roof, there were fires raging everywhere. In the beginning, she could hear fire engines rushing past, their bells ringing, but this had now stopped. There were too many fires in too many places.

The nights had become particularly frightening. The sky was always lit by conflagrations like giants spitting out flames. Then there were the slogans which rent the air with terrifying frequency—'Allaho Akbar', 'Har Har Mahadev'.

Sughra never expressed her fears to her father, because he had declared confidently that there was no cause for anxiety. Everything was going to be fine. Since he was generally always right, she had initially felt reassured.

However, when the power and water supplies were suddenly cut off, she expressed her unease to her father and suggested apologetically that, for a few days at least, they should move to Sharifpura, a Muslim locality, where many of the old residents had already moved to. Mian sahib was adamant. 'You're imagining things. Everything is going to be normal very soon.'

He was wrong. Things went from bad to worse. Before long there was not a single Muslim family to be found in Mian Abdul Hai's locality. Then one day Mian sahib suffered a stroke and was laid up. His son, Basharat, who used to spend most of his time playing self-devised games, now stayed glued to his father's bed.

All the shops in the area had been permanently boarded up. Dr Ghulam Hussain's dispensary had been shut for weeks and Sughra had noticed from the rooftop one day that the adjoining clinic of Dr Goranditta Mal was also closed. Mian sahib's condition was getting worse day by day. Sughra was almost at her wits' end. One day she took Basharat aside and said to him, 'You've got to do something. I know it's not safe to go out, but we must get some help. Our father is very ill.'

The boy went, but came back almost immediately. His face was pale with fear. He had seen a blood-drenched body lying in the street and a group of wild-looking men looting shops. Sughra took the terrified boy in her arms and said a silent prayer, thanking God for his safe return. However, she could not bear her father's suffering. His left side was now completely lifeless. His speech had been impaired and he mostly communicated through gestures, all designed to reassure Sughra that soon all would be well.

It was the month of Ramadan and only two days to Id. Mian sahib was quite confident that the troubles would be over by then. He was again wrong. A canopy of smoke hung over the city, with fires burning everywhere. At night the silence was shattered by deafening explosions. Sughra and Basharat hadn't slept for days.

Sughra in any case couldn't because of her father's deteriorating condition. Helplessly, she would look at him, then at her young, frightened brother and the seventy-year-old servant Akbar, who was useless for all practical purposes. He mostly kept to his bed, coughing and fighting for breath. One day Sughra told him angrily, 'What good are you? Do you realize how ill Mian sahib is? Perhaps you are too lazy to want to help, pretending that you are suffering from acute asthma. There was a time when servants used to sacrifice their lives for their masters.'

Sughra felt very bad afterwards. She had been unnecessarily

harsh on the old man. In the evening, when she took his food to him in his small room, he was not there. Basharat looked for him all over the house, but he was nowhere to be found. The front door was unlatched. He was gone, perhaps to get some help for Mian sahib. Sughra prayed for his return, but two days passed and he hadn't come back.

It was evening and the festival of Id was now only a day away. She remembered the excitement which used to grip the family on this occasion. She remembered standing on the rooftop, peering into the sky, looking for the Id moon and praying for the clouds to clear. But how different everything was today. The sky was covered in smoke and on distant roofs one could see people looking upwards. Were they trying to catch sight of the new moon or were they watching the fires, she wondered.

She looked up and saw the thin sliver of the moon peeping through a small patch in the sky. She raised her hands in prayer, begging God to make her father well. Basharat, however, was upset that there would be no Id this year.

The night hadn't yet fallen. Sughra had moved her father's bed out of the room on to the veranda. She was sprinkling water on the floor to make it cool. Mian sahib was lying there quietly looking with vacant eyes at the sky where she had seen the moon. Sughra came and sat next to him. He motioned her to get closer. Then he raised his right arm slowly and put it on her head. Tears began to run from Sughra's eyes. Even Mian sahib looked moved. Then with great difficulty he said to her, 'God is merciful. All will be well.'

Suddenly there was a knock on the door. Sughra's heart began to beat violently. She looked at Basharat, whose face had turned white like a sheet of paper. There was another knock. Mian sahib gestured to Sughra to answer it. It must be old Akbar who had come back, she thought. She said to Basharat, 'Answer the door. I'm sure it's Akbar.' Her father shook his head, as if to signal disagreement.

'Then who can it be?' Sughra asked him.

Mian Abdul Hai tried to speak, but before he could do so Basharat came running in. He was breathless. Taking Sughra aside, he whispered, 'It's a Sikh.'

Sughra screamed, 'A Sikh! What does he want?'

'He wants me to open the door.'

Sughra took Basharat in her arms and went and sat on her father's bed, looking at him desolately.

On Mian Abdul Hai's thin, lifeless lips, a faint smile appeared. 'Go and open the door. It is Gurmukh Singh.'

'No, it's someone else,' Basharat said.

Mian sahib turned to Sughra. 'Open the door. It's him.'

Sughra rose. She knew Gurmukh Singh. Her father had once done him a favour. He had been involved in a false legal suit and Mian sahib had acquitted him. That was a long time ago, but every year, on the occasion of Id, he would come all the way from his village with a bag of sawwaiyaan. Mian sahib had told him several times, 'Sardar sahib, you really are too kind. You shouldn't inconvenience yourself every year.' But Gurmukh Singh would always reply, 'Mian sahib, God has given you everything. This is only a small gift which I bring every year in humble acknowledgement of the kindness you did me once. Even a hundred generations of mine would not be able to repay your favour. May God keep you happy.'

Sughra was reassured. Why hadn't she thought of it in the first place? But why had Basharat said it was someone else? After all, he knew Gurmukh Singh's face from his annual visit.

Sughra went to the front door. There was another knock. Her heart missed a beat. 'Who is it?' she asked in a faint voice.

Basharat whispered to her to look through a small hole in the door.

It wasn't Gurmukh Singh, who was a very old man. This was a young fellow. He knocked again. He was holding a bag in his hand of the same kind Gurmukh Singh used to bring.

'Who are you?' she asked, a little more confident now.

'I am Sardar Gurmukh Singh's son Santokh.'

Sughra's fear had suddenly gone. 'What brings you here today?' she asked politely.

'Where is Judge sahib?' he asked.

'He is not well,' Sughra answered.

'Oh, I'm sorry,' Santokh Singh said. Then he shifted his bag from one hand to the other. 'Here is some sawwaiyaan.' Then after a pause, 'Sardarji is dead.'

'Dead!'

'Yes, a month ago, but one of the last things he said to me was, "For the last ten years, on the occasion of Id, I have always taken my small gift to Judge sahib. After I am gone, it will become your duty." I gave him my word that I would not fail him. I am here today to honour the promise made to my father on his deathbed.'

Sughra was so moved that tears came to her eyes. She opened the door a little. The young man pushed the bag towards her. 'May God rest his soul,' she said.

'Is Judge sahib not well?' he asked.

'No.'

'What's wrong?'

'He had a stroke.'

'Had my father been alive, it would have grieved him deeply. He never forgot Judge sahib's kindness until his last breath. He used to say, "He is not a man, but a god." May God keep him under his care. Please convey my respects to him.'

He left before Sughra could make up her mind whether or not to ask him to get a doctor.

As Santokh Singh turned the corner, four men, their faces covered with their turbans, moved towards him. Two of them held burning oil torches; the others carried cans of kerosene oil and explosives. One of them asked Santokh, 'Sardarji, have you completed your assignment?'

The young man nodded.

'Should we then proceed with ours?' he asked.

'If you like,' he replied and walked away.

# Mozail

TARLOCHAN LOOKED UP AT THE NIGHT SKY FOR THE FIRST TIME IN FOUR years, and only because he felt tired and listless. That was what had brought him out on the terrace of Advani Chambers to take the open air and think.

The sky was absolutely clear, free of cloud, stretched over the entire city of Bombay like a huge dust-coloured tent. As far as the eye could see, there were lights. Tarlochan felt as if a lot of stars had fallen from the sky and lodged themselves in tall buildings that looked like huge trees in the dark of the night. The lights shimmered like glow-worms.

This was a new experience for Tarlochan, a new feeling, his being under the open night sky. He felt that he had been imprisoned in his flat for four years and thus deprived of one of nature's great blessings. It was close to three and the breeze was light and pleasant after the heavy, mechanically stirred air of the fan under which he always slept. In the morning when he got up, he always felt as if he had been beaten up all night. But in the natural morning breeze, he felt every pore in his body happily sucking in the air's freshness. When he had come up, he was restless and agitated but now, half an hour later, he felt relaxed. He could think clearly.

He began to think of Kirpal Kaur. She and her entire family lived in a mohalla, which was predominantly and ferociously Muslim. Many houses had been set on fire there and several lives had been lost. Tarlochan would have evacuated the entire family except that a curfew had been clamped down——probably a forty-eight-hour one——and Tarlochan was helpless. There were Muslims all around, and pretty bloodthirsty Muslims they were. News was pouring in from the Punjab about atrocities being committed on Muslims by Sikhs. Any hand——easily a Muslim hand——could grab hold of the soft and delicate wrist of Kirpal Kaur and push her into the well of death.

Kirpal Kaur's mother was blind and her father was a cripple. There was a brother, who lived in Deolali, where he took care of the contract he had recently won.

Tarlochan was really annoyed with Kirpal's brother, Naranjan, who read about the riots every day in the newspaper. In fact, a week ago, he had been told of the rapidity and intensity with which the riots were spreading. He was warned in clear words: 'Forget about your business for the time being. We are passing through difficult times. You should stay with your family or, better still, move to my flat. I know there isn't enough space, but these are not normal times. We'll manage somehow.'

Naranjan had merely smiled through his thick moustache. 'Yaar, you are unduly worried. I have seen many such riots here. This is not Amritsar or Lahore: it is Bombay. You have only been here four years; I have lived here for twelve, a full twelve years.'

God knows what Naranjan thought Bombay was. To him it was a city which would recover from the effects of riots by itself, in case they ever were to take place. He behaved as if he had some magic formula, or a fairy-tale castle that could come to no harm. As for Tarlochan, he could see quite clearly in the cool morning air that this mohalla was not safe. He was even mentally prepared to read in the morning papers that Kirpal Kaur and her parents had been killed.

He did not care much for Kirpal Kaur's crippled father or her blind mother. If they were killed and Kirpal survived, it would be good for Tarlochan. If her brother, Naranjan, was killed in Deolali, it would be even better, as the coast would be clear for Tarlochan. Naranjan was not only a hindrance in his way, but a huge, big boulder blocking his path. Whenever his name came up in a conversation with Kirpal Kaur, he would call him Khingar Singh—Punjabi for 'boulder'—instead of Naranjan Singh.

The breeze was blowing gently, imparting a cool, pleasant sensation to Tarlochan's head, shorn of its long hair, religiously ordained. But his heart was full of apprehensions. Kirpal Kaur had newly entered his life. Although she was the sister of the rough and ruddy Khingar Singh, she was soft, delicate and willowy. She had grown up in the village, lived through its summers and winters, but she did not have that hard, tough, masculine quality that is common to average Sikh village girls, who have to do hard, physical work. She had delicate features as if they were still in the making and her breasts were small, still in need of a few more layers of creamy fat. She was fairer than most Sikh village girls are, fair as unblemished white cotton cloth. Her body was smooth like printed linen. She was very shy.

Tarlochan belonged to the same village but he had not lived there very long. After primary school, he had gone to the city to attend high school and never went back. High school done, he began his life at college and, although during those years he went to his village numerous times, he had never even heard of this girl called Kirpal Kaur. But that may have been because he was always in a hurry to get back to the city.

The building he lived in was called Advani Chambers and, as he stood on the balcony looking at the pre-morning sky, he thought of Mozail, the Jewish girl who had a flat here. There was a time when he was in love with her 'up to his knees', as he liked to say. Never in his thirty-five years had he felt that way about any woman.

But those college days were long in the past. Between the college campus and the terrace of the Advani Chambers lay ten years, a period full of strange incidents in Tarlochan's life: Burma, Singapore, Hong Kong—and Bombay, where he had now lived for four years. And it was for the first time in those four years that he had seen the sky at night, which was not a bad sight. In its dust-coloured canopy twinkled thousands of clay lamps while a cool breeze blew his way gently.

While thinking of Kirpal Kaur, he began to think about Mozail, the Jewish girl who lived in Advani Chambers and with whom he had fallen in love 'right up to the knees'. It was a love the like of which he had not known before. He had run into Mozail the very day he had moved into a second-floor flat at Advani Chambers, which a Christian friend of his had helped him rent. His first impression of her was that she was really quite mad. Her brown hair was cut short and looked dishevelled. She wore thick, unevenly laid lipstick that sat on her lips like congealed blood. She wore a loose white dress, cut so low at the neck that you could see three-quarters of her big breasts with their faint blue veins. Her thin arms were covered with a fine down. She seemed to have just stepped out of a hairdresser's after a haircut. Her lips were not as thick as they looked, but it was the liberal quantities of crimson-red lipstick she plastered on them that gave them the appearance of thick beefsteaks.

Tarlochan's flat faced hers, divided by a narrow passage. When he stepped forward to go into his flat, she stepped out of hers in

wooden sandals. He heard their clatter and stopped. She looked
at him with her big eyes through her dishevelled hair and laughed.
This made Tarlochan nervous and he pulled out his key from the
pocket and moved towards his door. One of Mozail's wooden
sandals slipped from her foot and came skidding across the floor
towards him. Before he could recover, he was on the floor and
Mozail was over him, pinning him down. Her trussed-up dress
revealed two bare, strong legs which had him in a scissors-like
grip. He tried to get up and, in so doing, brushed against her
entire body as if soaping it. Breathless now, he apologized to her
in very proper words. Mozail straightened her dress and smiled.
'These wooden sandals *ek-dum kandam*, just no good.' Then she
carefully re-threaded her big toe in her sandal and walked out
of the corridor.

Tarlochan was afraid it might not be easy to get to befriend
her, but she became quite close to him before long. She was
headstrong and she did not take Tarlochan too seriously. She
would make him take her out to dinner, the cinema or Juhu
beach, where she would spend the entire day with him, but
whenever he tried to go beyond hands and lips she would tell
him to lay off. She would do it in such a way that all his resolve
would get entangled in his beard and moustache.

Tarlochan had never been in love before. In Lahore, Burma,
Singapore, he would pick up girls and pay for the service. It
would never have occurred to him that one day he would find
himself plunged 'up to the knees' in love with a wild Jewish girl
in Bombay. She treated him with strange indifference, although
she would dress up and get ready whenever he asked her to go
to the movies with him. Often they would hardly have taken
their seats when she would start looking around and, if she found

someone she knew, she would wave to him and go sit next to him without asking Tarlochan if he minded.

The same thing would happen in restaurants. He would order an elaborate meal and she would abruptly rise in the middle of it to join an old friend who had caught her eye. Tarlochan would get terribly jealous. And when he protested, she would stop meeting him for days on end and, when he insisted, she would pretend that she had a headache or her stomach was upset. Or she would say, 'You are a Sikh. You are incapable of understanding anything subtle.'

'Such as your lovers?' he would taunt her.

She would put her hands on her hips, spread out her legs and say, 'Yes, my lovers, but why does it burn you up?'

'We cannot carry on like this,' Tarlochan would say.

And Mozail would laugh. 'You're not only a real Sikh, you're also an idiot. In any case, who asked you to carry on with me? I have a suggestion. Go back to your Punjab and marry a Sikhni.' In the end Tarlochan would always give in because Mozail had become his weakness and he wanted to be around her all the time. Often she would humiliate him in front of some young 'Kristan' lout she had picked up that day from somewhere. He would get angry, but not for long.

This cat-and-mouse thing with Mozail continued for two years, but he was steadfast. One day when she was in one of her high and happy moods, he took her in his arms and asked, 'Mozail, don't you love me?'

Mozail freed herself, sat down in a chair, gazed intently at her dress, then raised her big Jewish eyes, batted her thick eyelashes and said, 'I cannot love a Sikh.'

'You always make fun of me. You make fun of my love,' he said in an angry voice.

She got up, swung her brown head of hair from side to side and said coquettishly, 'If you shave off your beard and let down your long hair which you keep under your turban, I promise you many men will wink at you suggestively, because you are very dishy.'

Tarlochan felt as if his hair was on fire. He dragged Mozail towards him, squeezed her in his arms and put his bearded lips on hers.

She pushed him away. 'Phew!' she said, 'I brushed my teeth this morning. You don't have to bother.'

'Mozail!' Tarlochan screamed.

She paid no attention, but took out her lipstick from the bag she always carried and began to touch up her lips which looked havoc-stricken after contact with Tarlochan's beard and moustache.

'Let me tell you something,' she said without looking up. 'You have no idea how to use your hirsute assets properly. They would be perfect for brushing dust off my navy-blue skirt.'

She came and sat next to him and began to unpin his beard. It was true he was very good-looking, but being a practising Sikh he had never shaved a single hair off his body and, consequently, he had come to assume a look which was not natural. He respected his religion and its customs and he did not wish to change any of its ritual formalities.

'What are you doing?' he asked Mozail. By now his beard, freed of its shackles, was hanging over his chest in waves.

'You have such soft hair, so I don't think I would use it to brush my navy-blue skirt. Perhaps a nice, soft woven handbag,' she said, smiling flirtatiously.

'I have never made fun of your religion. Why do you always mock mine? It's not fair. But I have suffered these insults silently because I love you. Did you know I love you?'

'I know,' she said, letting go of his beard.

'I want to marry you,' he declared, while trying to repin his beard.

'I know,' she said with a slight shake of her head. 'In fact, I have nearly decided to marry you.'

'You don't say!' Tarlochan nearly jumped.

'I do,' she said.

He forgot his half-folded beard and embraced her passionately. 'When . . . when?'

She pushed him aside. 'When you get rid of your hair.'

'It will be gone tomorrow,' he said without thinking.

She began to do a tap dance around the room. 'You're talking rubbish, Tarloch. I don't think you have the courage.'

'You will see,' he said defiantly.

'So I will,' she said, kissing him on the lips, followed by her usual 'Phew!'

He could hardly sleep that night. It was not a small decision. However, the next day he went out to a barber in the Fort area and had him cut his hair and shave off his beard. While this operation was in progress, he kept his eyes closed. When it was finished, he looked at his new face in the mirror. It looked good. Any girl in Bombay would have found it difficult not to take a long, second look at him.

He did not leave his flat on his first hairless day, but sent word to Mozail that he was not well and would she mind dropping in for a minute. She stopped dead in her tracks when she saw him. 'My darling Tarloch,' she cried and fell into his arms. She ran her hands over his smooth cheeks and combed his short hair with her fingers. She laughed so much that her nose began to run. She had no handkerchief and calmly she lifted her skirt and wiped it. Tarlochan blushed. 'You should wear something underneath.'

'Gives me a funny feeling. That's how it is,' she replied.

'Let's get married tomorrow,' he said.

'Of course,' she replied, rubbing his chin.

They decided to get married in Poona, where Tarlochan had many friends.

Mozail worked as a salesgirl in one of the big department stores in the Fort area. She told Tarlochan to wait for her at a taxi stand in front of the store the next day, but she never turned up. He later learnt that she had gone off with an old lover of hers who had recently bought a new car. They had moved to Deolali and were not expected to return to Bombay 'for some time'.

Tarlochan was shattered, but in a few weeks he had got over it.

And it was at this point that he had met Kirpal Kaur and fallen in love with her.

He now realized what a vulgar girl Mozail was and how totally heartless. He thanked his stars that he hadn't married her.

But there were days when he missed her. He remembered that once he had decided to buy her some gold earrings and had taken her to a jeweller's, but all she wanted was some cheap baubles. That was the way she was.

She used to lie in bed with him for hours and let him kiss and fondle her as much as he wanted, but she would never let him make love. 'You're a Sikh,' she would laugh, 'and I hate Sikhs.'

One argument they always had was over her habit of not wearing any underclothes. Once she said to him, 'You're a Sikh and I know that you wear some ridiculous shorts under your trousers because that is the Sikh religious requirement, but I think it's rubbish that religion should be kept tucked under one's trousers.'

Tarlochan looked at the gradually brightening sky.

'The hell with her,' he said loudly and decided not to think about her at all. He was worried about Kirpal Kaur and the danger which loomed over her.

A number of communal incidents had already taken place in the locality. The place was full of orthodox Muslims and, curfew or no curfew, they could easily enter her house and massacre everyone.

Since Mozail had left him, he had decided to grow his hair. His beard had flourished again, but he had come to a compromise. He would not let it grow too long. He knew a barber who could trim it so skilfully that it would not appear trimmed.

The curfew was still in force, but you could walk about in the street, as long as you did not stray too far. He decided to do so. There was a public tap in front of the building. He sat down under it and began to wash his hair and freshen up his face.

Suddenly he heard the sound of wooden sandals on the cobblestones. There were other Jewish women in that building, all of whom for some reason wore the same kind of sandals. He thought it was one of them.

But it was Mozail. She was wearing her usual loose gown under which he could see her breasts dancing. It disturbed him. He coughed to attract her attention, because he had a feeling she might just pass him by. She came towards him, examined his beard and said, 'What do we have here, a twice-born Sikh?'

She touched his beard. 'Still good enough to brush my navy-blue skirt with, except that I left it in that other place in Deolali.'

Tarlochan said nothing. She pinched his arm. 'Why don't you say something, Sardar sahib?'

He looked at her. She had lost weight. 'Have you been ill?' he asked.

'No.'

'But you look run down.'

'I am dieting. So you are once again a Sikh?' She sat down next to him, squatting on the ground.

'Yes,' he replied.

'Congratulations. Are you in love with some other girl?'

'Yes.'

'Congratulations. Does she live here, I mean, in our building?'

'No.'

'Isn't that awful?'

She pulled at his beard. 'Is this grown on her advice?'

'No.'

'Well, I promise you that if you get this beard of yours shaved off, I'll marry you. I swear.'

'Mozail,' he said, 'I have decided to marry this simple girl from my village. She is a good, observing Sikh, which is why I am growing my hair again.'

Mozail got up, swung herself in a semi-circle on her heel and said, 'If she's a good Sikh, why should she marry you? Doesn't she know that you once broke all the rules and shaved your hair off?'

'No, she doesn't. I started growing a beard the very day you left me—as a gesture of revenge, if you like. I met her some time later, but the way I tie my turban, you can hardly tell that I don't have a full head of hair.'

She lifted her dress to scratch her thigh. 'Damn these mosquitoes,' she said. Then she added, 'When are you getting married?'

'I don't know.' The anxiety in his voice showed.

'What are you thinking, Tarlochan?' she asked. He told her.

'You are a first-class idiot. What's the problem? Just go and get her here where she would be safe.'

'Mozail, you can't understand these things. It's not that simple. You don't really give a damn and that is why we broke up. I'm sorry,' he said.

'Sorry? Come off it, you silly idiot. What you should be thinking of now is how we can get . . . whatever her name is . . . to your flat. And here you go talking about your sorrow at losing me. It could never have worked. Your problem is that you are both stupid and cautious. I like my men to be reckless. OK, forget about that, let's go and get your whatever Kaur from wherever she is.'

Tarlochan looked at her nervously. 'But there's a curfew in the area,' he said.

'There's no curfew for Mozail. Let's go,' she said, almost dragging him.

She looked at him and paused. 'What's the matter?' he asked.

'Your beard, but it's not that long. However, take that turban off, then nobody will take you for a Sikh.'

'I won't go bareheaded,' he said.

'Why not?'

'You don't understand? It is not proper for me to go to their house without my turban.'

'And why not?'

'Why don't you understand? She has never seen me except

in a turban. She thinks I am a proper Sikh. I daren't let her think otherwise.'

Mozail rattled her wooden sandals on the floor. 'You are not only a first-class idiot, you are also an ass. It is a question of saving her life, whatever that Kaur of yours is called.'

Tarlochan was not going to give up. 'Mozail, you've no idea how religious she is. Once she sees me bareheaded, she'll start hating me.'

'Your love be damned. Tell me, are all Sikhs as stupid as you? On the one hand, you want to save her life and at the same time you insist on wearing your turban, and perhaps even those funny knickers you are never supposed to be without.'

'I do wear my knickers—as you call them—all the time,' he said.

'Good for you,' she said. 'But think, you're going to go to that awful area full of those bloodthirsty Muslims and their big maulanas. If you go in a turban, I promise you they will take one look at you and run a big, sharp knife across your throat.'

'I don't care, but I must wear my turban. I can risk my life, but not my love.'

'You're an ass,' she said exasperatedly. 'Tell me, if you're bombed off, what use will that Kaur be to you? I swear, you're not only a Sikh, you are an idiot of a Sikh.'

'Don't talk rot,' Tarlochan snapped.

She laughed, then she put her arms around his neck and swung her body slightly. 'Darling,' she said, 'then it will be the way you want it. Go put on your turban. I will be waiting for you in the street.'

'You should put on some clothes,' Tarlochan said.

'I'm fine the way I am,' she replied.

When he joined her, she was standing in the middle of the street. Her legs apart like a man, and smoking. When he came close, she blew the smoke in his face. 'You're the most terrible human being I've ever met in my life,' Tarlochan said. 'You know we Sikhs are not allowed to smoke.'

'Let's go,' she said.

The bazaar was deserted. The curfew seemed to have affected even the usually brisk Bombay breeze. It was hardly noticeable. Some lights were on but their glow was sickly. Normally at this hour the trains would start running and shops begin to open. There was absolutely no sign of life anywhere.

Mozail walked in front of him. The only sound came from the impact of her wooden sandals on the road. He almost asked her to take the stupid things off and go barefoot, but he didn't. She wouldn't have agreed.

Tarlochan felt scared, but Mozail was walking ahead of him nonchalantly, puffing merrily at her cigarette. They came to a square and were challenged by a policeman. 'Where are you going?' Tarlochan fell back, but Mozail moved towards the policeman, gave her head a playful shake and said, 'It's you! Don't you know me? I'm Mozail. I'm going to my sister's in the next street because she's sick. That man there is a doctor.'

While the policeman was still trying to make up his mind, she pulled out a packet of cigarettes from her bag and offered him one. 'Have a smoke,' she said.

The policeman took the cigarette. Mozail helped him light it with hers. He inhaled deeply. Mozail winked at him with her left eye and at Tarlochan with her right and they moved on.

Tarlochan was still very scared. He looked left and right as he walked behind her, expecting to be stabbed any moment.

Suddenly she stopped. 'Tarloch dear, it is not good to be afraid. If you're afraid, then something awful always happens. That's my experience.'

He didn't reply.

They came to the street which led to the mohalla where Kirpal Kaur lived. A shop was being looted. 'Nothing to worry about,' she told him. One of the rioters who was carrying something on his head ran into Tarlochan and the object fell to the ground. The man stared at Tarlochan and he knew he was a Sikh. He slipped his hand under his shirt to pull out his knife.

Mozail pushed him away as if she was drunk. 'Are you mad, trying to kill your own brother? This is the man I'm going to marry.' Then she said to Tarlochan, 'Karim, pick this thing up and help put it back on his head.'

The man gave Mozail a lecherous look and touched her breasts with his elbow. 'Have a good time, sali,' he said.

They kept walking and were soon in Kirpal Kaur's mohalla. 'Which street?' she asked.

'The third on the left. That building in the corner,' he whispered.

When they came to the building, they saw a man run out of it into another across the street. After a few minutes, three men emerged from that building, and rushed into the one where Kirpal Kaur lived. Mozail stopped. 'Tarloch dear, take off your turban,' she said.

'That I'll never do,' he replied.

'Just as you please, but I hope you do notice what's going on.'

Something terrible was going on. The three men had re-emerged, carrying gunny bags with blood dripping from them.

Mozail had an idea. 'Look, I'm going to run across the street and go into that building. You should pretend that you're trying to catch me. But don't think. Just do it.'

Without waiting for his response, she rushed across the street and ran into Kirpal Kaur's building, with Tarlochan in hot pursuit. He was panting when he found her in the front courtyard.

'Which floor?' she asked.

'Second.'

'Let's go.' And she began to climb the stairs, her wooden sandals clattering on each step. There were large bloodstains everywhere.

They came to the second floor, walked down a narrow corridor and Tarlochan stopped in front of a door. He knocked. Then he called in a low voice, 'Mehnga Singhji, Mehnga Singhji.'

A girl's voice answered, 'Who is it?'

'Tarlochan.'

The door opened slightly. Tarlochan asked Mozail to follow him in. Mozail saw a very young and very pretty girl standing behind the door trembling. She also seemed to have a cold. Mozail said to her, 'Don't be afraid. Tarlochan has come to take you away.'

Tarlochan said, 'Ask Sardar sahib to get ready, but quickly.'

There was a shriek from the flat upstairs. 'They must have got him,' Kirpal Kaur said, her voice hoarse with terror.

'Whom?' Tarlochan asked.

Kirpal Kaur was about to say something, when Mozail pushed her in a corner and said, 'Just as well they got him. Now take off your clothes.'

Kirpal Kaur was taken aback, but Mozail gave her no time to think. In one moment, she divested her of her loose shirt. The young girl frantically put her arms in front of her breasts. She was terrified. Tarlochan turned his face. Then Mozail took off the kaftan-like gown she always wore and asked Kirpal Kaur to put it on. She was now stark naked herself.

'Take her away,' she told Tarlochan. She untied the girl's hair so that it hung over her shoulders. 'Go.'

Tarlochan pushed the girl towards the door, then turned back. Mozail stood there, shivering slightly because of the cold.

'Why don't you go?' she asked.

'What about her parents?' he said.

'They can go to hell. You take her.'

'And you?'

'Don't worry about me.'

They heard men running down the stairs. Soon they were banging at the door with their fists. Kirpal Kaur's parents were moaning in the other room. 'There's only one thing to do now. I'm going to open the door,' Mozail said.

She addressed Tarlochan, 'When I open the door, I'll rush out and run upstairs. You follow me. These men will be so flabbergasted that they will forget everything and come after us.'

'And then?' Tarlochan asked.

'Then, this one here, whatever her name is, can slip out. The way she's dressed, she'll be safe. They'll take her for a Jew.'

Mozail threw the door open and rushed out. The men had no time to react. Involuntarily, they made way for her. Tarlochan ran after her. She was storming up the stairs in her wooden sandals with Tarlochan behind her.

She slipped and came crashing down, head first. Tarlochan stopped and turned. Blood was pouring out of her mouth and nose and ears. The men who were trying to break into the flat had also gathered round her in a circle, forgetting temporarily what they were there for. They were staring at her naked, bruised body.

Tarlochan bent over her. 'Mozail, Mozail.'

She opened her eyes and smiled. Tarlochan undid his turban and covered her with it.

'This is my lover. He's a bloody Muslim, but he's so crazy that I always call him a Sikh,' she said to the men.

More blood poured out of her mouth. 'Damn it!' she said.

Then she looked at Tarlochan and pushed aside the turban with which he had tried to cover her nakedness.

'Take away this rag of your religion. I don't need it.'

Her arm fell limply on her bare breasts and she said no more.

# The Return

THE SPECIAL TRAIN LEFT AMRITSAR AT TWO IN THE AFTERNOON, ARRIVING at Mughalpura, Lahore, eight hours later. Many had been killed on the way, a lot more injured and countless lost.

It was at ten o'clock the next morning that Sirajuddin regained consciousness. He was lying on bare ground, surrounded by screaming men, women and children. It did not make sense.

He lay very still, gazing at the dusty sky. He appeared not to notice the confusion or the noise. To a stranger, he might have looked like an old man in deep thought, though this was not the case. He was in shock, suspended, as it were, over a bottomless pit.

Then his eyes moved and, suddenly, caught the sun. The shock brought him back to the world of living men and women. A succession of images raced through his mind. Attack . . . fire . . . escape . . . railway station . . . night . . . Sakina. He rose abruptly and began searching through the milling crowd in the refugee camp.

He spent hours looking, all the time shouting his daughter's name . . . Sakina, Sakina . . . but she was nowhere to be found.

Total confusion prevailed, with people looking for lost sons, daughters, mothers, wives. In the end Sirajuddin gave up. He sat down, away from the crowd, and tried to think clearly. Where did he part from Sakina and her mother? Then it came to him in a flash—the dead body of his wife, her stomach ripped open. It was an image that wouldn't go away.

Sakina's mother was dead. That much was certain. She had died in front of his eyes. He could hear her voice: 'Leave me where I am. Take the girl away.'

The two of them had begun to run. Sakina's dupatta had slipped to the ground and he had stopped to pick it up and she had said, 'Father, leave it.'

He could feel a bulge in his pocket. It was a length of cloth. Yes, he recognized it. It was Sakina's dupatta, but where was she?

Other details were missing. Had he brought her as far as the railway station? Had she got into the carriage with him? When the rioters had stopped the train, had they taken her with them?

All questions. There were no answers. He wished he could weep, but tears wouldn't come. He knew then that he needed help.

A few days later, he had a break. There were eight of them, young men armed with guns. They also had a truck. They said they brought back women and children left behind on the other side.

He gave them a description of his daughter. 'She is fair, very pretty. No, she doesn't look like me, but her mother. About seventeen. Big eyes, black hair, a mole on the left cheek. Find my daughter. May God bless you.'

The young men had said to Sirajuddin, 'If your daughter is alive we will find her.'

And they had tried. At the risk of their lives, they had driven to Amritsar, recovered many women and children and brought them back to the camp, but they had not found Sakina.

On their next trip out, they had found a girl on the roadside. They seemed to have scared her and she had started running. They had stopped the truck, jumped out and run after her.

Finally, they had caught up with her in a field. She was very pretty and she had a mole on her left cheek. One of the men had said to her, 'Don't be frightened. Is your name Sakina?' Her face had gone pale, but when they told her who they were she had confessed that she was Sakina, daughter of Sirajuddin.

The young men were very kind to her. They had fed her, given her milk to drink and put her in their truck. One of them had given her his jacket so that she could cover herself. It was obvious that she was ill at ease without her dupatta, trying nervously to cover her breasts with her arms.

Many days had gone by and Sirajuddin had still not had any news of his daughter. All his time was spent running from camp to camp, looking for her. At night, he would pray for the success of the young men who were looking for his daughter. Their words would ring in his ear: 'If your daughter is alive, we will find her.'

Then one day he saw them in the camp. They were about to drive away. 'Son,' he shouted after one of them, 'have you found Sakina, my daughter?'

'We will, we will,' they replied all together.

The old man again prayed for them. It made him feel better.

That evening there was sudden activity in the camp. He saw four men carrying the body of a young girl found unconscious near the railway tracks. They were taking her to the camp hospital. He began to follow them.

He stood outside the hospital for some time, then went in. In one of the rooms, he found a stretcher with someone lying on it.

A light was switched on. It was a young woman with a mole on her left cheek. 'Sakina,' Sirajuddin screamed.

The doctor, who had switched on the light, stared at Sirajuddin.

'I am her father,' he stammered.

The doctor looked at the prostrate body and felt for the pulse. Then he said to the old man, pointing at the window, 'Open it.'

The young woman on the stretcher moved slightly. Her hands groped for the cord which kept her shalwar tied round her waist. With painful slowness, she unfastened it, pulled the garment down and opened her thighs.

'She is alive. My daughter is alive,' Sirajuddin shouted with joy.

The doctor broke into a cold sweat.

# A Woman's Life

SHE HAD HAD A LONG DAY AND SHE FELL ASLEEP AS SOON AS SHE HIT THE bed. The city sanitary inspector, whom she always called Seth, had just gone home, very drunk. His love-making had been aggressive as usual and he had left her feeling bone-weary. He would have stayed longer but for his wife who, he always said, loved him very much.

The silver coins, which she had earned, were safely tucked inside her bra. Her breasts still bore the traces of the inspector's wet kisses. Occasionally the coins would clink as she took a particularly deep breath.

Her chest had felt on fire, partly because of the pint of brandy which she had drunk followed by the home-made brew they had downed with tap water after the brandy had run out.

She was sprawled face down on her wide, wooden bed. Her bare arms, stretched out on either side, looked like the frame of a kite which has come unstuck from the paper.

It was a small room and her things were everywhere. Three or four ragged pairs of sandals lay under the bed; a mangy dog lay sleeping with his head resting on them. There were bald patches on its skin and, from a distance, one could have mistaken it for a worn doormat.

On a small shelf lay her make-up things: face powder, a single lipstick, rouge, a comb, hairpins.

Swinging from a hook in the ceiling was a cage with a green parrot. The bird was asleep, its beak tucked under one of its wings. The cage was littered with pieces of raw guava and orange peels, with some black moths and mosquitoes hovering over them.

A wicker chair stood next to the bed, its back grimy with use. To its left was a small table with an antiquated His Master's Voice gramophone resting on it. On the wall were four pictures.

It was her habit, after being paid, to rub the money against the picture she had of the Hindu elephant god Ganesha, for good luck, before putting it away. However, whenever Madhu was expected from Poona, she hid most of the money under her bed. This had first been suggested by Ram Lal, who knew that every visit by Madhu was like a raid on Saugandhi's savings. One day he said to her, 'Where'd you pick up this sala? What kind of a lover boy is he? He never parts with a penny and he is back every other week having a good time at your expense. What's more, he cheats you out of your hard-earned money. Saugandhi, what is it about this sala that you find so irresistible? I've been in this business for seven years and I know you chhokris well but this one beats me, I have to admit.'

Ram Lal, who scouted around for men looking for a good time, had a range of girls worth anything from ten to a hundred rupees for the night. He said to her one day, 'Saugandhi, don't ruin your business; I warn you this scoundrel will take the shirt off your back if you don't watch out. Tell you what, keep your money hidden under your bed and the next time he is here tell him something like, "I swear on your head, Madhu, for days I haven't set eyes on so much as a penny. I haven't even eaten today. Can you get me something to eat and a cup of tea from that Iranian cafe across the street?"'

Ram Lal went on, 'Sweetheart, these are bad times. By bringing in prohibition, this sali Congress government has taken the life out of the bazaar. But how would you know? You get your drop somehow or the other. As God is my witness, whenever I see an empty liquor bottle in your room, I almost want to change places with you.'

Saugandhi liked to offer advice too. She had once said to her friend Jamuna, 'Let me give you some advice. For ten rupees, you let men pluck you like a chicken. Let someone so much as touch me in the wrong place and he will come to grief. You know what happened last night? Ram Lal brought a Punjabi man at about two in the morning. When we went to bed, I put out the light. I swear to you, Jamuna, he was scared! He couldn't do anything! "Come on," I said to him. "Don't you want it? It is nearly morning." But all he wanted was for the light to be switched on. I couldn't hold back my laughter. "No light," I teased him. Then I pinched him and he jumped out of bed and the first thing he did was to put the light back on. "Are you crazy?" I screamed, then I put out the light. He was scared. I tell you, it was such fun. No light, then light again. When he heard the first tram car rattle past in the morning, he hurriedly put on his clothes and ran. The sala must have won that money in gambling. Jamuna, you are still very naive. I know how to deal with men. I have my ways.'

This was true. She had her ways, which she often told her friends about. 'If the customer is nice, the quiet type, flirt with him, talk, tease him, touch him playfully. If he has a beard, comb it with your fingers and pull out a hair or two just for fun. If he is fat, then tease him about it. But never give them enough time to do what they really want; keep them occupied and they'll leave happily and you'll be spared possible misadventure. The quiet types are always dangerous. Watch them because they are often very rough.'

Actually, Saugandhi was not as clever as she pretended. She didn't have a great number of clients either. She liked men, which was why all her clever methods would desert her when it was time to use them. It only took a few sweet words, softly cooed into her ear, to make her melt. Although she was convinced that physical relations were basically pointless, her body felt otherwise. It seemed to want to be overpowered and left exhausted.

When she was a little girl, she used to hide herself in the big wooden chest which sat in a corner of her parents' home while the other children looked for her. The fear of being caught, mixed with a sense of excitement, would make her heart beat very fast. Sometimes she wanted to spend her entire life in a box, hidden from view yet dying to be found. The last five years had been like a game of hide-and-seek. She was either seeking or being sought. When a man said to her, 'I love you, Saugandhi,' she would go weak in the knees, although she knew he was lying. Love, what a beautiful word, she would think. Oh, if only one could rub love like a balm into one's body! However, she did like four of her regulars enough to have their framed pictures hanging on her wall.

She had lived intensely in the last five years. True, she hadn't had the happiness she would have wished but she had managed. Money had never interested her much. She charged ten rupees for what she did, out of which one-fourth went to Ram Lal. What she was left with was enough for her needs. In fact, when Madhu came from Poona, she spent ten to fifteen rupees on him quite happily. This was perhaps the price she paid for that certain feeling that Ram Lal had once said existed between the two of them.

He was right. There was something about Madhu which Saugandhi liked. When they met, the first thing Madhu had said to her was, 'Aren't you ashamed of selling yourself, putting a price on your body? Ten rupees you take with one-fourth going to that man, Ram Lal, which leaves you with seven rupees and eight annas, doesn't it? And for that you promise to give something which you can't love. And what about me? I have come looking for something which really cannot be had. I need a woman but do you need a man? I could do with any woman but could you do with any man? There is nothing between us except this sum of ten rupees, one-fourth of which is to go to Ram Lal and the rest to you. But I know we like each other. Shouldn't we do something about it? Perhaps we could fulfil our separate needs that way. Now listen. I am a sergeant in the police at Poona. I'll come once a month for three or four days. You don't have to be doing anything from now on. I'll look after all your expenses. What is the rent for this kholi of yours?'

Madhu had made her feel like the police sergeant's chosen woman. He had also rearranged everything in the room. There were posters showing half-clad women that she had stuck on the wall. He had removed them without her permission and then torn them up. 'Saugandhi, my dear, I won't have these. And look at this slimy earthen pitcher of yours. It needs to be scrubbed and cleaned. And what are those smelly rags lying around? Throw them out. And look at your hair. It is matted and in need of a wash. And . . . and . . .'

After three hours of conversation, mostly Madhu's, Saugandhi had felt as if she had known him for many years. Never before had anyone spoken to her like that, nor made her feel that her kholi was home. The men who came to her did not even notice that her bed sheets were soiled. Nobody had ever said to her, 'I think you are catching a cold; let me run along and get you something for it.' But Madhu was different; he told her things nobody ever had and she knew she needed him.

He would come once a month from Poona and before going back he would say, 'Saugandhi, if you resume that old business of yours, you'll never see me again. Yes, about this month's household expenses, the money will be on its way as soon as I get to Poona . . . so what did you say the monthly rent for this place was?'

Madhu had never sent her any money from Poona or elsewhere and Saugandhi had continued her business as usual. They both knew it but she never said, 'What rubbish you are talking! You have never given me so much as a bum penny.' And Madhu had never asked her how she was managing to survive. They were living a pretension and they were quite happy with it. Saugandhi had argued to herself that, if one was unable to buy real gold, one might as well settle for what looked like gold.

But now she was sound asleep. She was too tired to even bother to switch off the harsh, unshaded light over her bed.

There was a knock at the door. She only heard it as a faint, faraway sound. This was followed by a succession of knocks, which woke her up. She first wiped her mouth, still sodden with the aftertaste of bad liquor, and her eyes, then looked under the bed where the dog was still asleep, its head resting on her old sandals. The parrot was also in its cage, its beak tucked under its wing.

There was another impatient knock. She rose from her bed and realized that she had a splitting headache. She poured herself some water from the earthen pitcher and rinsed her mouth, then filled another glass and drank it down in one gulp. Carefully, she opened the door and whispered, 'Ram Lal?'

Ram Lal, who had almost given up, replied caustically, 'I thought you had been bitten by a snake. I have been out here for an hour. Didn't you hear me?' Then in his discreet voice he asked, 'Is anybody with you?' She told him no and let him in. 'If it is going to take me an hour getting you chhokris out of bed, I might as well change my line of work. What are you looking at me like that for? Put on that nice flower-print sari of yours and dust your face with powder, and a bit of lipstick too. Out there in a car I have a rich Seth waiting for you.'

Instead, Saugandhi fell into her armchair, picked up a jar of rubbing balm from the table, eased off its lid and said, 'Ram Lal, I don't feel well.'

'Why didn't you say so right away?'

Saugandhi, who was now rubbing her forehead with the balm, replied, 'I just don't feel good; maybe I had too much to drink.'

Ram Lal's expression changed. 'Is there some left? I'd love a drop.'

Saugandhi returned the balm to the table. 'If I had saved some, I would have done something about this awful headache. Look, Ram Lal, bring that man in.'

'I can't,' Ram Lal answered. 'He is an important man. He was even reluctant to park on the street. Look, sweetheart, put on those nice clothes and off we go. You won't be sorry.'

It was the usual deal: seven rupees eight annas. Had Saugandhi not been in need of money, she would have sent Ram Lal packing.

In the next kholi lived a Madrasi woman whose husband had recently died in an accident. She had a grown-up daughter and they wanted to go back to Madras but didn't have the train fare. Saugandhi had said to her, 'Don't you worry, sister, my man is expected from Poona any day. He'll give me some money and you'll be on your way.' While Madhu was indeed expected, the money, of course, was to be earned by Saugandhi herself. So she rose reluctantly from her chair and began to change. She put on the flower-print sari and a bit of make-up, and then drank another glass of water from the pitcher.

The street was very still. The lights had been dimmed because of the war. In the distance, she could see the outline of a car. They walked up to it and stopped.

Ram Lal stepped forward and said, 'Here she is, a sweet-tempered girl, very new to the business.' Then to her, 'Saugandhi, the Seth sahib is waiting.'

She moved closer, feeling nervous. A flashlight suddenly lit her face, blinding her. 'Ugh!' grunted the man in the car, then revved up his engine and drove off without another word.

Saugandhi had had no time to react because of the torch in her face. She hadn't been able to see the man; she had only heard him say, 'Ugh!' What did he mean by that?

Ram Lal was muttering to himself. 'You didn't like her; that's two hours of mine gone waste.' He left without speaking to her. Saugandhi was trembling, trying hard to deal with the situation. 'What did he mean by "Ugh"? That he did not like me? The son of a . . .'

The car was gone, the red glow from its fading tail-lights barely visible now. She wanted to scream, 'Come back . . . Stop . . . Come back!'

She was alone in the deserted bazaar wearing her grey flower-print sari which fluttered in the night air.

She began to walk back slowly but then she thought of Ram Lal and the man in the car and she stopped. Ram Lal had said the Seth didn't like her; he hadn't said it was because of her looks. Well, so what? There were people she did not like. There were men who came to her that she did not care for. Only the other night she had one who was so ugly that when he was lying next to her she had felt nauseated. But she hadn't shown it.

But the man in the car? He had practically spat in her face. 'Ram Lal,' he had implied, 'from what hole have you pulled out this scented reptile? And you want ten rupees for her? For her? Ugh!'

She was angry with herself and with Ram Lal who had woken her up at two in the morning, though he had meant well. It wasn't his fault and it wasn't hers but she wanted the whole scene replayed just one more time. Slowly, very slowly, she would move towards the car, then the torchlight would be flashed in her face to be followed by a grunt, and she, Saugandhi, would scratch that Seth's face with her long nails, pull him out of that car by his hair and hit him till she broke down exhausted.

Saugandhi, she said to herself, you are not ugly. While it was true that the bloom of her early youth was gone, nobody had ever said she was ugly. In fact, she was one of those women men always steal a second look at. She knew she had everything a man expects in a woman. She was young and she had a good body. She was nice to people. She couldn't remember a single man in the last five years who hadn't enjoyed himself with her.

She was soft-hearted. Last year at Christmas time when she was living in the Golpitha area, this young fellow from Hyderabad who had spent the night with her had found his wallet missing in the morning. Obviously, the servant boy, who was a rogue, had nicked it and disappeared. He was extremely upset because he had come all the way to Bombay to spend his holidays and he hadn't the fare to go back. She had simply returned him the money he had given her the night before.

She wanted to go home, take a long, cool drink, lie on her bed and go to sleep. She began to walk back.

However, once she was outside her kholi, the pain and humiliation came back. She just couldn't forget what had happened. She had been called out to the street and a man had slapped her across the face. She had been looked at as they look at sheep in a farmers' market. A torch had been shone on her face to see if she had any flesh on her or whether she was just skin and bones. And then she had been rejected.

If that man came back, she would stand in front of him, tear up her clothes and shout, 'This is what you came to buy! Well, here it is. You can have it free, but you'll never be able to reach the woman who is inside this body!'

The key was where she always kept it, inside her bra, but the lock on the door had been released. She pushed gently and it creaked on its hinges. Then it was unlatched from the inside and she went in.

She heard Madhu laugh through his thick moustache as he carefully closed the door. 'At last you have done what I've always suggested,' he said. 'Taken an early morning walk. There is nothing like that for good health. If you do it regularly, all your lassitude will disappear, also that back pain you are always going on about. Did you walk as far as the Victoria Gardens?'

Saugandhi said nothing, nor did Madhu appear to expect an

answer. His remarks were generally supposed to be heard, not answered.

Madhu sat in the cane chair, which bore much oily evidence of earlier contact with his greasy hair. He swung one leg on top of the other and began to play with his moustache.

Saugandhi sat on the bed. 'I was waiting for you today,' she said.

'Waiting?' he asked, a bit puzzled. 'How did you know I was coming today?'

Saugandhi smiled. 'Because last night I dreamt about you and that woke me up but you weren't there so I went for a walk.'

'And there I was when you came back,' Madhu said happily. 'Haven't the wise said that lovers' hearts beat together? When did you dream about me?'

'A few hours ago,' Saugandhi answered.

'Ah!' said Madhu. 'And I dreamt about you not too many hours earlier. You were wearing your flower-print sari. Yes, the same one you have on now. And there was something in your hands. Yes, a little bag full of money. And you said to me, "Madhu, why do you worry so much about money? Take it. What is mine is yours." And I swear on your head, Saugandhi, the next thing I knew I was out of Poona and on my way to Bombay. There is bad news though. I am in trouble. There was this police investigation I botched up and, unless I can get twenty or thirty rupees together and bribe my inspector, I can say good-bye to my job. But never mind that. You look tired. Lie down, darling, and I'll press your feet. If you are not used to taking walks, you get tired. Now lie down and turn your feet towards me.'

Saugandhi lay down, cradling her head in her arms. Then in a voice which wasn't really hers, she asked, 'Madhu, who's this person who has put you in trouble? If you are afraid of losing your job and going to jail, just let me know. In such situations, the higher the bribe, the better off you are. Since you gave me the bad news about your job, my heart has been jumping up and down. By the way, when are you going back?'

Madhu could smell liquor in Saugandhi's breath and thought this was a good time to make his pitch. 'I must take the afternoon train. By this evening, I should slip around a hundred rupees in my inspector's pocket; on second thoughts, perhaps fifty will do.'

'Fifty,' Saugandhi said. Then she rose from the bed and stood facing the four pictures on the wall. The third was Madhu's. He was sitting in a chair, his hands on his thighs and a black curtain with painted flowers forming the background. There was a rose in his lapel and two thick books lay on a small table next to his chair. He sat there, looking very conscious of being photographed. He was staring at the camera with an almost painful expression.

Saugandhi began to laugh. 'Is it the picture you find so amusing?' he asked.

Saugandhi touched the first, the sanitary inspector's. 'Look at that face. Once he told me that a rani had fallen in love with him. With him!' She pulled down the frame from the wall with such violence that some of the plaster came off; then she smashed it to the floor. 'When my sweeperess Rani comes in the morning, she will take away this raja with the rest of the rubbish,' Saugandhi said. Then she began to laugh, a light laugh like the first rain of summer. Madhu managed a smile with some difficulty and followed it with a forced guffaw.

By then Saugandhi had pulled down the second picture and

thrown it out of the window. 'What's this sala doing here? No one with a mug like his is allowed on this wall, is he Madhu?' she asked. Madhu laughed but the sound was unnatural.

She pulled down the fourth picture, a man in a turban, and then, as Madhu watched apprehensively, his own, throwing them out together through the window. They heard them fall on the street, the glass breaking. Madhu somehow managed to say, 'Well done! I didn't like that one of mine either.'

Saugandhi moved slowly towards him. 'You didn't like that one, yeah? Well, let me ask you, is there anything about you which you should like? This bulb of a nose of yours! This small, hairy forehead! Your swollen nostrils! Your twisted ears! And that awful breath! Your filthy, unwashed body! This oil that you coat yourself with! So you didn't like your picture, eh?'

Madhu was flinching away from her, his back against the wall. He tried to put some authority into his voice. 'Look, Saugandhi, it seems to me you have gone back to that dirty old profession of yours. I am telling you for the last time . . .'

Saugandhi mimicked him, 'If you return to that dirty old profession of yours, that'll be the end. And if I find out that another man has been in your bed, I'll drag you out by your hair and throw you out on the street. As for your monthly expenses, a money order will be on its way as soon as I return to Poona. And what is the monthly rent of this kholi of yours?'

Madhu listened in total disbelief.

Saugandhi had not finished with him yet. 'Let me tell you what it costs me every month—fifteen rupees. And you know what my own rental is? Ten rupees. Out of that two rupees and eight annas go to Ram Lal, which leaves me with seven rupees and eight annas exactly, in return for which I sleep with men.

What was our relationship anyway? Nothing! Ten rupees, perhaps. Every time you came you took away what you wanted——and the money too. It used to be ten rupees; now it is fifty.' She flicked away his cap with one finger and it fell to the floor.

'Saugandhi!' Madhu yelled.

She ignored him. Then she pulled out his handkerchief from his pocket, raised it to her nose, made a face and said with disgust, 'It stinks! Look at yourself, at your filthy cap and these rags that you call clothes. They all smell! Get out!'

'Saugandhi!' Madhu screamed again.

But she screamed right back. 'You creep! Why do you come here? Am I your mother, who will give you money to spend? Or are you such a ravishing man that I'd fall in love with you? You dog, you wretch, don't you dare raise your voice at me! I am nothing to you! You miserable beggar, who do you think you are? Tell me, are you a thief or a pickpocket? What are you doing in my house at this hour anyway? Should I call the police? There may or may not be a case against you in Poona but there will be a case against you here in Bombay!'

Madhu was scared. 'What has come over you, Saugandhi?'

'Who are you to put such questions to me? Get out of here . . . this instant!' The mangy dog, who had so far slept undisturbed, suddenly woke up and began to bark at Madhu, which made Saugandhi laugh hysterically.

Madhu bent down to pick up his cap from the floor but Saugandhi shouted, 'Leave it there! As soon as you get to Poona, I'll money-order it to you.' She began to laugh again as she fell into the chair. The dog, in the meanwhile, had chased Madhu out of the room and down the stairs.

He came back wagging his short, ugly tail and flapping his ears and sat down at Saugandhi's feet. Everything was very still and for a minute she was terrified. She also felt empty, like a train which having discharged its passengers is shunted into the yard and left there.

For a long time she sat in the chair. Then she rose, picked up her dog from the floor, put it carefully on the bed, laid herself next to him, threw an arm across his wasted body and went to sleep.

# Odour

IT WAS ABOUT THIS TIME OF YEAR. THE MONSOONS HAD COME AND, outside his window, the leaves of the peepal tree danced as the raindrops fell on them. On the mahogany bed with the spring mattress that had now been pushed away from the window, a girl lay next to Randhir, their bodies clinging. Outside, in the milky dankness of the evening, the leaves of the peepal tree swung in the breeze like a golden ornament on a woman's forehead.

This was how it had happened. Having already read everything in the day's paper, including the advertisements, he had stepped out on the balcony. That was when he had seen her. She stood under the tamarind tree to stay dry. She must have been one of the workers in the sweatshop next door that made rope. To attract her attention, he coughed a couple of times and, when she looked up, he waved to her to come to him.

He was tired of being lonely because, since the war, most of the young Anglo-Indian girls of Bombay had joined the army's women's auxiliary corps, while some had opened private dance places in the Fort area to which only whites were admitted.

Randhir felt bored and a little sorry for himself. His ego hurt because he was far more cultured, far better educated and much better looking than those British tommies who were welcome in these clubs while he wasn't because of his colour. Before the war, Randhir had had several flings with the better-known hookers from the Nagpara area and the Taj Hotel. He always thought those Christian chhokras who ran after them, sometimes ending up marrying them, offered no competition.

He wanted the girl who stood under the tree as his revenge on Hazel, who lived on the ground floor and left every morning for work in her new, crisp uniform with a khaki cap sitting at a jaunty angle on her fashionably coiffeured hair. She was proud and flirtatious, expecting any man she came across to pay court to her. She had also decided to ignore Randhir.

When Randhir made a sign to the girl who stood under the tree to come upstairs, he wasn't sure if he wanted her. But she had come anyway. He noticed that her clothes were wet and he was afraid she might catch a chill, so he said to her, 'Take your wet clothes off unless you want to catch something.' He could see from her eyes that she knew why she was there. He gave her a dry towel to wrap herself in. She hesitated but only for a second. Then she took off her lehnga that was tied around her waist with a cord, placed it aside, hurriedly covered her thighs with the towel he had handed her and tried to wriggle out of her choli which was knotted in the front. She couldn't undo it because it was wet. She worked at the knot that was half embedded in her deep cleavage but it didn't yield. Finally she gave up. 'I can't; it won't give.'

Randhir made her sit next to him on the bed and began to struggle with the knot. In exasperation, he tugged at it and it snapped, revealing a pair of throbbing breasts like new clay cups from a potter's wheel: soft, round, cool, fragile and sensual. Dusky and virginal, they glowed like two floating lamps in a muddy pond.

It was the same time of year as it is now. The monsoons had come, and the leaves of the peepal tree danced as the raindrops fell on them. The wet clothes of the girl lay in a heap on the floor as she clung to Randhir, her naked body radiating a strange heat, a feeling of goodness and warmth that one gets in a steam bath. She never let go of him as long as she stayed. They said no more than a few words. There was no need to because their breath, their lips, their bodies had made that unnecessary. Randhir's hands moved over her breasts like breeze over open land. Her nipples were small and there were dark circles around them. They pressed their throbbing bodies together and he felt as if he was engulfed by fire.

Randhir was no novice to such encounters. He had slept with scores of girls and he knew the ecstasy of fulfilled desire. He had spent many nights lying next to beautiful women, his hard chest pressed against their tender breasts. He had known women who had no experience of men and who told him things one doesn't tell strangers. Then there were those who asked him to just lie back while they did all the work. But this girl who only a few minutes ago was standing under the tamarind tree trying to stay dry was different.

All through the night, Randhir remained aware of the odour that her body emitted, a smell both pleasant and unpleasant, a smell he drank all night. The odour that came out of her armpits, her breasts, her hair, her belly, in fact, from every part of her body, was overwhelming. Had she smelt different, he would have felt nothing for her. But this odour had penetrated the inner recesses of his being and gone beyond anything he had ever experienced. It was the odour that had welded their two bodies together. He felt as if he were drowning in a bottomless sea of desire, the closest a man can come to total physical satisfaction, a state both transitory and timeless. At moments he felt as if the two of them were flying high in an indescribably blue sky.

The odour cascaded out of every pore of her body and every pore of Randhir's body opened up to drink it in, but there was nothing he could compare it with. Perhaps it was closest to the smell of dry earth when sprinkled with water. Perhaps it wasn't. Her odour was not artificial like perfume: it was strong and earthy, like the physical union between man and woman that is both sacred and eternal.

Randhir had always hated the smell of perspiration and after a shower he would rub his body with talcum powder and put deodorant in his armpits. But wasn't it strange that he had kissed her repeatedly in her armpits and felt no nausea? In fact, a deep sense of satisfaction had washed over him. He was profoundly aware of the powerful smell of her body, something impossible to explain.

The monsoons had come as they had come that year. He looked out of the window. The peepal tree was where it had been that day. The raindrops fell over its leaves and the breeze blew over them gently as they fluttered. The sky was dark, yet there was a glow everywhere as if the rain had brought down starlight with it.

The rains had come as they had come that day, except that there were now two beds in the room, lying next to each other. There was also a new dressing table in one corner. One bed was empty and on the other lay Randhir, watching the rain fall on the leaves of the peepal tree. A fair-complexioned girl was stretched out next to him. She had fallen asleep while trying to cover her naked body with a bed sheet but had only half succeeded. Her red shalwar lay heaped at the foot of the bed, its silken cord dangling. Her other clothes also lay on the bed: the gold-coloured flowered jumper, the brassiere, the panties, the dupatta. Her clothes were bridal red and they were perfumed. There were bits of glitter in her black hair that, off and on, caught the light. Her face was rouged and made up, and her brassiere had left a faint red imprint on her white, slightly bluish breasts. Her armpits were shaved and the skin was steel gray.

Randhir looked at the girl who lay next to him. She could have been sent to him in a wooden crate and he would have pulled out the nails to examine the contents. She had fine lines on her skin like old porcelain. Randhir had relieved her of her brassiere and seen its faint red imprint on her skin. Around her waist, the tight cord of her red shalwar had also left an imprint. There were also marks on her skin left by the heavy necklace she had been wearing.

It was the same time of year as it was then. He could hear the rain coming down on the leaves of the peepal tree, the same sound he had heard that night. He felt a cool breeze rise and carry the girl's perfume with it. Randhir fondled her breasts gently and a current ran through her body. He was conscious of the excitement embedded in her limbs. He lay next to her, their breasts touching. He heard her body hum but no odour leapt out of it. He remembered that dark girl to whom he had made love all night. Her odour had called out to him, as had her body, the same way a child calls out to its mother when hungry for her milk.

Randhir looked out of the window. The leaves of the peepal tree, now wet and washed, danced in the breeze. Beyond the trees he could see clouds in the sky that glowed as the breasts of the dark girl he had made love to all night had glowed. Their bodies had bonded.

He looked at the girl lying next to him. Her body was soft as if it were made of milk and melted butter, but the perfume she wore had a tired smell now, even a sour smell, a sad, colourless smell. He looked at her again. Her white skin with scratch marks reminded him of milk gone bad. He recoiled from the perfume she exuded. His mind went back to that night when that dark girl had lain next to him, her odour overwhelming his senses. It was something that leapt out of her body at him with a primeval force, far sweeter than the perfume his bride wore. The dark girl's odour had penetrated his body like an arrow, he remembered.

Randhir ran his hands over her white body but felt nothing. There was no sense of gathering excitement under his skin. His bride was the daughter of a judge, a college graduate and the heartthrob of her fellow students, but for Randhir she may as well not have been there. He had sought in her perfumed body that lost, remembered odour that had cascaded out of the unwashed body of that dark girl on a certain evening when the rain had begun to fall gently on the wet and dancing leaves of the peepal tree outside his window.

# Kingdom's End

THE PHONE RANG. MANMOHAN PICKED IT UP. 'HELLO, 44457.'

'Sorry, wrong number,' said a woman's voice.

Manmohan put the receiver down and returned to his book. He had read it about twenty times, not because it was anything extraordinary, but because it was the only book in this room.

For one week now, Manmohan had been the sole occupant of this office room. It belonged to a friend of his who had gone out of town to raise a business loan. Since Manmohan was one of this big city's thousands of homeless people who slept nights on its footpaths, his friend had invited him to stay here in his absence to keep a watch on things.

He hardly ever went out. He was permanently out of work because he hated all employment. Had he really tried, he could easily have got himself hired as director with some film company, which is what he once was when he had decided to drop out. However, he had no desire to be enslaved again. He was a nice, quite harmless man. He had almost no personal expenses. All he required was a cup of tea in the morning with two slices of toast, a little bit of curry and chapatti in the afternoon and a packet of cigarettes. That was all. Luckily, he had enough friends who were quite happy to provide for these simple needs.

Manmohan had no family or close relations. He could go without food for days on end if the going got hard. His friends didn't know much about him except that he had run away from home as a boy and had lived on the broad footpaths of Bombay for many years. There was only one thing missing in his life—women. He used to say, 'If a woman were to fall in love with me, my life would change.' Friends would retort, 'But even then you wouldn't work.'

'It would be nothing but work from then on,' he would answer.

'Why not have an affair then?'

'What good is an affair when the initiative comes from the man?'

It was afternoon now, almost time for lunch. Suddenly, the phone rang.

He picked it up. 'Hello, 44457.'

'44457?' a woman's voice asked.

'That's right,' Manmohan answered.

'Who are you?' the voice asked.

'I am Manmohan.'

There was no response. 'Who do you wish to speak to?' he asked.

'You,' the voice said.

'Me?'

'Unless you object.'

'No . . . not at all.'

'Did you say your name was Madan Mohan?'

'No. Manmohan.'

'Manmohan?'

There was a silence. 'I thought you wanted to talk to me,' he said.

'Yes.'

'Then go ahead.'

'I don't know what to say. Why don't you say something?'

'Very well,' Manmohan said. 'I have already told you my name. Temporarily, this office is my headquarters. I used to sleep on the city's footpaths, but for the last one week I have been sleeping on a big office table.'

'What did you do to keep the mosquitoes away at night? Use a net on your footpath?'

Manmohan laughed. 'Before I answer this, let me make it clear that I don't tell lies. I have slept on footpaths for years. Since this office came under my occupation, I have been living it up.'

'How are you living it up?'

'Well, there's this book I have. The last pages are missing, but I've read it twenty times. One day, when I can lay my hand on the missing pages, I will finally know what end the two lovers met.'

'You sound like a very interesting man,' the voice said.

'You are only being kind.'

'What do you do?'

'Do?'

'I mean, what is your occupation?'

'Occupation? None at all. What occupation can a man have when he doesn't work? But to answer your question, I loaf around during the day and sleep at night.'

'Do you like your life?'

'Wait,' Manmohan said. 'That is one question I have never asked myself. And now that you have put it to me, I'm going to put it to myself for the first time. Do I like the way I live my life?'

'And what is the answer?'

'Well, there is no answer, but I suppose if I've lived my life the way I've lived it for so long, then it's reasonable to assume that I like it.'

There was laughter. 'You laugh so beautifully,' Manmohan said.

'Thank you.' The voice was shy. The call was disconnected. For a long time, he kept holding the receiver, smiling to himself.

The next day at about eight in the morning, the phone rang again. He was fast asleep, but the noise woke him up. He yawned and picked it up.

'Hello, this is 44457.'

'Good morning, Manmohan sahib.'

'Good morning . . . oh it's you. Good morning.'

'Were you asleep?'

'I was. You know I have become spoilt since I moved here. When I return to the footpath, I'm going to run into difficulties.'

'Why?'

'Because if you sleep on the footpath, you have to get up before five in the morning.'

There was laughter.

'You rang off abruptly yesterday,' he said.

'Well, why did you say I laugh beautifully?'

'What a question! If something is beautiful, it should be praised, shouldn't it?'

'Not at all.'

'You are not to impose conditions. I have never accepted conditions. If you laugh, I'm going to say that you laugh beautifully.'

'In that case, I'll hang up.'

'Please yourself.'

'Don't you really care if I get upset?'

'Well, to begin with, I don't wish to upset myself, which means that if you laugh and I don't say that you laugh beautifully, I would be doing an injustice to my good taste.'

There was a brief silence. Then the voice came back: 'I'm sorry, I was having a word with our maid. So you were saying that you were partial to your good taste. What else is your good taste partial to?'

'What do you mean?'

'I mean . . . what hobby or work . . . . or, shall I ask, what can you do?'

Manmohan laughed. 'Nothing much except that I am fond of photography—just a bit.'

'That's a very good hobby.'

'I have never thought of it in terms of its being good or bad.'

'You must have a very nice camera.'

'I have no camera. Off and on, I borrow one from a friend. Anyway, if I'm ever able to earn some money, there is a certain camera I am going to buy.'

'What camera?'

'Exacta. It's a reflex camera. I like it very much.'

There was silence. 'I was thinking of something.'

'What?'

'You have neither asked me my name nor my phone number.'

'I haven't felt the need.'

'Why not?'

'What does it matter what your name is? You have my number. That's enough. When you want me to phone you, I'm sure you will give me your name and number.'

'No, I won't.'

'Please yourself. I'm not going to ask.'

'You're a strange man.'

'That's true, I am.'

There was another silence.

'Were you thinking again?' he asked.

'I was, but I just can't think of anything to think about.'

'Then why don't you hang up? Another time.'

There was a touch of annoyance in the voice. 'You're a very rude man. I am hanging up.'

Manmohan smiled and put the phone down. He washed his face, put on his clothes and was about to leave, when the phone rang. He picked it up. '44457.'

'Mr Manmohan?' asked the voice.

'What can I do for you?'

'Well, I wanted to tell you that I'm not annoyed any more.'

'That's very nice.'

'You know while I was having breakfast, it occurred to me that I shouldn't be annoyed with you. Have you had breakfast?'

'No, I was just about to go out when you phoned.'

'Oh, then I won't keep you.'

'I'm in no particular hurry today, because I have no money. I don't think there'll be any breakfast this morning.'

'Why do you say such things? Do you enjoy hurting yourself?'

'No, I'm quite used to the way I am and the way I live.'

'Should I send you some money?'

'If you want to. That will be one more name on the list of my financiers.'

'Then I won't.'

'Do what you like.'

'I am going to hang up.'

'Hang up then.'

Manmohan put down the phone and walked out of the office. He came back very late in the evening. He had been wondering about his caller all day. She sounded young and educated and she laughed beautifully. At eleven o'clock the phone rang.

'Hello.'

'Mr Manmohan.'

'That's him.'

'I've been phoning all day. Could you please explain where you were?'

'Although I don't have a job, I still have things to do.'

'What things?'

'Loafing about.'

'When did you come back?'

'An hour ago.'

'What were you doing when I called?'

'I was lying on the table and trying to imagine what you looked like, but I have nothing to go on except your voice.'

'Did you succeed?'

'No.'

'Well, don't try. I'm very ugly.'

'If you are ugly, then kindly hang up. I hate ugliness.'

'Well, if that's the case, I am beautiful. I don't want you to nurture hatred.'

They didn't speak for some time. Then Manmohan asked, 'Were you thinking?'

'No, but I was going to ask you . . .'

'Think before you ask.'

'Do you want me to sing for you?'

'Yes.'

'All right, wait.'

He heard her clear her throat, then in a very soft, low voice she sang him a song.

'That was lovely.'

'Thank you.' She rang off.

All night long he dreamt about her voice. He rose earlier than usual and waited for her call, but the phone never rang. He began to pace around the room restlessly. Then he lay down on the table and picked up the book he had read twenty times. He read it once again. The whole day passed. At about seven in the evening, the phone rang. Hurriedly, he picked it up.

'Who's that?'

'It's me.'

'Where were you all day?' he asked sharply.

'Why?' the voice trembled.

'I've been waiting. I haven't had anything to eat, although I had money.'

'I'll phone when I want to . . .'

Manmohan cut her short. 'Look, either put an end to this business or let me know when you will call. I can't stand waiting.'

'I apologize for today. From tomorrow I promise to phone both morning and evening.'

'That's wonderful.'

'I didn't know you were . . .'

'Well, the thing is that I simply can't bear to wait and, when I can't bear something, I begin to punish myself.'

'How do you do that?'

'You didn't phone this morning. I should have gone out, but I didn't. I sat here all day fretting.'

'I didn't phone you deliberately.'

'Why?'

'To find out if you miss my call.'

'You are very naughty. Now hang up. I must go out and eat.'

'How long will you be?'

'Half an hour.'

He returned after an hour. She phoned. They talked for a long time. He asked her to sing him the same song. She laughed and sang it.

She would now ring regularly, morning and evening. Sometimes they would talk for hours. But, so far, Manmohan had neither asked her her name nor her phone number. In the beginning he had tried to imagine what she looked like, but that had now become unnecessary. Her voice was everything—her face, her soul, her body. One day she asked him, 'Mohan, why don't you ask me my name?'

'Because your voice is your name.'

Another day she said, 'Mohan, have you ever been in love?'

'No.'

'Why?'

He grew sad. 'To answer this question, I'll have to clear away the entire debris of my life and I would be very unhappy if I found nothing there.'

'Then don't.'

A month passed. One day Mohan had a letter from his friend. He said he had raised the money and would be returning to Bombay in a week. When she phoned that evening, he said to her, 'This is my kingdom's end.'

'Why?'

'Because my friend is coming back.'

'You must have friends who have phones?'

'Yes, I have friends who have phones, but I can't give you the numbers.'

'Why?'

'I don't want anyone else to hear your voice.'

'Why?'

'Let's say I'm jealous.'

'What should we do?'

'Tell me.'

'On the day your kingdom ends, I'll give you my number.'

The sadness he had felt was suddenly gone. He again tried to picture her, but there was no image, just her voice. It was only a matter of days now, he said to himself, before he would see her. He could not imagine the immensity of that moment.

When she called next day, he said to her, 'I'm curious to see you.'

'Why?'

'You said you would give me your phone number on the day my kingdom ends.'

'Yes.'

'Does that also mean you'll tell me where you live? I want to see you.'

'You can see me whenever you like. Even today.'

'Not today. No, I want to see you when I am wearing nice clothes. I have asked a friend of mine to get me some.'

'You're like a child. When we meet, I'll give you a present.'

'There can be no greater present in the world than meeting you.'

'I have bought you an Exacta camera.'

'Oh!'

'But there's a condition. You'll have to take my picture.'

'That I'll decide when we meet.'

'I shan't be phoning you for the next two days.'

'Why?'

'I'm going to be away with my family. It's only two days.'

Manmohan did not leave the office that day. The next morning he felt feverish. At first he thought it was boredom because she hadn't phoned. By the afternoon, his fever was high. His body felt on fire. His eyes were burning. He lay down on the table. He was very thirsty. He kept drinking water all day. There was heaviness in his chest. By the next morning, he felt completely exhausted. He had trouble in breathing. His chest hurt.

His fever was so high that he went into a delirium. He was talking to her on the phone, listening to her voice. By the evening, his condition had deteriorated. There were voices in his head and strange sounds as if thousands of phones were ringing at the same time. He couldn't breathe.

When the phone rang, he did not hear it. It kept ringing for a long time. Then suddenly there was a moment of clarity. He could hear it. He rose, stumbling uncertainly on his feet. He almost fell but, steadying himself against the wall, he picked it up with trembling hands. He ran his tongue over his lips. They were dry like wood.

'Hello.'

'Hello, Mohan,' she said.

'It is Mohan,' his voice fluttered.

'I can't hear you.'

He tried to say something, but his voice dried up in his throat.

She said, 'We came back earlier than I thought. I've been trying to call you for hours. Where were you?'

Manmohan's head began to spin.

'What is wrong?' she asked.

With great difficulty he said, 'My kingdom has come to an end today.'

Blood spilled out of his mouth, making a thin red line down his chin, then along his neck.

She said, 'Take my number down. 50314 . . . 50314. Call me in the morning. I have to go now.'

She hung up. Manmohan collapsed over the phone, blood bubbling out of his mouth.

# Upstairs Downstairs

HUSBAND: 'IT IS AFTER AGES THAT WE ARE SITTING DOWN LIKE THIS, together and alone.'

Wife: 'Yes.'

Husband: 'Engagements . . . as much as I try to avoid them, there is no let-up. Being aware of the incompetents with whom we are surrounded and conscious of my responsibilities to the nation, I have to keep working.'

Wife: 'Actually, you just happen to be far too tender-hearted, when it comes to these things. Just like me.'

Husband: 'Yes, I keep myself abreast of your social activities. When you find a minute, do let me read the speeches you have been making on several recent occasions. I would like to go through them when I find time.'

Wife: 'Very well.'

Husband: 'Yes, Begum, you recall my mentioning that business to you the other day.'

Wife: 'What business?'

Husband: 'Perhaps I did not. Yesterday, by chance I happened to find myself in our middle son's room and found him reading *Lady Chatterley's Lover*.'

Wife: 'You mean that scandalous book!'

Husband: 'Yes, Begum.'

Wife: 'What did you do?'

Husband: 'I snatched the book from him and hid it.'

Wife: 'You did the right thing.'

Husband: 'I am going to consult a doctor and ask him to suggest a different diet for him.'

Wife: 'That would be absolutely the right thing to do.'

Husband: 'And how are you feeling?'

Wife: 'Fine.'

Husband: 'I was playing with the idea of . . . requesting you today . . .'

Wife: 'Oh, you are getting too bold.'

Husband: 'And all because of your winning ways.'

Wife: 'But . . . your health?'

Husband: 'Health? . . . I feel well . . . but unless I consult the doctor, I won't make any move . . . and I should be fully satisfied about that being all right from your side.'

Wife: 'I will have a word with Miss Saldhana today.'

Husband: 'And I will speak to Dr Jalal.'

Wife: 'That's the way it should be.'

Husband: 'If Dr Jalal permits.'

Wife: 'And if Miss Saldhana has no objection . . . Do wrap your scarf around your neck carefully. It is cold outside.'

Husband: 'Thank you.'

*

Dr Jalal: 'Did you say yes?'

Miss Saldhana: 'Yes.'

Dr Jalal: 'So did I . . . but out of mischief.'

Miss Saldhana: 'Out of mischief, I almost said no.'

Dr Jalal: 'But then I took pity.'

Miss Saldhana: 'So did I.'

Dr Jalal: 'After one full year.'

Miss Saldhana: 'Yes, after one full year.'

Dr Jalal: 'When I said yes, his pulse quickened.'

Miss Saldhana: 'She was the same way.'

Dr Jalal: 'He said to me, the fear showing in his voice, "Doctor, it seems to me my heart is not going to keep up with me. Please take a cardiogram."'

Miss Saldhana: 'That is exactly what she said to me.'

Dr Jalal: 'I gave him an injection.'

Miss Saldhana: 'I too, except that it was simple distilled water.'

Dr Jalal: 'Water is the best thing in the world.'

Miss Saldhana: 'Jalal, if you were married to that woman?'

Dr Jalal: 'And if you were married to that man?'

Miss Saldhana: 'I would have become a nymphomaniac.'

Dr Jalal: 'And I would have met my Maker by now.'

Miss Saldhana: 'You don't say.'

Dr Jalal: 'When we examine these high society idiots, they put some funny ideas in our heads.'

Miss Saldhana: 'Today as well?'

Dr Jalal: 'Today of all days.'

Miss Saldhana: 'The trouble with these people is that these funny ideas come to them after year-long intervals.'

**\***

Wife: '*Lady Chatterley's Lover*? Why is that book under your pillow?'

Husband: 'I wanted to see for myself how obscene it is.'

Wife: 'Let me take a peek also.'

Husband: 'No, I will read out from it; you do the listening.'

Wife: 'That would be very nice.'

Husband: 'I have had our son's diet changed as recommended by the doctor after I spoke to him.'

Wife: 'I was sure you would not let this matter go unattended.'

Husband: 'I have never put off till the next day what needed to be done today.'

Wife: 'I know that . . . And what is to be done today, I am sure you will not . . .'

Husband: 'You seem to be in a very pleasant mood.'

Wife: 'All because of you.'

Husband: 'I am obliged. And now if you permit . . .'

Wife: 'Have you brushed your teeth?'

Husband: 'Yes, not only have I brushed my teeth, I have also gargled with Dettol.'

Wife: 'So have I.'

Husband: 'The two of us were made for each other.'

Wife: 'That goes without saying.'

Husband: 'I will now slowly read from this infamous book.'

Wife: 'But wait, please take my pulse.'

Husband: 'It is fast . . . feel mine.'

Wife: 'Yours is racing too.'

Husband: 'Reason?'

Wife: 'A weak heart?'

Husband: 'Has to be that . . . but Dr Jalal had said there was nothing the matter.'

Wife: 'That was what Miss Saldhana also told me.'

Husband: 'He examined me thoroughly before giving his permission.'

Wife: 'I was examined thoroughly too.'

Husband: 'Then I suppose there is no harm . . .'

Wife: 'You know better . . . but your health . . .'

Husband: 'And yours?'

Wife: 'We should exercise the greatest care before . . .'

Husband: 'Did Miss Saldhana take care of that thing?'

Wife: 'What thing? . . . Oh, yes. She took care of that.'

Husband: 'So there should be no worry on that score?'

Wife: 'None.'

Husband: 'Feel my pulse now.'

Wife: 'Feels normal . . . and mine?'

Husband: 'Yours feels normal too.'

Wife: 'Read something out of that scandalous volume.'

Husband: 'Very well, but I can feel my heart racing.'

Wife: 'So is mine.'

Husband: 'Do we have all we need?'

Wife: 'Yes, everything.'

Husband: 'If you don't mind, could you take my temperature?'

Wife: 'There is a stopwatch around . . . the pulse rate should be measured.'

Husband: 'I agree.'

Wife: 'Where are the smelling salts?'

Husband: 'Should be with the other things.'

Wife: 'Yes, on the side table.'

Husband: 'I think we should raise the room thermostat as well.'

Wife: 'I agree.'

Husband: 'If I am overcome by weakness, don't forget my medicine.'

Wife: 'I will try, if . . .'

Husband: 'Yes . . . but only if necessary.'

Wife: 'Read out the whole page.'

Husband: 'Get ready to listen then.'

Wife: 'You sneezed.'

Husband: 'I don't know why.'

Wife: 'Strange.'

Husband: 'I find that strange also.'

Wife: 'Oh, I know what happened. Instead of raising the thermostat, I lowered it by mistake.'

Husband: 'I am glad I sneezed. That way we just found out in time.'

Wife: 'I am sorry.'

Husband: 'Not to worry, a dozen drops of brandy will do the needful.'

Wife: 'Let me measure the brandy; you are prone to get the count wrong.'

Husband: 'You are right there . . . why don't you then?'

Wife: 'Please swallow it very slowly.'

Husband: 'Can't do it any slower.'

Wife: 'Do you feel restored?'

Husband: 'I am coming round.'

Wife: 'Take some rest.'

Husband: 'Yes, I feel that I need to rest.'

*

Servant: 'What is the matter with the mistress today? Haven't seen her.'

Maid: 'Not feeling well.'

Servant: 'The master is not feeling well either.'

Maid: 'We knew that would happen.'

Servant: 'Yes . . . but can't understand.'

Maid: 'What?'

Servant: 'Nature plays tricks . . . both of us should be on our deathbeds, considering . . .'

Maid: 'Don't say such things . . . let the deathbed be theirs.'

Servant: 'Their deathbed would be rather grand. I would want to move it to the tiny hovel they have put us in.'

Maid: 'Where are you going?'

Servant: 'To look for a cabinetmaker. Our bed is practically broken down.'

Maid: 'And tell him to use more hardy wood this time.'

# A Man of God

CHAUDHRY MAUJOO SAT ON A STRING COT UNDER A LEAFY PEEPAL TREE, smoking his hookah. The afternoon was hot, but a gentle breeze blew across the fields, wafting the blue smoke away.

He had been ploughing his field since early morning, but was quite tired now. The sun was harsh, but it did not seem to bother him. He was enjoying his well-earned rest.

He sat there waiting for his only daughter, Jeena, to bring him his midday meal—tandoori roti and buttermilk. She was always on time, though there was nobody to help her with the housework. He had divorced her mother in a fit of temper about two years ago after a bitter domestic fight.

Jeena was a very obedient daughter who took good care of her father. She was never idle. When household chores were done, she would occupy herself with her spinning wheel. Only occasionally would she gossip with her friends.

Chaudhry Maujoo did not have much land, but it was enough to take care of his modest needs. The village was small and the nearest railway station was miles away. A mud road linked it to another village to which Chaudhry Maujoo rode twice a month to buy provisions.

He used to be a happy man, but since his divorce it had often troubled him that he had no other children. However, being a very religious man, he had managed to console himself with the thought that it was God's will.

His faith was deep, but he knew very little about religion, except that there was no God but God and He must be worshipped, and Muhammad was His Prophet and the Quran was God's word revealed to Muhammad. That was all.

He had never fasted or prayed. In fact, the village was so small that it did not even have a mosque. The people prayed at home and were generally God-fearing. Every household had a copy of the Quran but nobody knew how to read. It was kept wrapped up on the top shelf, to be used only when someone was required to take an oath.

A maulvi would be invited to the village to solemnize marriages. Funeral prayers were offered by the villagers themselves, not in Arabic, but in their own language, Punjabi.

Chaudhry Maujoo was much in demand on such occasions. He had developed a style of his own for funeral orations.

For instance, the year before when his friend Dinoo had lost his son, Chaudhry Maujoo had addressed the villagers after the body had been lowered into the grave.

'What a strong, handsome young man he was! When he spat, it landed at a distance of twenty yards and he had such strength in his abdomen that he could urinate farther than any other young man in the village. He never lost an arm-wrestling competition. He could fight free of a hold as easily as you unbutton a shirt.

'Dinoo my friend, for you, judgement day is already here. I doubt if you will survive it. I think you should die, because how are you going to live through this great shock! Oh, what a handsome young man your son was! I know for a fact that Neeti, the goldsmith's daughter, cast many spells on him to win his love but he spurned her. He was not tempted by her youth and beauty. May God grant him a houri in paradise and may he remain as untempted by her as he was by Neeti, the goldsmith's daughter. God bless his soul.'

This brief address was so effectively delivered that everyone broke down, including Chaudhry Maujoo himself.

When Maujoo decided to divorce his wife, he did not bother to send for a maulvi. He had heard from his elders that all it required was for the man to say thrice: I divorce you. And that was exactly what he had done. He had felt sorry the next day and even a bit ashamed of himself. It was no more serious than everyday quarrels between husband and wife and should not have ended in divorce.

It was not that he wasn't fond of Phatan, his wife. He liked her, and though she was no longer young her body was still well preserved. What was more, she was the mother of his daughter. But he had made no effort to get her back and life had gone on.

Jeena was beautiful like her mother had been in her youth, and in two years she had grown from a little girl into a young and luscious woman. He often worried about her marriage and on such occasions he particularly missed his wife.

He was still reclining on his string cot, enjoying his smoke, when he heard a voice: 'May the blessings and peace of God be upon you.'

He turned round and found an old man with a flowing beard and shoulder-length hair, all dressed in white, standing there. Maujoo greeted him, wondering where he had materialized from.

The man was tall and his eyes were the most striking feature of his face—large and tinged with kajal. He wore a big white turban on his head and a yellow silk scarf was thrown over one of his shoulders. He held a silver-headed staff in his hand. His shoes were made of soft leather.

Chaudhry Maujoo was immediately impressed. In fact, he

felt a deep respect bordering on awe for this imposing elderly figure. He rose from his cot and said, 'Where did you come from and when?'

The man smiled. 'We men of God come from nowhere and have no home to go to. No particular moment is ordained for our arrival and none for our departure. It is the Lord who directs us to move in fulfilment of His will and it is the Lord who orders us to break our journey at a particular point.'

Chaudhry Maujoo was deeply affected by these words. He took the holy man's hand, kissed it with great reverence and put it to his eyes. 'My humble house is yours,' he said.

The holy man smiled and sat down on the cot. He held his silver-tipped staff in both hands, and resting his head against it said, 'Who can say what particular deed of yours found approval in the eyes of the Lord that he directed this sinner to come to you?'

Chaudhry Maujoo asked, 'Maulvi sahib, have you come to me on orders from the Lord?'

The holy man raised his head and said in an angry tone, 'And do you think we came at your orders? Do we obey you or that supreme being whom we have humbly worshipped for forty years and can at last count ourselves among those He has chosen to favour?'

Chaudhry Maujoo was terrified. In his simple, rustic manner he whimpered, 'Maulvi sahib, we illiterate people know nothing about these matters. We do not even know how to say our prayers. Were it not for men of God like you, we would never find forgiveness in His eyes.'

'And that's why we are here,' the holy man said, his eyes half-shut.

Chaudhry Maujoo sat down on the ground and began to press his visitor's legs. Presently, Jeena appeared with his food. When she saw the stranger, she covered her face.

'Who is that, Chaudhry Maujoo?'

'My daughter, Jeena, Maulvi sahib.'

Maulvi sahib glanced at Jeena through slanted eyes. 'Ask her why she is hiding her face from holy mendicants like us.'

'Jeena,' he said to his daughter, 'Maulvi sahib is God's special emissary. Uncover your face.'

Jeena did what she was told. Maulvi sahib sized her up and said, 'Your daughter is beautiful, Chaudhry Maujoo.'

Jeena blushed. 'She takes after her mother,' Maujoo said.

'Where is her mother?' Maulvi sahib asked, surveying Jeena's young and virginal body.

Chaudhry Maujoo hesitated, not knowing how to answer that.

'Where is her mother?' Maulvi sahib asked again.

'She is dead,' Maujoo replied hurriedly.

Maulvi sahib looked at Jeena, carefully noting her startled reaction. Then he thundered, 'You are lying.'

Maujoo fell at his feet and said in a guilty voice, 'Yes, I told you a lie. Please forgive me. I am a liar. The truth is that I divorced her, Maulvi sahib.'

'You are a great sinner. What was the fault of that poor woman?'

'I don't know, Maulvi sahib. It was really nothing, but it ended up in my divorcing her. I am indeed a very sinful man. I realized my error the very next day, but by then it was too late. She had already returned to her parents.'

Maulvi sahib touched Maujoo's shoulder with his silver-tipped staff and said, 'God is great and He is merciful and kind. All

wrongs can be righted if He wishes. And if that is His command,
perhaps this servant of His will be empowered to lead you to
your salvation and find you forgiveness.'

A grateful and totally humiliated Chaudhry Maujoo threw
himself at Maulvi sahib's feet and began to weep. Maulvi sahib
looked at Jeena and found tears rolling down her cheeks as well.

'Come here, girl,' he ordered.

There was such authority in his voice that she found it
impossible not to obey. She placed the food aside and walked up
to him. Maulvi sahib grabbed her arm and said, 'Sit down.'

She was about to sit on the ground, but Maulvi sahib pulled
her up. 'Sit next to me here,' he commanded.

Jeena sat down. Maulvi sahib put his arm around her waist
and, pressing her close, asked, 'And what have you brought
for us?'

Jeena wanted to move away, but Maulvi sahib's hold was vice-
like. 'I have some tandoori roti and buttermilk and some greens,'
she said in a low voice.

Maulvi sahib squeezed her slim waist once again and said,
'Then go get it and feed us.'

As Jeena rose, Maulvi sahib struck Maujoo gently on the
shoulder with his staff and said, 'Maujoo, help us wash our hands.'

Maujoo went to the well, which was nearby and came back
with a bucket of fresh water. He helped Maulvi sahib wash his
hands like a true disciple. Jeena put the food in front of him.

Maulvi sahib ate everything. Then he ordered Jeena to pour
water on his hands. She obeyed, such was the authority of his
manner.

Maulvi sahib belched loudly, thanked God even more loudly,
ran his wet hand over his beard and lay down on the cot. With

one eye he watched Jeena, and with the other her father. She picked up the utensils she had brought the food in and left. Maulvi sahib said to Maujoo, 'Chaudhry, we are going to take a nap.'

Chaudhry Maujoo pressed his legs and feet for some time and when he was sure he had fallen asleep he stepped aside and warmed up his hookah. He was very happy. He felt as if a great weight had been lifted off his chest. In his heart, he thanked God in his simple words for having sent to him in the form of Maulvi sahib one of His angels of mercy.

He sat there for some time watching Maulvi sahib resting, then he returned to his field and got down to work. He hadn't even noticed his hunger. In fact, he was thrilled that the honour of feeding Maulvi sahib with food meant for him had fallen to his lot.

When he returned in the evening, he was gravely disappointed to see Maulvi sahib gone. He cursed himself. By walking off, he had offended that man of God. Perhaps he had put a curse on him before leaving. He trembled with fear and tears welled up in his eyes.

He looked for Maulvi sahib around the village but did not find him. The evening deepened into night, but there was no trace of Maulvi sahib. He was walking back to his house, his head down, feeling the weight of the world on his shoulders, when he came upon two boys from the village. They looked scared. First they wouldn't tell him what was wrong, but when he insisted they told him their story.

Some time earlier, they had brewed strong country liquor, put it in an earthen pitcher and buried it under a tree. That evening they had gone to the spot, unearthed their forbidden treasure and were about to imbibe it when an old man, whose face radiated a strange light, had suddenly appeared and asked them what they were doing.

He had admonished them for the evil deed they were about to commit. He had asked them how they could even think of drinking something which God Himself had forbidden men to touch. They had been so terrified that they had run away, leaving the earthen pitcher behind.

Chaudhry Maujoo told them that the old man with the radiant face was a holy man of God and, since he had been offended, he was likely to put a curse on the entire village.

'May God save us my sons, may God save us my sons,' he murmured and began to walk back to his house. Jeena was home, but he did not speak to her. He was convinced that the village would not escape Maulvi sahib's wrath.

Jeena had prepared extra food for Maulvi sahib. 'Where is Maulvi sahib, father?' she asked. 'Gone . . . he is gone. How could a man of God abide along with sinners like us?' he told her in a grief-stricken voice.

Jeena was sorry too because Maulvi sahib had promised he would find a way to have her mother come back. And now that he was gone, who was going to reunite her with her mother? Jeena sat down on a low stool. The food kept getting cold.

There was a sound of approaching feet at the door. Both father and daughter sprang up. Suddenly Maulvi sahib entered. In the dim light of the earthen lamp, Jeena noticed that he was staggering. In his hands he held a small pitcher.

Maujoo helped him to a cot. Handing over the pitcher to him, Maulvi sahib said, 'God put us through a severe test today. We chanced upon two youngsters from your village who were about to commit the grave sin of drinking liquor. When we admonished them, they ran away. We were deeply grieved. So young, and in such deep mortal error. But we felt that their youth was to blame for what they were about to do. So we prayed in the heavenly court of the Lord that they be forgiven. And do you know what reply we received?'

'No,' Chaudhry Maujoo said, greatly moved.

'The reply was: are you prepared to face the consequences of their sin? And we said: yes, Almighty God. And then we heard a voice: you are commanded to drink this entire pitcher of liquor. We forgive the boys.'

Maujoo's hair stood on end. 'Did you then drink it?'

Maulvi sahib's tongue became even thicker. 'Yes, we drank to save the souls of those two young sinners and to gain merit in the eyes of God, who alone is to be honoured. There is still some left and that too we have been commanded to drink. Now put it away carefully and make sure that not a drop is wasted.'

Maujoo picked up the pitcher, secured its top with a clean length of cloth and took it into one of the small, dark rooms of his modest house. When he returned, Maulvi sahib was sprawled on the cot and Jeena was massaging his head. He was telling her, 'He who helps others wins the Lord's favour. He is pleased with you at this moment . . . and we are pleased with you too.'

Then Maulvi sahib made her sit next to him and planted a generous kiss on her forehead. She tried to get up, but was unable to wrest herself free. Maulvi sahib then embraced her and said to Maujoo, 'Chaudhry, I have awakened your daughter's sleeping destiny.'

Maujoo was so overwhelmed that he couldn't even express his gratitude properly. All he managed to say was, 'It is all a result of your prayers and your kindness.'

Maulvi sahib squeezed Jeena against his chest once again and said, 'Truly, God has touched you with His grace. Jeena, tomorrow we will teach you a holy prayer and if you recite it regularly you will forever find acceptance in the eyes of the Lord.'

Maulvi sahib rose late the next day. Maujoo had not gone to the fields, afraid he might be needed. Dutifully, he waited and, when Maulvi sahib was ready, he helped him wash his face and hands and, in accordance with his wishes, brought out the earthen pitcher.

Maulvi sahib mumbled a prayer, then he untied the cloth which covered its top and blew into it three times. He drank three large cups, mumbled another prayer, looked up at the sky and declaimed, 'God, You will not find us wanting in the test You have put us through.'

Then he addressed Maujoo, 'Chaudhry, we have just received divine orders that you should proceed to your wife's village and bring her back. The signal we were seeking has come through.'

Maujoo was thrilled. He saddled his horse and promised to be back by the next day. He instructed Jeena to leave no stone unturned to keep Maulvi sahib happy and comfortable.

After her father had left, Jeena got busy with housework. Maulvi sahib kept drinking steadily. Then he produced a thick rosary from his pocket and began to run it through his fingers. When Jeena was through, he ordered her to perform her ablutions.

Jeena replied innocently, 'Maulvi sahib, I don't know how to.'

Maulvi sahib reprimanded her gently on her lack of knowledge of essential religious practices. Then he began to teach her how to do her ablutions. This intricate exercise was performed with the help of close physical contact.

After the ablutions, Maulvi sahib asked for a prayer mat. There was none in the house. Maulvi sahib was not pleased. He told her to get him a clean bed sheet. He spread it on the floor of the inside room, summoned Jeena in and instructed her to bring the pitcher and cup with her.

Maulvi sahib poured out a large quantity and drank half of it. Then he started to run his rosary through his fingers, while Jeena watched in silence.

For a long time, Maulvi sahib was busy with his rosary. His eyes were closed. Then he blew into the cup three times and ordered Jeena to drink it.

Jeena took it with trembling hands. Maulvi sahib said in a thundering voice, 'We order you to drink it. All your pain and suffering will come to an end.'

Jeena lifted the cup to her lips and drank it down in one go. Maulvi sahib smiled. 'We are going to resume our special prayers, but when we raise our index finger pour out half a cup from the pitcher and drink it.'

He did not allow her to react and went into a deep reverie. There was an awful taste in Jeena's mouth and a fire blazing in her chest. She wanted to get up and drink buckets of cold water, but she did not dare. Suddenly Maulvi sahib's index finger rose. Hypnotized, she poured herself the ordained quantity and drank it in one gulp.

Maulvi sahib kept praying. She could hear the rosary beads rubbing against each other. Her head was spinning and she felt very sleepy. She had a vague, almost unconscious feeling that she was in the lap of a young, clean-shaven man who was telling her that he was taking her on a trip through paradise.

When she came to, she was lying on the floor inside the room. Bleary-eyed, she looked around. Why was she lying here and since when? Everything was in a mist. She wanted to go back to sleep, but she got up. Where was Maulvi sahib? And where had that paradise vanished to?

She walked into the open courtyard and was surprised to see that it was almost evening. Maulvi sahib was performing ablutions. He heard her and turned with a smile on his face. She went back to the room, sat down on the floor and began to think about her mother, who was going to come home. There was only one night left. She was very hungry but she didn't want to cook. Her mind was full of strange and unanswered questions.

Suddenly, Maulvi sahib appeared at the door. 'We have to offer special prayers for your father. We will pray in a graveyard all night and return in the morning. We will be praying for you too.'

He appeared next morning. His eyes were very red and he stammered a little when he spoke. He wasn't steady on his feet either. He walked into the courtyard and hugged and kissed Jeena with great warmth. Jeena sat on a low stool in a corner trying to untangle the strange, half-remembered events of the last twenty-four hours. She wanted her father to return . . . and her mother, who had been gone for two years. And then there was that paradise . . . what sort of paradise was it she had been taken to . . . and the Maulvi sahib . . . was it he who had taken her? It couldn't be because she remembered a young man who had no beard.

Maulvi sahib addressed her, 'Jeena, your father has not returned yet.'

She said nothing.

He spoke again, 'All night long he has been in our prayers. He should have returned by now . . . with your mother.'

All Jeena could say was, 'I don't know. He should be on his way . . . and mother too. I really don't know.'

The front door opened. Jeena rose. It was her mother. The two fell into each other's arms, weeping profusely. Maujoo followed his wife. With great respect, he greeted Maulvi sahib and then said to his wife, 'Phatan, you haven't greeted Maulvi sahib.'

Phatan disengaged herself from her daughter, wiped her eyes and greeted Maulvi sahib, who examined her through bloodshot eyes. 'We have been praying all night for you and have just returned. God has answered our prayers. All will be well.'

Chaudhry Maujoo sat down on the ground and began to press Maulvi sahib's feet. With a lump in his throat, he said to his wife, 'Phatan, come here and express your gratitude to Maulvi sahib. I don't know how to.'

Phatan came forward. 'We are poor and humble folk. There is nothing we can do for you, holy man of God.'

Maulvi sahib looked at her penetratingly. 'Maujoo Chaudhry, you were right. Your wife is beautiful and even at this age she looks young. She is another Jeena, even better. We will set everything right, Phatan. God has decided to be kind and merciful to you.'

Chaudhry Maujoo kept pressing Maulvi sahib's feet, while Jeena got busy with cooking.

After a while, Maulvi sahib rose, patted Phatan's head affectionately and said to Maujoo, 'It is the Almighty's law that when a man divorces his wife and then wants to bring her back he may not do so unless the woman first marries another man and is divorced by him to be reunited with her first husband.'

Maujoo said in a low voice, 'That I've heard, Maulvi sahib.'

Maulvi sahib asked him to rise, put his hand on his shoulder and said, 'Last night, we begged of the Almighty to spare you the punishment due to you because of your error. And the voice from beyond said, "How long are we going to accept your intercession on behalf of others? Ask something for yourself and it shall be granted." We begged again, "King of the universe, sovereign of all the lands and seas, we ask nothing for ourselves. You have given us enough. Maujoo Chaudhry is in love with his wife." And the voice said, "We are going to put his love and your faith to the test. You are to wed her for one day and divorce her the next and return her to Maujoo. That's all we can grant you, because for forty long years you have worshipped us faithfully."'

Maujoo was ecstatic. 'I accept, Maulvi sahib . . . I accept.' Then he looked at Phatan, his eyes shining with inner happiness. 'Right, Phatan?' He didn't wait for her answer. 'We both accept.'

Maulvi sahib closed his eyes, recited a prayer, blew it in their faces and raised his eyes heavenwards. 'God of all the skies, grant us the strength not to fail the test You are putting us through.'

Then he said to Maujoo, 'We are leaving now, but we want you and Jeena to go away somewhere for the night. We shall return later.'

When he came back in the evening, Jeena and Maujoo were ready to leave. Maulvi sahib was reciting something under his breath. He didn't speak to them, but made a sign that they were to leave. They left.

Maulvi sahib bolted the door and said to Phatan, 'For one night you are our wife. Go inside, get the bedding and spread it on this cot. We wish to take a nap.'

Phatan went inside, brought out the bedding and spread it neatly on the string cot. Maulvi sahib asked her to wait for him. He went inside.

An earthen lamp cast a shadowy light around the little room. The pitcher stood in a corner. Maulvi sahib shook it to see if there was anything left in it. There was. He raised the pitcher to his lips and took a few quick swigs. He wiped his mouth with his yellow silk scarf and went out.

Phatan sat on the cot. Maulvi sahib carried a cup in his hand. He blew some holy words on it thrice and offered it to Phatan. 'Drink it down.'

She drank and was almost immediately sick, but Maulvi sahib patted her on the back vigorously and said, 'You will be all right.' Then he lay down.

Next morning, when Jeena and Maujoo returned, they found Phatan sleeping on the cot in the courtyard. Maulvi sahib was not around. Maujoo thought he had gone for a walk in the fields. He woke up his wife, who opened her eyes and mumbled, 'Paradise . . . paradise.' When she saw Maujoo, she sat up.

'Where is Maulvi sahib?' he asked.

Phatan was still a little groggy. 'Maulvi sahib, which Maulvi sahib . . . I don't know where he is . . . he is not here.'

'No,' Maujoo exclaimed, 'I'll go and look for him.'

He was at the door when he heard Phatan scream. She was fumbling with something she had found under the pillow.

'What is it?' she asked.

'Looks like hair,' Maujoo said.

Phatan threw away the black bunch on the floor. Maujoo picked it up, examined it and said, 'Looks like human hair.'

'Maulvi sahib's beard and shoulder-length hair,' Jeena exclaimed.

Maujoo was confused. 'And where is Maulvi sahib?' he asked. Then his simple and believing heart provided him with the answer. 'Jeena, Phatan you don't understand. He was a man of God who could perform miracles. He brought us what our hearts desired and he has left us something of his person to remember him by.'

He kissed the false beard and hairpiece, touched his eyes with them reverently and handed them to Jeena. 'Go and wrap them up in a clean piece of cloth and place them on top of the big wooden chest. The grace of God shall never abandon our house.'

Jeena went in. Maujoo sat down next to Phatan and said, 'I am going to learn how to pray and I will remember that saint in my prayers every day.'

Phatan remained silent.

# The Gift

BEFORE SULTANA MOVED TO DELHI, SHE LIVED IN THE AMBALA cantonment, where many of her regulars were British goras. She had, consequently, picked up bits of English but she used the language most sparingly, and never in day-to-day conversation. When she realized that business in the new city was almost non-existent—at least her sort of business—she said to her friend and neighbour, Tamancha Jan, in English one day, 'This laif very bad,' which meant that this was no way to live when there was no work and you weren't even sure where your next meal was coming from.

Ambala cantonment had been different; she had more business than she could handle. The goras, all British tommies, would hit her place roaring drunk most evenings and, in a matter of three to four hours, she would have them on their way to the barracks, lighter in the pocket by twenty to thirty rupees. She preferred the goras to her own countrymen though she had some visiting her off and on. While it was true that she did not understand the language the Brits spoke, in a way it suited her fine. For instance, when one of them was keen to bargain to bring down the price, she would pretend she didn't understand. She would shake her head and tell him in Urdu, 'Sahib, I don't know what you are saying.' And if they tried to take more liberties than she normally allowed, she would start cursing them in Urdu. They would look at her, quite puzzled as to what she was going on about, and she would say, 'Sahib, you are *ek-dum, ulloo ka patha*, an owl's

offspring, and a *haramzada*, of illegitimate birth. Understand?'
The goras would laugh and Sultana would chuckle, 'Oh! They
do look like the owl's offspring when they laugh.'

However, not one gora had been to visit her in the three
months she had lived in Delhi. All the stories she had been told
about this big city when she was in Ambala had turned out to be
false. Where were all the big laat sahibs who lived here, who
reportedly moved to Simla in the summer where it was cool?
All she had had here by way of business were six men in three
months. Just six, which came to two a month. What was funny
was that even these six had told her the same old story about
Delhi being the city of the burra sahibs and the rich, who moved to
Simla in the summer. From these six visits she had made a total sum
of eighteen rupees and eight annas. Not one of them was willing to
fork out a penny more than three rupees, which appeared to be
the upper limit here. From the first five, she had initially
demanded ten rupees but it was strange that they had all insisted
that three rupees was what she was going to get and no more.

Why they considered her worth visiting she couldn't say.
Anyway, by the time the sixth man turned up, she had decided
to save her breath. 'Look,' she had told him in her no-nonsense
voice, 'three rupees is what I charge and not a penny less. Take it
or leave it.' The man had said nothing and stepped into her room.
When he was taking off his jacket, Sultana had said, 'Let's have
an extra rupee, shall we?' Instead, he had given her a newly
minted eight anna coin with the Emperor of India's head on it.
Sultana had accepted it on the sound principle that something
was better than nothing.

The arithmetic is all wrong, Sultana thought. Only eighteen
rupees and eight annas in three months. And against that she

had to pay twenty rupees for her kotha, this hovel of a place that the landlord insisted on describing as a flat. It had one of those modern WCs with a chain. Sultana had never seen, much less used, one before. The first time she did, she thought the chain was meant to help heave you up. She had a backache that day and as she reached for the chain there was a tremendous explosion. She screamed.

Khuda Bux was in the next room sorting out his photographic paraphernalia. He rushed out to see what had happened. 'Sultana,' he shouted, 'was that you?' Her heart was beating rapidly. 'My God,' she said. 'Is this a lavatory or a railway station? I thought I would die!' Khuda Bux began to laugh. 'Silly, this is a big city vilayati bathroom. Understand?'

How Sultana and Khuda Bux met was interesting. He came from Rawalpindi. After passing high school, he became a lorry driver and took a job with a bus company, which operated a fleet between Rawalpindi and the Kashmir Valley. In Kashmir he met a woman who ran away with him to Lahore. However, he failed to find any work in the new city and decided to enrol her in the world's oldest profession for the sake of survival. This arrangement lasted for a couple of years till one day she left him for another man. Somebody had told him she was in Ambala and he had gone there looking for her. Instead, he had found Sultana, who took an immediate fancy to him.

Khuda Bux's arrival brought Sultana luck. Business started booming. Since she was a superstitious woman, she attributed her good fortune to Khuda Bux.

Khuda Bux was hard-working. He hated to be idle. There was a street photographer outside the local railway station whom he befriended. In a few months, he managed to learn to take pictures. Sultana gave him sixty rupees and he bought an old camera, an ornate backdrop, a couple of chairs and some basic chemicals. Then he launched a business of his own. One day he told Sultana that he was going to move from the city to the cantonment area. Within a month, he had got to know most of the goras stationed there, and his business began to flourish. Soon he had persuaded Sultana to leave the city and they found themselves a nice place to live in the cantonment. Many of Khuda Bux's gora customers became Sultana's clients as well.

Sultana had by now saved enough money to buy herself a pair of silver earrings and eight gold bracelets. She had also built up a wardrobe of fifteen nice saris. She also bought some decent furniture for the house. Everything was going well till one day Khuda Bux decided on a whim that they should move to Delhi. Sultana had agreed enthusiastically because she really had come to believe that he brought her good luck.

Sultana was well aware that it took time before a business got going. During the first month, she had not worried but, by the end of the second month, she was beginning to. Not one customer had materialized so far. 'What do you think is going on? It is two months now and not one man has come to the kotha. I know things are tough these days but are they that tough?' she said to Khuda Bux.

Although he hadn't spoken to her about it, Khuda Bux too had been feeling the strain. 'I have been thinking about it myself and I have come to the conclusion that because of the war our business has ceased to interest people. It is also possible that . . .' He did not finish the sentence. They heard footsteps. Then there was a knock at the door. Khuda Bux leapt up and undid the latch. Sultana's first customer had arrived but all he paid was three rupees. The other five had done the same. So there she was, richer in three months by no more than eighteen rupees and eight annas.

The situation had become difficult. The rent on the flat was twenty rupees a month. Then there were the water and electricity bills, followed by food, clothes and odds and ends. And there was no income. You couldn't call eighteen rupees and eight annas income, could you? The eight gold bangles she had bought herself in Ambala had been sold one by one. When she was selling the last one, she had said to Khuda Bux, 'Let's return to Ambala. There's nothing for us in this city. It hasn't been good to us. What we have lost is lost. Let's just convince ourselves that we gave it to charity. Go sell this last bangle; I'll pack in the meanwhile and we'll take the night train to Ambala.'

Khuda Bux had taken the bangle. 'No, sweetheart, we won't go to Ambala. We'll stay in Delhi and earn money. All your gold bangles will be bought back. Just have trust in God. He will show us the way.' Sultana had not argued and only stared disconsolately at her bare wrists.

Two more months went by with earnings covering only a tiny percentage of expenses. Sultana just didn't know what to do. Khuda Bux would spend most of his time away from home, which was an added reason for her unhappiness. In the beginning, she used to spend her day gossiping with friends but after a while she had begun to feel uneasy in their company and stopped seeing them almost altogether. All day long she would sit alone in her flat, trying to while away her time by preparing betel leaf condiments or darning and adjusting her old clothes. Sometimes she would stand on her balcony staring for hours at the railway yard across the street with its stationary and shunting engines and wagons.

The railway goods godown was also part of the yard. Hundreds of bales and crates of different sizes lay scattered around under a huge shed with a tin roof. To its left was an open space with a criss-crossing railway track. The noonday sun would make the blue steel shimmer, reminding Sultana of her hands with their increasingly protuberant blue veins. There was always something going on there: an engine being shunted about or a goods train moving slowly towards the yard to unload its cargo, only to chug away later.

There were always engines blowing their steam hooters, their rhythmic chug chug fading in the distance. When she came out on the balcony very early in the morning, she was always struck by the sight. Through the hazy light, she would see an engine belching smoke, then she would look up at the sky and watch it rise in a thick column. Sometimes she would see a long wagon just disconnected from an engine, which would be sent rolling down the track, and would think of herself. Had she too not been pushed on the track, of life? She was moving, but not of her own volition. The levers were in the hands of others and one day the momentum would begin to weaken and, at some unknown point at an unknown place, she would slowly come to a stop, never to move again.

Her time was now increasingly spent standing on the balcony, looking at the railway track, the stillness frequently broken by an engine chugging past. Strange thoughts would crowd her head. In the Ambala cantonment, her house was not too far from the station but she had never noticed trains or anything of the sort. There were times now when she felt that the railway yard was like a vast, smoky, steamy brothel, its fat engines much like the rich traders who would occasionally visit her in Ambala.

Sometimes an engine, all by itself, slowly shunting past stationary wagons, would look to her like a man walking past women sitting at their windows waiting for customers. Such sensations were disturbing in the extreme and she had stopped going out on the balcony altogether because it distracted her.

Not once, not twice, but several times she had tried to talk to Khuda Bux. 'Look, have pity on me. What do you think I do here all day? Like a bedridden patient I am confined indoors from morning to night. Please!' But every time, he would say, 'Sweetheart, I am trying to work out something. God willing, it is only a matter of time; our days are going to change.'

Five months had passed and nothing had changed. Khuda Bux was still out there all day, trying to work out something and she was still cooped up in the flat. The month of Muharram was only a few days away. That was one time of the year when Sultana observed every sombre ritual commemorating the martyrdom of Hussain, the Prophet's grandson, and his companions at Karbala fourteen hundred years ago. She always wore black, the colour of mourning.

But what was she going to do this year? She had no money for new clothes. Mukhtar, the girl across the street who was in the same line of work as herself, had got herself a black Lady Hamilton shirt stitched, and very elegant it was too, with the sleeves fashioned out of georgette. She also had a matching black silk shalwar which shimmered. Another girl, Anwari, had bought herself a georgette sari. She had also told Sultana that she would have a white silk petticoat to go with it as that was the latest fashion. Anwari had even found herself a new pair of very delicate-looking black velvet shoes. Sultana had never felt more depressed. For the first time in her life, she had nothing to wear for Muharram.

She came home after visiting Mukhtar and Anwari that
morning and just stretched herself out on the floor, which was
covered with a coarse cotton carpet, feeling very sorry for
herself. The house was empty. Khuda Bux was out as usual. She
had kept lying there for a long time, her head propped up against
a large pillow. Then she had felt her neck stiffen and stepped out
on the balcony involuntarily. She was very sad.

The railway yard wore a desolate look. There was no
movement at all, just a few old bogies without any engines.
They had sprinkled the street with water, as on most evenings,
and there was no dust hanging in the air. A few men were walking
past but they all looked like the kind who liked to ogle women
like Sultana and then went straight home to their wives. One of
them looked up at her and she gave him a smile. Then she turned
her eyes towards the yard, but she had a feeling he was still
there, looking at her, which he was. Sultana waved to him to
come up, pointing to the stairs which led to the flat.

He walked up looking diffident. 'Were you afraid to come?'
Sultana asked. 'Why do you say that?' he replied with a smile.
'Well, you have probably been in the street for some time
wondering if you should make a move,' she said. He smiled again.
'Not at all. I was actually watching a woman in the flat above
yours using body language to communicate with a man in the
flat across. Then you switched on the green light in your room
and came out on the balcony. I love green; it is so soothing to
the eyes.' He began to look around the room. 'Are you leaving?'
Sultana asked. 'No, no, I just wanted to see the flat. Would you
like to show me around?'

Sultana showed him around the flat, which had just three
rooms. Then they came back to the main room with the cushions

on the floor. 'My name is Shanker,' the man said.

For the first time, Sultana really looked at him. He was a man of average height with average looks but his eyes were extraordinarily clear and bright. His temples had a touch of grey and he was wearing a pair of beige trousers and a white shirt with a raised collar.

Shanker sat down on the floor, which was covered by a simple cotton rug. He was so much at home that it seemed to Sultana as if their roles had been reversed—she the client and he the one dispensing the service. 'And what can I do for you?' she asked him at last. He stretched himself on the floor. 'What can I say? I leave it to you. Didn't you ask me over?' When Sultana did not answer, he got up. 'All right, since you ask, I'll tell you. What you thought I was, I am not. I am not one of those who leave money or what have you. I am like a doctor; I have a fee. When I am asked over, the fee has to be paid.'

Sultana began to laugh. 'What is your line of work?'

'The same as yours,' Shanker replied.

'What?'

'What do you do?' he asked.

'I . . . I . . . I don't do anything.'

'I don't do anything either.'

'That doesn't make sense!' she said sharply. 'There must be something you do.'

'So do you, I am sure,' Shanker retorted calmly.

'I fritter myself away,' she said.

'So do I.'

'Then let's do some frittering together.'

'I am willing but I must tell you I never pay for it.'

'Are you out of your mind! This is not a soup kitchen for the homeless!'

'Neither am I volunteer.'

'What's a volunteer?' she asked.

'A volunteer is an owl's offspring,' Shanker answered.

'Well, I'm not an owl's offspring.'

'But that man Khuda Bux who lives with you is.'

'Why?'

'Because for several weeks now he has been spending his time in the company of a fake holy man, begging him to make fortune smile on him, not realizing that he whose own fortune is like a permanently rusted lock cannot help others.'

'Because you are a Hindu, you can't understand these things. You can only make fun of our Muslim fakirs,' she said.

Shanker smiled. 'It is not a Hindu–Muslim thing at all.'

'God knows what nonsense you talk,' she said, then added, 'Would you like to . . .'

'Yes, but on my terms.'

Sultana stood up. 'Then let me show you to the door.'

Shanker rose, put his hands in his pockets and said, 'I pass this way off and on. Whenever you need me, just say so . . . . I am a very useful man.'

Shanker left and Sultana, Muharram's black clothes momentarily forgotten, kept thinking about him. She felt somehow better. She thought if he had come to her in Ambala, she would have had him thrown out but Delhi was different. She felt lonely and Shanker's strange and amusing conversation had made her feel quite good.

When Khuda Bux returned in the evening, Sultana asked him

where he had been all day. He looked totally exhausted. 'I was in the city's old fort area. For some days past, a holy man has taken up residence there. I go to him every day so that our luck will change,' he said.

'Has he said anything so far?'

'No, not yet. He hasn't made up his mind about me but I tell you, Sultana, my devotion to him will never go waste. By the grace of God, times are about to change.'

Sultana's mind went back to Muharram. In a tearful voice she said to him, 'You are out all day, leaving me alone to fend for myself in this cage. I can't even go anywhere. Muharram is round the corner. Has it occurred to you that I would need new black clothes? There is not a penny in the house. The last gold bangle is also gone. Tell me, what is going to happen to us? As for you, all day long you keep chasing these beggars and that fake holy man. It seems in Delhi even God has turned His face away from us. Why don't you start your old street photo business again? It'll bring in something at least.'

Khuda Bux lay down on the floor. 'But to start I'd need some capital. Maybe it was a mistake to leave Ambala, but it was God's will and I am sure it was all for the best. Who knows? He may be testing us . . .'

Sultana cut him short. 'I beg you, get me a length of black cloth for a shalwar. I have a white satin shirt which I'll have dyed black. I also still have the white chiffon dupatta you brought me in Ambala at Diwali. That can be dyed too. All I am missing is a black shalwar. I don't care whether you steal it; I want that shalwar. Swear on my head that you'll get it for me, and if you don't, may I die.'

Khuda Bux stood up abruptly. 'Stop that, please! Where do

you think I am going to get the money? I don't have a single penny.'

'I don't care as long as I get four and a half yards of black satin,' Sultana said with finality.

'Let's pray to God to send three or four customers tonight,' Khuda Bux suggested.

'What about you? Won't you do anything yourself? If you tried, you could easily make enough to buy the cloth. It used to cost twelve to fourteen annas a yard before the war. I don't think it is more than a rupee and a quarter now. Look, how much can four and a half yards cost?'

'Well, since you insist, I will think of something. Now let me run down to that food stand across the street and get us something to eat,' Khuda Bux said. They ate the bazaar food quietly and went to bed. In the morning Khuda Bux was off to see the holy man, leaving Sultana to herself again. She slept for a while, then rose, and walked about from room to room to stretch her legs and kill time. She ate around noon, then pulled out her white chiffon dupatta and white satin shirt from the old box and took them to the laundry which also dyed clothes. She came back to read for a while from one of her books which contained scripts with the dialogue and lyrics of her favourite films. At some point she must have dozed off, because when she woke up it was nearly four. She bathed, put on fresh clothes, threw a light woollen stole over her shoulders and stepped out on the balcony. She stood there for an hour. The street had begun to show early signs of evening life and it had become a bit chilly. Suddenly she saw Shanker, who smiled at her. Without quite meaning to, she asked him to come up.

When Shanker came, she was somewhat embarrassed, not

knowing what to say to him. However, he was totally relaxed, as if he were in his own home. Without much formality, he stretched himself on the floor, a cushion under his head. Sultana still hadn't said a single word to him. 'Look, you can invite me to come up a hundred times and ask me to leave each time. I'll not mind at all.'

'No one is asking you to leave,' Sultana answered.

'So it is on my terms then,' Shanker said with a smile.

'What terms? Are you going to marry me?' Sultana asked with a laugh.

'Marriage? You and I won't be involved in that sort of nonsense as long as we live. Such things are not for people like us.'

'Cut out this rubbish. Say something useful,' Sultana suggested.

'What do you want me to say? You are the woman. Say something which should help us while away the time nicely. There is more to life than talking shop.'

'Tell me frankly what you want,' Sultana asked.

'The same as other men,' he said, sitting up.

'Then what's the difference between you and them?'

'Between you and me there is no difference but between me and them, well, we are worlds apart. Not everything should be reduced to a question. There is much one can try to comprehend oneself,' Shanker said.

'I understand,' Sultana said after a pause.

'Well then?'

'You win, but I very much doubt if this sort of thing ever takes place,' Sultana remarked.

'You are wrong there. In this very neighbourhood, there must be thousands of families who will never believe that a woman will accept the sort of degradation of her body that you do without even thinking. But despite that, there are thousands of women in your profession in this city alone. Your name is Sultana, isn't it?'

'Sultana it is.'

Shanker laughed. 'And mine is Shanker. Names are rubbish. Let's go to the next room.'

When they returned, they were both laughing. When he was leaving, Sultana said, 'Will you do something for me?'

'Say it first,' he replied.

Sultana hesitated, 'You might think I was trying to charge for what we just did.'

'Come on, say it,' he encouraged her.

Sultana plucked up her courage. 'Muharram is not too far and I do not have any money to get a new black shalwar stitched. Well, what can I say? I have the dupatta and the shirt, which are now at the dyer's.'

'Do you want me to give some money for the black shalwar?' Shanker asked.

'I didn't mean that,' she answered. 'You could get me a black shalwar.'

Shanker smiled. 'It is rare for me to have any money. However, I promise you will have the shalwar on the first day of Muharram. Cheer up now.' He looked at Sultana's earrings. 'Can you give me those?'

'What'd you want with them?' Sultana said with a smile. 'They are ordinary silver, worth no more than five rupees.'

'I asked you for the earrings. I did not ask what they cost.'

'Here you are then,' Sultana said. After he was gone she felt sorry she had parted with the earrings but it was too late.

Sultana was quite sure Shanker would not keep his word. On the morning of the first day of Muharram, there was a knock at the door. It was Shanker. He had something in his hand, wrapped in a newspaper. 'The black satin shalwar. Could be a bit long— see you later.'

He looked a bit dishevelled. It seemed he had just hopped out of bed. They didn't talk.

When he was gone, Sultana unwrapped the package. It was a lovely black silk shalwar, much like the one her friend Mukhtar had shown her. She forgot about her earrings.

In the afternoon, she went down to pick up her dyed dupatta and shirt from the laundry. Then she put on her new clothes. There was a knock at the door. It was Mukhtar. After sizing up Sultana carefully, she said, 'The dupatta and shirt appear to be dyed but the shalwar looks new. Did you have it stitched?'

'Only today. The tailor brought it first thing this morning,' Sultana lied. Suddenly she noticed Mukhtar's ears. 'When did you get those earrings?'

'This very morning,' Mukhtar said.

For a long time neither of them spoke.

# The Room with the Bright Light

HE STOOD QUIETLY BY A LAMP-POST OFF THE QAISER GARDENS, THINKING how desolate everything looked. A few tongas waited for customers who were nowhere in evidence.

A few years ago, this used to be such a gay place, full of bright, happy, carefree men and women, but everything seemed to have gone to seed. The area was now full of louts and vagabonds with nowhere to go. The bazaar still had its crowds, but it had lost its colour. The shops and buildings looked derelict and unwashed, staring at each other like empty-eyed widows.

He stood there wondering what had turned the once fashionable Qaiser Gardens into a slum. Where had all the life and excitement gone? It reminded him of a woman who had been scrubbed clean of all her make-up.

He remembered that many years ago when he had moved to Bombay from Calcutta to take up a job, he had tried vainly for weeks to find a room in this area. There was nothing going.

How times had changed. Judging by the kind of people in the streets, just anybody could rent a place here now——weavers, cobblers, grocers.

He looked around again. What used to be film company offices were now bed-sitters with cooking stoves, and where the elegant people of the city used to gather in the evenings were now washermen's backyards.

It was nothing short of a revolution, but a revolution which had brought decay. In between, he had left the city, but knew through newspaper reports and friends who had stayed back what had happened to Qaiser Gardens in his absence.

There had been riots, accompanied by massacres and rapes. The violence Qaiser Gardens had witnessed had left its ugly mark on everything. The once splendid commercial buildings and residential houses looked sordid and unclean.

He was told that during the riots women had been stripped naked and their breasts chopped off. Was it then surprising that everything looked naked and ravaged?

He was here this evening to meet a friend who had promised to find him a place to live.

Qaiser Gardens used to have some of the city's best restaurants and hotels. And if one was that way inclined, the best girls in Bombay could be obtained through the good offices of the city's high-class pimps who used to hang out here.

He recalled the good times he had had here in those days. He thought nostalgically of the women, the drinking, the elegant hotel rooms. Because of the war, it was almost impossible to obtain Scotch whisky, but he had never had to spend a dry evening. Any amount of expensive Scotch was yours for the asking, as long as you were able to pay for it.

He looked at his watch. It was going on five. The shadows of the February evening had begun to lengthen. He cursed his friend who had kept him waiting. He was about to slip into a roadside place for a cup of tea when a shabbily dressed man came up to him.

'Do you want something?' he asked the stranger.

'Yes,' he replied in a conspiratorial voice.

He took him for a refugee who had fallen on bad times and wanted some money. 'What do you want?' he asked.

'I don't want anything.' He paused, then drew closer and said, 'Do you need something?'

'What?'

'A girl, for instance?'

'Where is she?'

His tone was none too encouraging for the stranger, who began to walk away. 'It seems you are not really interested.'

He stopped him. 'How do you know? What you can provide is something men are always in need of, even on the gallows. So look, my friend, if it is not too far, I am prepared to come with you. You see, I was waiting for someone who hasn't turned up.'

The man whispered, 'It is close, very close, I assure you.'

'Where?'

'That building across from us.'

'You mean that one?' he asked.

'Yes.'

'Should I come with you?'

'Yes, but please walk behind me.' They crossed the road. It was a run-down building with the plaster peeling off the walls and rubbish heaps littering the entrance.

They went through a courtyard and then through a dark corridor. It seemed that construction had been abandoned at some point before completion. The bricks in the walls were unplastered and there were piles of lime mixed with cement on the floor.

The man began to ascend a flight of dilapidated stairs. 'Please wait here. I'll be back in a minute,' he said.

He looked up and saw a bright light at the end of the landing.

He waited for a couple of minutes and then began to climb the stairs. When he reached the landing, he heard the man who had brought him screaming, 'Are you going to get up or not?'

A woman's voice answered, 'Just let me sleep.'

The man screamed again, 'You heard me, are you getting up or not? Or you know what I'll do to you.'

The woman's voice again: 'You can kill me but I won't get up. For God's sake, have mercy on me.'

The man changed his tone. 'Darling, don't be obstinate. How are we going to make a living if you don't get up?'

'Living be damned. I'll starve to death, but for God's sake, don't drag me out of bed. I'm sleepy,' answered the woman.

The man began to roar with anger, 'So you're not going to leave your bed, you bitch, you filthy bitch . . . !'

The woman shouted back, 'I won't, I won't, I won't!'

The man changed his tone again. 'Don't shout like that. The whole world can hear you. Come on now, get up. We could make thirty, even forty rupees.'

The woman began to whimper, 'I beg of you, don't make me go. You know how many days and nights I have gone without sleep. Have pity on me, please.'

'It won't be long,' the man said, 'just a couple of hours and then you can sleep as long as you like. Look, don't make me use other methods to persuade you.'

There was a brief silence. He crossed the landing on tiptoe and peeped into the room where the very bright light was coming from. It was not much of a room. There were a few empty cooking pots on the floor and a woman stretched out in the middle with the man he had come with crouching over her. He was pressing her legs and saying, 'Be a good girl now. I promise you, we'll be back in two hours and then you can sleep to your heart's content.'

He saw the woman suddenly get up like a firecracker which has been shown a match. 'All right,' she said, 'I'll come.'

He was suddenly afraid and ran down the stairs. He wanted to put as much distance between this place and himself as he could, between himself and this city.

He thought of the woman who wanted to sleep. Who was she? Why was she being treated with such inhumanity?

And who was that man? Why was the room so unremittingly bright? Did they both live there? Why did they live there?

His eyes were still partly blinded by the dazzling light bulb in that terrible room upstairs. He couldn't see very well. Couldn't they have hung a softer light in the room? Why was it so nakedly, pitilessly bright?

There was a noise in the dark and a movement. All he could see were two silhouettes, one of them obviously that of the man whom he had followed to this awful place.

'Take a look,' he said.

'I have,' he replied.

'Is she all right?'

'She is all right.'

'That will be forty rupees.'

'All right.'

'Can I have the money?'

He could no longer think clearly. He put his hand in his pocket, pulled out a fistful of bank notes and handed them over. 'Count them,' he said.

'There's fifty there.'

'Keep it.'

'Thank you.'

He had an urge to pick up a big stone and smash his head.

'Please take her, but be nice to her and bring her back in a couple of hours.'

'OK.'

He walked out of the building with the woman, and found a tonga waiting outside. He jumped quickly in the front. The woman took the back seat.

The tonga began to move. He asked him to stop in front of a ramshackle, customerless hotel. They went in. He took his first look at the woman. Her eyes were red and swollen. She looked so tired that he was afraid she would fall to the floor in a heap.

'Raise your head,' he said to her.

'What?' She was startled.

'Nothing, all I said was raise your head.'

She looked up. Her eyes were like empty holes topped up with ground chilli.

'What is your name?' he asked.

'Never mind.' Her tone was like acid.

'Where are you from?'

'What does it matter?'

'Why are you so unfriendly?'

The woman was now wide awake. She stared at him with her blood-red eyes and said, 'You finish your business because I have to go.'

'Where?'

'Where you picked me up from,' she answered indifferently.

'You are free to go.'

'Why don't you finish your business? Why are you trying to ridicule me?'

'I'm not trying to ridicule you. I feel sorry for you,' he said in a sympathetic voice.

'I want no sympathizers. You do whatever you brought me here for and then let me go,' she almost screamed.

He tried to put his hand on her shoulder, but she shook it off rudely.

'Leave me alone. I haven't slept for days. I've been awake ever since I came to that place.'

'You can sleep here.'

'I didn't come here to sleep. This isn't my home.'

'Is that room your home?'

This seemed to infuriate her even more.

'Cut out the rubbish. I have no home. You do your job or take me back. You can have your money returned by that . . .'

'All right, I'll take you back,' he said.

And he took her back to that big building and left her there.

The next day, sitting in a desolate hotel in Qaiser Park, he told the story of that woman to a friend, who was greatly moved by it. Expressing sorrow, he asked, 'Was she young?'

'I don't know,' he replied. 'The fact is that I didn't really look at her. I only had this savage desire to pick up a rock and smash the head of the man who had brought me there.'

His friend said, 'That would have been a most worthy deed.'

He did not stay with his friend for very long in that hotel. He felt greatly depressed by the events of the day before. They finished their tea and left.

He quietly walked to the tonga stand, his eyes searching for that procurer, who was nowhere to be found. It was now six o'clock and the big building was right across, just a few yards from him. He began to walk towards it and, once there, went in.

. There were people walking in. Quite calmly, taking steps

through the dark, he came to the stairway and noticed a light at the top. He looked up and began to climb very quietly. For a while, he stood at the landing. A bright light was coming out of the room, but there was no sound, not even a stir. He approached the wide open doors and, standing aside, peeped in. The first thing he saw was a bulb whose light dazzled his eyes. He abruptly moved aside and turned towards the dark to get the dazzle out of his eyes.

Then he advanced towards the doors but in a way that his eyes should not meet that blinding light. He looked in. On the bit of floor he could see, there was a woman lying on a mat. He looked at her carefully. She was asleep, her face covered with her dupatta. Her bosom rose and fell with her rhythmic breathing. He moved deeper into the room and screamed but he quickly stifled it. Next to that woman, on the bare floor, lay a man, his head smashed into a pulp. A bloodied brick lay close by. He saw all this in one rapid sequence, then he leapt towards the stairs but lost his foothold and fell down. Without caring for his injuries, while trying to keep his sanity intact, he managed to get home with great difficulty. All night, he kept seeing terrifying dreams.

# Siraj

THERE WAS A SMALL PARK FACING THE NAGPARA POLICE POST AND AN Iranian teahouse next to it. Dhondoo was always to be found in this area, leaning against a lamp-post, waiting for custom. He would come here around sunset and remain busy with his work until four in the morning.

Nobody knew his real name, but everyone called him Dhondoo—the one who searches and finds—which was most appropriate because his business consisted of procuring women of every type and description for his clients.

He had been in the trade for the last ten years and during this period hundreds of women had passed through his hands, women of every religion, race and temperament.

This had always been his hangout, the lamp-post facing the Iranian teahouse which stood in front of the Nagpara police headquarters. The lamp-post had become his trademark. Often, when I passed that way and saw the lamp-post, I felt as if I was actually looking at Dhondoo, besmeared like him with betel juice and much the worse for wear.

The lamp-post was tall, and so was Dhondoo. A number of power lines ran in various directions from the top of this ugly steel column into adjoining buildings, shops and even other lamp-posts.

The telephone department had tagged on a small terminal to the post and technicians could be seen checking it out from time to time. Sometimes I felt that Dhondoo was also a kind of terminal, attached to the lamp-post to verify the sexual signals of his customers. He not only knew the locals, but even some of the big seths of the city who would come to him for an evening to get their sexual cables straightened out.

He knew almost all the women in the profession. He had intimate knowledge of their bodies, since they constituted the wares he transacted, and he was familiar with their temperaments. He knew exactly which woman would please which customer. But there was one exception—Siraj. He just had not been able to fathom her out.

Dhondoo had often said to me, 'Manto sahib, this one is off her rocker. I just cannot make her out. Never seen a chhokri like her. She is so changeable. When you think she is happy and laughing her head off, just as suddenly she bursts into tears. She simply cannot get along with anyone. Fights with every "passenger". I have told her a million times to sort herself out, but it has had absolutely no effect on her. Many times I have had to tell her to go back to wherever she first came from to Bombay. Have you seen her? She has practically nothing to wear and not a penny to her name, and yet she simply will not play ball with the men I bring her. What an obstinate, mixed-up piece of work!'

I had seen Siraj a few times. She was slim and rather pretty. Her eyes were like outsize windows in her oval face. You simply could not get away from them. When I saw her for the first time on Clare Road, I felt like saying to her eyes, 'Would you please step aside for a minute so that I can see this girl?'

She was slight and yet there was so much of her. She reminded me of a glass goblet, which had been filled to the brim with strong, under-diluted spirits, and the restlessness showed. I say strong spirits because there was something sharp and tangy about her personality. And yet I felt that in this heady mixture someone had added a bit of water to soften the fire. Her femininity was strong, despite her somewhat irate manner. Her hair was thick and her nose was aquiline. Her fingers reminded me of the sharpened pencils draughtsmen use. She gave the impression of being slightly annoyed with everything, with Dhondoo and the lamp-post he always stood against, with the gifts he brought her and even with her big eyes which ran away with her face.

But these are the impressions of a storyteller. Dhondoo had his own views. One day he said to me, 'Manto sahib, guess what that sali Siraj did today? Boy, am I lucky! Had it not been for God's mercy and the fact that the Nagpara police are always kind to me, I would have found myself in the jug. And that could have been one big, blooming disaster.'

'What happened?'

'The usual. I don't know what the matter with me is. I must be off my head. It is not the first time she has got me in a spot and yet I continue to carry her along. I should just wash my hands off her. She is neither my sister nor my mother that I should be running around trying to get her a living. Seriously, Manto sahib, I no longer know what to do.'

We were both sitting in the Iranian teahouse, sipping tea. Dhondoo poured from his cup into the saucer and began slurping up the special mixture he always blended with coffee. 'The fact is that I feel sorry for this sali Siraj.'

'Why?'

'God knows why. I wish I did.' He finished his tea and put the cup back on the saucer, upside down. 'Did you know she is still a virgin?'

'No, I didn't, Dhondoo.'

Dhondoo felt the scepticism in my voice and he didn't like it. 'I am not lying to you, Manto sahib. She is a hundred per cent virgin. You want to bet on that?'

'How's that possible?' I asked.

'Why not? A girl like Siraj. I tell you she could stay in this profession the rest of her life and still be a virgin. The thing is she simply does not let anyone so much as touch her. I know her whole bloody history. I know that she comes from the Punjab. She used to be on Lymington Road in the private house run by that memsahib, but was thrown out because of her endless bickerings with the passengers. I am surprised she lasted three months there, but that was because madam had about twenty girls at the time. But Manto sahib, how long can people feed you? One day madam pushed her out of the house with nothing on her except the clothes she was wearing. Then she moved to that other madam on Faras Road. She did not change her ways and one day she actually bit a passenger.

'She lasted no more than a couple of months there. I don't know what is wrong with her. She is full of life and nobody can cool it. From Faras Road she found her way into a hotel in Khetwari and created the usual trouble. One day the manager gave her marching orders. What can I say, Manto sahib, the sali doesn't seem to be interested in anything—clothes, food, ornaments, you name it. Doesn't bathe for months until lice start crawling over her clothes. If someone gives her hash, she smokes a couple of joints happily. Sometimes I see her standing outside a hotel, listening to music.'

'Why don't you send her back? I mean it's obvious she's not interested in the business. I'll pay her fare if you like,' I suggested.

Dhondoo didn't like it. 'Manto sahib, it's not a question of paying the sali's fare. I can do that. Won't kill me.'

'Then why don't you send her back?'

He lit a cigarette, which he had tucked above his ear, drew on it deeply, exhaled the smoke through his nose and said, 'I don't want her to go.'

'Do you love her?' I asked.

'What are you talking about, Manto sahib!' He touched both his ears. 'I swear by the Quran that such a vile thought has never entered my head. It is just . . . just that I like her a bit.'

'Why?'

'Because she's not like the others who are only interested in money—the whole damn lot of them. This one is different. When I make a deal on her behalf, she goes most willingly. I put her in a taxi with the passenger and off they go.

'Manto sahib, passengers come for a good time. They spend money. They want to see what they are getting and like to feel it with their hands. And that's when the trouble starts. She doesn't let anyone even touch her. Starts hitting them. If it's a gentleman, he slinks away quietly. If it's the other kind, then there's hell to pay. I have to return the money and go down on my hands and knees. I swear on the Quran. And why do I do it? Only for Siraj's sake. Manto sahib, I swear on your head that because of this sali my business has been reduced by half.'

One day I decided to see Siraj without Dhondoo's good offices. She lived in a no-good locality near the Byculla station, dumping ground for garbage and other refuse. The city corporation had built a large number of tin huts here for the poor. I do not want to write here about those tall buildings which stood not too far from this dump of filth because that has nothing to do with this story. This world after all is but another name for the high and the low. I knew roughly through Dhondoo where her hut was located. I went there—feeling apologetic about the good clothes I was wearing—but then this is not a story about me.

Outside her door a goat was tethered. It bleated when I approached. An old woman hobbled out, bent over her stick. I was about to leave when, through a hole in the coarse length of tattered cloth which hung over the door and served as a curtain, I saw large eyes in an oblong face.

She had recognized me. She must have been doing something, but she came out. 'What are you doing here?' she asked.

'I wanted to meet you.'

'Come in.'

'No, I want you to come with me.'

The old woman said, 'That'll cost you ten rupees.'

I pulled out my wallet and gave her the money. 'Come,' I said to Siraj.

She looked at me with those big window-like eyes of hers. It once again occurred to me that she was pretty, but in a withdrawn, frozen kind of way, like a mummified but perfectly preserved queen.

I took her to a hotel. There she sat in front of me in her not-quite-clean clothes, staring at the world through eyes which were so big that her entire personality had become secondary to them.

I gave Siraj forty rupees.

She was quiet and, to make a pass at her, I had to drink something quickly. After four large whiskies, I put my hands on her like passengers are expected to, but she showed me no resistance. Then I did something quite lewd and was sure she would go up like a keg of gunpowder but, surprisingly, she did not react at all. She just looked at me with her big eyes. 'Get me a joint,' she said.

'Take a drink,' I suggested.

'No, I want a joint.'

I sent for one. It was easy to get. She began to drag on it like experienced hash smokers. Her eyes had somehow lost their overpowering presence. Her face looked like a ravaged city. Every line, every feature suggested devastation. But what was this devastation? Had she been ravaged before even becoming whole? Had her world been destroyed long before the foundations could be raised?

Whether she was a virgin or not, I didn't care. But I wanted to talk to her, and she did not seem interested. I wanted her to fight with me, but she was simply indifferent.

In the end, I took her home.

When Dhondoo came to learn of my secret foray, he was upset. His feelings, both as a friend and as a man of business, had been hurt. He never gave me an opportunity to explain. All he said was, 'Manto sahib, this I did not expect of you.' And he walked away.

I didn't see him the next day. I thought he was ill, but he did not appear the day after either. One week passed. Twice a day I used to go to work past Dhondoo's headquarters and whenever I saw the lamp-post I thought of him.

I even went looking for Siraj one day, only to be greeted by the old woman there. When I asked her about Siraj, she smiled the million-year-old smile of the procuress and said, 'That one's gone, but I can always get you another.'

The question was: Where was she? Had she run away with Dhondoo? But that was quite impossible. They were not in love and Dhondoo was not that sort of person. He had a wife and children whom he loved. But the question was: Where had they disappeared to?

I thought that maybe Dhondoo had finally decided that Siraj should go home, a decision he had always been ambivalent about. One month passed.

Then one evening, as I was passing by the Iranian teahouse, I saw him leaning against his lamp-post. When he saw me, he smiled.

We went into the teahouse. I did not ask him anything. He sent for his special tea, mixed with coffee, and ordered plain tea for me. He turned around in his chair and it seemed as if he was going to make some dramatic disclosure, but all he said was, 'And how are things, Manto sahib?'

'Life goes on, Dhondoo,' I replied.

'You are right, life goes on,' he smiled. 'It's a strange world, isn't it?'

'You can say that again.'

We kept drinking tea. Dhondoo poured his into the saucer, took a sip and said, 'Manto sahib, she told me the whole story. She said to me that that friend of yours, meaning you, was crazy.'

I laughed. 'Why?'

'She told me that you took her to a hotel, gave her a lot of money and didn't do what she thought you would do.'

'That was the way it was, Dhondoo,' I said.

He laughed. 'I know. I'm sorry if I showed annoyance that day. In any case, that whole business is now over.'

'What business?'

'That Siraj business, what else?'

'What happened?'

'You remember the day you took her out? Well, she came to me later and said that she had forty rupees on her and would I take her to Lahore. I said to her, "Sali, what has come over you?" She said, "Come on Dhondoo, for my sake, take me." And Manto sahib, you know I could never say no to her. I liked her. So I said, "OK, if that's what you want."

'We bought train tickets and arrived in Lahore. She knew what hotel we were going to stay in.

'The next day she says to me, "Dhondoo, get me a burqa." I went out and got her one. And then our rounds began. She would leave in the morning and spend the entire day on the streets of Lahore in a tonga, with me keeping company. She wouldn't tell me what she was looking for.

'I said to myself, "Dhondoo, have you gone bananas? Why did you have to come with this crazy girl all the way from Bombay?"

'Then, Manto sahib, one day, she asked me to stop the tonga in the middle of the street. "Do you see that man there? Can you bring him to me? I am going to the hotel. Now."

'I was confused but I stepped down from the tonga and began to follow the man she had pointed out. Well, by the grace of God, I am a good judge of men. I began to talk to him and it did not take me long to find out that he was game for a good time.

'I said to him, "I have a very special brand of goods from Bombay." He wanted me to take him with me right away, but I said, "Not that fast, friend, show me the colour of your money." He brandished a thick wad of bank notes in my face. What I couldn't understand was why, of all the men in Lahore, Siraj had picked this one out. In any case, I said to myself, "Dhondoo, everything goes." We took a tonga to the hotel.

'I went in and told Siraj I had the man waiting outside. She said, "Bring him in but don't go away." When I brought him in and he saw her, he wanted to run away, but Siraj grabbed hold of him.'

'She grabbed hold of him?'

'That's right. She grabbed hold of the *sala* and said to him, "Where are you going? Why did you make me run away from home? You knew I loved you. And remember you had said to me that you loved me too. But when I left my home and my parents and my brothers and my sisters and came with you from Amritsar to Lahore and stayed in this very hotel, you abandoned me the same night. You left while I was asleep. Why did you bring me here? Why did you make me run away from home? You know, I was prepared for everything and you let me down. But I have come back and found you. I still love you. Nothing has changed."

'And Manto sahib, she threw her arms around him. That *sala* began to cry. He was asking her to forgive him. He was saying he had done her wrong. He had got cold feet. He was saying he would never leave her again. He kept repeating he would never leave her again. God knows what rot he was talking.

'Then Siraj asked me to leave the room. I lay on a bare cot outside and went to sleep at some point. When she woke me up, it was morning. "Dhondoo," she said, "let's go." "Where?" I asked. She said, "Let's go back to Bombay." I said, "Where is that *sala*?" "He is sleeping, I have covered his face with my burqa," she replied.'

Dhondoo ordered himself another cup of tea mixed with coffee. I looked up and saw Siraj enter the hotel. Her oval face was glowing, but her two big eyes looked like fallen train signals.

# The Wild Cactus

THE NAME OF THE TOWN IS UNIMPORTANT. LET US SAY IT WAS IN THE suburbs of the city of Peshawar, not far from the frontier, where that woman lived in a small mud house, half hidden from the dusty, unmetalled, forlorn road by a hedge of wild cactus.

The cactus was quite dry but it had grown with such profusion that it had become like a curtain shielding the house from the gaze of passers-by. It is not clear if it had always been there or whether it was the woman who had planted it.

The house was more like a hut with three small rooms, all kept very spick and span. There wasn't much in it by way of furniture, but what there was was nice. In the backroom was a big bed, and beside it an alcove where an earthen lamp burned all night. It was all very orderly.

Let me now tell you about the woman who lived there with her young daughter.

There were various stories. Some people said the young girl was not really her daughter, but an orphan whom she had taken in and raised. Others said she was her illegitimate child, while there were some who believed her to be her real daughter. One does not know the truth.

I forgot to tell you the woman's name, not that it matters. It could be Sakina, Mehtab, Gulshan or something else, but let's call her Sardar for the sake of convenience.

She was in her middle years, and must have been beautiful in her time. Her face had now begun to wrinkle, though she still looked years younger than she was.

Her daughter—if she was her daughter—was extremely beautiful. There was nothing about her to suggest that she was a woman of pleasure, which is what she was. Business was brisk. The girl, whom I will call Nawab, was not unhappy with her life. She had grown up in an atmosphere where no concept of marital relations existed.

When Sardar had brought her her first man in the big bed in the backroom, it had seemed to her quite a natural thing to have happened to a girl who had just crossed the threshold of puberty. Since then it had become the pattern of her life and she was happy with it.

And although, according to popular definition, she was a prostitute, she had no knowledge or consciousness of sin. It simply did not exist in her world.

There was a physical sincerity about her. She used to give herself completely, without reservations, to the men who were brought to her. She had come to believe that it was a woman's duty to make love to men, tenderly and without inhibitions.

She knew almost nothing about life as it was lived in the big cities, but through her men she had come to learn something of their city habits, like the brushing of teeth in the morning, drinking a cup of tea in bed and taking a quick bath before dressing up and driving off.

Not all men were alike. Some only wanted to smoke a cigarette in the morning, while others wanted nothing but a hot cup of tea. Some were bad sleepers; others slept soundly and left at the crack of dawn.

Sardar was a woman without a worry in the world. She had faith in the ability of her daughter—or whoever she was—to look after the clients. She generally used to go to bed early herself happily drugged on opium. It was only in emergencies that she was woken up. Often customers had to be revived after they had had too much to drink. Sardar would say philosophically, 'Give him some pickled mango or make him drink a glass of salt water so that he can vomit. Then send him to sleep.'

Sardar was a careful woman. Customers were required to pay in advance. After collecting the money she would say, 'Now you two go and have a good time.'

While the money always stayed in Sardar's custody, presents, when received, were Nawab's. Many of the clients were rich and gifts of cloth, fruit and sweets were frequent.

Nawab was a happy girl. In the little three-bed mud house, life was smooth and predictable. Not long ago, an army officer had brought her a gramophone and some records which she used to play when alone. She even used to try to sing along, but she had no talent for music, not that she was aware of it. The fact was that she was aware of very little, and not interested in knowing more. She might have been ignorant, but she was happy.

What the world beyond the cactus hedge was like, she had no idea. All she knew was the rough, dusty road and the men who drove up in cars, honked once or twice to announce their arrival and when told by Sardar to park at a more discreet distance, did so, then walked into the house to join Nawab in the big bed.

The regulars numbered not more than five or six, but Sardar had arranged things with such tact that never had two visitors been known to run into each other. Since every customer had his fixed day, no problems were ever encountered.

Sardar was also careful to ensure that Nawab did not become

pregnant. It was an ever-present possibility. However, two and a half years had passed without any mishap. The police were unaware of Sardar's establishment and the men were discreet.

One day, a big Dodge drove up to the house. The driver honked once and Sardar stepped out. It was no one she knew, nor did the stranger say who he was. He parked the car and walked in as if he was one of the old regulars.

Sardar was a bit confused, but Nawab greeted the stranger with a smile and took him into the backroom. When Sardar followed them in, they were sitting on the bed, next to each other, talking. One look was enough to assure her that the visitor was rich and, apart from that, handsome. 'Who showed you the way?' she asked, nevertheless.

The stranger smiled, then put his arm amorously around Nawab and said, 'This one here.' Nawab sprung up flirtatiously and said, 'Why, I never saw you in my life!' 'But I have,' the stranger answered, grinning.

Surprised, Nawab asked, 'When and where?' The stranger took her hand in his and said, 'You won't understand; ask your mother.' 'Have I met this man before?' Nawab asked Sardar like a child. By now Sardar had come to the conclusion that the tip had come from one of her regulars. 'Don't worry about it. I'll tell you later,' she said to Nawab.

Then she left the room, took some opium and lay on her bed, satisfied. The stranger did not look the kind to make trouble.

His name was Haibat Khan, the biggest landlord in the neighbouring district of Hazara. 'I want no men visiting Nawab in future,' he said to Sardar on his way to his car after a few hours. 'How's that possible, Khan sahib? Can you afford to pay for all of them?' Sardar asked, being the woman of the world she was.

Haibat Khan did not answer her. Instead, he pulled out a lot of money from his pocket and threw it on the floor. He also removed a diamond ring from his finger and slipped it on Nawab. Then he walked out hurriedly, past the cactus hedge.

Nawab did not even look at the money, but she kept gazing at the ring with the big resplendent diamond. She heard the car start and move away, leaving clouds of dust in its wake.

When she returned, Sardar had picked up the money and counted it. There were nineteen hundred rupees in bank notes. One more, and it would have been two thousand, she thought, but it didn't worry her. She put the money away, took some opium and went to bed.

Nawab was thrilled. She just couldn't take her eyes off the diamond ring. A few days passed. In between, an old client came to the house, but Sardar sent him packing, saying she anticipated a police raid and had therefore decided to discontinue business.

Sardar's logic was simple. She knew Haibat Khan was rich and money would keep coming in, as before, with the added advantage that there would be only one man to deal with. In the next few days she was able to get rid of all her old clients, one by one.

A week later, Haibat Khan made his second appearance, but he did not speak to Sardar. The two of them went to the backroom, leaving Sardar with her opium and her bed.

Haibat Khan was now a regular visitor. He was totally enamoured of Nawab. He liked her artless approach to love-making, untinged by the hard-baked professionalism common to prostitutes. Nor was there anything housewifely about her. She would lie in bed next to him as a child lies next to its mother, playing with her breasts, sticking his little finger in her nose and then quietly going off to sleep.

It was something entirely new in Haibat Khan's experience. Nawab was different, she was interesting and she gave pleasure. His visits became more frequent.

Sardar was happy. She had never had so much money coming in with such regularity. Nawab, however, sometimes felt troubled. Haibat Khan always seemed to be vaguely apprehensive of something. It showed in little things. A slight shiver always seemed to run through his body when a car or bus went speeding past the house. He would jump out of bed and run out, trying to read the number plate.

One night, a passing bus startled Haibat Khan so much that he suddenly wrested himself free from her arms and sat up. Nawab was a light sleeper and woke up too. He looked terrified. She was frightened. 'What happened?' she screamed.

By now, Haibat Khan had composed himself. 'It was nothing. I think I had a nightmare,' he said. The bus had gone, though it could still be heard in the distance.

Nawab said, 'No, Khan, there is something. Whenever you hear a noise, you get into a state.'

Haibat Khan's vanity was stung. 'Don't talk rubbish,' he said sharply. 'Why should anyone be afraid of cars and buses?'

Nawab began to cry, but Haibat Khan took her in his arms and she stopped sobbing.

He was a handsome man, strong of limb and a passionate lover, who ignited the fires in Nawab's young body every time he touched her. It was really he who had initiated her into the intricacies of love-making. For the first time in her life, she was experiencing the state called love. She used to pine for him when he was gone, and would play her records endlessly.

Many months went by, deepening Nawab's love for Haibat

Khan, and also her anxiety. His visits had of late become somewhat erratic. He would come for a few hours, look extremely ill at ease and leave suddenly. It was clear he was under some pressure. He never seemed willing or happy to leave, but he always left.

Nawab tried to get to the truth many times, only to be given evasive answers.

One morning his Dodge drove up to the house, stopping at the usual place. Nawab was asleep but she woke up when she heard him honk the horn. She rushed out and ran into Haibat Khan at the door. He embraced her passionately, picked her up and carried her inside.

They kept talking to each other for a long time about things lovers talk about. For the first time in her life, Nawab said to him, 'Khan, bring me some gold bangles.'

Haibat Khan kissed her fleshy arms many times and said, 'You will have them tomorrow. For you I can even give my life.'

Nawab squirmed coquettishly. 'Oh no Khan, it is poor me who'll have to give her life.'

Haibat Khan kissed her and said, 'I'll return tomorrow with your gold bangles and I'll put them on you myself.'

Nawab was ecstatic. She wanted to dance with joy. Sardar watched her contentedly, then reached for her opium and went to bed.

Nawab rose the next morning, still in a state of high excitement. This is the day he will bring me my gold bangles, she said to herself, but she felt uneasy. That night she couldn't sleep.

She said to her mother, 'The Khan hasn't come. He promised and he hasn't come.' Her heart was full of foreboding.

Had he had an accident? Had he been suddenly taken ill? Had he been waylaid? She heard cars passing and thought of Haibat Khan and how these noises used to terrify him.

One week passed. The house behind the cactus hedge continued to remain without visitors. Off and on, a car would go by, leaving clouds of dust behind. In her mind, passing cars and buses were now associated with Haibat Khan. They had something to do with his absence.

One afternoon, while both women were about to take a nap after lunch, they heard a car stop outside. It honked, but it was not Haibat Khan's car. Who was it then?

Sardar went outside to make sure it was not one of the old customers, in which case she would send him on his way. It was Haibat Khan. He sat in the driver's seat but it was not his car. With him was a well-dressed, rather beautiful woman.

Haibat Khan stepped out, followed by the woman. Sardar was confused. What was this woman doing with him? Who was she? Why had he brought her here?

They entered the house without taking any notice of her. She followed them inside after a while and found all three of them sitting next to one another on the bed. There was a strange silence about everything. The woman, who was wearing heavy gold ornaments, appeared to be somewhat nervous.

Sardar stood at the door and when Haibat Khan looked up she greeted him, but he made no acknowledgement. He was in a state of great and visible agitation.

The woman said to Sardar, 'Well, we are here; why don't you get us something to eat?'

'I'll have it ready in no time, whatever you wish,' Sardar replied, suddenly the hostess.

There was something about the woman which suggested authority. 'Go to the kitchen,' she ordered Sardar. 'Get the fire going. Do you have a big cooking pot?'

'Yes.' Sardar shook her head.

'Rinse it well. I'll join you later,' she said. Then she rose from the bed and began examining the gramophone.

Apologetically, Sardar said, 'One cannot buy meat around here.'

'It'll be provided,' the woman said. 'And look, I want a big fire. Now, go and do what you have been told.'

Sardar left. The woman smiled and addressed Nawab, 'Nawab, we have brought you gold bangles.'

She opened her handbag and produced heavy, ornate gold bangles, wrapped in red tissue paper.

Nawab looked at Haibat Khan, who sat next to her, very still. 'Who is this woman, Khan?' she asked in a frightened voice.

Playing with the gold bangles, the woman said, 'Who am I? I am Haibat Khan's sister.' Then she looked at Haibat Khan, who seemed to have suddenly shrunk. 'My name is Halakat,' she said, addressing Nawab.

Nawab could not understand what was going on, but she felt terrified.

The woman moved towards Nawab, took her hands and began to slip the gold bangles on them. Then she said to Haibat Khan, 'I want you to leave the room. Let me dress her up nicely and bring her to you.'

Haibat Khan looked mesmerized. He did not move. 'Leave the room. Didn't you hear me?' she told him sharply.

He left the room, looking at Nawab as he walked out.

The kitchen was outside the house. Sardar had got the fire

going. He did not speak to her, but walked past the cactus hedge, out on the road. He looked half-demented.

A bus approached. He had an urge to flag it down, get on board and disappear. But he did no such thing. The bus sped by, coating him with dust. He tried to shout after it, but his voice seemed to have gone.

He wanted to rush back into the house where he had spent so many nights of pleasure, but his feet seemed to be embedded in the ground.

He just stood there, trying to take stock of the situation. The woman who was now in the house, he had known a long time. He used to be a friend of her husband, who was dead. He remembered their first encounter many years ago. He had gone to console her after her husband's death and had ended up being her lover. It was very sudden. She had simply commanded him to take her, as if he was a servant being asked to perform a simple task.

Haibat Khan had not been very experienced with women. When Shahina, who had told Nawab her name was Halakat, or death, had become his lover, he had felt as if he had accomplished something in his life. She was rich in her own right and now had her husband's money. However, he was not interested in that. She was the first real woman in his life and he had let her seduce him.

For a long time he stood on the road. Finally, he went back to the house. The front door was closed and Sardar was cooking something in the kitchen.

He knocked and it was opened. All he could see was blood on the floor and Shahina leaning against the wall. 'I have dressed up your Nawab for you very nicely,' she said.

'Where is she?' he asked, his throat dry with terror.

'Some of her is on the bed, but most of her is in the kitchen,' she replied.

Haibat Khan began to tremble. He could now see that there was blood on the floor and a long knife. There was someone on the bed, covered with a bloodstained sheet.

Shahina smiled. 'Do you want me to lift the sheet and show you what I have there? It is your Nawab. I have made her up with great care. But perhaps you should eat first. You must be hungry. Sardar is cooking the most delicious meat in the world. I prepared it myself.'

'What have you done?' Haibat Khan screamed.

Shahina smiled again. 'Darling, this is not the first time. My husband, like you, was also faithless. I had to kill him and then throw his severed limbs for wild birds to feast on. Since I love you, instead of you, I have . . .'

She did not complete the sentence, but removed the sheet from the heap on the bed. Haibat Khan fainted and fell to the floor.

When he came to, he was in a car. Shahina was driving. They seemed to be in a wild country.

# It Happened in 1919

'IT HAPPENED IN 1919. THE WHOLE OF PUNJAB WAS UP IN ARMS AGAINST the Rowlatt Act. Sir Michael O'Dwyer had banned Gandhiji's entry into the province under the Defence of India rules. He had been stopped at Pulwal, taken into custody and sent to Bombay. I believe if the British had not made this blunder, the Jallianwala Bagh incident would not have added a bloody page to the black history of their rule in India.'

I was on a train and the man sitting next to me had begun talking to me, just like that. I hadn't interrupted him and so he had gone on.

'Gandhiji was loved and respected by the people, Muslims, Hindus and Sikhs alike. When news of the arrest reached Lahore, the entire city went on strike. Amritsar, where the story I am going to narrate happened, followed suit.

'It is said that by the evening of 9 April, the deputy commissioner had received orders for the expulsion from Amritsar of the two leaders, Dr Satyapal and Dr Kitchlew, but was unwilling to implement them because, in his view, there was no likelihood of a breach of the peace. Protest meetings were being organized and no one was in favour of using violent methods.

'I was a witness to a procession taken out to celebrate a Hindu festival, and I can assure you it was the most peaceful thing I ever saw. It faithfully kept to the route marked out by the officials, but this Sir Michael was half-mad. They said he refused to follow the deputy commissioner's advice because he was convinced that Kitchlew and Satyapal were in Amritsar waiting for a signal from Gandhiji before proceeding to topple the government. In his view the protest meetings and processions were all part of this grand conspiracy.

'The news of the expulsion of the two leaders spread like wildfire through the city, creating an atmosphere of uncertainty and fear. One could sense that disaster was about to strike. But, my friend, I can tell you that there was also a great deal of enthusiasm among the people. All businesses were closed. The city was quiet like a graveyard and there was a feeling of impending doom in the air.

'After the first shock of the expulsions had died down, thousands of people gathered spontaneously to go in a procession to the deputy commissioner and call for the withdrawal of the orders. But, my friend, believe me, the times were out of joint. That this extremely reasonable request would be even heard was out of the question. Sir Michael was like a pharaoh and we were not surprised when he declared the gathering itself unlawful.

'Amritsar, which was one of the greatest centres of the liberation struggle and which still proudly carries the wound of Jallianwala Bagh, is now of course changed . . . but that is another story. Some people say that what happened in that great city in 1947 was also the fault of the British. But if you want my opinion, we ourselves are responsible for the bloodshed there in 1947. Anyway.

'The deputy commissioner's house was in the Civil Lines. In fact, all senior officers and the big toadies of the Raj lived in that exclusive area. If you know your Amritsar, you will recall that

bridge which links the city with the Civil Lines. You cross the
bridge from the city and you are on the Mall, that paradise on
earth created by the British rulers.

'The protest procession began to move towards the Civil
Lines. When I reached Hall Gate, word went round that British
mounted troops were on guard at the bridge, but the crowd
was undeterred and kept moving. I was also among them. We
were all unarmed. I mean there wasn't even a stick on any of us.
The whole idea was to get to the deputy commissioner's house
and protest to him about the expulsion of the two leaders and
demand their release. All peacefully.

'When the crowd reached the bridge, the tommies opened
fire, causing utter pandemonium. People began to run in all
directions. There were no more than twenty to twenty-five
soldiers, but they were armed and they were firing. I have never
seen anything like it. Some were wounded by gunshot; others
were trampled.

'I stood well away from the fray at the edge of a big open
gutter and someone pushed me into it. When the firing stopped,
I crawled out. The crowd had dispersed. Many of the injured
were lying on the road and the tommies on the bridge were
having a good laugh. I'm not sure what my state of mind at the
time was, but I think it couldn't have been normal. In fact, I
think I fainted when I fell in. It was only later that I was able to
reconstruct the events.

'I could hear angry slogans being chanted in the distance. I
began to walk. Going past the shrine of Zahra Pir, I was in Hall
Gate in no time, where I found about thirty or forty boys
throwing stones at the big clock which sits on top of the gate.
They finally shattered its protective glass and the pieces fell on
the road.

'"Let's go and smash the queen's statue," someone shouted.

'"No, let's set fire to the police headquarters."

'"And all the banks too."

'"What would be the point of that? Let's go to the bridge and fight the tommy soldiers," suggested another.

'I recognized the author of the last proposal. He was Thaila kanjar—kanjar, because he was the son of a prostitute—otherwise Mohammad Tufail. He was quite notorious in Amritsar. He had got into the habit of drinking and gambling while still a boy. He had two sisters, Shamshad and Almas, who were considered the city's most beautiful singing and dancing girls.

'Shamshad was an accomplished singer and big landlords and the like used to travel from great distances to hear her perform. The sisters were not exactly enamoured of the doings of their brother, Thaila, and it was said that they had practically disowned him. However, through one excuse or the other, he was always able to get enough money from them to live in style. He liked to dress and eat well and drink to his heart's content. He was a great storyteller, but unlike other people of his type he was never vulgar. He was tall, athletic and quite handsome, come to think of it.

'However, the boys did not show much enthusiasm for his suggestion of taking on the tommies. Instead, they began to move towards the queen's statue. Thaila was not the kind to give up so easily. He said to them, "Why are you wasting your energy? Why don't you follow me? We'll go and kill those tommies who have shot and killed so many innocent people. I swear by God, if we're together, we can wring their necks with our bare hands."

'Some were already well on their way to the queen's statue, but there were still some stragglers who began to follow Thaila

in the direction of the bridge where the tommies stood guard. I
thought the whole thing was suicidal and I had no desire to be
part of it. I even shouted at Thaila, "Don't do it, yaar, why are
you bent upon getting yourself killed?"

'He laughed. "Thaila just wants to demonstrate that he's not
afraid of their bullets," he said cavalierly. Then he told the few
who were willing to follow him, "Those among you who are
afraid can leave now."

'No one left, which is understandable in such situations. Thaila
started to walk briskly, setting the pace for his companions. There
seemed to be no question of turning back now.

'The distance between Hall Gate and the bridge is negligible,
maybe less than a hundred yards. The approach to the bridge
was being guarded by two mounted tommies. I heard the sound
of fire as Thaila closed in, shouting revolutionary slogans. I
thought he'd been hit, but no, he was still moving forward with
great resolution. Some of the boys began to run in different
directions. He turned and shouted, "Don't run away . . . Let's
go get them."

'I heard more gunfire. Thaila's back was momentarily towards
the tommies, since he was trying to infuse some life into his
retreating entourage. I saw him veer towards the soldiers and
there were big red spots of blood on his silk shirt. He had been
hit, but he kept advancing, like a wounded lion. There was more
gunfire and he staggered, but then he regained his foothold and
leapt at the mounted tommy, bringing him down to the ground.

'The other tommy became panic-stricken and began to fire
his revolver recklessly. What happened afterwards is not clear,
because I fainted.

'When I came to, I found myself home. Some men who knew

me had picked me up and brought me back. I heard from them that angry crowds had ransacked the town. The queen's statue had been smashed and the town hall and three of the city bands had been set on fire. Five or six Europeans had been killed and the crowd had gone on a rampage.

'The British officers were not bothered about damage to property, but the fact that European blood had been shed. And as you know, it was avenged at Jallianwala Bagh. The deputy commissioner handed the city over to General Dyer, so on 12 April the general marched through the streets at the head of columns of armed soldiers. Dozens of innocent people were arrested. On 13 April a protest meeting was organized in Jallianwala Bagh which General Dyer "dispersed" by ordering his Gurkha and Sikh soldiers to open fire on the unarmed crowed.

'However, I was telling you about Thaila and what I saw with my own eyes. Only God is without blemish and Thaila was, let's not forget, the son of a prostitute and he used to practise every evil in the book. But he was brave. I tell you he had already been hit when he exhorted his companions not to run away but to move forward. He was so intoxicated with enthusiasm at the time that he did not realize he had been hit. He was shot twice more, once in the back and then in the chest. They pumped his young body full of molten lead.

'I didn't see it, but I'm told that when Thaila's bullet-ridden body was pulled away both his hands were dug into the tommy's throat. They just couldn't get his grip to loosen. The tommy had of course been well and truly dispatched to hell.

'Thaila's bullet-torn body was handed over to his family the next day. It seemed the other tommy had emptied the entire magazine of his revolver into him. He must have been dead by then, but the devil had nevertheless gone on.

'It is said that when Thaila's body was brought to his mohalla it was a shattering scene. It's true he wasn't exactly the apple of his family's eye, but when they saw his minced-up remains, there wasn't a dry eye to be seen anywhere. His sisters, Shamshad and Almas, fainted.

'My friend, I have heard that in the French Revolution, it was a prostitute who was the first to fall. Mohammad Tufail was also a prostitute's son, so whether it was the first bullet of the revolution which hit him or the tenth or the fiftieth, nobody really bothered to find out because socially he did not matter. I have a feeling that when they finally make a list of those who died in this bloodbath in Punjab, Thaila kanjar's name won't be included. As a matter of fact, I don't think anyone would even bother about a list.

'Those were terrible days. The monster they call martial law held the city in its grip. Thaila was buried amid great hurry and confusion, as if his death was a grave crime which his family should obliterate from the record. What can I say except that Thaila died and Thaila was buried.'

My companion stopped speaking. The train was moving at breakneck speed. Suddenly I felt as if the clickety-clack of its powerful wheels was intoning the words 'Thaila died, Thaila buried . . . Thaila died, Thaila buried . . . Thaila died, Thaila buried.' There was no dividing line between his death and his burial. He had died and in the next instant he had been buried. 'You were going to say something,' I said to my companion.

'Yes,' he replied, 'yes . . . there is a sad part of the story which I haven't yet come to.'

'And what's that?'

'As I have already told you, he had two sisters, Shamshad and Almas, both very beautiful. Shamshad was tall, with fine features, big eyes, and she was a superb thumri singer. They say she had taken music lessons from the great Khan Sahib Fateh Ali Khan. Almas, the other one, was unmusical, but she was a fantastic dancer. When she danced it seemed as if every cell of her body was undulating with the music. Oh! They say there was a magic in her eyes which nobody could resist . . .

'Well, my friend, it is said that someone who was trying to make his number with the British told them about Thaila's sisters and how beautiful and gifted they were. So it was decided that to avenge the death of that English woman . . . what was the name of that witch? Miss Sherwood I think . . . the two girls should be summoned for an evening of pleasure. You know what I mean.'

'Yes.'

'These are delicate matters, but I would say that when it comes to something like this, even dancing girls and prostitutes are like our sisters and mothers. But I tell you, our people have no concept of national honour. So, you can guess what happened.

'The police received orders from the powers that be and an inspector personally went to the house of the girls and said that the sahib log had expressed a desire to be entertained by them.

'And to think that the earth on the grave of their brother was still fresh. He hadn't even been dead two days and there were these orders: come and dance in our imperial presence. No greater torture could have been devised! Do you think that it even occurred to those who issued these orders that even women like Shamshad and Almas could have a sense of honour? What do you think?'

But he was speaking more to himself than to me. Nevertheless, I ventured, 'Yes, surely they too have a sense of honour.'

'Quite right. After all, Thaila was their brother. He hadn't lost his life in a gambling brawl or a fit of drunkenness. He had volunteered to drink the cup of martyrdom like a valiant national hero.

'Yes, it's true he was born of a prostitute, but a prostitute is also a mother and Shamshad and Almas were his sisters first and dancing girls later. They had fainted when they had brought Thaila's bullet-ridden body home, and it was heart-breaking to hear them bewail the martyrdom of their brother.'

'Did they go?' I asked.

My companion answered after a pause, 'Yes, yes, they went all right. They were dressed to kill.' There was a note of bitterness in his voice.

'They went to their hosts of the evening and they looked stunning. They say it was quite an orgy. The two sisters displayed their art with fascinating skill. In their silks and brocades they looked like Caucasian fairy queens. There was much drinking and merrymaking and they danced and sang all night.

'And it is said that at two in the morning the guest of honour indicated that the party was over.'

'The party was over, the party was over' the wheels intoned as the train ran headlong along the tracks. I cleared my mind of this intrusion and asked my companion, 'What happened then?'

Taking his eyes away from the passing phantasmagoria of trees and power lines, he said in a determined voice, 'They tore off their silks and brocades and stood there naked and they said . . . look at us . . . we are Thaila's sisters . . . that martyr whose beautiful body you peppered with your bullets because inside that body dwelt a spirit which was in love with this land . . . yes, we are his beautiful sisters . . . come, burn our fragrant bodies with the red-hot irons of your lust . . . but before you do that, allow us to spit in your faces once.' He fell silent as if he did not wish to say any more.

'What happened then?'

Tears welled up in his eyes. 'They . . . they were shot dead.'

I did not say anything. The train stopped. He sent for a porter and asked him to pick up his bags. As he was about to leave, I said to him, 'I have a feeling that the story you have just told me has a false ending.'

He was startled. 'How do you know?'

'Because there was indescribable agony in your voice when you reached the end.'

He swallowed. 'Yes, those bitches . . .' he paused, 'they dishonoured their martyred brother's name.'

He stepped on the platform and was gone.

# The Woman in the Red Raincoat

THIS DATES BACK TO THE TIME WHEN BOTH EAST AND WEST PUNJAB WERE being ravaged by bloody communal riots between Hindus and Muslims. It had been raining hard for many days and the fire which men had been unable to put out had been extinguished by nature. However, there was no let-up in the murderous attacks on the innocent, nor was the honour of young women safe. Gangs of young men were still on the prowl and abductions of helpless and terrified girls were common.

On the face of it, murder, arson and looting are really not so difficult to commit as some people think. However, my friend 'S' had not found the going so easy.

But before I tell you his story, let me introduce 'S'. He's a man of ordinary looks and build and is as much interested in getting something for nothing as most of us are. But he isn't cruel by nature. It is another matter that he became the perpetrator of a strange tragedy, though he did not quite realize at the time what was happening.

He was just an ordinary student when we were in school, fond of games, but not very sporting. He was always the first to get into a fight when an argument developed during a game. Although he never quite played fair, he was an honest fighter.

He was interested in painting, but he had to leave college after only one year. Next we knew, he had opened a bicycle shop in the city.

When the riots began, his was one of the first shops to be

burnt down. Having nothing else to do, he joined the roaming bands of looters and arsonists, nothing extraordinary at the time. It was really more by way of entertainment and diversion than out of a feeling of communal revenge, I would say. Those were strange times. This is his story and it is in his own words.

'It was really pouring down. It seemed as if the skies would burst. In my entire life, I had never seen such rain. I was at home, sitting on my balcony, smoking a cigarette. In front of me lay a large pile of goods I had looted from various shops and houses with the rest of the gang. However, I was not interested in them. They had burnt down my shop but, believe me, it did not really seem to matter, mainly because I had seen so much looting and destruction that nothing made any sense any longer. The noise of the rain was difficult to ignore but, strangely enough, all I was conscious of was a dry and barren silence. There was a stench in the air. Even my cigarette smelt unpleasant. I'm not sure I was thinking even. I was in a kind of daze. Very difficult to explain. Suddenly a shiver ran down my spine and a powerful desire to run out and pick up a girl took hold of me. The rain had become even heavier. I got up, put on my raincoat and, fortifying myself with a fresh tin of cigarettes from the pile of loot, went out in the rain.

'The roads were dark and deserted. Not even soldiers—a common sight in those days—were around. I kept walking about aimlessly for hours. There were many dead bodies lying on the streets, but they seemed to have no effect on me. After some time, I found myself in the Civil Lines area. The roads were without any sign of life. Suddenly I heard the sound of an approaching car. I turned. It was a small Austin being driven at breakneck speed. I don't know what came over me, but I placed myself in the middle of the road and began to wave frantically for the driver to stop.

'The car did not slow down. However, I was not going to move. When it was only a few yards away, it suddenly swerved to the left. In trying to run after it, I fell down, but got up immediately. I hadn't hurt myself. The car braked, then skidded and went off the road. It finally came to a stop, resting against a tree. I began to move towards it. The door was thrown open and a woman in a red raincoat jumped out. I couldn't see her face, but her shimmering raincoat was visible in the murky light. A wave of heat gripped my body.

'When she saw me moving towards her, she broke into a run. However, I caught up with her after a few yards. "Help me," she screamed as my arms enveloped her tightly, more her slippery raincoat than her, come to think of it.

'"Are you a Englishwoman?" I asked her in English, realizing too late that I should have said 'an', not 'a'.

'"No," she replied.

'I hated Englishwomen, so I said to her, "Then it's all right."

'She began to scream in Urdu, "You're going to kill me. You're going to kill me."

'I said nothing. I was only trying to guess her age and what she looked like. The hood of her raincoat covered her face. When I tried to remove it, she put both her hands in front of her face. I didn't force her. Instead, I walked towards the car, opened the rear door and pushed her in. I started the car and the engine caught. I put it in reverse and it responded. I steered it carefully back on to the road and took off.

'I switched off the engine when we were in front of my house. My first thought was to take her to the balcony, but I changed my mind, not being sure if she would willingly walk up all those stairs. I shouted for the houseboy. "Open the living room door," I told him. After he had done that, I pushed her into the room. In the dark, I caught hold of her and gently pushed her on to the sofa.

'"Don't kill me. Don't kill me please," she began to scream.

'It sounded funny. In a mock-heroic voice I said, "I won't kill you. I won't kill you, darling."

'She began to cry. I sent the servant, who was still hanging around, out of the house. I pulled out a box of matches from my pocket, but the rain had made it damp. There hadn't been any power for weeks. I had a torch upstairs but I didn't really want to bother. "I'm not exactly going to take pictures that I should need a light," I said to myself. I took off my raincoat and threw it on the floor. "Let me take yours," I suggested to her.

'I fumbled for her on the sofa but she wasn't there. However, I wasn't worried. She had to be in the room somewhere. Methodically, I began to comb the place and in a few minutes I found her. In fact, we had a near collision on the floor. I touched her on the throat by accident. She screamed. "Stop that," I said. "I'm not going to kill you."

'I ignored her sobbing and began to unbutton her raincoat, which was made of some plastic material and was very slippery. She kept wailing and trying to struggle free, but I managed to get her free of that silly coat of hers. I realized that she was wearing a sari underneath. I touched her knee and it felt solid. A violent electric current went through my entire body. But I didn't want to rush things.

'I tried to calm her down. "Darling, I didn't bring you here to murder you. Don't be afraid. You are safer here than you would be outside. If you want to leave, you are free to do so. However, I would suggest that as long as these riots last, you should stay here with me. You're an educated girl. Out there, people have become like wild beasts. I don't want you to fall into the hands of those savages."

"'You won't kill me?" she sobbed.

"'No sir," I said.

'She burst out laughing because I had called her sir. However, her laughter encouraged me. "Darling, my English is rather weak," I said with a laugh.

'She did not speak for some time. Then she said, "If you don't want to kill me, why have you brought me here?"

'It was an awkward question. I couldn't think of an answer, but I heard myself saying, "Of course I don't want to kill you for the simple reason that I don't like killing people. So why have I brought you here? Well, I suppose because I'm lonely."

"'But you have your live-in servant."

"'He is only a servant. He doesn't matter."

'She fell silent. I began to experience a sense of guilt, so I got up and said, "Let's forget about it. If you want to leave, I won't stop you."

'I caught hold of her hand, then I thought of her knee which I had touched. Violently, I pressed her against my chest. I could feel her warm breath under my chin. I put my lips on hers. She began to tremble. "Don't be afraid, darling. I won't kill you," I whispered.

"'Please let me go," she said in a tremulous voice.

'I gently pulled my arms away, but then on an impulse I lifted her off the ground. The flesh on her hips was extremely soft, I noticed. I also found that she was carrying a small handbag. I laid her down on the sofa and took her bag away. "Believe me, if it contains valuables, they will be quite safe. In fact, if you like, there are things I can give you," I told her by way of reassurance.

'"I don't need anything," she said.

'"But there is something I need," I replied.

'"What?" she asked.

'"You," I answered.

'She didn't say anything. I began to rub her knee. She offered no resistance. Feeling that she might think I was taking advantage of her helplessness, I said, "I don't want to force you. If you don't want it, you can leave, really."

'I was about to get up, when she grabbed my hand and put it on her breast. Her heart was beating violently. I became excited. "Darling," I whispered, taking her into my arms again.

'We began to kiss each other with reckless abandon. She kept cooing "darling" and God knows what nonsense I myself spoke during that mad interlude.

'"You should take those things off," I suggested.

'"Why don't you take them off yourself?" she answered in an emotional voice.

'I began to caress her. "Who are you?" she asked.

'I was in no mood to tell her, so I said, "I am yours, darling."

'"You're a naughty boy," she said coquettishly, while pressing me close to her. I was now trying to take off her blouse, but she said to me, "Please don't make me naked."

'"What does it matter? It's dark," I said.

'"No, no!"

'She lifted my hands and began to kiss them. "No, please no. I just feel shy."

'"Forget about the blouse," I said. "It's all going to be fine."

'There was a silence, which she broke. "You're not annoyed, are you?"

'"No, why should I be? You don't want to take off your blouse, so that's fine, but . . ." I couldn't complete the sentence, but then with some effort, I said, "But anyway something should happen. I mean, take off your sari."

'"I am afraid." Her throat seemed to have gone dry.

'"Who are you afraid of?" I asked flirtatiously.

'"I am afraid," she replied and began to weep.

'"There is nothing to be afraid of," I said in a consoling voice. '"I won't hurt you, but if you are really afraid, then let's forget about it. You stay here for a few days and, when you begin to feel at home and are not afraid of me any longer, then we'll see."

'"No, no," she said, putting her head on my thighs. I began to comb her hair with my fingers. After some time, she calmed down, then suddenly she pulled me to her with such force that I was taken aback. She was also trembling violently.

'There was a knock at the door and streaks of light began to filter into the dark room from outside.

'It was the servant. "I have brought a lantern. Would you please take it?"

'"All right," I answered.

'"No, no," she said in a terrified, muffled voice.

'"Look, what's the harm? I will lower the wick and place it in a corner," I said.

'I went to the door, brought the lantern in and placed it in a corner of the room. Since my eyes were not yet accustomed to the light, for a few seconds I could see nothing. Meanwhile, she had moved into the farthest corner.

'"Come on now," I said, "we can sit in the light and chat for a few minutes. Whenever you wish, I will put the lantern out."

'Picking up the lantern, I took a few steps towards her. She had covered her face with her sari. "You're a strange girl," I said, "after all, I'm like your bridegroom."

'Suddenly there was a loud explosion outside. She rushed forward and fell into my arms. "It's only a bomb," I said. "Don't be afraid. It's nothing these days."

'"My eyes were now beginning to get used to the light. Her face began to come into focus. I had a feeling that I had seen it before, but I still couldn't see it clearly.

'I put my hands on her shoulders and pulled her closer. God, I can't explain to you what I saw. It was the face of an old woman, deeply painted and yet lined with creases. Because of the rain, her make-up had become patchy. Her hair was coloured, but you could see the roots, which were white. She had a band of plastic flowers across her forehead. I stared at her in a state bordering on shock. Then I put the lantern down and said, "You may leave if you wish."

'She wanted to say something, but when she saw me picking up her raincoat and handbag, she decided not to. Without looking at her, I handed her things to her. She stood for a few minutes staring at her feet, then opened the door and walked out.'

After my friend had finished his story, I asked him, 'Did you know who that woman was?'

'No,' he answered.

'She was the famous artist Miss "M",' I told him.

'Miss "M",' he screamed, 'the woman whose paintings I used to try to copy at school?'

'Yes. She was the principal of the art college and she used to teach her women students how to paint still lifes. She hated men.'

'Where is she now?' he asked suddenly.

'In heaven,' I replied.

'What do you mean?' he asked.

'That night when you let her out of your house, she died in a car accident. You are her murderer. In fact, you are the murderer of two women. One, who is known as a great artist, and the other who was born from the body of the first woman in your living room that night and whom you alone know.'

My friend said nothing.

# The Dog of Titwal

THE SOLDIERS HAD BEEN ENTRENCHED IN THEIR POSITIONS FOR SEVERAL weeks, but there was little, if any, fighting, except for the dozen rounds they ritually exchanged every day. The weather was extremely pleasant. The air was heavy with the scent of wild flowers and nature seemed to be following its course, quite unmindful of the soldiers hiding behind rocks and camouflaged by mountain shrubbery. The birds sang as they always had and the flowers were in bloom. Bees buzzed about lazily.

Only when a shot rang out, the birds got startled and took flight, as if a musician had struck a jarring note on his instrument. It was almost the end of September, neither hot nor cold. It seemed as if summer and winter had made their peace. In the blue skies, cotton clouds floated all day like barges on a lake.

The soldiers seemed to be getting tired of this indecisive war where nothing much ever happened. Their positions were quite impregnable. The two hills on which they were placed faced each other and were about the same height, so no one side had an advantage. Down below in the valley, a stream zigzagged furiously on its stony bed like a snake.

The air force was not involved in the combat and neither of the adversaries had heavy guns or mortars. At night, they would light huge fires and hear each others' voices echoing through the hills.

The last round of tea had just been taken. The fire had gone cold. The sky was clear and there was a chill in the air and a sharp, though not unpleasant, smell of pine cones. Most of the soldiers were already asleep, except Jamadar Harnam Singh, who was on night watch. At two o'clock, he woke up Ganda Singh to take over. Then he lay down, but sleep was as far away from his eyes as the stars in the sky. He began to hum a Punjabi folk song:

Buy me a pair of shoes, my lover
A pair of shoes with stars on them
Sell your buffalo, if you have to
But buy me a pair of shoes
With stars on them.

It made him feel good and a bit sentimental. He woke up the others one by one. Banta Singh, the youngest of the soldiers, who had a sweet voice, began to sing a lovelorn verse from 'Heer Ranjha', that timeless Punjabi epic of love and tragedy. A deep sadness fell over them. Even the grey hills seemed to have been affected by the melancholy of the songs.

This mood was shattered by the barking of a dog. Jamadar Harnam Singh said, 'Where has this son of a bitch materialized from?'

The dog barked again. He sounded closer. There was a rustle in the bushes. Banta Singh got up to investigate and came back with an ordinary mongrel in tow. He was wagging his tail. 'I found him behind the bushes and he told me his name was Jhun Jhun,' Banta Singh announced. Everybody burst out laughing.

The dog went to Harnam Singh, who produced a cracker from his kitbag and threw it on the ground. The dog sniffed at it and was about to eat it, when Harnam Singh snatched it away . . .

'Wait, you could be a Pakistani dog.'

They laughed. Banta Singh patted the animal and said to Harnam Singh, 'Jamadar sahib, Jhun Jhun is an Indian dog.'

'Prove your identity,' Harnam Singh ordered the dog, who began to wag his tail.

'This is no proof of identity. All dogs can wag their tails,' Harnam Singh said.

'He is only a poor refugee,' Banta Singh said, playing with his tail.

Harnam Singh threw the dog a cracker, which he caught in mid-air. 'Even dogs will now have to decide if they are Indian or Pakistani,' one of the soldiers observed.

Harnam Singh produced another cracker from his kitbag. 'And all Pakistanis, including dogs, will be shot.'

A soldier shouted, 'India Zindabad!'

The dog, who was about to munch his cracker, stopped dead in his tracks, put his tail between his legs and looked scared. Harnam Singh laughed. 'Why are you afraid of your own country? Here, Jhun Jhun, have another cracker.'

The morning broke very suddenly, as if someone had switched on a light in a dark room. It spread across the hills and valleys of Titwal, which is what the area was called.

The war had been going on for months but nobody could be quite sure who was winning it.

Jamadar Harnam Singh surveyed the area with his binoculars. He could see smoke rising from the opposite hill, which meant that, like them, the enemy was busy preparing breakfast.

Subedar Himmat Khan of the Pakistan army gave his huge moustache a twirl and began to study the map of the Titwal sector. Next to him sat his wireless operator, who was trying to establish contact with the platoon commander to obtain instructions. A few feet away, the soldier Bashir sat on the ground, his back against a rock and his rifle in front of him. He was humming:

Where did you spend the night, my love, my moon?
Where did you spend the night?

Enjoying himself, he began to sing more loudly, savouring the words. Suddenly he heard Subedar Himmat Khan scream, 'Where did *you* spend the night?'

But this was not addressed to Bashir. It was a dog he was shouting at. He had come to them from nowhere a few days ago, stayed in the camp quite happily and then suddenly disappeared last night. However, he had now returned like a bad coin.

Bashir smiled and began to sing to the dog. 'Where did *you* spend the night, where did you spend the night?' But he only wagged his tail. Subedar Himmat Khan threw a pebble at him. 'All he can do is wag his tail, the idiot.'

'What has he got around his neck?' Bashir asked.

One of the soldiers grabbed the dog and undid his makeshift rope collar. There was a small piece of cardboard tied to it. 'What does it say?' the soldier, who could not read, asked.

Bashir stepped forward and with some difficulty was able to decipher the writing. 'It says Jhun Jhun.'

Subedar Himmat Khan gave his famous moustache another mighty twirl and said, 'Perhaps it is a code. Does it say anything else, Bashirey?'

'Yes sir, it says it is an Indian dog.'

'What does that mean?' Subedar Himmat Khan asked.

'Perhaps it is a secret,' Bashir answered seriously.

'If there is a secret, it is in the word Jhun Jhun,' another soldier ventured in a wise guess.

'You may have something there,' Subedar Himmat Khan observed.

Dutifully, Bashir read the whole thing again. 'Jhun Jhun. This is an Indian dog.'

Subedar Himmat Khan picked up the wireless set and spoke to his platoon commander, providing him with a detailed account of the dog's sudden appearance in their position, his equally sudden disappearance the night before and his return that morning. 'What are you talking about?' the platoon commander asked.

Subedar Himmat Khan studied the map again. Then he tore up a packet of cigarettes, cut a small piece from it and gave it to Bashir. 'Now write on it in Gurmukhi, the language of those Sikhs . . .'

'What should I write?'

'Well . . .'

Bashir had an inspiration. 'Shun Shun, yes, that's right. We counter Jhun Jhun with Shun Shun.'

'Good,' Subedar Himmat Khan said approvingly. 'And add: This is a Pakistani dog.'

Subedar Himmat Khan personally threaded the piece of paper through the dog's collar and said, 'Now go join your family.'

He gave him something to eat and then said, 'Look here, my friend, no treachery. The punishment for treachery is death.'

The dog kept eating his food and wagging his tail. Then Subedar Himmat Khan turned him round to face the Indian position and said, 'Go and take this message to the enemy, but come back. These are the orders of your commander.'

The dog wagged his tail and moved down the winding hilly track that led into the valley dividing the two hills. Subedar Himmat Khan picked up his rifle and fired in the air.

The Indians were a bit puzzled, as it was somewhat early in the day for that sort of thing. Jamadar Harnam Singh, who in any case was feeling bored, shouted, 'Let's give it to them.'

The two sides exchanged fire for half an hour, which of course was a complete waste of time. Finally, Jamadar Harnam Singh ordered that enough was enough. He combed his long hair, looked at himself in the mirror and asked Banta Singh, 'Where has that dog Jhun Jhun gone?'

'Dogs can never digest butter, goes the famous saying,' Banta Singh observed philosophically.

Suddenly the soldier on lookout duty shouted, 'There he comes.'

'Who?' Jamadar Harnam Singh asked.

'What was his name? Jhun Jhun,' the soldier answered.

'What is he doing?' Harnam Singh asked.

'Just coming our way,' the soldier replied, peering through his binoculars.

Subedar Harnam Singh snatched them from him. 'That's him all right and there's something around his neck. But, wait, that's the Pakistani hill he's coming from, the motherfucker.'

He picked up his rifle, aimed and fired. The bullet hit some rocks close to where the dog was. He stopped.

Subedar Himmat Khan heard the report and looked through his binoculars. The dog had turned round and was running back. 'The brave never run away from battle. Go forward and complete your mission,' he shouted at the dog. To scare him, he fired at the same time. The bullet passed within inches of the dog, who leapt in the air, flapping his ears. Subedar Himmat Khan fired again, hitting some stones.

It soon became a game between the two soldiers, with the dog running round in circles in a state of great terror. Both Himmat Khan and Harnam Singh were laughing boisterously. The dog began to run towards Harnam Singh, who abused him loudly and fired. The bullet caught him in the leg. He yelped, turned around and began to run towards Himmat Khan, only to meet more fire, which was only meant to scare him. 'Be a brave boy. If you are injured, don't let that stand between you and your duty. Go, go, go,' the Pakistani shouted.

The dog turned. One of his legs was now quite useless. He began to drag himself towards Harnam Singh, who picked up his rifle, aimed carefully and shot him dead.

Subedar Himmat Khan sighed, 'The poor bugger has been martyred.'

Jamadar Harnam Singh ran his hand over the still-hot barrel of his rifle and muttered, 'He died a dog's death.'

# The Last Salute

THIS KASHMIR WAR WAS A VERY ODD AFFAIR. SUBEDAR RAB NAWAZ OFTEN felt as if his brain had turned into a rifle with a faulty safety catch.

He had fought with distinction on many major fronts in the Second World War. He was respected by both his seniors and his juniors because of his intelligence and valour. He was always given the most difficult and dangerous assignments and he had never failed the trust placed in him.

But he had never been in a war like this one. He had come to it full of enthusiasm and with the itch to fight and liquidate the enemy. However, the first encounter had shown that the men arrayed against them on the other side were mostly old friends and comrades with whom he had fought in the old British Indian army against the Germans and the Italians. The friends of yesterday had been transformed into the enemies of today.

At times, the whole thing felt like a dream to Subedar Rab Nawaz. He could remember the day the Second World War was declared. He had enlisted immediately. They had been given some basic training and then packed off to the front. He had been moved from one theatre of war to another and, one day, the war had ended. Then had come Pakistan and the new war he was now fighting. So much had happened in these last few years at such breakneck speed. Often it made no sense at all. Those who had planned and executed these great events had perhaps deliberately maintained a dizzying pace so that the participants should get no time to think. How else could one explain one revolution followed by another and then another?

One thing Subedar Rab Nawaz could understand. They were fighting this war to win Kashmir. Why did they want to win Kashmir? Because it was crucial to Pakistan's security and survival. However, sometimes when he sat behind a gun emplacement and caught sight of a familiar face on the other side, for a moment he forgot why they were fighting. He forgot why he was carrying a gun and killing people. At such times, he would remind himself that he was not fighting to win medals or earn a salary, but to secure the survival of his country.

This was his country before the establishment of Pakistan and it was his country now. This was his land. But now he was fighting against men who were his countrymen until only the other day. Men who had grown up in the same village, whose families had been known to his family for generations. These men had now been turned into citizens of a country to which they were complete strangers. They had been told: we are placing a gun in your hands so that you can go and fight for a country which you have yet to know, where you do not even have a roof over your head, where even the air and water are strange to you. Go and fight for it against Pakistan, the land where you were born and grew up.

Rab Nawaz would think of those Muslim soldiers who had moved to Pakistan, leaving their ancestral homes behind, and come to this new country with empty hands. They had been given nothing, except the guns that had been put in their hands. The same guns they had always used, the same make, the same bore, guns to fight their new enemy with.

Before the Partition of the country, they used to fight one

common enemy who was not really their enemy perhaps but whom they had accepted as their enemy for the sake of employment and rewards and medals. Formerly, all of them were Indian soldiers, but now some were Indian and others were Pakistani soldiers. Rab Nawaz could not unravel this puzzle. And when he thought about Kashmir, he became even more confused. Were the Pakistani soldiers fighting for Kashmir or for the Muslims of Kashmir? If they were being asked to fight in defence of the Muslims of Kashmir, why had they not been asked to fight for the Muslims of the princely states of Junagarh and Hyderabad? And if this was an Islamic war, then why were other Muslim countries of the world not fighting shoulder to shoulder with them?

Rab Nawaz had finally come to the conclusion that such intricate and subtle matters were beyond the comprehension of a simple soldier. A soldier should be thick in the head. Only the thick-headed made good soldiers, but despite this resolution, he couldn't help wondering sometimes about the war he was now in.

The fighting in what was called the Titwal sector was spread across the Kishan Ganga river and along the road which led from Muzaffarabad to Kiran. It was a strange war. Often at night, instead of gunfire, one heard abuse being exchanged in loud voices.

One late evening, while Subedar Rab Nawaz was preparing his platoon for a foray into enemy territory, he heard loud voices from across the hill the enemy was supposed to be on. He could not believe his ears. There was loud laughter followed by abuse. 'Pig's trotters,' he murmured, 'what on earth is going on?'

One of his men returned the abuse in as loud a voice as he

could muster, then complained to him, 'Subedar sahib, they are abusing us again, the motherfuckers.'

Rab Nawaz's first instinct was to join the slanging match, but he thought better of it. The men fell silent too, following his example. However, after a while, the torrent of abuse from the other side became so intolerable that his men lost control and began to match abuse with abuse. A couple of times he ordered them to keep quiet, but did not insist because, frankly, it was difficult for a human being not to react violently.

They couldn't of course see the enemy at night, and hardly did so during the day because of the hilly country which provided perfect cover. All they heard was abuse, which echoed across the hills and valleys and then evaporated in the air.

Some of the hills were barren, while others were covered with tall pine trees. It was very difficult terrain. Subedar Rab Nawaz's platoon was on a bare, treeless hill which provided no cover. His men were itching to go into attack to avenge the abuse, which had been hurled at them without respite for several weeks. An attack was planned and executed with success, though they lost two men and suffered four injuries. The enemy lost three and abandoned the position, leaving behind food and provisions.

Subedar Rab Nawaz and his men were sorry they had not been able to capture an enemy soldier. They could then have avenged the abuse face to face. However, they had captured an important and difficult feature. Rab Nawaz relayed the news of the victory to his commander, Major Aslam, and was commended for gallantry.

On top of most hills one found ponds. There was a large one on the hill they had captured. The water was clear and sweet and, although it was cold, they took off their clothes and jumped in. Suddenly they heard firing. They jumped out of the pond and hit the ground—naked. Subedar Rab Nawaz crawled towards his binoculars, picked them up and surveyed the area carefully. He could see no one. There was more firing. This time he was able to determine its origin. It was coming from a small hill, lying a few hundred feet below their perch. He ordered his men to open up.

The enemy troops did not have very good cover and Rab Nawaz was confident they could not stay there much longer. The moment they decided to move, they would come in direct range of their guns. Sporadic firing kept getting exchanged. Finally, Rab Nawaz ordered that no more ammunition should be wasted. They should just wait for the enemy to break cover. Then he looked at his still naked body and murmured, 'Pig's trotters. Man does look silly without clothes.'

For two whole days, this game continued. Occasional fire was exchanged, but the enemy had obviously decided to lie low. Then suddenly the temperature dropped several degrees. To keep his men warm, Subedar Rab Nawaz ordered that the tea kettle should be kept on the boil all the time. It was like an unending tea party.

On the third day—it was unbearably cold—the soldier on the lookout reported that some movement could be detected around the enemy position. Subedar Rab Nawaz looked through his binoculars. Yes, something was going on. Rab Nawaz raised his rifle and fired. Someone called his name, or so he thought. It echoed through the valley. 'Pig's trotters,' Rab Nawaz shouted, 'what do you want?'

The distance that separated their two positions was not great;

the voice came back, 'Don't hurl abuse, brother.'

Rab Nawaz looked at his men. The word 'brother' seemed to hang in the air. He raised his hands to his mouth and shouted, 'Brother! There are no brothers here, only your mother's lovers.'

'Rab Nawaz,' the voice shouted.

He trembled. The words reverberated around the hills and then faded into the atmosphere.

'Pig's trotters,' he whispered, 'who was that?'

He knew that the troops in the Titwal sector were mostly from the old 6/9 Jat Regiment, his own regiment. But who was this joker shouting his name? He had many friends in the regiment, and some enemies too. But who was this man who had called him brother?

Rab Nawaz looked through his binoculars again, but could see nothing. He shouted, 'Who was that? This is Rab Nawaz. Rab Nawaz. Rab Nawaz.'

'It is me . . . Ram Singh,' the same voice answered.

Rab Nawaz nearly jumped. 'Ram Singh, oh, Ram Singha, Ram Singha, you pig's trotters.'

'Shut your trap, you potter's ass,' came the reply.

Rab Nawaz looked at his men, who appeared startled at this strange exchange in the middle of battle. 'He's talking rot, pig's trotters.' Then he shouted, 'You slaughtered swine, watch your tongue.'

Ram Singh began to laugh. Rab Nawaz could not contain himself either. His men watched him in silence.

'Look, my friend, we want to drink tea,' Ram Singh said.

'Go ahead then. Have a good time,' Rab Nawaz replied.

'We can't. The tea things are lying elsewhere.'

'Where's elsewhere?'

'Let me put it this way. If we tried to get them, you could blow us to bits. We'd have to break cover.'

'So what do you want, pig's trotters?' Rab Nawaz laughed.

'That you hold your fire until we get our things.'

'Go ahead,' Rab Nawaz said.

'You will blow us up, you potter's ass,' Ram Singh shouted.

'Shut your mouth, you crawly Sikh tortoise,' Rab Nawaz said.

'Take an oath on something that you won't open fire.'

'On what?'

'Anything you like.'

Rab Nawaz laughed. 'You have my word. Now go get your things.'

Nothing happened for a few minutes. One of the men was watching the small hill through his binoculars. He pointed at his gun and asked Rab Nawaz in gestures if he should open fire. 'No, no, no shooting,' Rab Nawaz said.

Suddenly, a man darted forward, running low towards some bushes. A few minutes later he ran back, carrying an armful of things. Then he disappeared. Rab Nawaz picked up his rifle and fired. 'Thank you,' Ram Singh's voice came.

'No mention,' Rab Nawaz answered. 'OK, boys, let's give the buggers one round.'

More by way of entertainment than war, this exchange of fire continued for some time. Rab Nawaz could see smoke going up in a thin blue spiral where the enemy was. 'Is your tea ready, Ram Singha?' he shouted.

'Not yet, you potter's ass.'

Rab Nawaz was a potter by caste and any reference to his origins always enraged him. Ram Singh was the one person who could get away with calling him a potter's ass. They had grown up together in the same village in the Punjab. They were the same age, had gone to the same primary school, and their fathers had been childhood friends. They had joined the army the same day. In the last war, they had fought together on the same fronts.

'Pig's trotters, he never gives up, that one,' Rab Nawaz said to his men. 'Shut up, lice-infested donkey Ram Singha,' he shouted.

He saw a man stand up. Rab Nawaz raised his rifle and fired in his direction. He heard a scream. He looked through his binoculars. It was Ram Singh. He was doubled up, holding his stomach. Then he fell to the ground.

Rab Nawaz shouted, 'Ram Singh' and stood up. There was rapid gunfire from the other side. One bullet brushed past his left arm. He fell to the ground. Some enemy soldiers, taking advantage of this confusion, began to run across open ground to securer positions. Rab Nawaz ordered his platoon to attack the hill. Three were killed, but the others managed to capture the position with Rab Nawaz in the lead.

He found Ram Singh lying on the bare ground. He had been shot in the stomach. His eyes lit up when he saw Rab Nawaz. 'You potter's ass, whatever did you do that for?' he asked.

Rab Nawaz felt as if it was he who had been shot. But he smiled, bent over Ram Singh and began to undo his belt. 'Pig's trotters, who told you to stand up?'

'I was only trying to show myself to you, but you shot me,' Ram Singh said with difficulty. Rab Nawaz unfastened his belt. It was a very bad wound and bleeding profusely.

Rab Nawaz's voice choked, 'I swear upon God, I only fired out of fun. How could I know it was you? You were always an ass, Ram Singha.'

Ram Singh was rapidly losing blood. Rab Nawaz was surprised

he was still alive. He did not want to move him. He spoke to his platoon commander, Major Aslam, on the wireless, requesting urgent medical help.

He was sure it would take a long time to arrive. He had a feeling Ram Singh wouldn't last that long. But he laughed. 'Don't you worry. The doctor is on his way.'

Ram Singh said in a weak voice, 'I am not worried, but tell me, how many of my men did you kill?'

'Just one,' Rab Nawaz said.

'And how many did you lose?'

'Six,' Rab Nawaz lied.

'Six,' Ram Singh said. 'When I fell, they were disheartened, but I told them to fight on, give it everything they'd got. Six, yes.' Then his mind began to wander.

He began to talk of their village, their childhood, stories from school, the 6/9 Jat Regiment, its commanding officers, affairs with strange women in strange cities. He was in excruciating pain, but he carried on. 'Do you remember that madam, you pig?'

'Which one?' Rab Nawaz asked.

'That one in Italy. You remember what we used to call her? Man-eater.'

Rab Nawaz remembered her. 'Yes, yes. She was called Madam Minitafanto or some such thing. And she used to say: no money, no action. But she had a soft spot for you, that daughter of Mussolini.'

Ram Singh laughed loudly, causing blood to gush out of his wound. Rab Nawaz dressed it with a makeshift bandage. 'Now keep quiet,' he admonished him gently.

Ram Singh's body was burning. He did not have the strength

to speak, but he was talking nineteen to the dozen. At times he would stop, as if to see how much petrol was still left in his tank.

After some time, he went into a sort of delirium. Briefly, he would come out of it, only to sink again. During one brief moment of clarity, he said to Rab Nawaz, 'Tell me truthfully, do you people really want Kashmir?'

'Yes, Ram Singha,' Rab Nawaz said passionately.

'I don't believe that. You have been misled,' Ram Singh said.

'No, you have been misled, I swear by the Holy Prophet and his family,' Rab Nawaz said.

'Don't take that oath . . . you must be right.' But there was a strange look on his face, as if he didn't really believe Rab Nawaz.

A little before sunset, Major Aslam arrived with some soldiers. There was no doctor. Ram Singh was hovering between consciousness and delirium. He was muttering, but his voice was so weak that it was difficult to follow him.

Major Aslam was an old 6/9 Jat Regiment officer. Ram Singh had served under him for years. He bent over the dying soldier and called his name, 'Ram Singh, Ram Singh.'

Ram Singh opened his eyes and stiffened his body as if he was coming to attention. With one great effort, he raised his arm and saluted. A strange look of incomprehension suddenly suffused his face. His arm fell limply to his side and he murmured, 'Ram Singh, you ass, you forgot this was a war, a war . . .' He could not complete the sentence. With half-open eyes, he looked at Rab Nawaz, took one last breath and died.

# The New Constitution

MANGU THE TONGAWALA WAS CONSIDERED A MAN OF GREAT WISDOM among his friends. He had never seen the inside of a school, and in strictly academic terms was no more than a cipher, but there was nothing under the sun he did not know something about. All his fellow tongawalas at the adda, or tonga stand, were well aware of his versatility in worldly matters. He was always able to satisfy their curiosity about what was going on.

Recently, when he had learnt from one of his fares about a rumour that war was about to break out in Spain, he had patted Gama Chaudhry across his broad shoulder and predicted in a statesmanlike manner, 'You will see, Chaudhry, a war is going to break out in Spain in a few days.' And when Gama Chaudhry had asked him where Spain was, Ustad Mangu had replied very soberly: 'In Vilayat, where else?'

When war finally broke out in Spain and everybody came to know of it, every tonga driver at the Station adda, smoking his hookah, became convinced in his heart of Ustad Mangu's greatness. At that hour, Ustad Mangu was driving his tonga on the dazzling surface of the Mall, exchanging views with his fare about the latest Hindu–Muslim rioting.

That evening when he returned to the adda, his face looked visibly perturbed. He sat down with his friends, took a long drag on the hookah, removed his khaki turban and said in a worried voice, 'It is no doubt the result of a holy man's curse that Hindus and Muslims keep slashing each other up every other day. I have heard it said by my elders that Akbar Badshah once showed disrespect to a saint, who angrily cursed him in these words: "Get out of my sight! And, yes, your Hindustan will always be plagued by riots and disorder." And you can see for yourselves. Ever since the end of Akbar's raj, what else has India known but riot after riot!'

He took a deep breath, drew on his hookah reflectively and said, 'These Congressites want to win India its freedom. Well, you take my word, they will get nowhere even if they keep bashing their heads against the wall for a thousand years. At the most, the Angrez will leave, but then you will get maybe the Italywala or the Russiawala. I have heard that the Russiawala is one tough fellow. But Hindustan will always remain enslaved. Yes, I forgot to tell you that part of the saint's curse on Akbar which said that India will always be ruled by foreigners.'

Ustad Mangu had intense hatred for the British. He used to tell his friends that he hated them because they were ruling Hindustan against the will of the Indians and missed no opportunity to commit atrocities. However, the fact was that it was the gora soldiers of the cantonment who were responsible for Ustad Mangu's rather low opinion of the British. They used to treat him like some lower creation of God, even worse than a dog. Nor was Ustad Mangu overly fond of their fair complexion. He would feel nauseated at the sight of a fair and ruddy gora soldier's face. 'Their red wrinkled faces remind me of a dead body whose skin is rotting away,' he used to say.

After an argument with a drunken gora, he would remain depressed for the entire day. He would return to his adda in the evening and curse the man to his heart's content, while smoking his Marble brand cigarette or taking long drags at his hookah.

He would deliver himself of a heavyweight curse, shake his head with its loosely tied turban and say, 'Look at them, came to the door to borrow a light and the next thing you knew they owned the whole house. I am sick and tired of these offshoots of monkeys. The way they order us around, you would think we were their fathers' servants!'

But even after such outbursts, his anger would show no sign of abating. As long as a friend was keeping him company, he would keep at it. 'Look at this one, resembles a leper? Dead and rotting. I could knock him out cold with one blow, but the way he was throwing his git-pit at me, you would have thought he was going to kill me. I swear on your head, my first urge was to smash the damn fellow's skull, but then I restrained myself. I mean it would have been below my dignity to hit this wretch.' He would wipe his nose with the sleeve of his khaki uniform jacket and keep murmuring curses. 'As God is my witness, I'm sick of suffering and humouring these Lat sahibs. Every time I look at their blighted faces, my blood begins to boil in my veins. We need a new law to get rid of these people. Only that can revive us, I swear on your life.'

One day Ustad Mangu picked up two fares from district courts. He gathered from their conversation that there was going to be a new constitution for India and he felt overwhelmed with joy at the news. The two Marwaris were in town to pursue a civil suit in the local court and, while on their way home, they were discussing the new constitution, the India Act.

'It is said that from 1 April, there's going to be a new constitution. Will that change everything?'

'Not everything, but they say a lot will change. The Indians would be free.'

'What about interest?' asked one.

'Well, this needs to be inquired. Should ask some lawyer tomorrow.'

The conversation between the two Marwaris sent Ustad Mangu to seventh heaven. Normally, he was in the habit of abusing his horse for being slow and was not averse to making liberal use of the whip, but not today. Every now and then, he would look back at his two passengers, caress his moustache and loosen the horse's reins affectionately. 'Come on son, come on, show 'em how you take to the air.'

After dropping his fares, he stopped at the Anarkali shop of his friend, Dino the sweetmeat vendor. He ordered a large glass of lassi, drank it down, belched with satisfaction, took the ends of his moustache in his mouth, sucked at them and said in a loud voice, 'The hell with 'em all!'

When he returned to the adda in the evening, contrary to routine, no one that he knew was around. A storm was roaring in his breast and he was dying to share the great news with his friends, that really great news which he simply had to get out of his system. But no one was around to hear it.

For about half an hour, he paced about restlessly under the tin roof of the Station adda, his whip under his arm. His mind was on many things, good things that lay in the future. The news that a new constitution was to be implemented had brought him at the doorstep of a new world. He had switched on all the lights in his brain to carefully study the implications of the new law that was going to become operational in India from 1 April. The worried words of the Marwari about a change in the law governing interest or usury rang in his ears. A wave of happiness was coursing through his entire body. Quite a few times, he laughed under his thick moustache and hurled a few words of abuse at the Marwaris. 'The new constitution is going to be like boiling hot water is to bugs who suck the blood of the poor,' he said to himself.

He was very happy. A delightful cool settled over his heart when he thought of how the new constitution would send these white mice (he always called them by that name) scurrying back into their holes for all times to come.

When the bald-headed Nathoo ambled into the adda some time later, his turban tucked under his arm, Ustad Mangu shook his hand vigorously and said in a loud voice, 'Give me your hand, I have great news for you that would not only bring you immense joy but might even make hair grow back on your bald skull.'

Then, thoroughly enjoying himself, he went into a detailed description of the changes the new constitution was going to bring. 'You just wait and see. Things are going to happen. You have my word, this Russian king is bound to do something big.' And as he talked, he continued to slap Ganju's bald head, and with some force as well.

Ustad Mangu had heard many stories about the socialist system the Soviets had set up. There were many things he liked about their new laws and many of the new things they were doing, which was what had made him link the king of Russia with the India Act or the new constitution. He was convinced that the changes being brought in on 1 April were a direct result of the influence of the Russian king.

For the past several years, the Red Shirt movement in Peshawar and other cities had been much in the news. To Ustad Mangu, this movement was all tied up with the 'king of Russia' and, naturally, with the new constitution. Then there were the frequent reports of bomb blasts in various Indian cities. Whenever Ustad Mangu heard that so many had been caught somewhere for possessing explosives or so many were going to be tried for treason, he interpreted it all to his great delight as preparation for the new constitution.

One day he had two barristers at the back of his tonga. They were vigorously criticizing the new constitution. He listened to them in silence. One of them was saying, 'It is Section II of the Act that I still can't make sense of. It relates to the federation of India. No such federation exists in the world. From a political angle too, such a federation would be utterly wrong. In fact, one can say that this is going to be no federation.'

Since most of this conversation was being carried on in English, Ustad Mangu had only been able to follow the last bit. He came to the conclusion that these two barristers were opposed to the new constitution and did not want their country to be free. 'Toady wretches,' he muttered with contempt. Whenever he called someone a 'toady wretch' under his breath, he felt greatly elated that he had applied the words correctly and that he could tell a good man from a toady.

Three days after this incident, he picked up three students from Government College who wanted to be taken to Mozang. He listened to them carefully as they talked.

'The new constitution has raised my hopes. If so and so becomes a member of the assembly, I will certainly be able to get a job in a government office.'

'Oh! There are going to be many openings and, in that confusion, we will be able to lay our hands on something.'

'Yes, yes, why not!'

'And there's bound to be a reduction in the number of all

those unemployed graduates who have nowhere to go.'

This conversation was most thrilling as far as Ustad Mangu
was concerned. The new constitution now appeared to him to
be something bright and full of promise. The only thing he could
compare the new constitution with was the splendid brass and
gilt fittings he had purchased after careful examination a couple
of years ago for his tonga from Choudhry Khuda Bux. When the
fittings were new, the nickel-headed nails would shimmer and
where brass had been worked into the fittings it shone like gold.
On the basis of that analogy also, it was essential that the new
constitution should shine and glow.

By 1 April, Ustad Mangu had heard a great deal about the
new constitution, both for and against. However, nothing could
change the concept of the new constitution that he had formed
in his mind. He was confident that come 1 April, everything
would become clear. He was sure that what the new constitution
would usher in would soothe his heart.

At last, the thirty-one days of March drew to a close. There
were still a few silent night hours left before the dawn of
1 April and the weather was unusually cool, the breeze quite
fresh. Ustad Mangu rose early, went to the stable, set up his
tonga and took to the road. He was extraordinarily happy today
because he was going to witness the coming in of the new
constitution.

In the cold morning fog, he went round the broad and narrow
streets of the city but everything looked old, like the sky. His
eyes wanted to see things taking on a new colour but, except
for the new plume made of colourful feathers that rested on his
horse's head, everything looked old. He had bought this new
plume from Chaudhry Khuda Bux for fourteen annas and a half
to celebrate the new constitution.

The road lay black under his horse's hooves. The lamp-posts that stood on the sides at regular intervals looked the same. The shop signs had not changed. The way people moved about, the sound made by the tiny bells tied around his horse's neck were not new either. Nothing was new, but Ustad Mangu was not disappointed.

Perhaps it was too early in the morning. All the shops were still closed. This he found consoling. It also occurred to him that the courts did not start work until nine, so how could the new constitution be at work just yet.

He was in front of Government College when the tower clock imperiously struck nine. The students walking out through the main entrance were smartly dressed, but somehow their clothes looked shabby to Ustad Mangu. He wanted to see something startling and dramatic.

He turned his tonga left towards Anarkali. Half the shops were already open. There were crowds of people at sweetmeat stalls, and general traders were busy with their customers, their wares displayed invitingly in their windows. Overhead, on the power lines perched several pigeons, quarrelling with each other. But none of this held any interest whatever for Ustad Mangu. He wanted to see the new constitution as clearly as he could see his horse.

Ustad Mangu was one of those people who cannot stand the suspense of waiting. When his first child was to be born he had spent the last four or five months in a state of great agitation. While he was sure that the child would come to be born one day, he found it hard to keep waiting. He wanted to take a look at his child, just once. It could then take its time getting born. It was because of this desire that he could not overcome that he had pressed his sick wife's belly and put his ear to it in an attempt to find out something about the baby, but he had had no luck.

One day he had screamed at his wife in exasperation, 'What's the matter with you! All day long you lie in bed as if you were dead. Why don't you get up and walk about to gain some strength? If you keep lying there like a flat piece of wood, do you think you will be able to give birth?'

Ustad Mangu was temperamentally impatient. He wanted to see every cause have an effect, and he was always curious about it. Once his wife, Gangawati, watching his impatient antics, had said to him, 'You haven't even begun digging the well and already you're dying to have a drink.'

This morning he was not as impatient as he normally should have been. He had come out early to take a look at the new constitution with his own eyes, in the same way he used to wait for hours to catch a glimpse of Gandhiji and Pandit Jawaharlal Nehru being taken out in a procession.

Great leaders, in Ustad Mangu's view, were those who were profusely garlanded when taken out in public. Anyone bedecked in garlands of marigolds was a great man in Ustad Mangu's book. And if because of the milling crowds a couple of near-clashes took place, the leader's stature grew in Ustad Mangu's eyes. He wanted to measure the new constitution by the same yardstick.

From Anarkali he turned towards the Mall, driving his tonga slowly on its shiny surface. In front of an auto showroom, he found a fare bound for the cantonment. They settled the price and were soon on their way. Ustad Mangu whipped his horse into action and said to himself, 'This is just as well. One might find out something about the new constitution in the cantonment.'

He dropped his passenger at his destination, lit a cigarette, which he placed between the last two fingers of his left hand, and eased himself into a cushion in the rear of the tonga. When Ustad Mangu was not looking for a new fare, or when he wanted to think about some past incident, he would move into the rear seat of the tonga, with the reins of his horse wound around his left hand. On such occasions, his horse after neighing a little would begin to move forward at a gentle pace, glad to be spared the daily grind of cantering ahead.

Ustad Mangu was trying to work out if the present system of allotting tonga number plates would change with the new law, when he felt someone calling out to him. When he turned to look, he found a gora standing under a lamp-post at the far end of the road, beckoning to him.

As already noted, Ustad Mangu had intense hatred for the British. When he saw that his new customer was a gora, feelings of hatred rose in his heart. His first instinct was to pay no attention to him and just leave him where he was. But then he felt that it would be foolish to give the man's money a miss. The fourteen annas and a half he had spent on the plume should be recovered from these people, he decided.

He neatly turned around his tonga on the empty road, flicked his whip and was at the lamp-post in no time. Without moving from his comfortable perch, he asked in a leisurely manner, 'Sahib Bahadur, where do you want to be taken?'

He had spoken these words with undisguised irony. When he had called him 'Sahib Bahadur', his upper lip, covered by his moustache, had moved lower, while a thin line that ran from his nostril to his lower chin had trembled and deepened, as if someone had run a sharp knife across a brown slab of shisham wood. His entire face was laughing, but inside his chest roared a fire ready to consume the gora.

The gora, who was trying to draw on a cigarette by standing close to the lamp-post to protect himself from the breeze, turned and moved towards the tonga. He was about to place his foot on the foothold when his eyes met Ustad Mangu's and it seemed as if two loaded guns had fired at each other and their discharge had met in mid-air and risen towards the sky in a ball of fire.

Ustad Mangu freed his left hand of the reins that he had wrapped around it and glared at the gora standing in front of him, as if he would eat every bit of him alive. The gora, meanwhile, was busy dusting his blue trousers of something that couldn't be seen, or perhaps he was trying to protect this part of his body from Ustad Mangu's assault.

'Do you want to go or are you again going to make trouble?' the gora asked.

'It is the same man,' Ustad Mangu said to himself. He was quite sure it was the same fellow with whom he had clashed the year before. That uncalled for argument had happened because the gora was sozzled. Ustad Mangu had borne the insults hurled at him in silence. He could have smashed the man into little bits, but he had remained passive because he knew that in such quarrels it was tongawalas mostly who suffered the wrath of the law.

'Where do you want to go?' Ustad Mangu asked, thinking about the previous year's argument and the new constitution of 1 April. His tone was sharp like the stroke of a whip.

'Hira Mandi,' the gora answered.

'The fare would be five rupees,' Ustad Mangu's moustache trembled.

'Five rupees! Five rupees! Are you . . .?' the gora screamed in disbelief.

'Yes, yes, five rupees,' Ustad Mangu said, clenching his big right fist tightly. 'Are you interested or will you keep making idle talk?'

The gora, remembering their last encounter, had decided not to be awed by the barrel-chested Ustad Mangu. He felt that the man's skull was again itching for punishment. This encouraging thought made him advance towards the tonga. With his swagger stick, he motioned Ustad Mangu to get down. The polished cane touched Ustad Mangu's thigh two or three times. Ustad Mangu, standing up, looked down at the short-statured gora as if the sheer weight of a single glance would grind him down. Then his fist rose like an arrow leaving a bow and landed heavily on the gora's chin. He pushed the man aside, got down from his tonga and began to hit him all over his body.

The astonished gora made several efforts to save himself from the heavy blows raining down on him, but when he noticed that his assailant was in a rage bordering on madness and flames were shooting forth from his eyes, he began to scream. His screams only made Ustad Mangu work his arms faster. He was thrashing the gora to his heart's content while shouting, 'The same cockiness even on 1 April! Well, sonny boy, it is our Raj now.'

A crowd gathered. Two policemen appeared from somewhere and with great difficulty managed to rescue the Englishman. There stood Ustad Mangu, one policeman to his left and one to his right, his broad chest heaving because he was breathless. Foaming at the mouth, with his smiling eyes he was looking at the astonished crowd and saying in a breathless voice, 'Those days are gone, friends, when they ruled the roost. There is a new constitution now, fellows, a new constitution.'

The poor gora with his disfigured face was looking foolishly, sometimes at Ustad Mangu, other times at the crowd.

Ustad Mangu was taken by police constables to the station. All along the way, and even inside the station, he kept screaming, 'New constitution, new constitution!' but nobody paid any attention to him.

'New constitution, new constitution! What rubbish are you talking? It's the same old constitution.'

And he was locked up.

# Khushia

KHUSHIA WAS THINKING.

He had just got himself a paan laced with black tobacco from the shop across the road. He was sitting in his usual place, the cemented plinth by the roadside that served as a showroom for tyres and motor spares during the day. Evenings, it was his. He was masticating his black-tobacco-laced paan slowly and he was thinking of what had happened just half an hour earlier.

He had gone to the fifth street in Khetwari because around the corner lived his new girl, Kanta, who had come from Mangalore. Someone had told him that she was planning to move and he had gone to check it out. He had knocked at her door and she had asked who it was. 'It is I, Khushia,' he had answered. She had opened the door and what he had seen had nearly thrown him. She was naked, or nearly naked because all she had covering her was a skimpy towel which was simply not adequate because whatever women keep covered normally was there in full view.

'Khushia, what brings you here . . . I was about to take a bath . . . sit down . . . you should have ordered some tea from the shop across the road before you came in . . . that blasted boy Rama who used to work for me has run off.'

Khushia, who had never seen a woman naked or even half-naked, was confused. He did not know how to react or what to say. His eyes wanted to be elsewhere rather than on Kanta's body.

But all he could manage to mutter was, 'Why don't you go

and take your bath?' And then, 'If you were not quite dressed, why did you answer the door? You could just have said you were not ready and I would have come another time . . . But go and take your bath.'

Kanta smiled, 'When you said it was Khushia, I asked myself what harm there was in letting you in. After all, I thought, it is Khushia, our own Khushia . . .'

He sat there thinking of the smile on her face as she had spoken to him. The sensation was almost physical, electrifying his mind and body. He could see her standing in front of him naked like a wax figurine. Her body was beautiful. For the first time, Khushia had realized that women who rent out their bodies could be beautiful also. This was like a revelation. But what had thrown him was her standing in front of him without the least sense of shame or self-consciousness. Why?

But then had she not answered that question herself when she said that she had let him in because, after all, he was 'Khushia, our own Khushia'.

Both Kanta and Khushia were in the same line of work, she being the goods that he hawked. In that sense, he was her 'own' but did that justify her standing in front of him without her clothes? Khushia could not figure it out.

He could still see her as she had stood there. Her skin was taut like skin over a drum and her body did not seem to be aware of itself. He had gazed at her brown nakedness exploratively but there had been no reaction from her. She had just stood there like an emotionless statuette. She should have reacted to his gaze. After all, there was a man staring at her, and men's eyes could penetrate through a woman's clothes, but she had shown not the least nervousness. He also remembered that her eyes had a washed and laundered look. Whatever it was, he said to himself again, she should have felt some sense of self-consciousness, given some sign that her modesty had been outraged. Her face should have turned red with embarrassment. It is true she was a prostitute but did prostitutes stand undressed in front of men as she had done?

He had been in this business for ten years and he knew all the secrets of this profession and the women who worked it. He knew, for instance, that at the end of the street the girl who lived with a man she said was her brother, and who used to play a song from the movie *Achoot Kanya* on her broken harmonium, was in love with the actor Ashok Kumar. Many boys had taken her to bed on the promise that they would introduce her to Ashok. He also knew that the Punjabi girl who lived in Dadar wore a jacket and trousers because a customer had once told her about Marlene Dietrich, the star of the movie *Morocco*, who was said to wear trousers because her legs were so beautiful that they needed to be protected. They were said to be insured for a lot of money. She had seen that movie many times. The trousers sat tightly over her buttocks but it didn't matter. Then there was the girl from Daccan who lived in Mizgaon and who ensnared handsome college students because she wanted to have a good-looking baby, though she knew it was unlikely to happen as she was infertile. There was also the dark one from Madras with diamond earrings who wasted most of what she earned on lotions, creams and medicaments that promised to turn dark skin into fair, though in her heart of hearts she knew it would never happen and she was wasting her money.

All these women for whom he worked he knew inside out but what he did not know was that one day one of them, Kanta

Kumari, a name he found difficult to remember, would stand in front of him naked, an experience he had never had before. Beads of perspiration appeared on his brow. His pride had been hurt. When he thought of Kanta's bare body, he felt a deep sense of insult. He was speaking to himself. 'It is an insult, is it not! Here is a girl who is practically naked and she stands bang in front of me and says, "Come in, after all, you are Khushia, our own Khushia." As if I was not a man but that stupid cat which is always sprawled on her bed.'

As he sat there thinking, he became convinced that he had been insulted. He was a man and he expected women, whether housewives or the other kind, to treat him like a man, a male. He expected them to maintain the distance laid down by nature between man and woman. He had gone to Kanta's house to find out if she was really moving and, if so, where. It was a business call. When he knocked at her door, he had had no idea what she might be doing. He had thought maybe she was lying in bed with a bandage around her head to fight a headache or delicing her cat or removing the hair from her armpits with that foul-smelling powder he could not stand. She could even be playing a game of cards with herself.

She lived alone. It could not have even remotely occurred to him that Kanta, the girl whom he had always seen properly dressed, would open the door and stand there in front of him in her birthday suit. She was naked because that skimpy towel could hardly cover anything. But what had she really felt when she had let him in? As for himself, it was as if he had been holding a banana in his hand and suddenly the eatable part had slipped out and fallen on the ground and all he held now was its skin. Her words kept ringing in his ears. 'When you said it was Khushia, I said to myself that there was no harm in letting you in. After all, I said to myself, it is Khushia, our own Khushia.'

'The bitch was smiling,' he kept murmuring. It was a smile as naked as she was. He could not help thinking of her body, which was like smoothly polished wood. He suddenly remembered this woman from his childhood who used to say to him, 'Khushia, my son, go get me a bucket of water.' And when he returned with it, she would say from behind a makeshift curtain, 'Come, place it next to me. I cannot see because I have soaped my face.' He would lift the curtain from a corner and place the bucket next to her. He would see a naked woman with her entire body soaped, but it would mean nothing. He was only a child then and women did not hide themselves from children when they were naked.

But now he was a man, a twenty-eight-year-old man. How could a woman, even an old woman, bare herself in front of him? What did Kanta think he was? Was he not equipped with everything that a young man is supposed to be equipped with? While it was true that her bare body had startled him, he had looked at her stealthily. He could not help noticing that, despite the daily use to which her body was subjected, everything was where it should be, and in good shape too. She charged ten rupees for a throw and that was not much considering what she had on offer. The other day, the bank clerk who had gone back because she would not bring down the price by two rupees was surely an ass. He recalled experiencing a strange tautening of the body. He wanted to stretch out his arms and release the tension until his bones began to rattle. Why had this wheat-coloured girl from Mangalore not seen him as a male? Instead, she had let him gaze at her nakedness because to her he was Khushia, just Khushia.

He got up, spat on the road and jumped into the tram that he always took to get home.

Once there, he took a bath, put on fresh clothes, stepped into the neighbourhood barber shop, looked at himself in the mirror, combed his hair and, on second thought, sat down for a shave, his second that day. The barber said to him, 'Brother Khushia, have you forgotten? I shaved you only this morning.' Khushia ran his hand over his face and replied, 'Your razor was not sharp enough.'

After the shave, he rubbed his face with a bit of talcum powder and crossed the road to a taxi stand. 'Chi chi,' he said—the standard Bombay call for hailing a taxi. The driver opened the door for him, 'Where sahib?' he asked. Khushia was pleased at being called sahib. 'I will let you know. Go towards Pasera House first via Lemington Road, understand,' he replied in a friendly voice. The driver switched on his meter and took off. At the end of Lemington Road, Khushia asked him to turn left.

The taxi turned left and before the driver could change gears, Khushia had told him to stop. He then stepped out, walked across to a paan shop, exchanged a few words with a man who was standing there and after helping himself to a paan came back with the fellow he had talked to. They both got into the taxi. 'Go straight,' Khushia told the driver. The taxi drove for quite a while with Khushia doing the navigation. They went through brightly lit bazaars and, in the end, turned into an ill-lit street where some people had already settled in for the night on makeshift beds. Some were getting their heads massaged and looked contented. Khushia paid no attention to them. 'Stop here,' he told the driver as they went past a wooden hut. In a low voice, Khushia told the man he had picked up from the paan shop that he would wait for him in the car. The man got out without a word and went into the hut.

Khushia reclined into the seat and put one leg on top of the other. Then he pulled out a bidi from his pocket and lit it, but he took only a couple of drags before chucking it out of the window. He was restless. His heart was beating fast and for a moment he thought the driver had not killed the engine in order to increase the fare. 'How much extra do you think you will make by idling that engine?' he asked sharply.

The driver turned, 'Seth, the engine is not idling. It is switched off.'

As he realized his mistake, Khushia felt even more restless. He now began to bite his lips. Then he put on the black boat-like cap that lay tucked under his arm. He shook the driver by his shoulder. 'Look, a girl will soon come and get into the car. The moment she does so, drive off. And don't think anything odd is happening; everything is perfectly all right.'

The door of the hut opened and two people walked out, the man Khushia had picked up and Kanta, who was wearing a bright coloured sari.

Khushia sank further into his seat. It was quite dark in the car. The man opened the car door and gently pushed Kanta in. Then he banged the door shut. 'Khushia! You!' Kanta screamed. 'Yes, I, but you have already been paid, haven't you!' Then he told the driver to get moving.

The engine coughed and came to life. The car lurched forward and if Kanta said something it could not be heard. The man who had brought Kanta could be seen standing on the road, looking somewhat bewildered. The taxi soon disappeared into the night.

No one ever saw Khushia at his customary hangout again.

# Babu Gopi Nath

I THINK IT WAS IN 1940 THAT I FIRST MET BABU GOPI NATH. I WAS THE editor of a weekly magazine in Bombay. One day, while I was busy writing something, Abdul Rahim Sando burst into my office, followed by a short, nondescript man. Greeting me in his typical style, Sando introduced his friend. 'Manto Sahib, meet Babu Gopi Nath.'

I rose and shook hands with him. Sando was in his element. 'Babu Gopi Nath, you are shaking hands with India's number one writer.' He had a talent for coining words which, though not to be found in any dictionary, somehow always managed to express his meaning. 'When he writes,' Sando continued, 'it is dharan takhta. Nobody can get people's "continuity" together like him. Manto Sahib, what did you write about Miss Khurshid last week? "Miss Khurshid has bought a car. Verily, God is the great carmaker." Well, Babu Gopi Nath, if that's not the "anti" of pantipo, then what is, I put it to you!'

Abdul Rahim Sando was an original. Most of the words he used in ordinary conversation were strictly of his own authorship. After this introduction, he looked at Babu Gopi Nath, who appeared to be impressed. 'This is Babu Gopi Nath, from Lahore, but now of Bombay, accompanied by a "pigeonette" from Kashmir.'

Babu Gopi Nath smiled.

Abdul Rahim Sando continued, 'If you are looking for the world's number one innocent, this is your man. Everyone cheats

him out of his money by saying nice things to him. Look at me.
All I do is talk and he rewards me with two packets of Polson's
smuggled butter every day. Manto sahib, he is a genuine
"antifloojustice" fellow, if ever there was one. We are expecting
you at Babu Gopi Nath's flat this evening.'

Babu Gopi Nath, whose mind seemed to be elsewhere, now
joined the conversation. 'Manto sahib, I insist that you come.'
Then he looked at Sando. 'Sando, is Manto sahib . . . well, fond
of . . . you know what?'

Abdul Rahim Sando laughed. 'Of course, he is fond of that
and of many other things as well. Is it all settled then? May I add that
I have also started drinking because it can now be done free of cost.'

Sando wrote out the address and at six o'clock I presented
myself at the flat. It was nice and clean. Three rooms, good
furniture, all in order. Besides Sando and Babu Gopi Nath, there
were four others—two men and two women—to whom I was
presently introduced by Sando.

There was Ghaffar Sain, a typical Punjabi villager in a loose
tehmad, wearing a huge necklace of beads and coloured stones.
'He is Babu Gopi Nath's legal adviser, you know what I mean?'
Sando said. 'In Punjab, every lunatic is a man of God. Our friend
here is either already a man of God or about to be admitted to
that divine order. He has accompanied Babu Gopi Nath from
Lahore, because he had run out of suckers in that city. Here, he
drinks Scotch whisky, smokes Craven A cigarettes and prays for
the good of Babu Gopi Nath's soul.'

Ghaffar Sain heard this colourful description in silence, a smile
playing on his lips.

The other man was called Ghulam Ali, tall and athletic with
a pockmarked face. About him Sando provided the following

information: 'He is my shagird, my true apprentice. A famous singing girl of Lahore fell in love with him. She brought all manner of "continuities" in play to ensnare him, but the only response she received from Ghulam Ali was: "Women are not my cup of tea." Ran into Babu Gopi Nath at a Lahore shrine and has never left his side since. He receives a tin of Craven A cigarettes daily and all the food he can eat.'

Ghulam Ali smiled good-naturedly.

I looked at the women. One of them was young, fair and round-faced, the Kashmiri 'pigeonette' Sando had mentioned. She had short hair, which first appeared to be cropped, but was not. Her eyes were large and bright and her expression suggested that she was raw and inexperienced. Sando introduced her.

'Zeenat Begum, called Zeno, a love-name given by Babu sahib. This apple, plucked from Kashmir, was brought to Lahore by one of the city's most formidable madams. Babu Gopi Nath's private intelligence sources relayed the news of this arrival to him and, overnight, he decamped with her. There was litigation and for about two months the city police had a ball, thanks to Babu Gopi Nath's generosity. Naturally, Babu Gopi Nath won the suit. And so here she is. Dharan takhta.'

The other woman, who was quietly smoking, was dark and red-eyed. Babu Gopi Nath looked at her. 'Sando, and this one?' Sando slapped her thigh and declaimed, 'Ladies and gentlemen, this is mutton tippoti, fulful booti, Mrs Abdul Rahim Sando, alias Sardar Begum. Fell in love with me in 1936 and, inside of two years, I was done for—dharan takhta. I had to run away from Lahore. However, Babu Gopi Nath sent for her the other day to keep me out of harm's way. Her daily rations consist of one tin of Craven A cigarettes and two rupees eight annas every evening for her morphine shot. She may be dark, but, by God, she is a tit-for-tat lady.'

'What rubbish you talk,' Sardar said. She sounded like the hardened professional woman she was.

Having finished with the introductions, Sando began a lecture highlighting my greatness. 'Cut it out, Sando,' I said. 'Let's talk of something else.'

Sando shouted, 'Boy, whisky and soda. Babu Gopi Nath, out with the cash.'

Babu Gopi Nath reached in his pocket, pulled out a thick bundle of money, peeled off a bill and gave it to Sando. Sando stared at it reverently, raised his eyes to heaven and said, 'Dear God of the universe, bring unto me the day when I put my hand in my pocket and fish out a thick wad of money like this. Meanwhile, I am asking Ghulam Ali to run to the store and return post-haste with two bottles of Johnny Walker Still-Going-Strong.'

The whisky arrived and we began to drink, with Sando continuing to monopolize the conversation. He downed his glass in one go. 'Dharan takhta,' he shouted, 'Manto sahib, this is what I call honest-to-goodness whisky, inscribing "Long Live Revolution" as it blazes its way through the gullet into the stomach. Long live Babu Gopi Nath.'

Babu Gopi Nath did not say much, occasionally nodding to express agreement with Sando's opinions. I had a feeling that the man had no views of his own. His superstitious nature was evident from the presence of Ghaffar Sain, his legal adviser, in Sando's words. What it really meant was that Babu Gopi Nath was a born devotee of real and fake holy men. I learnt during the conversation that most of his time in Lahore was spent in the company of fakirs, mendicants, sadhus and the like.

'What are you thinking?' I asked him.

'Nothing, nothing at all.' Then he smiled, glanced at Zeenat amorously. 'Just thinking about these beautiful creatures. What else do people like us think about?'

Sando explained, 'Manto sahib, Babu Gopi Nath is a great man. There is hardly a singing girl or a courtesan worth the name in Lahore he has not had a "continuity" with.'

'Manto sahib, one no longer has the fire of youth in one's loins,' Babu Gopi Nath said modestly.

Then followed a long discussion about the leading families of courtesans and singing girls of Lahore. Family trees were traced, genealogy analysed, not to speak of how much Babu Gopi Nath had paid for the ritual deflowering of which woman in what year. These exchanges remained confined to Sando, Sardar, Ghulam Ali and Ghaffar Sain. The jargon of Lahore's kothas was freely employed, not all of it comprehensible to me, though the general drift of the conversation was clear.

Zeenat never said a word. Off and on, she smiled. It was quite clear that she was not interested in these things. She drank a rather diluted glass of whisky, and I noticed that she smoked without appearing to enjoy it. Strangely enough, she smoked the most. I could find no visible indication that she was in love with Babu Gopi Nath, but it was obvious that he was with her. However, one could sense a tension between the two, despite their physical closeness.

At about eight o'clock, Sardar left to get her morphine shot. Ghaffar Sain, three drinks ahead, lay on the floor, rosary in hand. Ghulam Ali was sent out to get some food. Sando had got tired of talking. Babu Gopi Nath, now quite tipsy, looked at Zeenat longingly and said, 'Manto sahib, what do you think of my Zeenat?'

I did not know how to answer that, so I said, 'She is nice.' Babu Gopi Nath was pleased. 'Manto sahib, she is a lovely girl and so simple. She has no interest in ornaments and things like that. Many times I have offered to buy her a house of her own and you know what her answer has been? "What will I do with a house? Who do I have in the world?"'

He asked suddenly, 'What does a motor car cost, Manto sahib?'

'I've no idea.'

'I don't believe it, Manto sahib, I'm sure you know. You must help me buy Zeno a car. I've come to the conclusion that one must have a car in Bombay.'

Zeenat's face was devoid of expression.

Babu Gopi Nath was quite drunk now and getting more sentimental by the minute. 'Manto sahib, you are a man of learning. I am nothing but an ass. Please let me know if I can be of some service to you. It was only by accident that Sando brought up your name yesterday. I immediately sent for a taxi and asked him to take me to meet you. If I have shown you any discourtesy, you must forgive me. I am nothing but a sinner, a man full of faults. Should I get you some more whisky?'

'No, we've all had much too much to drink,' I said.

He became even more sentimental. 'You must drink some more, Manto sahib!' He produced his bundle of money, but before he could peel some off, I thrust it back into his pocket. 'You gave a hundred rupees to Ghulam Ali earlier, didn't you?' I asked.

The fact was that I had begun to feel sorry for Babu Gopi Nath. He was surrounded by so many leeches and he was such a simpleton. Babu Gopi Nath smiled. 'Manto sahib, whatever is left of those hundred rupees will slip through Ghulam Ali's pocket.'

The words were hardly out of his mouth, when Ghulam Ali entered the room with the doleful announcement that some scoundrel had picked his pocket on the street. Babu Gopi Nath looked at me, smiled, and gave another hundred rupees to Ghulam Ali. 'Get some food quickly.'

After five or six meetings, I got to know a great deal more about Babu Gopi Nath's personality. First of all, my initial view that he was a fool and a sucker had turned out to be wrong. He was perfectly aware of the fact that Sando, Ghulam Ali and Sardar, his inseparable companions, were all selfish opportunists, but you could never guess his inner thoughts from his behaviour.

Once he said to me, 'Manto sahib, in my entire life, I have never rejected advice. Whenever someone offers it to me, I accept it with gratitude. Perhaps they consider me a fool, but I value their wisdom. Look at it like this. They have the wisdom to see that I am the sort of man who can be made a fool of. The fact is that I have spent most of my life in the company of fakirs, holy men, courtesans and singing girls. I love them. I just couldn't do without them. I have decided that when my money runs out, I would like to settle down at a shrine. There are only two places where my heart finds peace: prostitutes' kothas and saints' shrines. It's only a matter of time before I shall be unable to afford the former, because my money is running out, but there are thousands of saints' shrines in India. I will go to one.'

'Why do you like kothas and shrines?' I asked.

'Because both establishments are an illusion. What better refuge can there be for someone who wants to deceive himself?'

'You are fond of singing girls. Do you understand music?' I asked.

'Not at all. It doesn't matter in the least. I can spend an entire evening listening to the most flat-voiced woman in the world and still feel happy. It is the little things which go with these evenings that I love. She sings, I flash a hundred-rupee bill in front of her. She moves languorously towards me and, instead of letting her take it from my hand, I stick it in my sock. She bends and gently pulls it out. It's the sort of nonsense that people like us enjoy. Everybody knows, of course, that in a kotha parents prostitute their daughters and in shrines men prostitute their God.'

I learnt that Babu Gopi Nath was the son of a miserly moneylender and had inherited ten lakh rupees, which he had been frittering away ever since. He had come to Bombay with fifty thousand rupees, and though those were inexpensive times his daily outgoings were heavy.

As promised, he bought a car for Zeno—a Fiat—for three thousand rupees. A chauffeur was also employed—an unreliable ruffian—but they were the sort of people Babu Gopi Nath felt happy with.

Our meetings had become more frequent. Babu Gopi Nath interested me. In turn, he treated me with great respect and devotion.

One evening, I found among Babu Gopi Nath's regulars a man I had known for a long time—Mohammad Shafiq Toosi. Widely regarded as a singer and a wit, Shafiq had another unusual side to his character. He was the known lover of the most famous singing girls of the time. It was not so commonly known, however, that he had had affairs, one after the other with three sisters, belonging to one of the most famous singing families of Patiala.

Even less known was the fact that their mother, when she was young, had been his mistress. His first wife, who died a few years after their marriage, he did not care for, because she was too housewifely and did not act like a woman of pleasure. He had no use for housewives. He was about forty and, though he had gone through scores of famous courtesans and singing girls, he was not known to have spent a penny of his own on them. He was one of nature's gigolos.

Courtesans had always found him irresistible. When I walked into the flat, I found him engrossed in conversation with Zeenat. I couldn't understand who had introduced him to Babu Gopi Nath. I knew that Sando was a friend of his, but they had not been on speaking terms for some time. In the end, it turned out that the two had made up and it was actually Sando who had brought him here today.

Babu Gopi Nath sat in a corner, smoking his hookah. He never smoked cigarettes. Shafiq was telling stories, most of them ribald and all of them about courtesans and singing girls. Zeenat looked uninterested, but Sardar was all ears. 'Welcome, welcome,' Shafiq said to me, 'I did not know you too were a wayfarer of this valley.'

Sando shouted, 'Welcome to the angel of death. Dharan takhta.'

One could not fail to notice that Mohammad Shafiq Toosi and Zeenat were exchanging what could only be described as amorous glances. This troubled me. I had become quite fond of Zeenat, who had begun to call me Manto bhai.

I didn't like the way Shafiq was ogling Zeenat. After some

time, he left with Sando. I am afraid I was a bit harsh with Zeenat, because I expressed strong disapproval of the goings-on between Shafiq and her. She burst into tears and ran into the next room, followed by Babu Gopi Nath. A few minutes later, he came out and said, 'Manto sahib, come with me.'

Zeenat was sitting on her bed. When she saw us, she covered her face with both hands and lay down. Babu Gopi Nath was very sombre. 'Manto sahib, I love this woman. She has been with me for two years, and I swear by the saint Hazrat Ghaus Azam Jilani that she has never given me cause for complaint. Her other sisters, I mean women of her calling, have robbed me without compunction over the years, but she is a girl without greed or love of money. Sometimes, I go away for weeks, maybe to be with another woman, without leaving her any money. You know what she does? She pawns her ornaments to manage until I return.

'Manto sahib, as I told you once, I don't have long to go. My money has almost run out. I don't want her life to go to waste after I am gone. So often have I said to her, "Zeno, look at the other women and learn something from them. Today, I have money, tomorrow, I'll be a beggar. Women can't do with just one rich lover in their lives; they need several. If you don't find a rich patron after I leave, your life will be ruined. You act like a housewife, confined at home all day. That won't do."

'But Manto sahib, this woman is hopeless. I consulted Ghaffar Sain in Lahore and he advised me to take her to Bombay. He knows two famous actresses here who used to be singing girls in Lahore. I sent for Sardar from Lahore to teach Zeno a few tricks of the trade. Ghaffar Sain is also very capable in these matters.

'Nobody knows me in Bombay. She was afraid she would bring me dishonour, but I said to her, "Don't be silly. Bombay is a big city, full of millionaires. I have bought you a car. Why don't you find yourself a rich man who could look after you?"

'Manto sahib, I swear on God that it is my sincere wish that Zeno should stand on her own feet. I am prepared to put ten thousand rupees in a bank for her, but I know that within ten days that woman Sardar will rob her of the last penny. Manto sahib, you should try to persuade her to become worldly-wise. Since she has had the car, Sardar takes her out for a drive every evening to the Apollo Bandar beach, which is frequented by fashionable people. But there has been no success so far. Sando brought Mohammad Shafiq Toosi this evening, as you saw. What is your opinion about him?'

I decided to offer no opinion, but Babu Gopi Nath said, 'He appears to be rich, and he is good-looking. Zeno, did you like him?'

Zeno said nothing.

I simply could not believe what he was telling me: that he had brought Zeenat to Bombay so that she could become the mistress of a rich man, or, at least, learn to live off rich men. But that's the way it was. Had he wanted to get rid of her, it would have been the easiest thing in the world, but his intentions were exactly what he said they were. He had tried to get her into films, Bombay being India's movie capital. For her sake, he had entertained men who claimed to be film directors, but were no such thing. He even had had a phone installed in the flat. None of these things had produced the man he was looking for.

Mohammad Shafiq Toosi, a regular visitor for a month or so, suddenly disappeared one day. True to style, he had used the opportunity to seduce Zeenat. Babu Gopi Nath said to me, 'Manto sahib, it is so sad. Shafiq sahib was all show and no substance. Not only did he do nothing to help Zeno, but he cheated her out of many valuables and two hundred rupees. Now I am told he is having an affair with a girl called Almas.'

This was true. Almas was the youngest daughter of the famous courtesan Nazir Jan of Patiala. She was the fourth sister he had seduced in a row. Zeno's money had been spent on her, but like all his liaisons this too had turned out to be short-lived. It was later rumoured that Almas had tried to poison herself after being abandoned.

However, Zeenat had not given up on Mohammad Shafiq Toosi. She often phoned me, asking me to find Toosi and bring him to her. One day I accidentally ran into him at the radio station. When I gave him Zeenat's message, he said, 'This is not the first one. I have had several. The truth is that while Zeenat is a nice woman, she is too nice for my taste. Women who behave like wives are of no interest to me.'

Disappointed in Toosi, Zeenat resumed her visits to the beach in the company of Sardar. After two weeks of effort, Sardar was able to get hold of two men who appeared to be just the kind of gentlemen of leisure being sought. One of them, who owned a silk mill, even gave four hundred rupees to Zeenat and promised to marry her, but that was the last she heard from him.

One day, while on an errand on Hornsby Road, I saw Zeenat's parked car, with Mohammad Yasin, owner of the Nagina Hotel, occupying the back seat. 'Where did you get this car?' I asked.

'Do you know who it belongs to?'

'I do.'

'Then you can put two and two together.' He winked meaningfully.

A couple of days later, Babu Gopi Nath told me the story. Sardar had met someone at the beach and they had decided to go to Nagina Hotel to spend the evening. There was a quarrel and the man had walked out, which is how Yasin, the hotel's owner, had come into the picture.

Zeenat's affair with Yasin appeared to be progressing well. He had bought her some expensive gifts, and Babu Gopi Nath was mentally prepared to return to Lahore, because he was certain Yasin was the man Zeno could be entrusted to. Unfortunately, things did not work out that way.

A mother and daughter had recently moved into Nagina Hotel and Yasin was quick to see that Muriel, the daughter, was looking for someone to while away the time. So, while Zeenat sat in the hotel all day long, waiting for him, the two of them could be seen driving around Bombay in Zeenat's car. Babu Gopi Nath was hurt.

'What sort of men are these, Manto sahib?' he asked me. 'I mean if one has had one's fill of a woman, one just says so honestly. I no longer understand Zeenat. She knows what is going on, but she wouldn't even tell him that if he must carry on with that Christian chhokri then at least he should have the decency not to use her car. What am I to do, Manto sahib? She is such a wonderful girl, but she is so naive. She has to learn how to survive in this world.'

The affair with Yasin finally ended, but it seemed to have left no outward effect on Zeenat. One day I phoned the flat and learnt that Babu Gopi Nath had returned to Lahore, along with

Ghulam Ali and Ghaffar Sain. His money had run out, but he still had some property left, which he was planning to sell before returning to Bombay.

Sardar needed her morphine and Sando his Polson's butter. They had therefore decided to turn the flat into a whorehouse. Two or three men were roped in every day to receive Zeenat's sexual favours. She had been told to cooperate until Babu Gopi Nath's return. The daily takings were around a hundred rupees or so, half of them Zeenat's.

'You do realize what you are doing to yourself?' I said to her one day.

'I don't know, Manto bhai,' she answered innocently. 'I merely do what these people tell me.'

I wanted to say that she was a fool and the two of them would not even hesitate to auction her off, if it came to that. However, I said nothing. She was a woman without ambition and unbelievably naive. She simply had no idea of her own value or what life was all about. If she was being made to sell her body, she could at least have done so with some intelligence and style, but she was simply not interested in anything, drinking, smoking, eating, or even the sofa on which she was to be found lying most of the time, and the telephone which she was so fond of using.

A month later, Babu Gopi Nath returned from Lahore. He went to the flat, but found some other people living there. It turned out that, on the advice of Sando and Sardar, Zeenat had rented the top portion of a bungalow in the Bandara area. When Babu Gopi Nath came to see me, I told him of the new arrangement, but I said nothing about the establishment Sando and Sardar were running, thanks to Zeenat.

Babu Gopi Nath had come back with ten thousand rupees

this time. Ghaffar Sain and Ghulam Ali had been left in Lahore. When we met, he insisted that I should come with him to Zeenat's place. He had left a taxi waiting on the street.

It took us an hour to get to Bandara. As we were driving up Pali Hill, we saw Sando. 'Sando, Sando,' Babu Gopi Nath shouted. 'Dharan takhta,' Sando exclaimed when he saw who it was.

Babu Gopi Nath wanted him to get into the taxi, but Sando wouldn't. 'There is something I have to tell you,' he said.

I stayed in the taxi. The two of them talked for some time, then Babu Gopi Nath came back and told the driver to return to town.

He looked happy. As we were approaching Dawar, he said, 'Manto sahib, Zeno is about to be married.'

'To whom?' I asked, somewhat surprised.

'A rich landlord from Hyderabad, Sindh. May God keep both of them happy. The timing is perfect. The money I have can be used to buy Zeno her dowry.'

I was a bit sceptical about the story. I was sure it was another of Sando and Sardar's tricks to cheat Babu Gopi Nath. However, it all turned out to be true. The man was a rich Sindhi landlord who had been introduced to Zeno through the good offices of a Sindhi music teacher who had failed to teach her how to sing.

One day he had brought Ghulam Hussain—for that was the landlord's name—to Zeenat's place and she had received him with her usual hospitality. She had even sung for him at his insistence Ghalib's ghazal *'Nukta cheen hai gham-e-dil usko sunai na bana'*. Ghulam Hussain was smitten. The music teacher mentioned this to Zeenat, and Sardar and Sando joined hands to firm things up and a date for marriage was set.

One thing had led to another and now they were going to get married.

Babu Gopi Nath was ecstatic. He had managed to meet Ghulam Hussain, having had himself introduced as Sando's friend. He told me later, 'Manto sahib, he is handsome and he is intelligent. Before leaving Lahore, I went and prayed at the shrine of Data Ganj Baksh for Zeno and my prayer has been answered. May Bhagwan keep both of them happy.'

Babu Gopi Nath made all the wedding arrangements. Four thousand rupees was spent on ornaments and clothes and five thousand was to be given in cash to Zeenat.

The wedding guests from Zeenat's side were myself, Mohammad Shafiq Toosi, and Mohammad Yasin, proprietor of the Nagina Hotel. After the ceremony, Sando whispered, 'Dharan takhta.'

Ghulam Hussain was a handsome man. He was dressed in a blue suit and was graciously acknowledging the congratulations being offered to him. Babu Gopi Nath looked like a little bird in his presence.

There was a wedding dinner, with Babu Gopi Nath very much the host. At one point, he said to me, 'Manto sahib, you must see how lovely Zeno looks in her bridal dress.'

I went into the next room. There sat Zeenat, dressed in expensive, silver-embroidered red silk. She was lightly made up, but was wearing too much lipstick. She greeted me by bowing her head slightly. She did look lovely, I thought. However, when I looked in the other corner, I found a bed profusely bedecked with flowers. I just could not contain my laughter. 'What is this farce?' I asked her. 'You are making fun of me, Manto bhai,' Zeno said, tears welling up in her eyes.

I was still wondering how to react, when Babu Gopi Nath came in. Lovingly, he dried Zeno's tears with his handkerchief and said to me in a heartbroken voice, 'Manto sahib, I had always considered you a wise and sensitive man. Before making such fun of Zeno, you should at least have weighed your words.'

I suddenly had the feeling that the devotion he had always shown me had suffered a setback, but before I could apologize to him, he placed his hand affectionately over Zeenat's head and said, 'May God keep you happy.'

When he left the room, his eyes were wet and there was a look of disillusionment on his face.

# Mummy

HER NAME WAS STELLA JACKSON, BUT EVERYONE CALLED HER MUMMY. A short, active woman in her middle years, whose husband had been killed in the last great war. His pension still came every month.

I had no idea how long she had lived in Poona. The fact was that she was such a fascinating character that after meeting her once, such questions somehow became irrelevant. She herself was all that mattered. To say that she was an integral part of Poona may sound like an exaggeration, but as far as I am concerned all my memories of that city are inextricably linked with her.

I am a very lazy person by nature, which is not to say that I do not dream about great travels. If you hear me talking, you would think I was about to set out to conquer the Kanchenjunga peak in the Himalayas. It is another matter that once I get there I might decide not to move at all.

I can't really remember how many years I had been in Bombay when I decided one day to take my wife to Poona. Let me work it out. Our first child had been dead four years and it was another four years since I had moved to Bombay. So, actually, I had been living there for eight years, but not once had I taken the trouble to visit the famous Victoria Gardens or the museum. It was therefore quite unusual for me to get up one morning and take off for Poona. I had recently had a tiff at the film studio where I was employed as a writer. I wanted to get away—a change of scene, if you like. For one thing, Poona was not far and there were a number of my old movie friends living there.

We took a train, arrived, scampered out of the station and realized that the Parbhat Nagar suburb where we planned to stay with friends was quite far. We got into a tonga which turned out to be the slowest thing I had ever been in. I hate slowness, be it in men or animals. However, there was no alternative.

We were in no particular hurry to get to Parbhat Nagar, but I was getting impatient with the absurd conveyance we were in. I had never seen anything more ridiculous since Aligarh, which is notorious for its horse-drawn ikkas. The horse moves forward and the passengers slip backwards. Once or twice, I suggested to my wife that perhaps we should walk the rest of the way, or get hold of a better specimen of tonga, but she quite logically observed that there was nothing to choose from between one tonga and the next and, besides, the sun would be unbearable. Wives.

Another equally ridiculous-looking tonga was coming from the opposite direction. Suddenly, I heard someone shout, 'Hey Manto, you big horsie.' It was Chadda, my old friend, huddled in the back with a worn-out woman. My first reaction was regret. What had gone wrong with his aesthetic sense that he was now running around with a woman old enough to be his mother? I couldn't guess her age, but I noticed that despite her heavy make-up, the wrinkles on her face were visible. It was so grossly painted that it hurt the eye.

I had not seen Chadda for ages. He was one of my best friends and, had he not been with the sort of woman he was with, I would have greeted him with something equally mindless. In any case, both of us got down.

He said to the woman, 'Mummy, just a minute.' He pumped

my hand vigorously, then tried to do the same to my extremely formal wife. 'Bhabi, you have performed the impossible, I mean, getting this bundle of lazy bones all the way from Bombay to Poona.'

'Where are you headed for?' I asked.

'On important business. Now, listen, don't waste time. You are going straight to my place.' He began to issue instructions to the tongawala, adding, 'Don't charge the fare. It'll be settled.'

Then he turned to me. 'There is a servant around. See you later.' Without waiting for an answer, he jumped into his tonga, where the woman whom he had called Mummy sat waiting for him. The embarrassment I had felt earlier was gone.

His house was not far from where we had met. It looked like an old dak bungalow. 'This is it,' the tongawala said. 'I mean Chadda sahib's house.' I could see from my wife's expression that she was not overly enthusiastic about the prospects. As a matter of fact, she had not been overly enthusiastic about coming to Poona. She was afraid that once there I would team up with my drinking friends and, since I was supposed to be having a change of scene, most of my time would be spent in what was to her highly objectionable company. I got down and asked my wife to follow me, which she did after some hesitation, as it was clear to her that my mind was made up.

It was the kind of house the army likes to requisition for a few weeks and then abandon. The walls were badly in need of paint and the rooms could only have belonged to a careless bachelor, an actor most likely, paid every two or three months— and that, too, in instalments.

I was conscious that this was no place for wives, but there was nothing to do but wait for Chadda, and then move to Parbhat

Nagar, where this old friend of mine lived with his wife in more reasonable surroundings.

The servant in a way suited the place. When we arrived we found all the doors open and nobody in sight. When he finally materialized he took no notice of us, as if we had lived there for years. He came into the room and sailed past us without saying a word. I thought he was an out-of-work actor sharing the house with Chadda. However, when he came again and I asked him where the servant was to be found, he informed me gravely that he himself was the holder of that office.

We were both thirsty. When I asked him to get us a drink of water, he began looking for a glass. Finally, he produced a chipped glass mug from the bottom drawer of a cupboard and murmured, 'Only last night, sahib sent for half a dozen glasses. Now what on earth could have happened to them!'

My wife said she did not want a drink after all. He put the mug back exactly where he had unearthed it—in the bottom drawer of the cupboard—as if without this elaborate ritual the entire household would come tumbling down. Then he left the room.

While my wife took one of the armchairs, I made myself comfortable on the bed, which was probably Chadda's. We did not say anything to each other. After some time, Chadda arrived. He was alone. He seemed quite indifferent to the fact that we were his guests.

'What's what old boy,' he said. 'Let's run up to the studio for a few minutes. With you in tow, I'm sure I can pick up an advance, because this evening . . .' Then he looked at my wife. 'Bhabi, I hope you haven't made a mullah out of him.' He laughed. 'To hell with all the mullahs of the world. Come on, Manto, get moving. I am sure bhabi won't mind.'

My wife said nothing, although it wasn't difficult to guess what she was thinking. The studio was not far. After a noisy meeting with Mr Mehta the accountant, Chadda succeeded in making him cough up an advance of two hundred rupees. When we returned to the house, we found my wife sleeping in the armchair. We did not disturb her and moved into the next room, where I noticed everything was either broken or in an advanced state of disrepair. At least it gave the place a uniformity of sorts.

There was dust on everything, an essential touch to the bohemian character of Chadda's lodgings. From somewhere, he found the elusive servant, handed him a hundred rupees and said, 'Prince of Cathay, get us two bottles of third-class rum, I mean, 3-X rum and six new glasses.'

I later discovered that the servant was not only the Prince of Cathay, but the prince of practically very major country and civilization in the world. It all depended on Chadda's mood of the moment.

The Prince of Cathay left, fondling the money he had been given. Lowering himself on the bed, which had a broken spring mattress, Chadda ran his tongue over his lips in anticipation of the rum he had ordered and said, 'What's what. So you did hit Poona after all.' Then he added in a worried voice, 'But what about bhabi? I'm sure she's bloody upset.'

Chadda did not have a wife, but he was always worried about the wives of his friends. He used to say that he had remained single because he felt insecure when dealing with wives. 'When it's suggested to me that I should get married, my first reaction is always positive. Then I start thinking and in a few minutes come to the conclusion that I don't really deserve a wife. And that's how the project gets thrown into cold storage every time,' was one of his favourite explanations.

The rum arrived, and with it, the glasses. Chadda had sent for six, but the Prince of Cathay had dropped three on the way. Chadda was unconcerned. 'Praise be to the Lord that at least the bottles are unharmed,' he observed philosophically.

Then he opened the bottle hurriedly, poured the rum into virgin glasses and toasted me: 'To your arrival in Poona.' We downed our drinks in long swigs. Chadda poured more, then tiptoed into the other room to see if my wife was still asleep. She was. 'This is no good,' he announced 'Let me make some noise so that she wakes up . . . but before that let me organize some tea for her. Prince of Jamaica,' he shouted.

The Prince of Jamaica materialized at once. 'Go to Mummy's place and ask her to kindly prepare some first-class tea and have it sent over. Immediately.'

Chadda drank up, then poured himself a more civilized measure and said, 'For the time being, I am watching my drinking. The first four drinks make me very sentimental and we still have to go to Parbhat Nagar to dump bhabi.'

The tea came, set on a nice tray. Chadda lifted the lid of the teapot, smelled the brew and declared, 'Mummy is a jewel.' Then he sent for the Prince of Ethiopia and began screaming at him. When he was sure that the racket had awakened my wife, he picked up the tray daintily and told me to follow him. He put it down with an exaggerated flourish on a table and announced, 'Tea is served, madam.'

My wife did not appear too amused by Chadda's antics, but she drank two cups and said, not so ill-humouredly, 'I suppose the two of you have already had yours.'

'I must plead guilty to that charge, but we did it in the secure knowledge that we'd find forgiveness,' Chadda said.

My wife smiled, encouraging Chadda to continue. 'Actually, both of us are pigs of the purest breed who are permitted to eat every forbidden fruit on earth. It is therefore time that we took steps to move you to a holier place than this.'

My wife was not amused. She did not care for Chadda. The fact is that she did not care much for any of my friends, especially him because she thought he was always transgressing the limits of what she considered correct behaviour. I don't think it had ever occurred to Chadda how people reacted to him. He considered it a waste of time, like playing indoor games. He beamed at my wife and shouted, 'Prince of Kababistan, get us a Rolls-Royce tonga.'

The Rolls-Royce tonga came and we left for Parbhat Nagar. My friend Harish Kumar was not at home, but his wife was, which we found helpful. Chadda said, 'As melons influence melons, in the same way, wives influence wives. We are off to the studio now, but we will soon return to verify the results.'

Chadda's strategy was always simple. Create so much confusion that enemy forces get no opportunity to plan theirs. He pushed me towards the door, giving my wife no time to object. 'Operation successfully accomplished. What now? Yes, Mummy great Mummy,' Chadda declared.

I wanted to ask him who this Mummy of his was, daughter of what Tutankhamun, but he began to speak about totally unconnected matters, leaving my question to wither on the vine.

The tonga took us back to the house which was called Saeeda Cottage. Chadda had christened it Kabida Cottage, the abode of the melancholy, as it was his theory that all its residents were in a state of advanced melancholia. Like many of his other theories, this one too was not quite consistent with the facts.

Chadda was not the only resident of Saeeda Cottage. There were others, all actors, and all working for the same film company which paid salaries every third month——in the form of advance. Almost all the inmates of the establishment were assistant directors. There were chief assistant directors, their deputies and assistants who, in turn, had their own assistants. It seemed to me that everyone was everyone's assistant and on the lookout for a financier to help him set up his own film company.

Because of the war, food rationing was in effect, but none of the Saeeda Cottage residents had a ration card. When they had money, they used to buy from the black market at exorbitant prices. They always went to the movies and, during the season, to the races. Some even tried their luck at the stock exchange, but no one had so far made a killing.

Since space was limited, even the garage was used for residential purposes. It was occupied by a family. The husband was not an assistant director, but the film company chauffeur, who kept odd hours. His wife, a good-looking young woman, was named Shireen. She had a little boy who had been collectively adopted by the residents of Saeeda Cottage.

The more liveable rooms in the cottage were occupied by Chadda and two of his friends, both actors, who had yet to make the big time. One was called Saeed, but his professional name was Ranjeet Kumar, a quiet, nice-looking man. Chadda often referred to him as the tortoise because he did everything very, very slowly.

I do not now remember the real name of the other actor, but everybody called him Gharib Nawaz. He came from a well-to-do family of the princely state of Hyderabad. He had come to Poona to get into the movies. He was paid two hundred and fifty rupees a month, but since being hired a year earlier had been paid only once—an advance against salary. The money had gone to rescue Chadda from the clutches of a very angry Pathan moneylender. There was hardly anyone in Saeeda Cottage who did not owe money to Gharib Nawaz.

Despite Chadda's theory, none of them was particularly melancholy. In fact they lived fairly happily, and even when they talked of their straitened circumstances it was in an offhand, cheerful manner.

When Chadda and I returned, we ran into Gharib Nawaz outside the front gate. Chadda pulled out some money from his pocket and gave it to him—without counting—and said, 'Four bottles of Scotch. If I've given you less, then I know you'll make up for it. If I've given you more, I know I'll get it back. Thank you.'

Gharib Nawaz smiled. 'This is Mr—one two,' he said to him, meaning me. 'Detailed discussions are not possible at this stage because he has had a few rums. But wait until the evening when the Scotch begins to flow.'

We went inside. Chadda yawned, picked up the half-empty bottle of rum, took stock of its contents and shouted for the Prince of the Cossacks. There was no answer. 'I think he is drunk,' he observed, pouring himself another drink.

Chadda's room was like an old junk shop. However, it had a window or two, through one of which I now saw Venkutrey the music director, another old friend of mine, peeping in. It was difficult to tell by looking at him what race he belonged to— whether he was Mongol, Negroid, Aryan or something completely unknown to anthropology.

While one particular feature might, for a moment, suggest certain origins, it was immediately cancelled out by another feature, pointing at entirely different possibilities. However, he was from Maharashtra. His nose, unlike that of his famous forebear, the warrior Shivaji, was flat, which he always assured people was a great help in reproducing certain notes.

'Manto seth,' he screamed when he saw me.

'The hell with seths,' Chadda said. 'Don't stand there. Come in.' Venkutrey appeared, put a bottle of rum on the table and said he was at Mummy's when he was told that one of Chadda's friends was in town. 'I was wondering who that could be. Didn't know it was sala Manto the old sinner.'

Chadda slapped his head. 'Shut your trap. You've produced a bottle of rum, that's enough.' Venkutrey picked up my empty glass and poured himself a large measure. 'Manto, this sala Chadda was telling me this morning, "Venkutrey, I want to get drunk tonight. Get some booze." Now I was broke and I was wondering where I was going to get the money . . .'

'You are an imbecile,' Chadda said.

'Is that so, then where do you think I managed to get this big bucket of rum from? It wasn't a gift from your father, I can tell you that.' He finished his glass. 'What did Mummy say?' Chadda asked. 'Was Polly there, and Thelma . . . and that platinum blonde?'

Chadda didn't wait for his answer. 'Manto, what a bundle of goods that one is! I had always heard of platinum blondes, but by God I had never set eyes on one, that is, until yesterday. She's lovely. Her hair is like threads of fine silver. She is great, Manto. I tell you she's great. Mummy zindabad. Mummy zindabad.' Then he said to Venkutrey, 'You bloody man, say Mummy zindabad.'

Chadda grabbed my arm. 'Manto, I think I am getting very sentimental. You know in tradition the beloved is supposed to have black hair like a rain cloud, but what we have here is an entirely different bill of fare. Her hair is like finely spun silver . . . or maybe not . . . now I don't know what platinum looks like. I have never seen the bloody thing in my life. How can I describe the colour! Just try to imagine blue steel and silver mixed together.'

'And a shot of 3-X rum,' Venkutrey suggested, knocking back his.

'Shut up,' Chadda told him. 'Manto, I am really going bananas over this girl. Oh, the colour of her hair. What are those things fish have on their bellies, or is it all over? The pomfret fish. What are those things called? Damn fish, I think snakes have them too, those tiny, shimmering things. Scales, that's right, they're called scales. In Urdu they're called "khaprey", which is a ridiculous name for something so beautiful. We have a word for them in Punjabi. I know it. Yes . . . "chanay". What a lovely word. It sounds right. It sounds just right. That's what her hair is like . . . small, brilliant, slithering snakes.'

He got up. 'To hell with small, brilliant, slithering snakes. I'm going out of my mind. I'm getting sentimental.'

'What was that?' Venkutrey asked absent-mindedly.

'Beyond your feeble powers of comprehension, my friend,' Chadda replied.

Venkutrey mixed himself another drink. 'Manto, this sala Chadda thinks I don't understand English. You know I'm matriculate. My father loved me. He sent me to . . .'

'Your father was mad. He made you the greatest musician in the world. He twisted your nose and made it flat so that you could sing flat notes. Manto, whenever he has had a couple of drinks, he starts talking about his father. Yes, he's a matriculate, but should I then tear up my BA degree?'

I drank. 'Manto,' Chadda said, 'if I fail to conquer this platinum blonde, I promise you Mr Chadda will renounce the world, go to the highest peak in the Himalayas and contemplate his navel.'

He said he was throwing a big party that night. 'Had you not hit town, that rascal Mehta would never have given me the advance. Well, tonight is the night.' He began to sing in his highly unmusical voice. Before Venkutrey could protest at this most foul murder of music, the door opened to reveal Gharib Nawaz and Ranjeet Kumar, each holding two bottles of Scotch. We poured them some rum.

It turned out that the name of this jewel was Phyllis. She worked in a hairdressing salon and was generally to be seen with a young fellow, who, everybody assured me, looked like a sissy. The entire male population of Saeeda Cottage was infatuated with her.

Gharib Nawaz had declared that morning that he might rush back to Hyderabad, sell some property, return with the proceeds and sweep her off her feet. Chadda's only plus was his good looks. Venkutrey was of the view that she would fall into his lap the moment she heard him sing. Ranjeet Kumar was in favour of a more direct approach. However, in the end, it was clear that success would depend on whom Mummy favoured.

Chadda looked at his watch. 'Let the bloody platinum blonde go to blazes. We have to be in Parbhat Nagar, because I am sure by now Mrs Manto is angry. Now, if I get a sentimental fit in her presence, you'll have to look after me.' He finished his drink and called for the Prince of Egypt, the land of mummies.

The prince appeared, rubbing his eyes as if he had just been disinterred from the earth after hundreds of years. Chadda sprinkled his face with some rum and told him to conjure up two royal Egyptian chariots.

The chariots came and soon we were on our way to Parbhat Nagar. My friend Harish Kumar was home and my wife seemed to be in a good mood. Chadda winked at him as we entered to indicate that something was on the cards for the evening.

Harish asked my wife if she'd like to come to the studio to watch him shoot a couple of scenes. She wanted to know if a musical sequence was being filmed. When told that it would be the next day, she seemed to lose interest. 'Why not tomorrow then?' Harish's wife suggested. The poor woman was sick of taking guests to the studios. She told my wife, 'You look tired. I think you should take some rest.'

Harish said it was a good idea. 'Manto, you'd better come with me to see the studio chief. He has expressed an interest in your writing a film for him.' My wife was pleased. Chadda provided the final touch to the drama. He said he was leaving as he had something important to do. We said our good-byes. When we met later on the road, Chadda shouted lustily, 'Raja Harish Chander zindabad.'

Harish did not come with us. He had to meet his girlfriend.

From the outside, Mummy's house looked like Saeeda Cottage, but there the resemblance ended. I had expected to find myself in a sort of brothel, but it was a perfectly normal, middle-class Christian household. It looked a bit younger than Mummy, perhaps because it was simple and wore no make-up. When she walked in, I felt that while everything around her had remained the same age as the day it was bought, she had moved on and grown old. She was wearing the same bright make-up.

Chadda introduced her briefly: 'This is Mummy the great.'
She smiled, then admonished him gently. 'You sent for tea in
such an unholy hurry that I am sure Mrs Manto could not have
found it drinkable. It was all your friend Chadda's fault,' she
told me.

I said the tea was great. Then she said to Chadda, 'I fixed
dinner, otherwise you always get impatient at the last moment.'
Chadda threw his arms around her. 'You are a jewel, Mummy.
Of course we are going to eat that dinner.'

Mummy wanted to know where my wife was. When we told
her that she was with friends in Parbhat Nagar, she said, 'That's
awful, why didn't you bring her?'

'Because of the party tonight,' Chadda replied.

'What party? I decided to call it off the moment I saw Mrs
Manto.'

'What have you done, Mummy?' Chadda exclaimed. 'And to
think that we planned this entire charade just for that!'

Then on an impulse he jumped up. 'But you only thought of
calling the party off. You didn't actually call it off. As such, hereby
I call off your decision to call off the party. Cross your heart.'
He drew a cross across Mummy's heart and shouted, 'Hip hip
hurray!'

The fact was that Mummy had called off the party. I could
also see that she didn't want to disappoint Chadda. She touched
him on the cheek affectionately and said, 'Let me see what I can
do.'

She left. Chadda's spirits rose. 'General Venkutrey, report to
headquarters and arrange immediate transportation of all heavy
guns to the battlefront.'

Venkutrey saluted smartly and left for Saeeda Cottage. He

was back in ten minutes with the heavy guns—the four bottles of Scotch—with the servant bringing up the rear. 'Come in, come in, my Caucasian prince. The girl with hair the colour of snake scales is coming tonight. You too can try your luck.'

I was thinking about Mummy. Chadda, Gharib Nawaz and Ranjeet Kumar were like little children waiting for their mother who had gone out to buy them toys. Chadda was more confident because he was the favourite child and he knew that he would get the best toy. The others were not altogether without hope. Every situation has its own music. The one in Mummy's home had no harsh notes. Drinking did not feel like something which should not be done. It was like imbibing milk.

Her make-up still bothered me, however. Why did she have to paint her face like that? It was an insult to the love she showered with such generosity on Chadda, Gharib Nawaz and Venkutrey . . . and who knew how many more.

I asked Chadda, 'Why does your Mummy look so flashy?'

'Because the world likes flashy things. There are not many idiots around like you and me who wish colours to be sober and understated, music to be soft, who don't want to see youth clad in the garments of childhood and age in the mantle of youth. We who call ourselves artists are actually second-class asses, because there is nothing first class on this earth. It is either third or second class, except . . . except Phyllis. She alone is first class.'

Venkutrey poured his drink over Chadda's head. 'Snakes scales . . . you have gone mad.'

Chadda lapped it up. 'This has cooled me down.'

Venkutrey began his long, rambling story about how much his father loved him, but Chadda was having none of that.

'To hell with your entire family,' he said. 'I want to talk about Phyllis.' He looked at Gharib Nawaz and Ranjeet Kumar, who were huddled together in a corner whispering in each other's ears. 'You leaders of the great gunpowder plot, your conspiracies will never succeed. Victory in battle will kiss Chadda's feet. Isn't that so, my Prince of Wales?'

The Prince of Wales seemed more worried about the bottle of rum, which was getting emptier by the minute. Chadda laughed and poured him a hefty measure.

The lights had been switched on, and outside, the evening had fallen. Then we heard Mummy on the veranda. Chadda shouted a slogan and ran out. Ranjeet Kumar and Gharib Nawaz exchanged glances, waiting for the door to open.

Mummy came in, followed by four or five Anglo-Indian girls—Polly, Dolly, Kitty, Elma, Thelma—and a young man who answered to the description that had been provided to me of Phyllis's friend.

Phyllis was the last to appear. Chadda had his arm around her. He had already declared victory. Gharib Nawaz and Ranjeet Kumar looked positively unhappy at this unsporting behaviour.

All hell broke loose. Suddenly everyone was jabbering away in English, trying to impress the girls. Venkutrey failed his matriculation several times in a row. Soon he went into a corner with Thelma, offering free instruction in Indian classical dance.

Chadda was surrounded by a bevy of giggling girls. He was reciting dirty limericks which he knew by the hundred. Mummy was busy with her arrangements. Ranjeet Kumar sat alone, smoking cigarette after cigarette. Gharib Nawaz was asking Mummy if she needed any money.

The Scotch was brought in ceremoniously. Phyllis was offered a drink, but she shook her head. She said she did not like whisky. Even Chadda was refused. Finally, Mummy prepared a light drink, put the glass to her lips and said, 'Now be a brave girl and gulp it down.'

Chadda was so thrilled that he recited another twenty limericks. I was thinking. Man must have got bored with nakedness when he decided to don clothes, which is why sometimes he gets bored with them and reverts to his original state. The reaction to good manners is certainly bad manners.

I watched Mummy. She was surrounded by the girls and was giggling with the rest of them at Chadda's antics. She was wearing the same vulgar, tasteless make-up under which her wrinkles could be seen in high relief. She looked happy. I wondered why people thought escape to be a bad thing. Here was an act of escape. The exterior was unattractive, but the soul was beautiful. Did she need all those unguents, lotions and colouring liquids?

Polly was telling Ranjeet Kumar about her new dress, which she had picked up as a bargain and had done something to at home. And now it was perfectly lovely. Ranjeet Kumar was offering to buy her two new ones, although he was unlikely to get an advance in the near future. Dolly was trying to talk Gharib Nawaz into lending her some more money. He knew perfectly well that he would never see it again, but was still trying to convince himself to the contrary.

Thelma was being tutored in the intricacies of Indian classical dance by Venkutrey, who knew that she would never make a dancer. She knew that too, but she was still listening to him with great concentration. Elma and Kitty were drinking steadily.

In this tableau it was difficult to be sure about the rights and wrongs. Was Mummy's flashiness right or a part of the situation? Who could say? In her heart there was love for everyone. Perhaps she had coloured her face, I said to myself, so that the world should not see what she was really like. Maybe she did not have the emotional strength to play mother to the whole world. She had just chosen a few.

Mummy did not know that during her absence in the kitchen, Chadda had persuaded Phyllis to take a massive drink, not on the sly, but in front of the others. Phyllis was slightly high, but only slightly. Her hair was like polished steel, waving gently from side to side like her young sinuous body.

It was midnight. Venkutrey was no longer trying to make a classical dancer out of Thelma. Now he was telling her about his father, who loved him to the point of distraction. Gharib Nawaz had forgotten that he had already lent some more money to Dolly. Ranjeet Kumar had disappeared with Polly. Elma and Kitty were sleepy.

Around the table sat Phyllis, her friend and Mummy. Chadda was no longer sentimental. He sat next to Phyllis and it was evident he was determined to take her tonight.

At some point, Phyllis's friend got up, laid himself down on the sofa and went to sleep. Gharib Nawaz and Dolly left the room. Elma and Kitty said their goodnights and went home. Venkutrey, after praising his wife's beauty one more time, cast a longing look at Phyllis, put his arm around Thelma and took her out into the garden.

Suddenly a loud argument developed between Mummy and Chadda. He was drunk, angry and foul-mouthed. He had never spoken to her like that. Phyllis had given up her feeble efforts to make peace between the two. Chadda wanted to take her to

Saeeda Cottage and Mummy had told him that she would not
permit that. He was screaming at her now. 'You old pimp, you
have gone mad. Phyllis is mine. Ask her.'

'Chadda, my son, why don't you understand? She is young,
she is very young,' Mummy said to him, but Chadda was beyond
reason. For the first time it occurred to me how young Phyllis
was, hardly fifteen. Her face was like a raindrop surrounded by
silver clouds.

Chadda pulled Phyllis towards him, squeezed her against his
chest in a passionate B-grade movie embrace. 'Chadda, leave
her alone. For God's sake let her go,' Mummy screamed, but he
paid no attention to her.

Then it happened. She slapped him across the face. 'Get out,
get out!' she shouted.

Chadda pushed Phyllis aside, gave Mummy a furious look
and walked out. I followed him.

When I arrived at Saeeda Cottage, he was lying on his bed,
face down, fully clothed. We did not speak. I went to my room
and slept.

I got up late next morning. Chadda was not in his room. I
washed and as I was coming out of the bathroom I heard his
voice outside. 'She is unique. By God, she is great. You should
pray that when you reach her age you should become like her.'

I did not want to hang around much longer. I waited for him
to come back to the house, but after about half an hour I left for
Parbhat Nagar.

Harish hadn't returned home. I told his wife that we had had
a late night, so he had decided to sleep at Saeeda Cottage. We
took our leave and on the way I told my wife about the night's
incident. Her theory was that Phyllis was either related to

Mummy or the old woman wanted to save her for some better client. I kept quiet.

After several weeks I had a letter from Chadda. All it said was, 'I behaved like a beast that evening. Damn me.'

I went to Poona a few months later on business. When I called at Saeeda Cottage, Chadda was out. Gharib Nawaz was playing with Shireen's son. We shook hands. I learnt from him that Chadda hadn't spoken to Mummy after that night, nor had she visited Saeeda Cottage.

She had sent Phyllis back to her parents. It turned out that she had run away from home with that young fellow. Ranjeet Kumar—who had just walked in—was confident that had Phyllis stayed on, he would have scored. Gharib Nawaz had no such illusions, but he was sorry she was gone.

They said Chadda had not been well for some time, but refused to see a doctor. As we were talking, Venkutrey rushed in. He looked very nervous. He had met Chadda on the street, found him feeling groggy and put him in a tonga to get him home, but Chadda had fainted on the way. We ran out. Chadda lay in the tonga looking very ill. We brought him in. He was unconscious.

I told Gharib Nawaz to get a doctor. He consulted Venkutrey and left. They returned a little later with Mummy. 'What has happened to my son?' she asked. 'What kind of friends are you? Why didn't you send me word?' she said.

She immediately took charge. 'Get hold of some ice and rub his forehead. Massage his feet. Fan his face.' Then she went out to get a doctor. Everyone looked relieved, as if the entire responsibility of bringing Chadda back to health was now Mummy's.

Chadda had begun to regain consciousness when Mummy

returned with the doctor. The doctor examined him, then took Mummy aside. She told us there was no cause for worry. Chadda was still a bit disoriented. He saw Mummy. He took her hand in his and said, 'Mummy, you are great.'

She ran her hand gently over Chadda's burning face. 'My son, my poor son,' she said.

Tears came to Chadda's eyes. 'Don't say that. Your son is a scoundrel of the first order. Go get your husband's old service revolver and shoot him.'

'Don't talk rubbish,' she said. She rose. 'Boys, Chadda is very ill. I'm going to take him to the hospital.'

Gharib Nawaz sent for a taxi. Chadda could not understand why he was being taken to hospital, but Mummy told him that he would be more comfortable there than at home. 'It's nothing,' she said.

He was laid up for many days, with Mummy spending most of her time with him. However, he did not seem to be getting better. His skin had become sallow and he was losing strength. The doctors were of the view that he should be taken to Bombay, but Mummy said, 'No, I'm going to take him home and he's going to get well.'

I had to leave Poona, but I phoned from Bombay every other day. I had started to lose hope, but slowly, very slowly, Chadda began to come round. I had to go to Lahore for a few weeks. When I returned to Bombay there was a letter from Chadda. 'The great Mummy has reclaimed her unworthy son from the dead,' he had written. There was so much love in that line. When I told my wife, she observed icily, 'Such women are generally good at these things.'

I wrote to Chadda a few times, but he didn't answer. Later,

somebody told me that Mummy had sent him to the hills to stay with friends. He was soon better—and bored—and returned to Poona. I was there that day.

He looked weak, but nothing else had changed. He talked about his illness as if he had had a minor bicycle accident. Saeeda Cottage had seen a few changes in his absence. A Bengali music director called Sen had moved in. He shared his room with Ram Singh, a young boy from Lahore who had come to Bombay, like so many others, to get into films.

Ranjeet Kumar had been picked up to play the lead in a movie. He had been promised the direction of the next one, provided the one under production did well. Chadda had finally managed to raise an advance of one thousand five hundred rupees from the studio. Gharib Nawaz had just come back from Hyderabad and the general finances of Saeeda Cottage were in good shape as a result of that. Shireen's boy had new clothes and new toys.

My friend Harish was currently trying to seduce his new leading lady, who was from Punjab. He was, however, afraid of her husband, who had a formidable moustache and looked like a wrestler. Chadda's advice to Harish had been sound: 'Don't worry about him at all. He may be a wrestler, but in the field of love he is bound to fall flat on his face. All you need to learn are a few heavyweight Punjabi swear words from me. I'll settle for one hundred rupees per lesson. You'll need them in awkward situations.'

Harish had struck a deal and, at the rate of a bottle of rum per choice Punjabi swear word, had learnt half a dozen of them. However, there had been no occasion to test his new powers. His affair was doing well without them.

Mummy's parties had been reconvened and the old crowd—

Polly, Dolly, Elma, Thelma etc.——was back. Venkutrey had still
not given up his efforts to induct Thelma into the mysteries of
Indian classical dance. Gharib Nawaz was still lending money
and Ranjeet Kumar, who was about to hit the big screen, was
using his new position to ingratiate himself with the girls.
Chadda's dirty limericks were still flowing.

There was only one thing missing——the girl with the platinum
blonde hair, the colour of snake scales and blue steel and silver.
Chadda never mentioned her. Occasionally, one would see him
looking at Mummy, then lowering his eyes, recalling the events
of that night. Off and on, after his fourth drink, he would say,
'Chadda, you are a damned brute.'

Mummy was still the Mummy——Polly's Mummy, Dolly's
Mummy, Chadda's Mummy, Ranjeet Kumar's Mummy——still the
wonderful manageress of her unique establishment. Her make-
up was still flashy, and her clothes even flashier. Her wrinkles
still showed, but for me they had come to assume a sacred
dimension.

It was Mummy who had come to the rescue of Venkutrey's
wife when she had had a miscarriage. She had taken charge of
Thelma when she had caught a dangerous infection from a dance
director who had promised to put her in the movies. Recently,
Kitty had won five hundred rupees in a crossword puzzle
competition and Mummy had persuaded her to give some of it
to Gharib Nawaz, who was a bit short. 'Give it to him now and
you can keep taking it back,' she had advised her.

There was only one man she didn't like: the music director
Sen. She had told Chadda repeatedly, 'Don't bring him to my
house. There is something about him that makes me uneasy. He
doesn't fit.'

I returned to Bombay carrying with me the warmth of Mummy's parties. Her world was simple and beautiful and reassuring. Yes, there was drinking and sex and a general lack of seriousness, but one felt no emotional unease. It was like the protruding belly of a pregnant woman: a bit odd, but perfectly innocent and immediately comprehensible.

One day I read in the papers that the music director Sen had been found murdered in Saeeda Cottage. The suspect was said to be a young man named Ram Singh.

Chadda wrote me an account of the incident later.

'I was sound asleep that night. Suddenly, I felt someone slump into my bed. It was Sen. He was covered in blood. Then Ram Singh rushed into the room holding a knife. By this time, everyone was up. Ranjeet Kumar and Gharib Nawaz ran in and disarmed Ram Singh. Sen's breathing grew uneven and then stopped. "Is he dead?" Ram Singh asked. I nodded my head. "Please let go of me. I won't run away," he said calmly.

'We didn't know what to do, so we immediately sent for Mummy. She took stock of the situation in her unruffled manner and escorted Ram Singh to the police, where he made a statement confessing to the killing. The next few weeks were awful. Police, courts, lawyers, the works. There was a trial and the court acquitted Ram Singh.

'He had made the same statement under oath that he had made to the police. Mummy had said to him, "Son, speak the truth. Tell them what happened." Ram Singh had spoken the truth. He had told the court that Sen had promised to get him to sing for films, provided he would sleep with him. He had let himself be persuaded, but was always troubled by what he was doing. One day he had told Sen that if he tried to force him to perform the unnatural act again, he would kill him. And that was exactly what had happened that night. Sen had tried to force him and Ram Singh had stabbed him repeatedly with a kitchen knife.'

Chadda had written, 'In this age of untruth, the triumph of truth is astonishing.'

A party had been organized to celebrate Ram Singh's acquittal and when it was over Mummy had suggested that he should return to his parents in Lahore. Gharib Nawaz had bought him a ticket and Shireen had prepared food for him to take on the long journey. Everyone had gone to the station to see him off.

A week or so after this, I was asked by the studio to come to Poona to complete an assignment. Nothing had changed at Saeeda Cottage. It was still the way it always was. When I arrived, a minor party was in progress to celebrate the birth of another son to Shireen. Venkutrey had got hold of two tins of Glaxo baby food from somewhere, not an easy thing at the time. Suggestions were also being invited on a name for the child.

Everybody was trying to look cheerful, but I couldn't help feeling that there was something the matter with Chadda, Gharib Nawaz and Ranjeet Kumar. A vague sadness hung in the air. Was it the weather which was beginning to turn chilly or was it Sen's murder? I could not decide.

For one week I was shut up in Harish's house because I was in a hurry to complete my assignment. I was a bit surprised that Chadda hadn't come to see me all this time, nor Gharib Nawaz for that matter.

Then one afternoon Chadda burst into the house. 'This rubbish you've been writing, have you been paid something for it yet?' he asked. I told him I had received two thousand rupees only the other day and the money was in my jacket. He took out four hundred rupees and rushed out, pausing just long enough to tell me that there was a party at Mummy's house that evening and I was expected.

When I arrived, it was already in full swing. Ranjeet and Venkutrey were dancing with Polly and Thelma. Kitty was dancing with Elma, and Chadda was jumping around like a rabbit with Mummy in his arms. Everyone was quite drunk. My entrance was greeted with guffaws and slogans. Mummy, who had always maintained a certain formality with me, took hold of my hand and said, 'Kiss me, dear.'

'That's enough dancing,' Chadda announced above the din. 'I want to do some serious drinking now. Open a new bottle, my Prince of Scotland.' The prince, who was very drunk, appeared with a bottle and dropped it on the floor. 'It is only a bottle, Mummy. What about broken hearts?' Chadda said before she could scold the servant.

A chill fell over the party. A new bottle was duly produced. Chadda poured everyone a huge drink. Then he began to make a speech: 'Ladies and gentlemen, we have among us this evening this man called Manto. He thinks he's great story writer, but I think that's rubbish. He claims that he can fathom the depths of the human soul. That too is a lot of rubbish. This world is full of rubbish. I met someone yesterday after ten years and he assured me that we had met only the other week. That too is rubbish. That man was from Hyderabad. I pronounce a million curses on the Nizam of Hyderabad who has tons of gold but no Mummy.'

Someone shouted, 'Manto zindabad,' but Chadda continued with his speech. 'This is a conspiracy hatched by Manto, otherwise my instructions were clear. We should have greeted him with catcalls. I have been betrayed. But let me talk of that evening when I behaved like a beast with Mummy because of that girl with hair the colour of snake scales. Who did I think I was? Don Juan?

'Be that as it may, but it could have been done. With one kiss, I could have sucked in all her virginity with these big fat lips of mine. She was very young, very weak . . . what's the word, Manto? . . . yes, very unformed. After a night of love, she would either have carried the guilt with her the rest of her life, or she would have completely forgotten about it the next morning.

'I am glad Mummy threw me out that night. Ladies and gentlemen, now I end my speech. I've already talked lot of rubbish. Actually, I was planning a longer speech, but I can't speak any longer. I'm going to get myself a drink.'

Nobody spoke. It occurred to me that he had been heard in complete silence. Mummy also looked a bit lost. Chadda sat there nursing his drink. He was quiet. His speech seemed to have drained him out. 'What's with you?' I asked.

'I don't know—tonight the whisky is not battering in the buttocks of my brain as it always does,' he answered philosophically.

The clock struck two. Chadda, who in the meanwhile had begun a dance with Kitty, pushed her aside and said to Venkutrey, 'Sing us something, but I warn you, none of your classical mumbo-jumbo.'

Venkutrey sang a couple of songs, set to the melancholy evening raga Malkauns. The atmosphere grew even sadder. Gharib Nawaz was so moved that his eyes became wet. 'These Hyderabadis have weak eye-bladders. You never know when they might start dripping,' Chadda observed.

Gharib Nawaz wiped his eyes and took Elma on to the floor. Venkutrey put a record on. Chadda picked up Mummy and began to bounce around.

At four o'clock, Chadda suddenly said, 'That's it.' He picked up a bottle from the table, put it to his mouth and drank what was left of it. 'Let's go, Manto.'

When I tried to say goodbye to Mummy, he pulled me away. 'There are going to be no goodbyes tonight.'

When we were outside, I thought I heard Venkutrey crying. I wanted to go back, but Chadda stopped me. 'He too has a faulty eye-bladder.'

Saeeda Cottage was only a few minutes' walk. We did not speak. Before going to bed, I tried to ask Chadda about the strange party, but he said he was sleepy.

When I got up the next morning, I found Gharib Nawaz standing outside the garage wiping his eyes.

'What's the matter?' I asked him.

'Mummy's gone.'

'Where?'

'I don't know.'

Chadda was still in bed, but it seemed he hadn't slept at all. He smiled when I asked him if it was true. 'Yes, she's gone. Had to leave Poona by the morning train.'

'But why?' I asked.

'Because the authorities did not approve of her ways. Her parties were considered objectionable, outside the limits of the law. The police tried to blackmail her. They offered to leave her alone if she would do their dirty work for them. They wanted to use her as a procuress, an agent. She refused. Then they dug up an old case they had registered against her. They had her charged with moral turpitude and running a house of ill repute and they obtained court orders expelling her from Poona.

'If she was a procuress, a madam, and her presence was bad for society's health, then she should have been done away with altogether. Why, if she was a heap of filth, was she removed from Poona and ordered to be dumped elsewhere?'

He laughed bitterly. 'Manto, with her a purity has vanished from our lives. Do you remember that awful night? She cleansed me of my lust and meanness. I am sorry she's gone, but I shouldn't be sorry. She has only left Poona. She will go elsewhere and meet more young men like me and she will cleanse their souls and make them whole. I hereby bestow my Mummy on them.

'Now, let's go and look for Gharib Nawaz. He must have cried himself hoarse. As I told you, these Hyderabadis have weak eye-bladders. You never know when they might start dripping.'

I looked at Chadda. Tears were floating in his eyes like corpses in a river.

# The Patch

WHEN A SUPPURATED BOIL APPEARED ON GOPAL'S THIGH, HE WAS terrified.

It was summer and mangoes were in season and plentiful: in bazaars, streets, shops and even with street vendors. Wherever you looked, you saw mangoes. They came in all colours: red, yellow, green, multi-hued. Heaps upon heaps of them—and in all varieties—were on sale in the fruit and vegetable market at throwaway prices. The shortage experienced a year earlier had been more than made up for.

Outside the school, Gopal had had his fill of them at fruitseller Chootu Ram's stand. All the money he had saved during the month he had spent on those mangoes, saturated as they were with juice and honey. After school closed that day, Gopal, the taste of mangoes still in his mouth, had decided to stop by at Ganda Ram, the sweetmeat seller's, for a glass of buttermilk. He had asked him to prepare the drink but the man had refused, saying, 'Babu Gopal, settle the old account first and you can have fresh credit, not otherwise.'

Had Gopal not gorged himself on mangoes or had he had any money on him, he would have settled Ganda Ram's account there and then. He would then have paid for his glass of buttermilk which had in fact been prepared by Ganda Ram, and a piece of ice could be seen floating about in it. This sweetmeat seller had made a face and put the glass behind his back on a round iron dish. There was little Gopal could do and then, on the fourth day precisely, this big boil had appeared on his thigh. It had kept growing for the next three to four days. This had made Gopal very nervous, not quite knowing what to do. The boil itself did not bother him as much as the pain it was beginning to cause. What made things worse was that with each passing day the boil was getting redder and redder and some of the skin that covered it had begun to come off. At times Gopal felt as if under all that red there was a pot on the boil and whatever was in it wanted to burst out all in one go. So big had it become that once he felt as if one of his glass marbles had jumped out of his pocket and ledged itself in his thigh.

Gopal said nothing about the boil to anyone at home. He knew that if his father found out, all the anger that he felt over his fly-infested police station would be taken out on him. It was also possible that he might thrash him with the stick that the lawyer Girdhari Lal's assistant had brought for him from Wazirabad the other day. His mother was no less hot-tempered. Had she chosen not to punish him for eating all those mangoes, she would have boxed his ears red for having wolfed down all those mangoes all by himself. The principle his mother had laid down was, 'Gopal, even if it is poison that you want to take, you should do so at home.' Gopal knew what was behind this: her wish to sample the same delights that Gopal was enjoying.

Be that as it may, the fact was that this boil was destined to appear on Gopal's thigh and it had done so. As far as Gopal could work it out, it was the mangoes he had eaten that had caused this boil to appear. He had made no mention of it to anyone at home, because he still remembered the dressing-down he had got from his father, Lala Prashotam Das, police inspector, as he sat under the big municipal tap wearing only a loincloth, with the water gushing over his bald head and his big belly jutting forth. He was sucking mango after mango through the filter of his moustache. A dozen mangoes lay in front of him in a pail that he had taken from a street fruitseller in return for tearing up the ticket he had earlier given him. Gopal was rubbing his father's back, peeling away layers of dirt from it. When he had dipped a clean hand into the pail to quietly pull out a mango, Lalaji had prised the tiny fruit from his hand and put it in his mouth, along with his moustache, and said, 'How shameless! When will you learn to be respectful of your elders?'

And when with a weepy face Gopal had replied, 'Father, I too want to eat mangoes,' the Inspector sahib, chucking away the stone in an open drain that ran in the street, said, 'Gopu mangoes are just too hot for you, but if you want boils and carbuncles, then you are most welcome to them. Let it rain three or four times and then you can eat them to your heart's content. I will ask your mother to make you some buttermilk. Now get back to rubbing my back.' Gopal, having run into this roadblock, quietly resumed his assigned chore. The very thought of the mango's sour taste had made his mouth water and he kept swallowing it for a long time.

The very next day he gorged himself on those mangoes and four days later a boil appeared on his thigh. What his father had said had come true. Now, had Gopal mentioned his boil to anyone at home, he would have received a good beating, which was why he had kept quiet, while all the time thinking of some way of stopping the boil from growing any further.

One day on returning home from the police station, his father called out Gopal's mother and announced, as he handed her a packet, 'This Bombay balm is something of great value, one remedy that equals a hundred remedies. This is the time of year when boils and carbuncles are common, so all you need to be rid of them is just one single application. That's all. This is something special from Bombay, so tuck it away somewhere safe.'

Gopal was playing cricket in the courtyard with his sister, Nirmala. It just happened that, when the Inspector sahib was busy explaining to his wife something about the balm he had given her, Nirmala lobbed the ball towards him and since Gopal was trying to listen to his father the ball hit him precisely on the spot where his boil was. The pain was excruciating but he said not a word as he was used to bear pain in silence. He had become used to being caned at school by his teacher, Hari Ram. Pain was nothing new to him. Just as the ball landed on his boil, he heard his father say, 'Just apply a little balm on the boil and all will be well in a jiffy. Like this!' As he snapped his fingers, something clicked in Gopal's mind. Now he knew how to be rid of his pain.

His mother placed the balm in her sewing basket, where Gopal knew she kept all things she considered vauable. The most carefully guarded thing in that basket was a pair of tweezers, which she used every ten or fifteen days to pull out hair over her forehead to make it appear broader than it was. The white ash she used to apply afterwards at the spots from where she had pulled out the hair was also kept in this basket. However, to be absolutely certain, Gopal lobbed the ball under the bed and while retrieving it made sure that the balm had been duly placed in the sewing basket.

In the afternoon, with Nirmala in tow, he went to the rooftop, where sacks of coal used to be stored under a rain shelter, duly armed with the small pair of scissors with which his father used to clip his nails, the balm and a bit of cotton cloth that his mother has saved to finish the sewing of his father's loose pyjamas. They sat down on the floor next to the sacks of coal. Nirmala produced the piece of cotton and spread it out on her thigh, over the sleek, silken surface of her shalwar. When Gopal looked at her with his dancing eyes, it seemed as if this eleven-year-old girl, who was lissome as a reed growing on a river bank, was readying herself for a great task. Her little heart, which used to beat in fear of her parents' admonitions and her dolls getting soiled, was now all aflutter with the thought that she was about to view the boil on her brother's thigh. Her ear lobes had gone red and they felt warm.

Gopal, who had not whispered a word about his boil to anyone, had told her his secret and how he had eaten all those mangoes without letting anyone know, how he had not been able to drink any buttermilk after and how this boil as big as a coin had appeared on his thigh. After he had told her his story, he said to her in a confidential voice, 'Look, Nirmala, no one at home is to know this.' A serious look appeared on Nirmala's face. 'I am not mad that I should.' Gopal, being sure that Nirmala would keep the confidence, rolled up his trouser over one leg and showed her the boil, which she touched lightly with her finger, keeping herself at as much distance as she could. She trembled involuntarily, made a whistling noise, looked at the quite red boil and said, 'How red it is!' 'It is going to get even redder,' Gopal bragged with manly courage. 'Really?' Nirmala exclaimed with astonishment. 'This is nothing, the boil I saw on Charanji was much bigger and redder than this,' Gopal replied, while running two of his fingers across the boil. 'So, is it going to grow in size?' Nirmala asked, slipping closer. 'Who knows, it's still growing,' Gopal answered, pulling out the balm from his pocket. Nirmala was scared. 'Will this balm make it right?' Gopal uncovered the balm by peeling away the paper that covered it and shook his head affirmatively. 'One application and it will burst open.' 'Burst open!' Nirmala felt as if a balloon had just popped next to her ear. Her heart was beating fast. 'And whatever is in there will gush out,' Gopal said, dabbing his finger with balm.

Nirmala's pink complexion by now was pale like the Bombay balm. With her heart in her mouth, she asked, 'But why do these boils spring up, brother?' 'By eating things with hot properties,' Gopal replied like an expert physician. Nirmala remembered the two eggs she had eaten two months ago. She began to think. They talked some more and then they got down to the business at hand. With great delicacy, Nirmala cut a round patch of cloth, which was faultless. It was round like the round roti her mother baked every day. Gopal applied some balm on the round patch, spread it out and examined his boil with great care. Nirmala, bent over Gopal, was watching everything he was doing with great interest. When Gopal placed the patch on his boil, she trembled as if someone had put a piece of ice on her body. 'Will it get all right now?' Nirmala asked, but half-questioningly. Gopal had not yet answered her when they heard steps, which were their mother's who was coming up to pick up some coal. Gopal and Nirmala looked at each other at the same time and, without saying a word, hid everything under the box in which their cat Sundri used to give birth to her kittens. Then without a word, they slunk away.

When Gopal ran down the stairs, his father sent him out on a buying errand. When he returned, he ran into Nirmala on the street. He handed over the cold, sweet drink he had brought for his father to her and went over to Charanji's house. In the process, he forgot to put back the things he and Nirmala had hidden under that box when they had heard their mother walking up. He was at Charanji's quite long, playing cards. After they had had their fill, the two left the room, hand in hand. Something that made Charanji laugh highlighted an old mark on his left cheek, which reminded Gopal of his boil and the things he had hidden under the box. Wresting himself free, he ran towards home.

He studied the situation. His mother was sitting in the courtyard, while his father read out the day's news from the newspaper *Milap*. They were both laughing over something. Gopal went past them and, though they looked at him, they did not say anything. This reassured Gopal that his mother had not taken a look at her sewing basket yet. Quietly, he walked upstairs to the rooftop. He was about to step out on it when something he saw made him stop.

Nirmala was sitting next to the box. Gopal stepped back so that he could see without being seen what was up. With great concentration, Nirmala, her long, thin fingers delicately working the scissors they held, was cutting a piece of cloth into a round patch. After she was done, she applied a little balm on it, then bending her neck, she unbuttoned her shirt to uncover a protrusion on the right side of her chest, which resembled a half bubble in a faucet.

Nirmala blew on the patch and placed it on that slight protrusion.

# The Blouse

FOR SOME DAYS PAST, MOMIN HAD BEEN FEELING VERY RESTLESS. HIS ENTIRE body was like a boil about to erupt. A strange pain had taken hold of him, whether he was working, talking or even thinking. Had he tried to explain what he felt, he would not have been able to do that. He would suddenly jump up and faint; silent thoughts which normally rise in the mind like bubbles and disappear as quickly would come thundering down to him only to explode noisily. On the delicate membranes of his heart and brain, he would feel thorn-footed ants crawling all the time. He had developed a strange and painful stiffness in his limbs. Sometimes the pain would become unbearable, and he would feel like asking someone to throw him in a big cauldron and beat him down with heavy blows.

In the kitchen, when spices were being pounded in a deep mortar with a metal-tipped pestle, the impact produced would bounce back from ceiling to the floor and it would feel good to Momin's bare feet. The sensation would travel to his stiff legs, and go right through his thighs to his heart, which would begin to throb like the flame of a clay lamp in the wind.

Momin was fifteen, going on sixteen, but he wasn't really sure about his age. He was a strong and healthy boy whose boyhood was racing towards youth, a race of which Momin was utterly unaware, but every drop of his blood was affected by this. Sometimes, he would try to work it all out but without success.

Several changes were taking place in his body. His neck had thickened and the muscles of his arms felt taut. His voice was breaking and there was an extra layer of fat on his chest. For some days now, his nipples had felt swollen and when he touched them they were painful. Sometimes, while at work, he would touch his nipples without wanting to, and his body would shudder. Even the thick and rough cloth of his shirt caused him pain when it touched those sensitive spots.

At times, while washing himself in the bathroom or when he was alone in the kitchen, he would unbutton his shirt and look at his marble-like nipples and rub them, producing sharp darts of pain. His body would shake like a fruit-laden tree. But he would continue with that pain-generating exercise. When pressed harder, his nipples would flatten out and exude a sticky discharge. On such occasions, his face would redden up to the lobes of his ears and he would feel that he had committed a sin.

Momin's knowledge of sin and virtue was extremely limited. Anything that a person could not do in front of others was a sin in his view. He would quickly button up his shirt and promise himself never to do such a bad thing again. However, every second or third day, when alone, he would engage in the same old game. The family he worked for was pleased with him. He was a hard-working boy who would do what was assigned to him at the appointed time. He would provide no opportunity for anyone to complain. He had worked at the Deputy sahib's house for only three months but, in this brief period, he had impressed every member of the family with his natural industry. He had been hired as domestic help at six rupees a month but had earned a raise of two rupees in the second month of service, something that had made him very happy because he knew that he was being appreciated. However, for the last several days, he had been restless. He felt like walking about the bazaars all day without any purpose, or go to some lonely spot and lie down.

Although his heart was no longer in his work and he felt listless, by nature he was not lazy, which was why no one in the house was aware of his troubled mental state. There was Razia, who spent her entire day playing the harmonium, learning the latest movie tunes and reading magazines. She had never bothered Momin. Shakeela, however, would use Momin to do her odd jobs and even scold him sometimes. For the last several days, she had been busy copying different blouse designs, having borrowed a number of blouses from a friend who was fond of wearing new-fangled clothes. Shakeela had borrowed eight of her friend's blouses and was busy making notes so that she could replicate them. That was why for the last several days she had paid no attention to Momin.

The Deputy sahib's wife was not a harsh woman. There were two servants in the house besides Momin, and an old woman who mostly worked in the kitchen. Momin would help her off and on. If the Deputy sahib's wife had noticed some slackening in Momin's work, she had not mentioned it. In any case, she could not possibly be aware of the storm blowing across Momin's heart and mind because she did not have a son. She was therefore unable to understand the physical and mental changes which Momin was undergoing. And then Momin was only a house boy. Who cares about servants anyway! They pass from childhood to old age without those around them even noticing it.

This was also Momin's situation. In the last few days, he had taken a turn on the road of life that had put him on a course which, though not long, was extremely hazardous. Sometimes, he would take quick steps; at other times, he would slow down. He did not really know how to walk the stretch where life had brought him. Should he hurry or should be take his time while negotiating this road? Under Momin's bare feet lay the round, slippery pebbles of adolescence, which made it hard for him to keep his balance. This was why he felt so restless. Sometimes, while at work, he would grab hold of a hook in the wall with both hands and use it to lift himself from the ground. At such times, he would wish someone would pull him down by his legs and keep stretching them till his legs turned into a fine wire. All these thoughts came to life in a corner of his brain, though he did not fully understand them.

Subconsciously, he wanted something to happen, but what? The fact was that he just wanted whatever was to happen to happen. Dishes stacked on the table should start jumping up and down; the kettle should come to a boil in one go and its lid should fly away; a little pressure on the water faucet should bend it like a pin causing it to expel a fountain; or his body should stretch so much that every joint should come apart and relax. Or something should happen that had not happened before. Momin was one restless boy.

Razia was busy learning new tunes and Shakeela was busy with her blouse designs. When she was done, she picked out the one that had pleased her most and began to cut one from a length of azure satin. It also made Razia leave her harmonium and songbook to find out what her sister was up to. Shakeela did everything with great aplomb and care. When sewing, she would seat herself in a calm, comfortable position, not like her younger sister Razia, who was always rushing about. Shakeela sewed every stitch diligently to rule out mistakes. The measurements she took were precise. She would first make a paper cutout of the design and then cut the cloth accordingly. Time consuming though it all was, the end product was an exact copy.

Shakeela was a well-built girl. Her hands were well padded and at the base of each long finger was a tiny dimple. When she worked her sewing machine, these dimples would appear and disappear in quick succession. She would work the machine calmly turning the handle with her long, shapely hand. She would bend her wrist slightly and put her neck at an angle, while a lock of her hair that seemed to have no place to go would come hanging down. So busy would Shakeela be with her work that she would make no attempt to shake it back. When she was ready to cut the azure length of satin for the blouse, she realized that she needed a measuring tape. Their old tape had been used so long that it had fallen to pieces. There was a measuring rod but it was useless for measuring her waist and chest. She had her old blouses of course, but as she had put on a little weight since, she wanted everything remeasured.

She took off her shirt and shouted for Momin. When he came into the room, she told him to run out and borrow a measuring tape from flat No. 6. 'Tell them it is Shakeela bibi who needs it.' Momin's eyes rested on Shakeela's white vest. He had seen her in a vest many times in the past but today he felt a certain hesitation in looking at her, and turned his eyes away. Then he asked nervously, 'Bibiji, what kind of tape?' 'A tape to measure cloth . . . the measuring rod is lying right here in front of you. It is made of steel; but what is needed is a soft tape. Now run and get it from No. 6. Tell them Shakeela bibi needs it.'

Flat No. 6 lay close and Momin was back in no time with the tape, which Shakeela took from him and said, 'Just stay here so that you can return it.' Then she spoke to her sister Razia, 'If you keep anything you have borrowed from these people, that old woman can't stop bugging you for its return . . . Come here now, take this tape and measure me.' Razia began to measure Shakeela's waist and chest as the two talked, with Momin standing by the door listening to them. 'Razia, why don't you tighten it a bit . . . that's what happened last time when you measured me and the blouse turned out to be all wrong. If the fit on the top is not precise, the bits under the armpits begin to hang down.' Razia said, 'Where should I measure you and where should I not? You confuse me. I had begun to take a measurement here and you said I should move lower. The thing is if the finished product is a bit loose, that won't exactly be a calamity.' 'Why, the beauty of good clothing is that it should fit. Look at Surayya. What a tight fit her clothes are, nothing loose anywhere, even if you look for it! Now measure me.' After saying this, Shakeela took a deep breath to expand her chest and held it there. 'Get it now,' she said in a strangled voice. When Shakeela exhaled, Momin felt as if several balloons had exploded in his chest. Nervously he said, 'Give me the measuring tape bibiji and I will return it.' 'Just wait,' Shakeela said sternly.

As she spoke, the tape measure got wrapped around her arm and, when she tried to get rid of it, Momin saw a bunch of black hair under her fair armpit. Similar hair had begun to sprout in Momin's own armpits, but he liked the bunch he had glimpsed. His body felt electrified. He wanted that the bunch of hair he had seen should turn into a moustache and grow on him. As a child, he used to pretend that he had a blond or black moustache with hair you find on a corn cob. When he placed that hair over his upper lip, he would tremble slightly, which was what was happening now to his upper lip and nose. Shakeela had lowered her arm now and her armpit could no longer be seen, but he could not banish from his mind's eye the image of that bunch of black hair he had seen in her armpit.

After a few minutes, Shakeela handed over the tape measure to Momin, saying, 'Go, return it and say thank you very much.' After returning the tape, Momin came back and sat down in the courtyard. Vague thoughts had begun to rise in his head and for a long time he tried to understand them, but he failed. He then opened his small trunk in which he kept the new clothes he was going to wear for Id. When he lifted the lid, and the smell of his unworn cotton clothes hit his nose, he felt an urge to wash himself thoroughly, put on those new clothes and go straight to Shakeela bibi to say, 'Salam bibiji.' His new cotton shalwar would produce a rustling noise and his Rumi cap would . . .

As he thought of his cap, its black tassle at the top turned into the bunch of black hair that he had seen in Shakeela bibi's armpit. He pulled out his Rumi cap and began to run his hand over its soft, black silken tassle. Then he heard Shakeela bibi call, 'Momin!' He returned the cap to the trunk, closed the lid and went into the room where Shakeela had already cut several pieces of soft, slippery azure satin, which lay in a corner. 'I called you several times, had you gone to sleep?' she asked. Momin stuttered, 'No, bibiji.' 'So what were you doing?' 'What . . . nothing at all.' 'You must have been doing something,' Shakeela was firing all these questions at him but what was really on her mind was the blouse in which she had put temporary stitches. 'I was looking at my new clothes in my trunk,' Momin said, laughing bashfully. Shakeela burst out laughing too, as did Razia.

Shakeela's laughter gave Momin a strange sense of satisfaction

and he felt an urge to do something silly which should make
Shakeela laugh even more. Lisping like a girl, he said shyly, 'And
I will take some money from the elder Bibiji and buy myself a
silk handkerchief.' 'And what will you do with that handkerchief?'
Shakeela asked, still laughing. Momin replied awkwardly, 'I will
tie it around my neck, bibiji . . . it will feel good.' Both Shakeela
and Razia began to laugh at his reply. 'If you tie it around your
neck, I will hang you with it,' Shakeela said, trying to control
her laughter. 'The wretch has made me forget why I had called
him Razia,' Shakeela said.

Razia did not answer and began to hum a new popular song
that she had learnt two days earlier. Meanwhile, Shakeela
remembered why she had called Momin. 'Look Momin, I will
take off my vest, which I want you to take to that new store
next to the pharmacy and ask them what six such vests would
cost. You remember you went with me there that day. Ask them
for a discounted price. Understand!'

'Yes,' Momin answered.

'Go, be on your way now.'

Momin came out of the room and stood behind the half-
open door. In a few moments the vest landed at his feet, followed
by Shakeela's voice, 'Tell them this is exactly what we need.
There should be no dissimilarity.'

Momin picked up the vest, which was slightly damp because
of perspiration, as if somebody had placed it over a steaming
pot and then removed it quickly. The lingering body odour in
the garment and its sweet warmth felt good to Momin. Rubbing
the undershirt, which was soft like a kitten, between his hands,
he went to the bazar, found out the price and by the time he
came back Shakeela had begun stitching the azure satin blouse,

which was brighter and softer than the tassle on Momin's cap.

This blouse was probably being readied for Id, which was coming up. Momin was now being summoned several times a day, to get thread, to fetch the iron, to pick up a new needle because the one in use had snapped. In the evening, when Shakeela was done for the day, she asked Momin to pick up the loose bits of thread and satin trimmings which could be put to no further use. Momin swept the place up nicely and threw out the waste, but the shiny satin trimmings he put in his pocket, without quite knowing what he would do with them.

The next day, he pulled out the trimmings from his pocket, found a bit of privacy and began to dethread them. He spent a lot of time doing that and finally he had a tiny ball of thread in his hand, which he kept rubbing and pressing, while thinking of Shakeela's armpit and the bunch of black hair he had caught a glimpse of. The other trimmings he put back in his pocket. That day too, Shakeela called out to him a number of times. He watched the azure blouse through its various stages of production, from being cut to being stitched. These images kept popping up before his eyes, from the point where temporary white stitches were threaded through it to its being ironed to smooth out the wrinkles and make it appear even shinier to Shakeela putting it on and showing it to Razia, then standing in front of the dressing table and examining herself from every angle. When she was fully satisfied, she took it off and made what adjustments were necessary, so that it would fit perfectly. She tried it one more time before she began to apply the final stitches.

While the blouse was being readied, the stitches in Momin's brain were coming undone. When summoned to the room, his eyes wouldn't leave the shiny garment, wanting all the time to touch it, and not merely that, but to keep caressing its silken smooth texture with his rough hand. He knew from the satin trimmings in his pocket how smooth the blouse was. The tiny ball of thread he had made was even smoother with its rubber-like elasticity. Whenever he walked into the room and looked at the blouse, his mind would race back to the sight of the black hair he had seen in Shakeela's armpit. Momin wondered if it was as smooth as satin.

The blouse was ready at last. Momin was cleaning the floor with a wet rag, when Shakeela came into the room and took off her shirt, throwing it on the bed. She was wearing the white vest that Momin had been sent out to find the price of. She stood in front of the mirror and put on her new blouse. While continuing to clean the floor, Momin looked up at the mirror. The blouse had come to life and at one or two places it was stretched so tight as to have lost colour. Shakeela's back was turned owards Momin and he could see the deep cleft of her spine. He could not help himself and said, 'Bibiji, you have excelled even master tailors.' Shakeela was pleased by the praise, but she was restless because she wanted to know what Razia thought of her handiwork, so all she said to him was, 'Good, isn't it!' and ran out of the room. Momin kept staring at the mirror where he could still see an image of the shimmering blouse.

At night, when he went to the stitching room to place a pitcher of water there, he saw the blouse hanging there by a hook. There was no one in the room, so he stepped forward, looked at it carefully and then, apprehensively, ran his hand over it, which made him feel as if someone was caressing his entire body with

an exceedingly light and airy touch. When he went to bed that
night, he had many meaningless dreams. There was the Deputy
sahib who, standing in front of a heap of coal, was asking him to
break the larger pieces into smaller ones. When Momin picked
up a piece, put it on the ground and hit it with a hammer, it
turned first into a ball of fine black hair and then into a ball of
spun black sugar, which rose to the sky to break up into several
balloons. High up, very high up, the balloons burst. At that point,
a violent wind rose. Momin dreamt that he had lost the black
tassle on top of his Rumi cap, so he began to look for it, going
from place to place, some known, some utterly strange to him.
He could smell something that he identified as fresh white cotton
cloth. Next he found himself clutching a black satin blouse in
his hand. He could also feel a throbbing object that lay under his
hand. He woke up with a start and for a few minutes he could
not understand what had happened. A spasm of fear, surprise
and sweet pain shook his body. It was a most strange feeling.
First he felt a painful warmth come over him, which was replaced
after a few moments by a cool wave that crawled all over his
body.

# On the Balcony

SHE COMES TO THE BALCONY, WEARING A WHITE, SEQUINED SARI THAT seems to set off silver-hued fireworks. The sequins embedded in the undulating silken fabric of the garment shimmer and my entire body feels titillated. For quite some time now, she has been my titillation.

I have seen her nearly two hundred times and each one of those images is engraved in my mind. Once I saw her chasing a butterfly in her courtyard. She flashed past my eyes only once. Whenever I think of that incident, it feels as if a bird is fluttering in my heart, which might fly away suddenly out of fear. One day, I saw her standing on the balcony in the sun, shaking her wet hair dry. When I try to summon that image, I see it sometimes in dark outline; other times it appears brightly lit.

I have seen her so many times that I can summon her whenever I wish, even without appearing before her. At first, I found this exercise difficult but that is no longer true. Only last evening, while I was sitting at a friend's place, I felt a sudden desire to see her. Without even closing my eyes, I had her standing in front of me. She looked exactly as she normally does. Neither my friend nor his sister, who was sitting in a chair in front of me, could guess anything. For a moment, I pulled her out of the tiny box in my mind where I keep her and then put her back immediately so that no one should know what I had done. I kept talking to them while I looked at her, and not for a minute did my mind wander. And what was I saying? 'Yes, dried fish smells. God knows how people eat it! My nose can't . . .' And for a long time afterwards, we talked about noses and how different they all are.

I like her nose. I have a light pink tea service which I like because the handles of its cups resemble her nose. You will laugh but one morning when I saw her from close, a strange desire rose in me to hold her by the nose and drink the nectar of her lips. I find her lips lovely, maybe because they always look moist, like a peeled orange. If I feel a desire to kiss them, it is not because that is what I have read in books or that is what I have heard from others about kissing women's lips, no, that's not it. Had I known none of those things, I would still have wanted to kiss them. That's the way her lips are—they form an incomplete kiss.

She is the only daughter of my neighbour who is a doctor. All day long, she sits in her father's dispensary. Sometimes when passing by, I have seen her standing next to the medicine cabinet, looking like a long-necked bottle with something colourful and bubbly inside. One day I walked into the dispensary to ask the doctor for a cold remedy. Doctor sahib said to her, 'Child, sprinkle a few drops of eucalyptus on his handkerchief.' She took my handkerchief from me, pulled out a small bottle from the cabinet and put a few drops on it. At that moment, I wanted to get up, hold her by the hand and say, 'Please cork this bottle; instead give me a single teardrop from your eyes and I will be healed of all ailments.' But I sat there silently, looking at the colourless drops which were being sprinkled on my handkerchief.

Since I began to notice her, it has been my heartfelt desire that she should cry and I should watch tears floating in her eyes.

In my imagination, I have seen her eyes getting melancholy many times, which is the real reason I want to see her cry. Tears flickering over her thick eyelashes will look lovely. It will be like raindrops dancing down a shuttered window. It is possible that you may not think tears to be necessary in women's eyes, but I cannot even imagine a woman's eyes without tears. Tears are the perspiration of the eyes. A worker's brow is only a worker's brow when it is shining with perspiration. A woman's eyes can only be a woman's eyes when they are drowned in tears.

She came in a white, sequined sari on the balcony, setting off silver-hued fireworks. The sequins embedded in the undulating fabric of the garment shimmered and my entire body felt titillated. She suddenly turned towards me, as if she had become aware of a presence other than her own in the silence of the night. Two pearls rolled down her eyes . . . she was crying . . . she . . . she was crying. And as I looked and before I could do anything, the tears from her eyes, the first perspiration of her youth, fell to the floor. Perhaps they could not bear my intrusive eyes. They may have wished to lie, like newborn babies, in the soft and tender swings of her eyes. It was my eyes that made them come down. She was crying, but I was happy. Her moist eyes looked like fog-covered lakes, very mysterious, very thought-provoking. Under the shallows of her tears, the black and white of her eyes shimmered like those tiny fish that are afraid to come to the surface.

I stopped looking at her, only concentrating on her eyes, which looked like two clay lamps flickering on a cold, wet December night. Her eyes looked at me from far, very far, as I began to move towards her . . . then two tears formed, came up, dangled over her thick eyelashes for a while and slowly rolled down her pale cheeks. In her right eye, another tear rose, rolled down, stayed for a fleeting moment on her cheek and like a traveller who, approaching the end of his journey, takes a breather, it slid past the corner of her lips whose moisture made it thin out. With her washed eyes, she looked at me intently and asked, 'Who are you?' She knew who I was, and in asking who I was she was asking herself who she was. I answered, 'You are Sheela.'

Her clenched lips trembled and she said between sobs, 'Sheela . . . Sheela . . . She . . .' She sat down on the balcony. She looked tired, but then suddenly she thought of something, as if in a dream. She shook it off and stood up. In an anxious voice she said, 'I . . . I . . . what was I saying? . . . Nothing is the matter with me . . . I am all right . . . And how did I come to be here?' I consoled her, 'Do not be worried, Sheela . . . you have said nothing to me . . . such things are neither said nor heard.' Sheela looked at me as if I had caught her doing something she shouldn't have been doing. 'What things . . . what things . . . there is nothing.'

I said to her, 'Day before yesterday in the dispensary when you were playing with that parrot, sticking out your red tongue at him, your crystal fingers were creating music when they touched the bars of his cage. At that moment, you were an incomplete woman. But today, when tears are rolling down your eyes, you are complete as a woman. Don't you feel the difference? You must. What you were yesterday, you are not today. And what is today will not be there tomorrow. But the mark the hot iron of happiness has left on your heart will always remain there, just as it is . . . isn't it a good thing to have happened? That will remain something in your life that will always be entirely yours.

Something over whose ownership there would be no doubts. I wish my heart could become your heart . . . a woman's heart . . . which struck once remains content thereafter . . . in the immensity of a woman's heart, many wildernesses can find space . . . these numberless wildernesses are by themselves a refuge and a settlement . . . you are fortunate . . . the day for which you would have had to wait has come so early in your life . . . you are fortunate.'

There was a look of astonishment on her face; she was like a hen which has laid an egg for the first time. She began to speak in a monologue. 'Fortunate . . . I am fortunate . . . how is that? How do you know?' I answered, 'When a kite is cut away and the boys are screaming from their rooftops in an attempt to grab the string, does anything have to be said? Where is the kite that you had flown into the immensity of the sky? Till yesterday, you held the string in your hand, but where is it now?' Tears began to roll down her eyes. 'I am fortunate,' she said in tear-drenched words. 'Please tell those boys who get on their rooftops and start screaming because they want the kite that has been cut away . . . that they are so noisy.' Her tears became more abundant and she looked at me through their rain and asked, 'Whose parched throat do you want to moisten with these tears? I know why you are subjecting me to these pinpricks.'

Then she turned her face away in disgust. Her rational mind at that moment resembled an oversharpened knife. I spoke to her calmly, 'All that has happened is in my knowledge, but if I had asked you then to forget it all, offered you false sympathy and like a juggler made your pain, your grief disappear with a magic spell, you would have thought of me as a friend, but I can't do that . . . your heart is yours and what it has experienced is also yours. Why should I rob your heart of its wealth? Why should I ask you to forget the pain which is the treasure of your life? This pain, this sad event that has come to pass, these are what you will have to lay the foundations of your future life on . . . I do not want to lie, Sheela, but if you want, I can do even that for your satisfaction. Tell me what you want to hear.' Her reply was sharp, 'I do not need anyone's sympathy.' I said, 'I know . . . in such situations, no sympathy is needed . . . if the game consists of jumping into the fire, no instructions are required. The cortege of love needs to be borne on no one's shoulders. This dead body we will have to carry on our backs for the rest of our lives.'

She cut me short. 'I will carry it . . . what is that to you . . . why are you trying to frighten me by saying such terrifying things? I have only loved him . . . And do I not love him still . . . He betrayed me . . . he was false to me . . . but this betrayal has come at the hands of the one I love . . . I know that he has destroyed my life. I have nowhere to go, but what does it matter . . . It was a game that I played and lost . . . You want to frighten me, taunt me, but I . . . I do not now care about death . . . I have spoken of death . . . and this has made you tremble. You fear women, but look at me, I am not afraid of death.'

I looked at her. There was a forced smile playing on her lips and from her eyes, under the tears, a strange light shone forth. She was trembling, ever so slightly. I looked at her intently once again and said, 'I am afraid of death because I want to live. You are not afraid of death because you do not know how to live. A person who does not know the art of living, for him to be alive is like being dead . . . If you want to die, then go ahead.'

She looked at me with surprise. I continued, 'You want to die because you think that you will not be able to free yourself of this mountain of grief that has fallen on you so suddenly . . . That is not true . . . If you have the strength to love, you also have the strength to survive heartbreak . . . The joy, the ecstasy that you drew from being in love, is the essence of your life. Take good care of it and spend the rest of your life by drinking deep of those magic moments . . . The one who loved you is not so important, or even necessary, as the love you bore him . . . forget him but remember your love and live on that remembrance . . . the remembrance of those moments for whose sake you destroyed the most precious thing in your life. Can you ever forget those moments which you bought with a pearl whose value was beyond imagining? No, never! Man can forget such moments, and does forget them, because he pays no price for them . . . but a woman cannot forget because in return for those fleeting moments she has sacrificed her entire life. Do you want to die? Do you want to abandon the refuge for which you paid such a high price? Live, make use of this life! We all have to die, which is why it is necessary to live.'

My words had left her exhausted and she sat down. 'I am tired,' she said.

'Go to sleep . . . rest and gather your courage to fight other calamities.' I was about to walk off after saying this when it suddenly occurred to me—and the thought made my heart miss a beat—that she might kill herself. If that happened, I would lose something. I turned, came close to her and said in the voice of a supplicant, 'Sheela, I've a request.'

Sheela lifted her head and looked at me. 'Look, Sheela, I beg of you to banish the thought of suicide . . . you should live, you must live.'

She asked, 'Why?'

'Why? Why do you ask me, Sheela? You know very well in your heart why I am making this request. But let's not talk about such things . . . I hold nothing against you, nor anything against myself . . . what we started, I want it to reach a conclusion. Am I selfish? Every man is selfish . . . I am begging you not to die . . . this is selfishness . . . Live, if you live, my love will always remain young . . . I want my love to be inseparable from every phase of your life . . . but only with your permission.'

She kept thinking for a long time; she had grown quite sombre. 'I will have to live,' she said in a soft voice.

Her voice was an indication of her determination. Leaving her tired youth in sleepy moonlight, I walked down from the rooftop to my flat and went to sleep.

# Two-Nation Theory

THE FIRST TIME MUKHTAR SAW SHARDA WAS FROM HIS ROOFTOP, WHERE he had gone to grab a kite that had landed there. It was only a glimpse. She lived in the house across the street, which was lower than theirs, and he had seen her through the open window of the bathroom where she was washing herself, pouring water on her body from a pitcher. This was a surprise. Where had this girl materialized from, because no girl lived in that house. The ones who used to had all been married off. The only female now left was Roop Kaur, with her flabby husband and their three boys.

Mukhtar picked up his kite and stole another look at the girl. She was beautiful. A shudder ran through him. The water drops on the golden down of her body were shimmering. Her complexion was light brown, but it had the glow of copper. The tiny droplets of water that sparkled on her skin were making her body melt, drop by drop, or that was how it appeared to him. He was watching her through one of the eyeholes in the low brick wall built on all four sides of the open roof. His eyes were glued to the body of this girl bathing herself. She was no more than sixteen and there were water drops on her small, round breasts, lovely to look at. But he did not feel aroused. He just kept watching this young, beautiful, naked girl with great concentration as if she were a painting. There was a large mole in the corner of her mouth, which just sat there, soberly, as if it was unaware of its being there, but others were aware of its existence and knew that it was exactly where it ought to have been.

The golden down on her arms was studded with sparkling water drops. Her hair was not golden but light brown. Perhaps her hair had refused to go golden. Her body was full and supple but no lascivious thoughts came to him. He just kept looking at her through the eyehole. She soaped her body and he could smell its aroma spreading over her light brown, copper-hued body. The foam on her skin looked lovely. When she poured water over herself to wash it away, he felt as is she had removed her foamy covering with one calm, smooth move. When she was done, she dried herself with a towel, put on her clothes unhurriedly and, placing both hands on the window sill, stood up. She blushed. Her eyes, Mukhtar felt, had taken a dip into a lake of shyness. She closed the window shut and, involuntarily, Mukhtar laughed.

Then she threw open the window and looked towards him angrily. Mukhtar spoke, 'Please don't blame me but why were you bathing with the window open?' She said nothing, cast another angry look at him and shut the window. Four days later, Roop Kaur came to their house, accompanied by that girl. Mukhtar's mother and sister were excellent knitters. Many girls from the neighbourhood would come to them to learn how to knit and do crochet work. This girl was fond of learning how to crochet and that was why she had come. Mukhtar stepped out of his room into the courtyard, smiled and left. She drew herself together when she saw him. Mukhtar learnt that her name was Sharda and she was Roop Kaur's cousin, daughter of her uncle. She lived in the small town of Chichoki Malyaan with her poor relatives, but Roop Kaur had asked her to come live with her family. She had finished high school and she was said to be very intelligent. It had taken her no time to learn how to crochet.

Several days passed. By now Mukhtar knew that he had fallen in love with her. It had happened gradually, from the moment he had first seen her through that eyehole to this point where her thought never left his heart for a moment. It occurred to Mukhtar several times that falling in love was wrong because Sharda was a Hindu. How could a Muslim dare fall in love with a Hindu? But the fact was that he just could not bear the thought of not being in love with her. Sharda would sometimes talk to him but somewhat diffidently. The first thing that would come to her mind on seeing him would be the memory of the day he had seen her through that eyehole taking a bath naked. One day, when Mukhtar's mother and sister had gone to offer condolences at a family friend's home, Sharda walked in, carrying the small bag she always did. It was about ten in the morning and Mukhtar was stretched on a cot in the courtyard reading a newspaper. 'Where is Behanji?' she asked, referring to his sister. Mukhtar's hands began to tremble, 'She has gone out.' 'And Mataji?' Sharda asked, which was what she called his mother. Mukhtar got down from the cot. 'She . . . she has gone with her.' 'All right then,' she said, looking worried. Joining her hands in a namaste, she was about to leave when Mukhtar said, 'Sharda!' 'Yes?' She looked like someone who had just received an electric shock. Mukhtar said, 'Sit down. They will be back very soon.' 'No, I am leaving,' she replied but kept standing.

Picking up his courage, Mukhtar pulled her towards him by the wrist and kissed her on the lips. It all happened so quickly that Sharda was taken by surprise. By now both of them were trembling. 'Please forgive me,' was all Mukhtar said. Sharda kept quiet but her copper complexion turned red and her lips began to quiver as if they were complaining about having been teased. Mukhtar drew Sharda close to his chest and she did not resist. But there was a look of astonishment on her face. She seemed to be asking herself, 'What is it that has happened? What is happening? Should it have happened? Is this what happens to others as well?'

Mukhtar made her sit on the cot and asked, 'Why don't you speak Sharda?' Under her dupatta, Sharda's heart was beating fast. She did not answer him. Mukhtar felt bothered by her silence. 'Please say something Sharda, if what I have done has offended you, as God is my witness, I'll apologize. I will never even raise my eyes towards you. I would never have had the courage but I don't know what came over me. The fact is, the fact is that I am in love with you.' Sharda's lips moved as if they were trying to form the word 'love'. Mukhtar began to talk animatedly, 'I don't know if you understand the meaning of love. I don't know much about it myself. All I know is that I love you. I want to hold all of you in one hand. If you want, I can place my life in your hands. Sharda, why don't you speak?'

Sharda's eyes became dreamy. Mukhtar began to talk again. 'I saw you that day through that eyehole. I saw you and that is a sight I will not forget till judgement day. Why are you so shy? My eyes never stole your beauty. They just beheld a splendid scene. If you can bring it back, I will kiss your feet.' And he kissed one of her feet.

She trembled. Then she rose from the cot and said, her voice quivering, 'What are you doing? In our religion . . .' Mukhtar said excitedly, 'Forget religion. All is right in the religion of love.' He wanted to kiss her again but she leapt aside and, still smiling, she ran out. Mukhtar wanted to run up to the roof and jump from there into the courtyard and start dancing. Some time later, Mukhtar's mother and sister returned and so did Sharda. Mukhtar slipped away, his eyes to the ground. He did not want his secret to get out. The next day, he walked up to the rooftop. She was standing by the window, combing her hair. 'Sharda,' Mukhtar called out. She was startled. The comb fell from her hand, landing in the street. 'You are so timid; look your comb has fallen.' 'Why don't you buy me a new one then; this one has fallen into the gutter,' Sharda said. 'Now?' Mukhtar asked. 'No, no, I was only joking.' 'I was also joking. Could I have left you to buy a comb? Never.' Sharda smiled, 'How am I going to do my hair?' Mukhtar slipped his finger through the eyehole from where he was watching her. 'Use my fingers.'

Sharda laughed. Mukhtar felt that he could happily spend his entire life under the shade of that laughter. 'Sharda, by God, you laughed and I am in ecstasy. Why are you so lovely? There is no girl in the whole wide world who is as lovely. I want to smash these curtains of clay that stand between us.' Sharda laughed again. Mukhtar said, 'No one else should hear you laugh, nor even watch you when you do. Sharda, you must only laugh for me. Whenever you want to laugh, just call me. I will raise protective walls around you with my kisses.' 'You know how to talk,' Sharda said. 'Then give me a reward, just a look of love from across there. I will save that look in my eyes and I'll keep it hidden.' He noticed someone's shadow behind her and he moved away. When he returned, she was not at the window.

They came close in the days that followed and whenever they got a chance they would talk the sweet nothings that lovers do. One day, Roop Kaur and her husband, Lala Kalu Mal, were out of the house. Mukhtar happened to be walking past when a pebble hit him. He looked up and saw Sharda. She motioned him to come up. They were completely alone and they talked intimately for a long time. Mukhtar said, 'I apologize for what I did that day. And I want to do the same thing today, but this time I won't apologize.' Then he placed his lips on Sharda's quivering lips. 'Say you are sorry,' Sharda said naughtily. 'No, those are not your lips, they are mine. Am I wrong?' Sharda lowered her eyes, 'Not only those lips, all of me is yours too.'

Mukhtar became grave. 'Look Sharda, we are standing on the top of a volcano. I assure you—and you should believe it— that no woman will ever come into my life except you. I swear that I will remain yours for the rest of my life. My love will be steadfast. Do you also make the same promise?' Sharda raised her eyes. 'My love is true.' Mukhtar threw his arms around her and squeezed her to his chest. 'Live, but only for me, for my love. By God, Sharda, if you had not returned my love, I would have killed myself. You are in my arms and I feel that every blessing of the world, every happiness, is in my lap. I am so fortunate.'

Sharda rested her head on Mukhtar's shoulder. 'You know how to talk; I cannot bring to my lips what is in my heart.' They were together for a long time, absorbed in one another. When Mukhtar left, his spirits were imbued with a new and delicious pleasure. He kept thinking all night and the next day he left for Calcutta, where his father ran a business. He returned after eight days. Sharda came for her crochet hour. They did not speak but he felt her eyes asking him, 'Where have you been all these days? Never said a word to me and left for Calcutta? What happened to those claims of love? I am not going to speak to you. Don't look at me. What do you want to say to me now?' There was much Mukhtar wanted to say to her but they could not find themselves alone. He wanted to talk to her for a long, long time. Two days passed. But their eyes talked whenever they ran into each other. On the third day, with Roop Kaur and her husband, Lala Kalu Mal, again out of the house, Sharda called him.

She met him on the stairs and, when Mukhtar tried to embrace her, she wrested herself free and ran upstairs. She was annoyed. Mukhtar said to her, 'Sweetheart, come sit with me. I have important things to talk to you, things which concern us both.' She sat next to him on a bed. 'Don't try to talk yourself out of it. Why did you go to Calcutta without telling me? Really, I wept so much.' Mukhtar kissed her eyes. 'That day when I went home, I kept thinking all night. After what took place that day, I had to think. We were like man and wife. I erred and you let yourself go. In one leap, we covered such vast distances. We never thought about the direction we should take. You understand, Sharda.'

She lowered her eyes. 'Yes.' 'I went to Calcutta to talk to my father and you will be happy to know that I have his blessings.' Mukhtar's eyes had lit up with joy. He took Sharda's hands in his and said, 'A weight has lifted from my heart; I can marry you now.' 'Marriage!' she said in a low voice. 'Yes, marriage.' Sharda asked, 'How can we marry?' Mukhtar smiled, 'Where is the difficulty? You become a Muslim.' Sharda was startled. 'Muslim!' Mukhtar replied calmly, 'Yes, yes, what else can it be? I know your family will be up in arms, but I have made arrangements. We will go to Calcutta. My father will do the rest. The day we arrive, he will send for a cleric who will make you a Muslim and we will get married right away.' Sharda clenched her lips, as if they were sewn up. Mukhtar looked at her. 'Why have you become quiet?' She said nothing. 'Sharda, tell me what is it?' Mukhtar asked in a worried voice.

With great difficulty, Sharda replied, 'You become a Hindu.' 'I become a Hindu?' he asked in an astonished voice. Then he laughed. 'How can I become a Hindu?' 'And how can I become a Muslim?' she asked in a low voice. 'Why can't you become a Muslim . . . I mean you love me. And then Islam is the best of religions. The Hindu religion is no religion. Hindus drink cow urine; they worship idols. I mean it is all right in its place, but it cannot compare with Islam. If you become a Muslim, everything will fall in place.' Sharda's copper face had gone white. 'You won't become a Hindu?' Mukhtar laughed, 'Are you mad!' Sharda's face had blanched. 'You should leave. They will be coming about now.' She rose from the bed. Mukhtar couldn't understand. 'But Sharda . . .' 'No, no, please leave, go quickly or they will be here,' she said in a cold, uncaring voice. Mukhtar's throat had gone dry but with great difficulty he said, 'We love each other, Sharda why are you upset?' 'Go, go away, our Hindu religion is very bad; you Muslims are the good ones.' There was hatred in her voice. She went into the other room and shut the door. Mukhtar, his Islam tucked inside his chest, left the house.

# The Price of Freedom

THE YEAR I DO NOT REMEMBER, BUT THERE WAS GREAT REVOLUTIONARY fervour in Amritsar. 'Inqilab Zindabad'—long live revolution—was the slogan of the day. There was excitement in the air and a feeling of restlessness and youthful abandon. We were living through heady times. Even the fearful memories of the Jallianwala Bagh massacre had disappeared, at least on the surface. One felt intensely alive and on the threshold of something great and final.

People marched through the streets every day raising slogans against the Raj. Hundreds were arrested for breaking the law. In fact, courting arrest had become something of a popular diversion. You were picked up in the morning and quite often released by the evening. A case would be registered, a hearing held and a short sentence awarded. You came out, raised a few more slogans and were put in gaol again.

There was so much to live for in those days. The slightest incident sometimes led to the most violent upheaval. One man would stand on a podium in one of the city squares and call for a strike. A strike would follow. There was of course the movement to wear only Indian-spun cotton with the object of putting the Lancashire textile mills out of business. There was a boycott of all imported cloth in effect. Every street had its own bonfire. People would walk up, take off every imported piece of clothing they were wearing and chuck it into the fire. Sometimes a woman would stand on her balcony and throw down her imported silk sari into the bonfire. The crowd would cheer.

I remember this huge bonfire the boys had lit in front of the town hall and the police headquarters, where in a wild moment my classmate Sheikhoo had taken off his silk jacket and thrown it into the flames. A big cheer had gone up because it was well known that he was the son of one of the richest men of the city, who also had the dubious distinction of being the most infamous 'toady', as government sympathizers were popularly called. Inspired by the applause, Sheikhoo had also taken off his silk shirt and sent it the way of his jacket. It was only later that he remembered the gold links that had gone with it.

I don't want to make fun of my friend, because in those days I too was in the same turbulent frame of mind. I used to dream about getting hold of guns and setting up a secret terrorist organization. That my father was a government servant did not bother me. I was restless and did not even understand what I was restless about.

I was never much interested in school, but during those days I had completely gone off my books. I would spend the entire day at Jallianwala Bagh. Sitting under a tree, I would watch the windows of the houses bordering the park and dream about the girls who lived behind them. I was sure one of these days one of them would fall in love with me.

Jallianwala Bagh had become the hub of the movement of civil disobedience launched by the Congress. There were small and big tents and colourful awnings everywhere. The largest tent was the political headquarters of the city. Once or twice a week, a 'dictator'—for that was what he was called—would be nominated by the people to 'lead the struggle'. He would be ceremoniously placed in the large tent; volunteers would provide him with a ragtag guard of honour, and for the next few days he would receive delegations of young political workers, all wearing homespun cotton. It was also the 'dictator's' duty to get donations of food and money from the city's big shopkeepers and businessmen. And so it would continue until one day the police came and picked him up.

I had a friend called Ghulam Ali. Our intimacy can be judged from the fact that both of us had failed our school leaving examination twice in a row. Once we had run away from home and were on our way to Bombay—from where we planned to sail for the Soviet Union—when our money ran out. After sleeping for a few nights on footpaths, we had written to our parents and promised not to do such a thing again. We were reprieved.

Shahzada Ghulam Ali, as he later came to be called, was a handsome young man, tall and fair as Kashmiris tend to be. He always walked with a certain swagger that one generally associates with 'tough guys'. Actually, he was no Shahzada— which means prince—when we were at school. However, after having become active in the civil disobedience movement and run the gamut of revolutionary speeches, public processions, social intercourse with pretty female volunteer workers, garlands, slogans and patriotic songs, he had for some reason come to be known as Shahzada.

His fame spread like wildfire in the city of Amritsar. It was a small place where it did not take you long to become famous or infamous. The natives of Amritsar, though by nature critical of the general run of humanity, were rather indulgent when it came to religious and political leaders. They always seemed to have this peculiar need for fiery sermons and revolutionary speeches.

Leaders had always had a long tenure in our city. The times were advantageous because the established leadership was in gaol and there were quite a few empty chairs waiting to be occupied. The movement needed people like Ghulam Ali who would be seen for a few days in Jallianwala Bagh, make a speech or two and then duly get arrested.

In those days, the German and Italian dictatorships were the new thing in Europe, which is what had perhaps inspired the Indian National Congress to designate certain party workers as 'dictators'. When Shahzada Ghulam Ali's turn came to go to gaol, as many as forty 'dictators' had already been put inside.

When I learnt that Ghulam Ali had been named the current 'dictator', I made my way to Jallianwala Bagh. There were volunteers outside the big tent. However, since Ghulam Ali had seen me, I was permitted to go in. A white cotton carpet had been laid on the ground and there sat Ghulam Ali, propped up against cushions. He was talking to a group of cotton-clad city shopkeepers about the vegetable trade, I think. After having got rid of them he issued a few instructions to his volunteers and turned to me. He looked too serious, which I thought was funny. When we were alone, I asked him, 'And how is our prince?'

I also realized that he had changed. To my attempt at treating the whole thing as a farce, he said, 'No, Saadat, don't make fun of it. The great honour which has been bestowed on me, I do not deserve. But from now on the movement is going to be my life.'

I promised to return in the evening as he told me that he would be making a speech. When I arrived, there was a large crowd of people around a podium they had set up for the occasion. Then I heard loud applause and there was Shahzada

Ghulam Ali. He looked very handsome in his spotless white and his swagger seemed to add to his appeal.

He spoke for an hour or so. It was an emotional speech. Even I was overcome. There were moments when I wished nothing more than to turn into a human bomb and explode for the glory of the freedom of India.

This happened many years ago and memory always plays tricks with detail, but as I write this I can see Ghulam Ali addressing that turbulent crowd. It was not politics I was conscious of while he spoke, but youth and the promise of revolution. He had the sincere recklessness of a young man who might stop a woman on the street and say to her without any preliminaries, 'Look, I love you.'

Such were the times. I think both the British Raj and the people it ruled were still inexperienced and quite unaware of the consequences of their actions. The government, without really fully comprehending the implications, was putting people in gaol by the thousands, and those who were going to gaol were not quite sure what they were doing and what the results would be.

There was much disorder. I think you could liken the general atmosphere to a spreading fire which leaps out into the air and then just as suddenly goes out, only to ignite again. These sudden eruptions that died just as suddenly, only to burst into flame once again, had created much heat and agitation in the lacklustre, melancholy state of slavery.

As Shahzada Ghulam Ali finished speaking, the entire Jallianwala Bagh came to its feet. I stepped forward to congratulate him, but his eyes were elsewhere. My curiosity was soon satisfied. It was a girl in a white cotton sari, standing behind a flowering bush.

The next day I learnt that Shahzada Ghulam Ali was in love with the girl I had seen the previous evening. And so was she with him, and just as much. She was a Muslim, an orphan, who worked as a nurse at the local women's hospital. I think she was the first Muslim girl in Amritsar to join the Congress movement against the Raj.

Her white cotton saris, her association with the Congress and the fact that she worked in a hospital had all combined to soften that slight stiffness one finds in Muslim girls. She was not beautiful, but she was very feminine. She had acquired that hard-to-describe quality so characteristic of Hindu girls—a mixture of humility, self-assurance and the urge to worship. In her, the beauty of ritualistic Muslim prayer and Hindu devotion to temple gods had been alchemized.

She worshipped Shahzada Ghulam Ali and he loved her to distraction. They had met during a protest march and fallen for each other almost immediately.

Ghulam Ali wanted to marry Nigar before his inevitable and almost eagerly awaited arrest. Why he wanted to do that I am unable to say as he could just as well have married her after his release. Gaol terms in those days varied between three months and a year. There were some who were let out after ten or fifteen days in order to make way for fresh entrants.

All that was really needed was the blessing of Babaji.

Babaji was one of the great figures of the time. He was camped at the splendid house of the richest jeweller in the city, Hari Ram. Normally, Babaji used to live in his village ashram, but whenever he came to Amritsar he would put up with Hari Ram, and the palatial residence, located outside the city, would turn into a sort of shrine, since the number of Babaji's followers was legion. You could see them standing in line, waiting to be admitted briefly to the great man's presence for what was called darshan, or a mere look at him. The old man would receive them sitting cross-legged on a specially constructed platform in a grove of mango trees, accepting donations and gifts for his ashram. In the evening, he would have young women volunteers sing him Hindu devotional songs.

Babaji was known for his piety and scholarship, and his followers included men and women of every faith—Hindus, Muslims, Sikhs and untouchables.

Although on the face of it Babaji had nothing to do with politics, it was an open secret that no political movement in the Punjab could begin or end without his clearance. To the government machinery, he was an unsolved puzzle. There was always a smile on his face, which could be interpreted in a thousand ways.

The civil disobedience movement in Amritsar with its daily arrests and processions was quite clearly being conducted with Babaji's blessing, if not his direct guidance. He was in the habit of dropping hints about the tactics to be followed and the next day every major political leader in the Punjab would be wearing Babaji's wisdom as a kind of amulet around his neck.

There was a magnetic quality about him and his voice was soft, persuasive and full of nuances. Not even the most trenchant criticism could ruffle his composure. To his enemies he was an enigma because he always kept them guessing.

Babaji was a frequent visitor to Amritsar, but somehow I had never seen him. Therefore, when Ghulam Ali told me one day that he planned to call on the great man to obtain his blessing for his intended marriage to Nigar, I asked him to take me along.

The next day, Ghulam Ali arranged for a tonga, and the three of us—Ghulam Ali, Nigar and I—found ourselves at Hari Ram's magnificent house.

Babaji had already had his ritualistic morning bath—ashnan—and his devotions were done. He now sat in the mango grove listening to a stirring patriotic song, courtesy of a young, beautiful Kashmiri Pandit girl. He sat cross-legged on a mat made from date-palm leaves, and though there were plenty of cushions around, he did not seem to want any. He was in his seventies but his skin was without blemish. I wondered if it was the result of his famous olive oil massage every morning.

He smiled at Ghulam Ali and asked us to join him on the floor. It was obvious to me that Ghulam Ali and Nigar were less interested in the revolutionary refrain of the song, which seemed to have Babaji in a kind of trance, than their own symphony of young love. At last the girl finished, winning in the bargain Babaji's affectionate approval, indicated with a subtle nod of his head, and he turned to us.

Ghulam Ali was about to introduce Nigar and himself, but he never got an opportunity, thanks to Babaji's exceptional memory for names and faces. In his low, soothing voice he inquired, 'Prince, so you have not yet been arrested?'

'No sir,' Ghulam Ali replied, his hands folded as a mark of respect.

Playing with a pencil, which he had pulled out from somewhere, Babaji said, 'But I think you have already been arrested.' He looked meaningfully at Nigar. 'She has already arrested our prince.'

Babaji's next remark was addressed to the girl who had earlier been singing. 'These children have come to seek my blessing.

Tell me, when are you going to get married, Kamal?'

Her pink face turned even pinker. 'But how can I? I am already at the ashram.'

Babaji sighed, turned to Ghulam Ali and said, 'So you two have made up your minds.'

'Yes,' they answered together. Babaji smiled.

'Decisions can sometimes be changed,' he said.

And despite the reverence-laden atmosphere, Ghulam Ali answered, 'This decision can be put off, but it can never be changed.'

Babaji closed his eyes and asked in a lawyer's voice, 'Why?'

Ghulam Ali did not hesitate. 'Because we are committed to it as we are committed to the freedom of India, and while circumstances may change the timing of that event, it is final and immutable.'

Babaji smiled. 'Nigar,' he said, 'why don't you join our ashram because Shahzada is going to gaol in a few days anyway?'

'I will,' she whispered.

Babaji changed the subject and began to ask us about political activities in Jallianwala Bagh. For the next hour or so, the conversation revolved around arrests, processions and even the price of vegetables. I did not join in these pleasantries, but I did wonder why Babaji had been so reluctant to accord his blessing to the young couple. Was he not quite sure that they were in love? Why had he asked Nigar to join the ashram? Was it to help her not to think of Ghulam Ali being in gaol, or did it mean that if she joined the ashram she would not be allowed to marry?

And what was going to happen to Nigar once she was admitted to the rarefied surroundings of the ashram? Would she spend her time intoning devotional and patriotic songs for the spiritual and political enlightenment of Babaji? Would she be happy? I had seen many ashram inmates in my time. There was something lifeless and pallid about them, despite their early morning cold baths and long walks. With their pale faces and sunken eyes, they somehow always reminded me of cows' udders. I couldn't see Nigar living among them, she who was so young and fresh, made up entirely, it seemed to me, of honey, milk and saffron. What had ashrams got to do with India's freedom?

I had always hated ashrams, seminaries, saints' shrines and orphanages. There was something unnatural about these places. I had often seen young boys walking in single file on the street, led by men who administered these institutions. I had visited religious seminaries and schools with their pious inmates. The older ones always wore long beards and the adolescents walked around with sparse, ugly hair sprouting out of their chins. Despite their five prayers a day, their faces never showed any trace of that inner light prayer is supposed to bring about.

Nigar was a woman, not a Muslim, Hindu, Sikh or Christian, but a woman. I simply could not see her praying like a machine every morning at the ashram. Why should she, who was herself pure as a prayer, raise her hands to heaven?

When we were about to leave, Babaji told Ghulam Ali and Nigar that they had his blessing and he would perform the marriage the next day in (where else?) Jallianwala Bagh. He arrived as promised. He was accompanied by his usual entourage of volunteers, with Hari Ram the jeweller in tow. A much-bedecked podium had been put up for the ceremony. The girls had taken charge of Nigar and she made a lovely bride. Ghulam Ali had made no special arrangements. All day long, he had been doing his usual chores, raising donations for the movement and the like. Both of them had decided to hoist the Congress flag after it was all over.

Just before Babaji's arrival, I had been telling Ghulam Ali that we must never forget what had happened in Jallianwala Bagh a few years earlier, in 1919 to be exact. There was a well in the park, which people say was full of dead bodies after General Dyer had ordered his soldiers to stop firing at the crowd. Today, I had told him, the well was used for drinking water, which was still sweet. It bore no trace of the blood which had been spilt so wantonly by the British general and his Gurkha soldiers. The flowers still bloomed and were just as beautiful as they had been on that day.

I had pointed out to Ghulam Ali a house which overlooked the park. It was said that a young girl, who was standing at her window watching the massacre, had been shot through the heart. Her blood had left a mark on the wall below. If you looked carefully, you could still perhaps see it. I remember that six months after the massacre, our teacher had taken the entire class to Jallianwala Bagh and, picking up a piece of earth from the ground, had said to us, 'Children, never forget that the blood of our martyrs is part of this earth.'

Babaji was given a military-style salute by the volunteers. He and Ghulam Ali were taken around the camp, and as the evening was falling the girls began to sing a devotional song and Babaji sat there listening to it with his eyes closed.

The song ended, and Babaji opened his eyes and said, 'Children, I am here to join these two freedom lovers in holy wedlock.' A cheer went up from the crowd. Nigar was in a sari, which bore the three colours of the flag of the Indian National Congress—saffron, green and white. The ceremony was a combination of Hindu and Muslim rituals.

Then Babaji stood up and began to speak. 'These two children will now be able to serve the nation with even greater enthusiasm. The true purpose of marriage is comradeship. What is being sanctified today will serve the cause of India's freedom. A true marriage should be free of lust and those who are able to exorcize this evil from their lives deserve our respect.'

Babaji spoke for a long time about his concept of marriage. According to him, the true bliss of marriage could only be experienced if the relationship between man and wife was something more than the physical enjoyment of each other's bodies. He did not think the sexual link was as important as it was made out to be. It was like eating. There were those who ate out of indulgence and there were those who ate to stay alive. The sanctity of marriage was more important than the gratification of the sexual instinct.

Ghulam Ali was listening to Babaji's rambling speech as if in a trance. He whispered something to Nigar as soon as Babaji had finished. Then, standing up on the podium, he said in a voice trembling with emotion, 'I have a declaration to make. As long as India does not win freedom, Nigar and I will live not as husband and wife but as friends.' He looked at his wife. 'Nigar, would you like to mother a child who would be a slave at the moment of his birth? No, you wouldn't.'

Ghulam Ali then began to ramble, going from subject to subject, but basically confining his emotional remarks to the freedom of India from the British Raj. At one point, he looked at Nigar and stopped speaking. To me he looked like a drunken man who realizes too late that he has no money left in his wallet. But he recovered his composure and said to Babaji, 'Both of us need your blessing. You have our solemn word of honour that the vow made today shall be kept.'

The next morning Ghulam Ali was taken in because he had threatened to overthrow the Raj and had declared publicly that he would father no children as long as India was ruled by a foreign power. He was given eight months and sent to the distant Multan gaol. He was Amritsar's fortieth 'dictator' to be gaoled and the forty thousandth prisoner of the civil disobedience movement against the Raj.

At that time most of us were convinced that the ousting of the British from India was a matter of days away. However, the Raj was cleverer than we were prepared to give it credit for. It let the movement come to a boil, then made a deal with the leaders, and everything simmered down.

When the workers began to come out of gaol, they realized that the atmosphere had changed. Wisely, most of them decided to resume their normal, humdrum lives. Shahzada Ghulam Ali was let out after seven months, and while it is true the old popular enthusiasm had gone, yet he was received by a large crowd at the Amritsar railway station from where he was taken out in a procession through the city. A number of public meetings were also held in his honour, but it was evident that the fire and passion had died out. There was a sense of fatigue among the people. It was as if they were runners in a marathon who had been told by the organizers to stop running, return to the starting point, and begin again.

Years went by, but that heady feeling never returned. In my own life, a number of small and big revolutions came and went. I joined college, but failed my exams twice. My father died and I had to run from pillar to post looking for a job. I finally found a translator's position with a third-class newspaper, but I soon became restless and left. For a time, I joined the Aligarh Muslim University, but fell ill and was sent to the more salubrious climate of Kashmir to recover. After three months there, I moved to Bombay. Disgusted with its frequent Hindu-Muslim riots, I made my way to Delhi, but found it too slow and dull and returned to Bombay, despite its impersonal inhabitants who seemed to have no time for strangers.

It was now eight years since I had left Amritsar. I had no idea what had happened to my old friend or the streets and squares of my early youth. I had never written to anyone and the fact was that I was not interested in the past or the future. I was living in the present. The past, it seemed to me, was like a sum of money you had already spent, and to think about it was like drawing up a ledger account of money you no longer had.

One afternoon—I had both time and some money—I decided to go looking for a pair of shoes. Once, while passing by the Army & Navy Store, I had noticed a small shop, which had a very attractive display window. I didn't find that shop, but I noticed another, which looked quite reasonable.

'Show me a pair of shoes with rubber soles,' I told the shop assistant.

'We don't stock them,' he replied.

Since the monsoons were expected any time, I asked him if he could sell me rubber ankle-boots.

'We don't stock those either,' he said. 'Why don't you try the store at the corner? We don't carry rubber or part-rubber footwear at all.'

'Why?' I asked, surprised.

'It's the boss's orders,' he answered.

As I stepped out of this strange place which did not sell rubber shoes, I saw a man carrying a small child. He was trying to buy oranges from a vendor.

'Ghulam Ali,' I screamed excitedly.

'Saadat,' he shouted, embracing me. The child didn't like it and began to cry. He went into the shop and told the assistant with whom I had just been talking to take the child home.

'It's been years, hasn't it?' he said.

He had changed. He was no longer the cotton-clad revolutionary who used to make fiery speeches in Jallianwala Bagh. He looked like a normal, homely man.

My mind went back to his last speech. 'Nigar, would you like to mother a child who would be a slave at birth?'

'Whose child was that?' I asked.

'Mine. I have another one who is older. How many children do you have?' he answered without hesitation.

What had happened? Had he forgotten the vow he had taken that day? Was politics no longer a part of his life? What had happened to his passion for the freedom of India? Where was that firebrand revolutionary I used to know? What had happened to Nigar? What had induced her to beget slave children? Had Ghulam Ali married a second time?

'Let us talk,' he said. 'We haven't seen each other for ages.'

I didn't know where to begin, but he didn't put me to the test.

'This shop belongs to me. I've been living in Bombay for the last two years. I'm told you are a big-time story writer now. Do you remember the old days? How we ran away from home to come to Bombay? God, how time flies!'

We went into the shop. A customer who wanted a pair of

tennis shoes was told that he would have to go to the shop at the corner.

'Why don't you stock them? You know I also came here looking for a pair,' I asked.

Ghulam Ali's face fell. 'Let's say I just don't like those things,' he replied.

'What things?'

'Those horrible rubber things. But I'll tell you why,' he said. The anxious look, which had clouded his handsome face suddenly, cleared. 'That life was rubbish. Believe me, Saadat, I have forgotten about those days when the demon of politics was in my head. I'm very happy. I have a wife and two children and my business is doing well.'

He took me to a room at the back of the store. The assistant had come back. Then he began to talk. I will let him tell his story.

'You know how my political life began. You also know what sort of person I was. I mean we grew up together and we were no angels. I wasn't a strong person and yet I wanted to accomplish something in my life. I swear upon God that I was prepared then, as I am prepared today, to sacrifice even my life for the freedom of India. However, after much reflection, I've come to the conclusion that both the politics of India and its political leadership are immature. There are sudden storms and then all is quiet. There is no spontaneity.

'Look, man may be good or evil, but he should remain the way God made him. You can be virtuous without having your head shaved, without donning saffron robes or covering yourself with ash. Those who advocate such things forget that these external manifestations of virtue, if that be indeed what they are, will only get lost on those who follow them. Only ritual will survive, what led to the ritual will be overlooked. Look at all the great prophets. Their teachings are no longer remembered, but we still have their legacy of crosses, holy threads and unshaven armpit hair. They tell you to kill your baser self. Well, if everyone went ahead and did it, what sort of a world would it be?

'You have no idea what hell I went through because I decided to violate human nature. I made a pledge that I would not produce children. It was made in a moment of euphoria. As time passed, I began to feel that the most vital part of my being was paralysed. What was more, it was my own doing. There were moments when I felt proud of my great vow, but they passed. As the pores of my consciousness began to open, reality seemed to want to defeat my resolve. When I met Nigar after my release, I felt that she had changed. We lived together for one year and we kept our promise to Babaji. It was hell. We were being consumed by the futility of our married life.

'The world outside had changed too. Spun cotton, tricolour flags and revolutionary slogans had lost their power. The tents had disappeared from Jallianwala Bagh. There were only holes in the ground where those grand gatherings used to take place. Politics no longer sent the blood cruising through my veins as it used to.

'I spent most of my time at home and we never spoke our minds to each other. I was afraid of touching her. I did not trust myself. One day, as we sat next to each other, I had a mad urge to take her in my arms and kiss her. I let myself go, but I stopped just in time. It was a tremendous feeling while it lasted. However, in the days that followed, I couldn't get rid of a feeling of guilt.

'There had to be a way out of this absurd situation. One day we hit upon a compromise. We would not produce children. We would take the necessary steps, but we would live like husband and wife.

'Thus began a new chapter in our lives. It was as if a blind man had been given back the sight of one eye. But our happiness did not last. We wanted our full vision restored. We felt unhappy and it seemed that everything in our lives had turned into rubber. Even my body felt blubbery and unnatural. Nigar's agony was even more evident. She wanted to be a mother and she couldn't be. Whenever a child was born in the neighbourhood, she would shut herself in a room.

'I wasn't so keen on children myself because, come to think of it, one did not really have to have them. There were millions of people in the world who seemed to be able to get by without them. I could well be one of them. However, what I could no longer stand was this clammy sensation in my hands. When I ate, it felt as if I was eating rubber. My hands always felt as if they had been soaped and then left unrinsed.

'I began to hate myself. All my sensations had atrophied except this weird, unreal sense of touch, which made everything feel like rubber. All I needed to do was to peel off my terrible affliction with the help of two fingers and throw it as far as possible. But I didn't have the courage.

'I was like a drowning man who clutches at straws. And one day I found the straw I was looking for. I was reading a religious text and there it was. I almost jumped. It said, "If a man and woman are joined in wedlock, it is obligatory for them to procreate." And that day I peeled off my curse and have never looked back.'

At this moment, a servant entered the room. He was carrying a child who was holding a balloon. There was a bang and all the child was left with was a piece of string with a shrivelled piece of ugly rubber dangling at the other end.

With two fingers, Ghulam Ali carefully picked up the deflated balloon and threw it away as if it were a particularly disgusting piece of filth.